PRAISE FOR THE CORRIGAN BROTHERS SERIES

"Hard-eyed characters and six-gun action."

— *PUBLISHERS WEEKLY*

"Characters are placed in realistic emotionally driven situations, bringing with them souls filled with concern, fear, joy and desire."

— *TRUE WEST MAGAZINE*

"Solid writing and superb storytelling."

— *AMERICAN COWBOY MAGAZINE*

"The traditional Western doesn't get much better..."

— *ROUNDUP MAGAZINE*

BLUE SKY RECKONING

BLUE SKY RECKONING

CORRIGAN BROTHERS
BOOK FIVE

SCOTT F. SMITH

WOLFPACK PUBLISHING
— EST 2013 —

Blue Sky Reckoning
Paperback Edition
Copyright © 2024 by Scott F. Smith

Wolfpack Publishing
1707 E. Diana Street
Tampa, FL 33610

www.wolfpackpublishing.com

Editing by My Brother's Editor

Paperback ISBN 978-1-63977-631-3
Ebook ISBN 978-1-63977-630-6
LCCN 2024950068

To Laura Faulkner and Stephanie Kissick

BLUE SKY RECKONING

CHAPTER ONE

"You two hustle down the alley and bust through that rear door." Texas Ranger Holt Corrigan's piercing blue eyes flashed as he instructed his partner, Ranger Orion Higbee, and the town marshal of their roles. "Keep that group at the back table from joining in."

"When we kick open that back door, you come marchin' through the front," Orion added. "Just like your buddy, Gen'rul Sherman." He winked.

The two Rangers chuckled at their inside joke. They had been colleagues for only a few months, but in that short time they had been through more action than most would face in a lifetime. Lanky and approaching middle age, Orion was an experienced Ranger who greatly admired and appreciated the savvy of his new associate.

After their first mission together, hunting down the brutal killer known as "The Angel," they were thrown into a tangled web to discover just who was pulling the evil priest's strings—a man by the name of Meden Taliff who fancied himself the next governor of Texas. The two

Rangers had helped bring him down as well. Now, Holt and Orion had been ordered here to Stebbins, Texas, to help capture a band of ruthless rustlers, a local family named the Viklunds.

The two Rangers had arrived in Stebbins under the cover of darkness just the night before. Joined by the town marshal, they now gathered midday at the far corner outside the Blue Sky Inn, one of the town's better establishments. A tip had alerted the lawmen that a long-wanted gunman, Casper Longley, had been hired as "foreman" for Lars Viklund. The information revealed Longley would be in town having Sunday dinner in the hotel's saloon. Grabbing this bandit would hopefully shed light on the Viklund's rustling operation.

The morning's cool breeze had long disappeared. A late July sun held promise of a hot day ahead. Holt's quick glance through the glare of a dusty window veri-fied the gunman was seated at a table against the back wall, eating with two other men.

"You know, riding with you is no picnic," Holt said, a smirk curling up one end of his thick mustache. He quickly checked the cartridges in both of his shoulder-holstered Russian Smith & Wessons. An ivory silhouette of a panther was inlaid in each black grip, a tribute to his belief in reincarnation. He was convinced that in one of his lives he had been a jaguar in South America.

"Watch yourself, peckerhead." Orion grinned his response. "No tellin' who or what's on the menu in there." He spun the cylinder of his Navy Colt, eyeing that it held a full load of rounds. The lanky Ranger adjusted the flat-brimmed hat covering his full shock of salt-and-pepper hair and holstered the pistol.

"When we move"—Holt nodded—"we move quickly, no hesitation."

"You ready, Marshal?" Orion looked back at Baxter Hollings, the town marshal of Stebbins.

The doughy Hollings looked like he was more ready to vomit than barge in on a suspect. "You shure 'bout roustin' Longley? He's a foreman fer th' Viklunds," he grumbled, tugging at his ear where the lobe had been shot off long ago. A habit when he was nervous.

"He may be a foreman in Stebbins, but everywhere else he's been a heller with a gun," Orion growled. "Let's go."

Hollings nodded and pulled at his dirty bowler hat. The older man was not sure about any of this, but he definitely was not going to let down a couple of Rangers. Despite any misgiving, the sawed-off Greener he wielded was not for show. He quickly patted a pocket of his unbuttoned vest to make sure the extra handful of shotgun shells were still tucked there.

Tag Along, Holt's dog, sat and sniffed at the departing lawmen as the two hurried swiftly around the corner of the Blue Sky and down the space between buildings to the back alley.

Holt retrieved a chunk of beef jerky from his coat pocket and kneeled to give it to his furry, gray-and-brown friend. "Tag, you stay right here until I come back." A few pats on the floppy-eared dog's head preceded Holt wagging his finger in Tag's face. "Got that, boy? Stay, Tag. Stay."

The young Ranger stood slowly, taking a deep breath and exhaling. Holt was an imposing figure even though he was only average height. His long brown hair swept along the shoulders of his loose-fitting duster. His rugged face was highlighted by light-blue eyes with high cheekbones of bronze. A long scar on his right cheek was a prominent testament to a previous battle. He reached through his leather vest to find a comforting bulge under his shirt. He found the Apache medicine pouch there and held it briefly to his heart. Holt felt his inner panther spirit filling his soul with warrior song. For luck, he ran his fingers across the cardinal feather in his hatband and stepped between the windows toward the saloon entrance.

He took one more deep breath before he heard a loud crash from inside, Orion making his presence known.

Without hesitation, Holt rushed through the louvered batwing doors. Both his pistols were drawn from their shoulder holsters. "Texas Rangers! Throw up your hands!"

The Sunday dinner crowd was sparse and everyone was confused at the dual commotions coming from the back and front of the inn. Most were not sure which way to look. Two women screamed.

Laudie Kate Hart, today's keeper of the saloon, was leaning against the end of the bar. She kept her composure as she observed both disturbances. The barmaid she was talking to screamed as a long-haired man in a trail coat busted into her place of business, weapons drawn, and hollering to throw up their hands. Laudie Kate smoothly drew her .31 Colt pocket revolver and fired.

Pop-Pop! Ba-Bang!

When the shots rang out, they were not from where Holt expected. He felt a sharp concussion along the right side of his head and his hat went flying. He spun sideways toward the gun flashes just as dust popped from his coat as a bullet punched his left shoulder. Another shot slammed into his left thigh causing him to throw himself down, firing as he dove. His bullet thudded harmlessly into bar wood, ripping off a piece of the border frame. Just before he fell completely to the floor, another bullet tore at his side near his right hip.

Holt pushed himself to his hands and knees, the pain of his wounds not yet reaching his brain. Through the shock he told himself he had to move.

Had to move.

Had to move.

He tried to stand, but his legs turned to jelly, and he fell forward onto his side.

He was unaware of the chaos unfolding around him. The grubby floor planks he laid on were covered in sawdust, now collecting a dark red puddle.

"Blue...Deed...come...find me..." he gasped as darkness closed in around him.

CHAPTER TWO

"**O**rion Higbee, Texas Ranger! Drop that weapon *now*!"

His order from the back of the saloon followed two warning shots from his Navy Colt that blistered the support beam near Laudie Kate's head. He could never shoot a woman, but this might be the day. She threw the gun away as if it were red-hot and immediately crumpled to her knees.

There was no doubt of his purpose; Orion looked like a Ranger. Black coat and vest, tall, confident, and intimidating, but generally not threatening—except in the din of battle, when he became a six-foot-two wolverine. His dark-brown eyes were usually genial and pleasant, but they now burned lava hot.

"Baxter, keep both barrels of that Greener pointed at *this* table!" he directed the wide-eyed marshal. "Any movement, send 'em to hell."

At the table sat Casper Longley, a man who—by his filthy appearance—looked more like a dirt farmer than gunfighter. With unkept brown hair that looked like it had been chewed rather than hand-cut, Longley wore dirty trousers that were shoved into scruffy mule-ear boots. A faded work shirt was covered by an oversized, beat-up brown sack coat with worn-through elbows. The coat did not quite cover the well-oiled, converted Army Colt handles peeking out from his waist. Although an eye patch concealed a gnarled and scarred socket, his one good eye did not miss a thing. Fury was now burning from it, scorching all it saw.

Two men were seated with him. On one side was a short, curly-headed cowboy with an unruly mustache that looked like an upside-down horseshoe stamped to his face. On the gunfighter's other side was a handsome young drover with long blonde hair.

Longley kept his eye on the Ranger, while the other two men glared at the marshal. The fast spread pattern of the lawman's sawed-off shotgun aimed in their direction was a threat that kept them all motionless.

Orion reached for his back waistband and drew a short-barreled Army Colt revolver, cocking it into readiness with the command, "Everybody else move to the front end of the bar, *now!*"

Under Orion's watchful glare and the barrels of his readied pistols, eight remaining customers and three employees were corralled toward the door, near where Laudie Kate now knelt, her face buried in her hands, crying. He kicked her revolver savagely away from anyone's reach.

Laudie Kate looked up and pled through tears, "I'm so, so sorry. I didn't…I didn't kn-know. Let me help. *Please!*"

"I think you've done enough already, missy," Orion snarled.

"No, I-I can help." She began sobbing again. "I-I heard him...I heard him yell 'Throw up your hands' and saw...and saw his guns. I had to...I thought he was going to rob us." She looked down at the floor. She stopped her blubbering, took a deep breath, and gathered her composure. She stood slowly, her bright blue eyes flashing through the wetness. A long scar, surprisingly similar to Holt's, ran down the right side of her face, from her cheekbone to her jawline. She wiped her eyes with a handkerchief and declared, "I'm Laudie Kate Hart. The owner here, Señor Navarro, put me in charge today. Look around, there's a lot of money to be grabbed. I need this job. I was...I was only trying to protect..." She caught herself before breaking into tears again. "I can't...I can't tell you how sorry I am. I didn't mean... this...this was a terrible misunderstanding. Please let me look after him."

Orion's eyes blazed like torches as they connected with hers. She blinked but did not look away.

"You have business to attend to." She gestured toward the back table with her eyes and head. "Please."

He continued to lock eyes with her. "Okay," he exhaled in a deep growl. "Don't let him die."

She hurried toward Holt's downed body and kneeled next to him. Her brow furrowed and she pursed her lips, not liking what she saw.

"You!" Orion redirected his attention to the bar and snapped at the waitress who had been talking to Laudie Kate prior to the gunshots. "Run an' get your doctor. Go!"

Laudie Kate looked up at the tall Ranger and spoke calmly. "Her name is Evie."

He glared at Laudie Kate, then glanced worriedly at

his partner lying motionless on the floor. "Evie, get the doctor," he corrected himself. *"Run!"*

After brushing the long, bloody hair off Holt's face, Laudie Kate quickly determined one bullet had burned across the side of his scalp, leaving a nasty gash. Fortunate. The hole in his torn trousers revealed that a bullet had lodged in his outer thigh, but not come out the other side. She pulled back Holt's coat and unfastened his vest to examine the damage to his body, only then seeing the Ranger badge pinned there. Looking at his now bloody duster coat, she could see a deep slash near Holt's shoulder. She ripped open the buttons on his shirt and discovered another wound—an ugly furrow along the fleshy part of his right side, just above his hip.

On their own, each of the rough, jagged tears to his head, arm, and side were not necessarily life-threatening, but all of them together were bleeding hard enough to put Holt in a critical situation. Cut flesh was angry and puffing. She could tell he was carrying lead in his thigh. With her first glance, she suspected nothing had hit vital areas. The loss of blood needed to be stopped right away. She took the handkerchief she had been crying into and held it to the wound on Holt's head.

"Daniel! John! Help me carry him upstairs," she hollered at the group in front of Orion. Both men stood still, eyes locked, the Ranger still holding them at gunpoint. "It's okay, Ranger," she urged, looking at Orion, "they work across the street at the mill."

Nodding his acceptance, Orion added, "Just unbuckle those gun belts an' leave 'em right here before you go."

The townsmen dropped their guns quickly and rushed over to Laudie Kate.

"Give me a bandanna!" she demanded. One of the

men immediately produced a neckerchief, which she stuffed into the wound in Holt's leg. "Easy now," she said. "He's been hit everywhere." The three lifted Holt carefully. "Send the doctor up as soon as he gets here," she directed Orion and the others. "Room six."

Orion watched as they carried his partner away, then gave a glance toward Marshal Hollings, ensuring that Longley and his friends were still held in place by the marshal's shotgun. Even with Holt down, he got right to business. Orion's attention quickly returned to the remaining people in front of him. Gesturing with his pistols, he commanded, "The rest of you, drop your weapons too. Add 'em to the pile."

Satisfied with their compliance, he pointed to a table by the door. "Everyone sit there, hands where I can see 'em," he hissed. "An' don't move," he called over his shoulder as he moved to the back of the room toward their original intended target.

The doughy marshal had watched all of this restlessly. However, his double-barreled shotgun had not moved from the suspected gunman Casper Longley and his two associates. The local lawman wished he was anywhere but here, but he was determined to show his mettle.

"You three, keep them hands out in the open," Orion barked as he walked up to the table. "All right, Longley," he grumbled, gesturing with one of his pistols. "Get up. You're under arrest."

"What for?"

"For starters, a whole string of murders from Kansas, through Indian Territory, an' down here in Texas."

"I work at the Windmill V for the Viklunds. Ask anyone."

"We already did. Lotta county sheriffs an' marshals say you were right busy before the Viklunds hired you."

"You've got the wrong man."

"You don't say." Orion met the gunman's dirty look with a deadly smile. "That's a new one. Now, you muddy runnin' pumpkin roller, I asked you once. Get up!" He took a menacing step closer to the suspect; one of his pistols aimed at the outlaw's chest, the other pointed directly at the man's face.

The scruffy outlaw stood, his one eye narrowing in gritted teeth anger.

"Baxter, if he does anythin' other'n what I say, cut him in two. Understand?"

The gunman glared briefly at the marshal, who was nodding his head in agreement. The outlaw's one-eyed scowl returned to the Ranger.

Orion met the gunman's sneer with one of his own. "Okay, Longley, real easy-like, unbuckle your guns an' let 'em drop."

Without taking his gaze off the Ranger, the killer smoothly unbuckled his gun belt. The holsters and guns fell heavily to the floor.

"Now, hands in the air."

A grimace on the outlaw's face preceded the raising of his hands to shoulder height.

"That gun in your back waistband too. Pull it with one hand and let it drop behind you."

With a quick exhale and tightening of his lips, Longley carefully reached back with one arm. A short-barreled revolver thudded twice as it bounced on the planking. He returned his hand to shoulder height.

"Goood," Orion continued. "Now, one at a time, slowly retrieve the hideaways in your boots. *Slowly*."

Longley's hands stayed up as he placed one foot on the chair next to him. Deliberately, he reached with one hand into the top of the elevated boot. His fingers retrieved a derringer, which he tossed to the side. He lowered that leg and repeated the move with his other one. This boot produced a Bowie knife, which clattered as it joined the collection on the floor. He returned to his two-legged stance.

"Now, keep those hands up high," Orion ordered as he eased the hammers forward on his pistols. He jammed the short-barreled revolver back into his waistband, keeping the big Navy Colt in one hand. With his free hand, he patted at the pockets of the outlaw's worn coat. Satisfied the dirty jacket held no danger, Orion then quickly reached over to undo the belt holding up Longley's pants and yanked the leather clear.

"Somethin' to keep your hands busy." He grinned, throwing the belt away, but the smile did not reach his eyes.

The outlaw instantly grabbed for the waistline to keep his trousers from falling down. Orion expected the sudden movement, hoping for this exact effect.

"Sure wish you had some help, Marshal," Orion said, turning part of his attention to the lawman. "Don't they give you any deputies around here?"

"My deputy's guardin' th' jail," the marshal answered. "But him sittin' right there be a county deputy," he said, motioning to the front table.

Orion looked incredulously at a man now slowly standing, rubbing his hands along his brown-and-white spotted cowhide vest, and looking sheepish.

"Ho-lee damn..." Orion's anger soared as his eyes shot daggers at the deputy. "This one...with the fancy

vest? You stu…you mothe…you flug-fisted…" he sputtered. "Why in hell's creation didn't you help? An' where
the hell is your badge?"

The man gulped. "I'm not on duty. And I don't…"

"Gawdamighty, boy," Orion interrupted. "Get your
gun an' help us out," he commanded. "What's the matter
with you?"

The deputy tried to match the intensity of Orion's
glare but couldn't. He glanced away to look at Longley
before returning his gaze at the Ranger.

"Are you waitin' for an engraved invitation?" Orion
bellowed. "Move!"

The deputy hastily recovered his gun belt and
strapped it in place.

Orion frowned as the deputy moved to take a position
near Longley. "Now, you two," the Ranger said, turning
his attention to the men who sat with the gunfighter. "I
dunno who you are, but you've already shown poor judgment in companions. Get up slowly an' unbuckle those
guns."

"Why us?" the short man with the horseshoe
mustache whined as he and his friend stood. He raised his
arm to point in the direction of Longley and the deputy.
"It was that man there who sho—"

The deputy in the flashy vest, who had finally taken
his place with the marshal, caught the movement out of
the corner of his eye.

Ba-Bang!

Orion aimed his pistol at the sounds.

Two shots from the deputy dropped the complaining
man to the floor like a stone. The long blonde-haired
drover did not move, standing with his hands held up

chest high. Longley had not moved a muscle, continuing to hold up his pants.

"I thought he had a gun and was drawing on you," the deputy said to Orion.

Orion looked at the body on the floor. There was no immediate sign of another gun, but nothing in this saloon was going well or making sense right now.

"We didn't do anything wrong," the young drover insolently retorted. "He sure as hell didn't." His eyes and head motioned to the floor at the curly-headed man lying there.

"Maybe so, but the sooner you get shut of those guns, the sooner you stop bein' a target, savvy?" Orion snarled.

"Jus' shut up, Christer, an' do what th' Ranger says," Marshal Baxter warned.

"Hollings, gotdammit, get this heller Longley locked up!" Orion roared.

"C'mon, Casper, you heard th' Ranger," the marshal announced in a voice a little shy of assertive.

"Keep those hands holdin' them pants, Longley," Orion called out. "One wrong move and the marshal paints the street with your insides." He paused. "Deputy, you lead the way. Make sure there aren't any friends keepin' this snapperhead from his cell."

As the two lawmen began their little convoy to the jail, Orion called out again. "Baxter, after you get him locked up, come back. Help me sort things out."

The Ranger watched the outlaw intently, even as he moved through the front door and down the boardwalk. Once Longley was out of sight, Orion trained his eyes back on the towheaded man. "Christer, is it? As in Christer Viklund?"

"This is a mistake you will regret, Ranger," the

blonde man warned, ignoring the questions. "You have no idea what you just bought into."

"A Ranger's been shot here, *boy*." Orion scowled. "An' your dinner partner is wanted for a half dozen outright murders, maybe more. That's what I know for sure. I also know that I'm gonna be extra careful until things make sense. So, for last time you little pissant, unbuckle your guns." The click-click on the hammer of his Navy Colt added an exclamation point to his order.

The eyes of the boyish-looking cattleman widened with alarm. His demeanor abruptly changed as his gun belt hit the floor in swift obeyance of the imposing Ranger.

"You can pick up your guns at the jail later on. For now, get over there with the rest of the bunch," he directed, not moving his pistol that was aimed at the young drover's chest.

Christer Viklund's eyes beseeched the Ranger if it was all right to retrieve his hat. Orion's slitted-eye countenance acknowledged the action with a nod. The young Viklund slowly picked up his hat off the table and joined the group at the front of the saloon.

Orion returned his Colt to its holster and stepped to the body of the man with the unruly mustache. He hooked his boot under the ankle of the prone figure to lift the leg. He let it drop with a heavy thud. No response. The deputy's shots were well placed. This man was dead.

Just then, a red-faced, white-haired gentleman in a dark, rumpled suit hustled through the entrance. Right behind him, equally red-faced, was Evie, the barmaid sent to fetch a doctor.

"I'm Dr. Sherrell Vaughn," the gentleman said, trying to catch his breath. He touched his short-brimmed black fedora with his finger and thumb. In his other hand, he held a large physician's bag.

"Orion Higbee," came the reply. "Texas Ranger."

"I understand we have a lawman who's been shot. Where is he?"

Orion held the doctor with his intense gaze and motioned to the upstairs rooms with a brief lift of his head. "Room six. Do your best, Doc."

CHAPTER THREE

T he long afternoon passed slowly into evening for Ranger Orion Higbee. The closed door of room six blocked any sight or news of what was going on with Holt Corrigan and the three people working on him. He sat in a rocking chair at the end of the dimming hallway, staring at the door. Holt's dog, Tag Along, lay at his feet, occasionally whimpering his concern over the disappearance of his master, which Orion soothed with gentle pats and scratches. An earlier conversation the Ranger had with Marshal Baxter Hollings was replaying in his mind...

———

The marshal had returned to the hotel saloon after securing Casper Longley in a jail cell. Hollings stood with Orion at the bar watching silently as workers cleaned up the area where Holt had fallen. Holt's hat, as well as the pistol wielded by Laudie Kate, rested on the bar between both lawmen.

The two lawmen could not have looked any less alike
—the marshal's stubby build in wrinkled trousers, open
vest and rumpled jacket, and Orion's tall whip frame in a
black trail coat and vest. Hollings may not have resembled the part of a gritty town marshal, but his earnest
commitment to keeping the peace, shown during the
arrest of Longley, was sincere and not to be underes-
timated.

Lots of time spent in the sun resulted in a ruddy
complexion and a squint to Orion's eyes that usually gave
a nearly perpetual smiling look to his face. Except for
now. Hat in-hand, his face was set in a grim expression as
he took in the aftermath of his partner's shooting.

After mopping, one of the workers sprinkled new
sawdust over the stain left behind where the wide circle
of Holt's dark blood had pooled.

Not wanting to watch anymore, Orion smoothed the
salt-and-pepper hair on his head away from his face and
put his hat back on. He looked at the items lying on the
bar and noticed the cardinal feather in Holt's hatband had
been broken. The shaft had splintered but it still hung
together. He hoped it was a positive sign that Holt's good
luck piece, although broken, was still holding fast.

The inaction of the county deputy during the fight
had been gnawing at Orion. He rubbed at his thick,
trimmed beard which was edging more toward white than
the hair under his hat. Finally, he could not hold it in.
"Dammit to hell, Baxter, you need to find yourself some
better men. Standin' an' watchin' is a mighty unhealthy
trait for a lawman," he had groused at the marshal.

"He ain't my deputy. Boone Mercer is th' sheriff's
deputy. County law," the marshal intoned.

"But law is law." Orion scowled. "A badge comes with an oath, don't it?"

The words that came from the marshal looked like they tasted bad. He uttered frustratingly, "Mercer never listens ta me, he helped only b'cuz a Ranger said to. He only follows Sheriff Carmichael's orders."

County Sheriff Linus Carmichael was an enigma. In addition to wearing a badge for St. Clair County, he also had made a name for himself as a lawyer. Most people were afraid of him—except outlaws. He disappeared for days at a time, ostensibly in the execution of his job, but no one knew for sure. Although they were never seen together, it was believed that Carmichael and Lars Viklund were friends. It certainly seemed that way due to the legal representations that the sheriff defended which favored Viklund and his Windmill V ranch. Gaunt and angular, always dressed in black, to most people Carmichael looked more boogeyman than lawman.

"I haven't met this Sheriff Carmichael yet," Orion sniffed disdainfully.

"Ya might not, dependin' on how long yer aroun' an' what ya git involved with," Baxter said. "He's usually purty scarce. Always seems ta be conveniently gone when ya need 'im most."

"A busy man, huh?"

Baxter shrugged and scratched the back of his neck. "St. Clair County is purty large territory. Let's jus' say he always seems ta have a lot goin' on somewheres else."

Orion's stare drilled into the town marshal.

Uneasy with the silence, Baxter added, "That blonde at th' table with Longley was Christer Viklund, Lars's youngest. I'd say ol' man Viklund already knows 'bout what happened here. He might've even known, ya know, beforehan'…"

"You don't say…"

"I ain't sayin', jus' speculatin'."

"What if I were to speculate you bein' part of that equation? You were the only one who knew Holt an' I were in town an' what we were up to."

The marshal's eyes flashed as he turned to face Orion. "*Ranger* Higbee, I'd be downright offended if'n ya think…"

"*Marshal* Hollings, you know a badge comes with askin' tough questions."

"Let's see here…two tough-lookin' strangers, ridin' inta town af'er dark with four hosses an' a dog," the marshal continued. "Lotta pryin' eyes in Stebbins, 'specially ones lookin' ta gain favor with th' likes o' th' Viklunds or th' sheriff. Mebbe y'all were spotted comin' to see me."

"I reckon there's that," Orion acknowledged.

"I'd have questions too, if'n someone I cared 'bout were lyin' bleedin' an' shot up," the marshal responded, calming down and settling back to his previous position next to the Ranger.

"Ho-lee damn, Baxter, you're holdin' a bag of crap here. No-show for a sheriff an' a poor excuse for a county deputy." Orion gave a derisive *harrumph* and looked down at Tag Along, who sat close by the tall Ranger's boots.

Silence had taken hold when the marshal did not know quite how to respond.

Finally, Baxter had motioned upstairs. "Is that really *the* Holt Corrigan?"

"It sure is. One of the best lawmen this state'll ever

see," Orion had noted with pride.

"Wasn't he…wasn't he…an…an outlaw?" Baxter stammered. "A Reb who never gave up? Robbed banks an' such? How…"

"What Ranger Corrigan did a long time ago was in the line of duty for the Confederacy," Orion interrupted. "I wore blue an' would have forcefully opposed his actions had we crossed paths, but a man fights for what he believes in. I can respect that part of it. He was given a full federal pardon an' was a damn good county sheriff for Cassidy County an' the good town of Wilkon. Cap'n Laird McCoy personally recruited Holt to the Rangers." His eyes had bored directly into the doughy marshal.

At this moment, Baxter had tugged on his bad ear and once again wanted to be anywhere but in the presence of a Ranger. "Got somethin' ya might wanna know 'bout," he said, quickly digging into a pocket and eagerly handing the Ranger a handbill. "Grabbed it from my desk when I took Longley to jail. Left *my own* deputy watchin' 'im. Anyway, this arrived jus' a coupla days ago."

Orion glanced at the marshal over the top of the paper. "Hmmm. You done anythin' about this yet?"

Baxter shook his head. "Jus' received it Friday, two days ago. We was busy with th' usual weekend shenanigans an' then yo'all Rangers showed up."

"All right, Hollings, I'll look into it." He grunted a dismissive exhalation and folded the wanted notice, then tucked it into his coat pocket.

"I'm guessin' I don' need ta tell ya ta be careful," Baxter had said.

"You too, Marshal."

Orion's silence and far-off gaze had told Baxter their conversation was over. The marshal was just as eager to be out of the intimidating presence of this Ranger anyway.

———————

After the marshal left, impatience had eventually drawn Orion upstairs. The passage of time had dulled into unhurried rocks of the chair he had grabbed and placed by the door to the room where Holt now lay. Orion was sure somewhere in literature he had read about this metaphor in which he now found himself. A waiting room of sorts, where one side of the door meant life and the other side, death. He was too tired and too worried to figure out which tale it had been. Living this nightmare was bad enough.

The waiting took long pulls on his memory. His mind journey settled on his recent adventures with the young Ranger who now lay on the wrong side of that door.

The older Ranger recalled the first morning they met. Lodgepole it was. Holt had entered the café where Orion was having breakfast. As Holt approached his table, the older Ranger noted the younger man's rugged face with a trim mustache and eyes that burned with intensity. Orion was impressed at the formidable presence this new Ranger radiated despite his ordinary physical stature. Orion guessed the long scar down the younger man's right cheek was a grim reminder of a saber that had gotten too close, likely from the war. A faded blue wing-tip shirt and leather rancher vest over worn, dark trousers made Holt look like a rawboned gunfighter. Knee-high boots adorned with old small-roweled cavalry spurs marked him as a man who knew his way around a horse.

A warrior by any definition, Orion had quickly surmised.

The café's big-bosomed waitress had taken a real shine to Holt that morning. Orion grinned slightly at the recollection of Holt's embarrassment over her bawdy attentiveness.

The older Ranger's thoughts turned to their first mission—to track down and capture the killer known as The Angel. He remembered the long trail-eating discussions they had about the war. Though he had served in the Federal Navy and Holt had been a Confederate cavalryman, they were able to look back and examine their life-altering experiences without judgment or animosity.

During these talks, Holt had once asked Orion, "What was he like? Sherman. I always wondered if he was as big a son of a bitch as we suspected," he had said, laughing.

Orion chuckled his response. "He was somethin' else. Actually, he was a pretty scary peckerhead, if you ask me. The man was *intense*. Had no tolerance for fools."

"That sounds like everything I've heard."

"He was about your height. Had a real presence. If he was nearby, you could *feel* him. Red hair, grizzly beard, he didn't care as much about his appearance like a lotta generals did, but he wasn't as grubby as Grant could be."

"Strutting peacocks, most generals," Holt had interjected.

"Fools, on both sides," Orion had added. "Too many politicians an' rich chuckleheads playin' soldier."

"And pissing matches between each other that got too many good men killed."

From there, "peckerhead" had become kind of a

watchword for the two Rangers. A shared acknowledgment, warm-hearted banter between warriors.

Orion admired Holt's imposing presence. He seemed like a cougar, all coiled strength—silent and cautious—yet ready to strike with ferocity. He also recalled their stumbling upon the odd town of Kendrick and Holt's being upset with himself over his unintentional treatment of a deaf bartender. That caring side was like him too.

Reflecting back on those memories as he sat in the rocking chair, Orion absentmindedly rubbed the right side of his own face. The long scratch there had long since scabbed and healed, but still retained a tenderness, a reminder of the piece of Ketchum grenade shrapnel that buzzed a little too close during his and Holt's stand against Comanches this past spring. Just one of the hurdles they faced in tracking down The Angel. Despite his wound, the grenades he packed had come in handy.

He shook his head and leaned forward. "Damn near took off the top of my own pumpkin with that Ketchum, didn't I?" he remarked to Tag, who was largely unimpressed and resumed his nap.

The tall Ranger sat back in the rocker, stifled a yawn and scratched at his mane of graying brown hair, brushing it back on his head with his hand. He smoothed his thick, trimmed beard and again rubbed the tender area along his face. He immediately flashed back to the day he and Holt faced down that war party of Comanche warriors.

Holt saved his life that day.

———

They had just finished a quick lunch of jerky and corn dodgers beside a small creek when Tag had begun to growl, a teeth-tightening warning.

Off in the distance, a sizable group of riders on horse-back had appeared over a shallow ridge. Even without field glasses, Holt knew they were Indians by the way they sat their mounts. Orion had retrieved his naval spyglass and surveyed the group to confirm what they suspected.

"Comanches," Orion had said coolly, looking through his glass and puffing on a cigar. "Twenny-four. Painted for war. Horses got feathers in their manes an' tails."

"They likely have been sniffing around our trail more than just this morning," Holt had said, stowing away their packages of food. "We aren't going to lose them."

Orion pointed at a big outcropping of rock and boul-ders about a half mile away in the opposite direction and declared they should make a stand there. "Looks like a good place to hole up an' fight if it comes to that."

"Oh, it'll come to that." Holt had chuckled grimly. "They see four good horses and only two men."

"We can protect the horses better there too," Orion added as they took off for the shelter. "We'll have the high ground."

Orion had taken a position to Holt's left. The imposing boulders at their backs rose too high for anyone to come down at them from behind. Their sides might be another story, though, they would have to be vigilant. Although they were on higher ground, they needed to take care to not get flanked and hit from several angles.

It was not long until the war party had unleashed their screaming attack.

Using their wits, withering fire from their rifles, and

two of Orion's exploding Ketchum grenades, the two Rangers had whittled down the war party by more than half. The remaining Comanches had regrouped out of range from the Rangers' position. Recovering their nerve, the remaining nine warriors raced forward with their war leader to comply with his command.

"Ho-lee damn," Orion exclaimed and brought up his Henry to begin firing. Three shots from his Henry took down a warrior wearing a Confederate infantry tunic. Two shots from Holt's Winchester dropped another.

A menacing warrior with black-and-white face paint and wearing a white woman's dress had veered off to the left; another Comanche wearing leggings and an unbuttoned Yankee jacket had peeled away to the right.

Holt's first two shots at the man in the blue coat missed. The warrior had slipped to the side of his pony, making him a difficult target as he positioned to fire a revolver from under the horse's neck. Holt had seen the maneuver many times before and had even used it himself. He stroked the cardinal feather in his hatband and aimed. His first shot brought a scream from the Indian pony. It stumbled and fell, toppling the Comanche under him. The warrior's pistol skidded into a scrubby mesquite bush. Holt fired two more times, making sure the horse did not suffer. The warrior under the horse was dead.

Orion had been focused on the war leader, who was screaming and exhorting his men in between firing shots from an old rifle. Shifting his cigar to bite down on it, Orion cocked and fired his Henry. The war leader's cry jerked to a stop and he folded from his horse, his head a bloody mess with a huge bullet hole in his forehead.

Orion remembered puffing on his cigar in relief.

But suddenly, the warrior in the woman's dress had appeared in the rocks just to his left, tomahawk raised to strike.

"Orion, look out!" Holt had yelled, swinging his Winchester at the shrieking attacker as the warrior leaped at Orion. Holt fired his rifle four times as fast as he could lever the gun and the man fell next to Orion.

"Much obliged, Holt!" Orion remembered shouting. "You saved my bacon." He recollected firing his Henry into the bloody body to make sure.

The older Ranger's thoughts floated safely back to the rocking chair. "Yes, you certainly did, my friend," Orion said softly into the dim hotel hallway. "You surely saved my bacon."

Orion's mind then flashed to the showdown with The Angel. Although it seemed mere days ago, it was now months since that brutal encounter. So much had happened between then and today.

The lunatic preacher was the reason Orion Higbee had even come to know Holt Corrigan in the first place. His brand new partner had resigned as county sheriff of Wilkon to become a Texas Ranger. Holt had swapped badges after three of his friends, one of them his godfather, were brutally murdered because of the evil killer. Captain McCoy had partnered Holt and Orion and hurled them on the trail of the brutal man of the cloth who had been on a killing rampage for more than a year. After surviving the Comanche raid, the two Rangers secretly tracked the psychotic priest across the border into

Mexico, shooting up the killer's gang, and taking him into custody.

Holt's dog, Tag Along, saved Orion's life that night. The Angel had the drop on him. "But you jumped on that muddy runnin' fog whacker, didn't you?" he said, leaning down to give Tag a vigorous rub all across the dog's head and back.

This time, the scrappy mutt returned the attention, standing with his tail slapping the air affectionately.

Yes, Orion had not known Holt Corrigan long, but he thought how his life had changed in these few months—and not just because the young Ranger and his dog had twice saved his old Navy butt. That was the hard-to-ignore truth. The other fact was that, in this short time, he had come to look upon Holt like a brother.

Partners and friends had come and gone, but Holt Corrigan was different. There was an aura about him, Orion thought. Indians—and Holt himself—would say spirits were strong with him. This younger man had an intensity about him that was palpable, not unlike the general they had often discussed.

"Your buddy an' Gen'rul Sherman would be a pair to draw to, that's for sure," he said softly to Tag, who now had raised up and put his front paws on Orion's knee.

Orion gently kneaded the dog's head and ears. For the first time in a long while, the older Ranger was truly fearful. Scared to lose his friend who lay on the other side of that door, wounded and bloody. Or worse.

Just then, the dog pulled down and resumed his four-legged stance, jolting Orion out of his contemplation. Tag stood stock-still, staring down the hallway. The beginning of a soft, growling *rrruff* tightened in this throat.

A large form was moving quietly toward them, clinging to the shadows.

"It's okay, Tag." Orion patted the dog's head reassuringly. "It's okay, boy. We know him."

Dusk was giving way to nighttime as Texas Ranger Moose Elkins moved down the darkening hallway toward his longtime friend. Orion stood and they slapped each other on the shoulders. "Wondered when I'd see you or that reprobate Frantze." Orion smiled.

Orion, a tall, lanky man himself, looked rather diminutive next to the hulking form of Elkins. For such a huge man, Moose Elkins had navigated up the stairs and down the hall without a sound.

"Heard anythin'?" Moose inquired. His enormous, checkered flannel shirt looked as though it could have been made from a saddle blanket.

"No. Startin' to worry me a little," Orion acknowledged quietly. "But don't tell the dog that."

Moose easily moved another rocking chair down to where Orion and Tag sat. Thick brown locks of hair cascaded over his forehead. As he sat, he slowly brushed them back with a smooth deliberate sweep of his hand.

"Tag, meet Moose. Moose, Tag," Orion said softly.

"Hearda this guy," Moose said as he sat, giving the dog some appreciated rubs along his back, ending with a couple of friendly thumps on Tag's side.

"Saved my life, this floppy-eared hound did. When we captured The Angel. That unholy bastard had me dead to rights," Orion began. "Middle of the night, in a cruddy little Mexican church. So damn dark you could feel it. That wicked preacher all but had me in the ground an' read over."

"Dammit, Orion. Heard you'n Holt tracked that

sumbitch down, but I hadn't gotten wind've that part o' it. That's some scary stuff."

"Yeah it was scary, all right. That preacher glided up on me, all wraith-like, gun cocked, evil death-gleam in his eyes...but outta nowhere, ol' Tag flew right through the darkness in a blur an' pounced on that no-good frog-squatter. Wouldn't let go. Wouldn't let him get a shot at me."

"You did all that, boy?" Moose addressed the dog and administered a few more ear scritches. Tag's happy tail waggled the entire back half of his body.

"Tag here clamped down on that sonuvabitch long enough so I could deliver a sermon with the stock of my Henry. I shoulda shot the bastard, but our plan was to bring him in alive. You know, take him back across the border, find out who he was answerin' to." Orion's voice trailed off. His and Holt's plan had been derailed when enraged citizens of the nearest Texas town, Sweetclover, stormed the jail and lynched the killer priest before many questions were answered. "Made our job a helluva lot tougher, but we ended up piecin' together that puzzle."

"We jus' read 'but that in th' paper. Didja really use Roman candles in a gunfight?" Moose asked, a chuckle in his voice.

"Sure did. We brought down that apple knockin' pig thumper an' his blood brother. Can you believe the miserable bastard thought he could be governor?"

Meden Taliff was the Wilkon attorney who had established himself as a successful businessman and philanthropist in the region. He had planned to run for governor until word got out that he was the brains behind the brutal and sadistic Angel murders. Taliff and his two blood brothers—Father Miguel Beltran, known as The Angel, and Kane Barlow, a sadistic monster who enjoyed killing for the fun of it—had carefully plotted and carried out Taliff's rise to fortune and power. Until Holt, Orion, and the lawmen of Wilkon began to figure out the complicated pieces to Taliff's bloody puzzle. So much for their delusions of grandeur. The Angel's savagery ended four months ago at the end of a lynch mob's robe. Taliff 's golden dream was extinguished in a fiery shootout just a few weeks ago. Holt's brother, Deed, had killed the monster Barlow with his bare hands.

"Y'all bin busy, that's fer sure."

"You can say that again." Orion grinned, but the smile didn't reach his eyes.

"Well, it's damn good ta see ya. Wish'n it were diff'rent circumstances though. Hope I git ta meet this Holt fella. Sounds like he's one ta ride th' river with."

"An' then some." Orion nodded.

Moose acknowledged through the trailing silence, "Bit o' th' Irish fer ya?" He held up a bottle of pale gold liquid by its neck, two glasses accompanied in the same large grip.

"Aye, me friend." Orion smiled wanly. "It's been a day."

Both Rangers sat quietly, sipping at their glasses. Elkins was operating in secret with another Ranger, Dal Frantze. Both were now working for the Viklunds as ranch hands at the Windmill V ranch. It was a tip from them that led Holt and Orion to Longley and where to find him. Moose sat here in the dark, secure in the idea that no one knew he was a Ranger, much less meeting with another one.

Tag now laid at their feet. The big question loomed unasked.

"Just like you said he'd be, Longley was eatin' right here. We had him in our crosshairs," Orion finally began, almost inaudibly. "Me an' Marshal Hollings kicked in through the back door. Holt came bustin' through the front. When he yelled for everyone to throw up their hands, this bar gal just drew a pocket gun an' fired quick as you please. In all the hubbub, she thought Holt was tryin' to rob the place. Lead found him, hard. Lotta blood."

"Damn," Moose said, wiping one of his huge, paw-like hands across his mouth and freshly shaved chin. "Which one? Which bar gal?"

"Said her name was Laudie Kate."

"Miss Laudie? Yeah, sounds like somethin' she'd do. Tough gal."

"You know her?"

"I kinda bin seein' 'nother gal who works here. Name o' Evie. Evie O'Neill. Those two is friends."

"Evie fetched the doc for Holt. Both gals are in there now, helpin' him."

"He's in good hands then, yessir." Moose nodded and took a sip. "Ya got Longley despite it all too."

"That we did," Orion mused dolefully. "That we did."

"Be interestin' ta see how long he stays caged."

Orion's hard glance was its own question.

"Sheriff Linus Carmichael." Elkins's words dripped with contempt. "Got this here town wrapped aroun' his finger, tight as a noose."

"That's the second time I've heard of this character today," Orion said, holding out his glass for a little more of the whiskey. "An' neither one in a sunshiny light."

"Carmichael's crooked as an old shillelagh," Elkins continued as he poured another for his friend. "He wears a badge an' all but hasn't made a full commitment ta keepin' th' peace, if'n ya know what I mean."

"Depends on which way the wind is blowin' an' money is flowin' huh?"

"He shore 'nuff plays on th' edge of law an' order. Makin' it worse, he's even more shady as an attorney. Like th' livin' embodiment of a double-barreled shotgun. He an' Lars Viklund are thick as, well, thieves." Elkins half-chuckled at his own observation.

"So who's runnin' this show? Lars Viklund or Sheriff Carmichael?"

"Chicken or egg…seems like it be Viklund's game, but I haven't quite figgered it all out yet," Elkins replied. "They's both in deep though."

"I guess it don't matter. As long as we round up everyone in the operation."

"Sure as sunrise, O-Ryun, this Lars Viklund bastird an' his sons are up ta their eyeballs in rustlin'."

"That where the gunfighter Longley figured in?"

"Yes indeed." Elkins nodded. "Lars brought 'im in ta be foreman, overseein' th' cattle operation. An' th' intimidation."

"Whatever they don't steal, they strong-arm?"

"That's 'bout th' size o' it. They dun run off two smaller ranch owners. Took over their lands. No one knows that…yet."

"Longley looked more like a farmer than cattleman."

"Damn mean farmer. Frantze seen 'im kill one drover at th' Half Moon 6 an' pistol whip 'nother. None o' that made it ta th' attention of any real law."

"You think news of Longley's capture has already made it out to Viklund's ranch?" Orion asked.

"Count on it."

"An' you don't think the marshal can hold him?"

"Count on that too. It ain't th' marshal's fault. Baxter Hollings is a decent sort, but he's ov'rmatched. Carmichael's badge an' lawyer smarts plus Viklund's money an' craftiness..." Moose took a good sip from his glass. "They'll figger a way ta git Longley out an' make it look all legal-like."

"An' Marshal Hollings won't be able to do a thing about it."

"Yep...that's why th' Cap'n sent all us Ranger boys here."

CHAPTER FOUR

S uddenly, the door to room six opened and Dr. Vaughn emerged. Warm, stale air, and the heavy stringent smell of alcohol and anesthetic rushed out with him. Orion jumped to his feet and hurried to the door. Moose Elkins moved furtively away from his friend and into a dark pocket of the hallway.

"Woooo, let's open some windows," Dr. Vaughn said, wiping off his glasses with a hanky. "The smell of that chloroform is making me sleepy." He removed his apron, once crisp and white, now wrinkled and smudged with blotches of dark red.

Moose used the shadows in the dim hallway to shift toward the stairs as Orion raised the window behind the rocking chairs. The sounds of windows in Holt's room were heard to be opening as well. Fresh, cool air began to chase away the ominous smell of oblivion.

Laudie Kate emerged from the room, along with Evie. Even though exhausted expressions covered their faces and bloody smears coated the fronts of their dresses, Orion could sense their deep sighs of relief as they stepped into the hallway. Laudie Kate headed across the hall into her room. Evie moved quietly down the hall near where Ranger Elkins stood.

Orion approached the doctor, the Ranger's face a cold, hard mask. "How is he?" Orion asked.

"That gash near his shoulder had me worried, it did," Dr. Vaughn said to no one in particular. "Yessir, shoulders are tricky things. Bullets can lodge in a bone and you can't quite get to 'em. Thought we just might have to clean it and sew up around it." Putting his spectacles back in place, he spoke to Orion directly, "But the slug decided to keep moving. Small caliber, only cut the fleshy part."

"And?" Orion pressed, frustrated at the doctor's meandering explanation.

"And we wait," the doctor said. "I got the bleeding stopped. Took the bullet out of his thigh. Got everything cleaned and bandaged. He's lost a lot of blood though."

"So, what're you sayin', Doc? Is he gonna live?" Orion was now nearly bursting at the seams.

"Bullets are an intrusion on a person's body and soul," the doctor said calmly. "You never know the havoc they cause, or the outcome, until that person decides inside whether to return to the living. I've seen men survive worse than what hit your friend. I've seen those hurt even less not make it." He gestured with his head back into the room. "It's up to that man and his maker."

Orion drew his breath in and out slowly, his shoulders rising and falling trying to release the tension. "Holt stands in good with the spirits," he declared, hands on his hips. "He'll make it." He nodded. "He'll make it." The first assertion was to assure himself. The second was a declaration to the spirits. "Can we see him?"

"Sure. Try not to wake him though."

The doctor followed as Orion and Tag entered the room where Holt lay. Laudie Kate reemerged from her room with a blanket and joined them.

Orion stood by the bed and watched Holt for a moment, listening to his partner breathe.

Tag stood next to Orion, not quite sure what was going on. Finally, he raised up on hind legs and put his front paws on the bed. He sniffed at his master, getting a full whiff of the aroma of chloroform and laudanum. He whimpered slightly at the smell and at the sight of Holt lying motionless, not acknowledging him.

Orion patted the dog on the head before leaning over to speak to his partner.

"Holt, it's Orion. I dunno if you can hear me…but you're gonna be all right. Doc fixed everythin'. You're gonna be just fine. You're gonna be fine, you hear? I got Tag with me. I'll take care of him, don't you worry. You rest now an' keep fightin', Holt. You hear me, Holt Corrigan? You keep fightin'."

Suddenly, Holt's entire body tensed. "My guns…my guns…wh-where're my guns…" he mumbled. He tried to rise, eyes fluttering, not really open, not really seeing; his head jerking left-and-right in a half-crazed search for his weapons.

Laudie Kate placed the blanket in her arms down by Holt's feet and then moved to lay her hands gently on his chest, trying to settle him.

Orion went to the nightstand where Holt's shoulder holster rig held his two Russian Smith & Wessons. He drew one of the guns and quickly emptied it of bullets. He laid the pistol across Holt's stomach and guided the young Ranger's uninjured right arm and hand to the ivory panther-inlaid grip. He watched his partner relax his tensed frame as the familiarity of touching the weapon brought a sense of peace to his anxious mind.

As Laudie Kate started to let go of his chest, something else triggered inside Holt and he tensed and jerked once more.

"My-my medicine pouch…Four Shields! Wh-where is…" he stammered.

She gently shushed him again. Not strong enough to continue his search, Holt returned to unconsciousness.

Orion glanced around the room. "Where's his medicine pouch?"

"If that's it, it's behind you, on the dresser there, with his clothes." Laudie Kate pointed. "We took it off so Dr. Vaughn could patch him up."

"I need to get it back on him," Orion said, walking around to the other side of the bed. He grabbed the elk skin pouch and gently put it around Holt's neck, arranging it so it lay neatly on his chest. "Dunno what's in it. He'll need it though…to come back."

In the pouch was Holt's personal sacred medicine—a small red stone with a white star-like spot in its center. The stone was a spiritual support, a belief he had adopted from the very Indians he sometimes had to fight.

It was during a fierce battle against a Kiowa war party in the early days of the war, that Holt and four other Confederate guerrilla fighters had been surrounded by eighteen warriors. He saw the stone laying at his feet and decided to put it in his pocket. All the Rebels survived the fight and Holt had kept the rock ever since. He knew that Indians believed in the strength of personal medicine, usually something of nature, something that gave them courage, strength and protection. Who was he to question the idea? It was also the reason he carried a mountain lion claw in his pocket—a gift from his mother when he was a boy.

He credited this special medicine with getting him through some tough times. Only his brother Deed knew about it. His brother, Blue, being a preacher, would frown on the native belief. Holt was certain the pebble was actually something that belonged to him in another life when he, too, was an Indian. The stone had waited for him to find it again.

The pouch had been a recent gift. At the beginning of his original journey to meet Orion and find The Angel, an eerie Apache holy man, Four Shields, had visited Holt's camp one night along the trail. Four Shields told Holt that there were many spirits following the young Ranger, spirits that were all around him and in him.

"Your spirit, the *ndołkah*, has served you well in times of difficulty," Four Shields had said.

"*Ndołkah*?" Holt questioned.

"Big cat," the medicine man had said. "The mountain lion is a warrior. It carries with it energy, power, and strength. This spirit gives you skill, cunning and stealth. It has led you through great turmoil and strife. Although…it almost left you when you struggled with choosing the proper path to travel."

He counseled that Holt now had new spirits walking with him as well. "These are protector spirits. They are those who looked upon you highly, in life. They are your *tsét'soyé*, your bear spirits. Your *ndołkah* helps you fight, but your *tsét'soyé* will help you fight for what is good and true. Listen to them well."

Four Shields then had reached into a medicine bag at his side and pulled out a small elk skin pouch with a long loop of elk string. The pouch had a painted circle on it. The circle was colored with plant and vegetable pigments in equal quarters of blue, white, red and yellow. He told Holt that these colors were sacred, symbolizing a balance of life and spirit. Inside the pouch was cattail pollen.

As he decorated Holt's neck with the pouch, the Apache pointed at Holt's shirt pocket and instructed, "Your medicine stone belongs inside the pouch too."

Later on, after the strange visit, Holt had wondered how the medicine man had known about his sacred stone.

———

The older Ranger looked down at his unconscious partner. A piece of Holt's hair had flopped outside the dressing surrounding his forehead. Orion smoothed the lock of hair to the side and adjusted the blanket around Holt's shoulders. Tag had heard his master's frantic voice and jumped up on the bed, his nose gently finding the side of Holt's bandaged head, trying to nuzzle some attention.

"Ohhh, he shouldn't be up there," the doctor warned, looking at the dog.

"C'mon, Tag." Orion hurried around the bed and carefully gathered the dog in his arms. Tag usually did not take to anyone but Holt holding him, but he seemed comfortable with this arrangement. The two stood like that for several moments looking at Holt. Orion spoke softly and soothingly to Tag, words only the dog could hear.

With Tag still in his arms, Orion turned to Laudie Kate. "Can we get an extra blanket an' maybe an

Arbuckles box? To make a bed for Tag. In here. He isn't gonna want to leave Holt."

She smiled and said, "We'll get something set up for him."

"Much obliged," Orion said. He and the dog resumed their observation of Holt.

The doctor put on his coat and hat. "Keep an eye on our patient, Laudie," he said. "Let me know if he bleeds through those bandages or spikes a fever."

She nodded, listening intently.

"Watch when he first wakes," Dr. Vaughn continued as he headed out the door. "You'll likely need to hold him down again. Don't let him move too sudden or he'll bust everything open."

At this, Laudie Kate looked less comfortable, but agreed, nevertheless.

Orion moved out to the hallway and set the dog down. "Thank you, Doc," he said, relief in his voice. "Looks like your best is pretty good."

"We'll know for sure in a day or so."

CHAPTER FIVE

As the doctor made his way downstairs, Orion looked around for Ranger Elkins. Moose's partner, Dal Frantze, had infiltrated an outlaw gang before. The group had ridden into a nearby town to a dance. Frantze had pretended to fall in love with a young lady there. He wanted the excuse of being able to ride to the town to see the girl so he could file reports. Frantze suggested that Moose do the same in Stebbins so he could send reports about the Viklunds to Captain McCoy. Moose had followed through on the idea and found Evie, only he had actually, truly fallen for her.

"Did I see a large cowboy up here looking for Miss Evie?" Laudie Kate asked. "You wouldn't have missed him, he's so big. He's taken quite a shine to her. Sneaks away from the ranch to see her whenever he can."

Orion did not react to Laudie Kate's information and studied her for a moment. He guessed she was in her mid twenties. There was a sense of high energy and self-confidence about her, with an independent, steely core.

She was not classically beautiful, but more than pleasant to look at.

She hollered toward the stairwell to the unseen barmaid, "Evie, grab a blanket and a coffee box for a dog bed, will you?"

"Tag'll appreciate that. Holt too," Orion noted.

It was her turn to not react. She stood, reading the Ranger standing in front of her.

Orion broke the silence. "Laudie Kate, Hart, is it?"

"Yes."

"I'd like to talk to you. You're in a bit of trouble."

"About the shooting?"

"No. That was a…misunderstanding." He reached into his coat. "I gotta handbill here from the marshal…'bout a gambler the law is interested in catchin' up with." He fished the paper out of his coat pocket and showed it to her. "You know him? The gambler? Says he had a woman along. About five-foot-four, good figure, blue eyes, brown hair an' a scar along her right cheek. Says she likes a card game an' a good saloon."

Laudie Kate didn't acknowledge the handbill, putting her hands on her hips and looking Orion square in the eyes.

"Now," he continued, "there was no one matchin' the gambler's description in the bar, but this woman sure could be you."

"Yes, it could be," Laudie Kate said, looking down briefly to smooth the front of her bloodied dress before locking her eyes back onto Orion's. Even in this state of disarray, there was no doubt of her allure. "As a matter of fact, it is me."

She looked up and down the hallway and stepped

back into her room to avoid being in the hall but could still see into Holt's room to keep an eye on her patient.

Orion followed and asked delicately, "How does a young woman like you get herself on a wanted poster?"

Laudie Kate drew in her breath. "She gets herself married," she said, then exhaled, "to a no-good gambler."

"The handbill says he's a cheat."

"Was a cheat."

"He reformed? Or'd you leave him?"

"Neither. He left me. Rather suddenly."

Orion's raised eyebrows continued the interrogation.

"He was shot."

He just looked at Laudie Kate, deciding to let her finish the story.

She smoothed back a strand of her hair with a blood-stained hand. "I didn't know about the cheating until he got caught. I just thought he was having a lucky streak. Then his luck truly ran out...playing poker in Chinnery. He was a big winner, stacking the deck. And they called him on it. With bullets."

Her voice began to fill with emotion. Orion held out a handkerchief. She shook her head and took another deep breath instead.

"I guess it was my fault," she continued. "He couldn't afford the lifestyle we had become accustomed to. Thought he needed to cheat to keep me."

"An' did he, need to?"

Laudie Kate's slap across Orion's face was rattler-quick.

"Guess I deserved that." Orion paused, not touching the fire rising in the cheek she struck. "When'd all this happen?" he asked gently.

"About six or seven months ago," she said, a stern look still in her eyes.

"An' you've been on the move ever since."

She looked intently into the Ranger's eyes. "Let's just say this isn't the first time that wanted notice has appeared."

"You could change your line of work—"

"No, Mr. Higbee," she interrupted. "I do like a good saloon. I like to gamble. Being on my own, calling my own shots…it's who I am."

"Was he…your husband…the one who taught you how to shoot?"

"He taught me how to protect myself. Draw smoothly. Take good aim. Make sure."

"You were a good pupil," Orion said wearily.

Silence closed in on them. Finally, Laudie Kate spoke. "You don't have to be concerned with me, Ranger Orion. I'm on that handbill because I chose poorly when it came to a man. That's all. What you really need to be asking about is why your friend in there has four bullet wounds when I only shot twice."

His eyes anchored onto hers, wondering if he heard her correctly.

"Check my gun. You've got it laying on the table there in the hallway. It's only been fired twice. My first shot clipped him in the head and my second caught him near his shoulder. That bullet in his thigh and crease along his hip came from someone else."

"I'll be damned…"

"Different sized rounds too. I noticed that after Dr. Vaughn took out the one in his thigh. It was a .45. My gun's a .31." She grabbed his hand and dropped a mishappen slug into his palm. "I figured someone would want this as a souvenir. Or evidence."

As the weight of her words sank in, a short man reached the top of the stairwell. They had heard the stairs creaking ahead of his appearance and now could hear him hurriedly moving down the hall. Orion stepped back out of the room, his hand across his chest grasping his shoulder-holstered Navy Colt.

"Señor Ranger, I am Miguel Navarro," the little man called out in his clipped English. "Thees ees my hotel. Honored I am to have you and the other brave Ranger here. I hope okay he will be."

The tall Ranger relaxed. "Thank you, Miguel. Orion Higbee," he replied, then motioned toward Holt's room with his thumb. "That's my partner, Holt Corrigan, in there. We only meant to arrest a gunman an' move on. Things went sideways."

"I hear Mees Hart shot the Ranger."

"That she did."

"Then she must go. You will arrest her, no?"

"No, I reckon not, Señor Navarro."

"No?"

"No. She thought he was a bandit, comin' to rob your place."

The little man cocked his head to the side. He had not heard this part of the story.

"By my estimation," Orion continued. "Had Ranger Corrigan actually been a bandit, she would've saved you a lotta money today."

Navarro placed his hand across his mouth, thoughts conflicted.

"She's got sand, Navarro. She needs to stay."

The innkeeper began to nod in contemplation, but

then noticed Tag. "Oh my. What's that, a dog? He can't be here. Shoo! Shoo!"

"Just a minute, Señor…"

"That dog, he cannot stay."

"*That dog*? He's a hero, as much a Ranger as I am."

Navarro looked at Orion, not sure of what he was hearing.

"He's saved my life…"

The little man tried to speak, but Orion would not let him.

"On top of that, he's Ranger Corrigan's dog."

"Ohhh…"

"His name is Tag Along."

Navarro looked at the dog, now beginning to understand.

"An' he stays."

"*Si.*"

"So does the lady. Both of them. *Comprende*, Señor Navarro?"

"*Si. Si.*"

"Good," Orion said, walking away from the little man back to his rocking chair. A brief glance caught Laudie Kate standing in her room, just out of sight from the hallway, listening in.

Her eyes caught his and she mouthed silently, "Thank you."

Orion returned the acknowledgment with a brief nod, then turned to face the hotel owner once again. "Oh, another thing, Señor Navarro, Tag needs to stay here. In Ranger Corrigan's room. Miss Hart an' Miss Evie are puttin' a bed together for him."

The diminutive hotel owner looked again at the dog.

"He'll be real quiet, I promise," Orion continued.

"He's also real partial to beef stew. You got good stew here?"

"*Si*, Meester Ranger."

"*Gracias*, Miguel. Holt's bill here will be settled when he can move on. Texas an' the Rangers thank you. I thank you."

The little man bobbed his head energetically and hurried down the stairs, eager to get away from the imposing lawman.

As the hallway quieted down, Orion spoke softly to Laudie Kate, "I'm sure you're wantin' to clean up, so I'll leave you alone now."

"Thank you, Ranger."

"Evie, you say it was? I'll check with her on the progress of Tag's bed. An' maybe find he an' I some of that stew."

CHAPTER SIX

As the night wore on, Orion found himself sitting in an isolated corner of the Blue Sky Inn's saloon. Maybe it was due to being a Sunday night or maybe the town was subdued by the news of the shooting of a Texas Ranger, but the Blue Sky was not particularly busy. Just a couple of tables were occupied and a small handful of drinkers stood at the bar.

Holt's dog, Tag Along, sat at the Ranger's feet eagerly enjoying a bowl of beef stew. Orion had thought eating sounded like a good idea, but his own bowl of stew was not being relished with nearly the same enthusiasm. The events of the day were now weighing heavily on his mind. Everything seemed so fresh, yet distant, like some strange memory. It was making him weary.

The reality of the extra shots being fired at Holt that Laudie Kate presented to him was a mystery with few answers.

"You look like you could use a friend," said a pleasant voice.

The storm clouds surrounding Orion's thoughts

cleared momentarily and he looked up into Laudie Kate's smiling face.

"May I?" she said, gesturing to an empty chair.

"Y-Yes please," Orion stammered, rising to a half-standing position. "I'm sorry...damn, forgot my manners."

"Forgot them only because your mind was somewhere else."

Orion's tired face stared back at Laudie Kate. She had scrubbed up and changed her clothes since finishing with Holt and the doctor.

"Anything I can do to help?" she asked.

"You've done plenty, Miss Laudie. I mean that sincerely this time."

"How about I buy you a drink?"

"Have one for me. I gotta feelin' I won't be drinkin' any more for a while. Gotta big puzzle here an' not enough pieces." He paused and leaned back in his chair. "As funny as it seems, you might be the only one here I can trust."

"Thank you? That's about as backhanded a compliment as I've ever received."

Orion continued with no apology. "Been chewin' on somethin'. Holt an' I arrived last night after dark. Supposedly, only the marshal knew we were in town. You now tell me that two other shots were fired at Holt. Seems obvious to me that someone else knew we were in town. So, did the marshal tell somebody accidentally or on purpose? How else did someone know we were comin' to arrest Longley? An' was it that much of a threat to arrest him?"

"My, my, that *is* a lot to chew on."

"An' worse, maybe I can't trust you an' I just opened

a nastier can of worms by tellin' you all this." The questions tore at his brain and his appetite.

"Are you sure you don't want that drink?" She smiled.

"Want? Yes. Should? No."

Laudie Kate smiled supportively.

Orion took off his hat with one hand and smoothed back his hair with the other before setting it on his head again and speaking, "Holt an' I been through a lot these past few months. Tracked down a killer, someone who'd been tearin' aroun' Texas murderin' people for more'n a year. Called himself, The Angel."

"I remember reading about all that in the newspaper. That was you two?"

"Yeah, it sure was. We got The Angel all right, but then we were stuck with an unsolved mystery. That crazy bastard hadn't acted alone. Someone was pullin' his strings. We went down a lotta ratholes until we discovered the miserable sonuvabitch was right under our noses. Holt's hometown justice of the peace was that evil priest's blood brother. An' a candidate for governor! Ho-lee damn."

"That was *big* news. It just happened. You two again?"

"Well, we had a lotta help, but we were right in the middle of it. Now, we get sent here on a simple mission to bring down some rustlers...and this happens..." He paused a moment, lost in thought, then continued softly, more to himself than to Laudie Kate, "Mebbe it's time... we get Holt healed up and ride off to help his brothers raise horses...somethin' less hazardous..."

"And here I thought you Rangers just tracked down cattle thieves and bank robbers," Laudie Kate said, breaking his reverie, concern on her face and in her voice.

"An' now they just brought me this." He picked up an official-looking piece of paper lying on the table—a telegram. Captain McCoy's response to Orion's earlier message was no-nonsense:

> HIGBEE:
>
>   RELIEVED CORRIGAN IS ALIVE.
>
>   ASSUME HE'S UNABLE TO CARRY ON DUTIES.
>
>   NO LONGER AN ACTIVE RANGER.
>
>   CONTINUE OPERATION. WIRE FINDINGS SOONEST.
>
> MCCOY

Holt not being an active Ranger as of this evening meant he would not be paid by the state, nor expected to assume his duties. It was standard protocol whenever any Ranger was wounded. A harsh reminder that the state would not help you if you weren't in a position to help the state.

Orion knew this would happen but was angered it happened so soon. He held the message over the flame of the table's small oil lamp, letting the stub of paper burn to ashes. Definitely no longer hungry, he set his bowl of stew down by Tag so at least one of them could enjoy the meal.

"That's a big puzzle, to be sure," Laudie Kate said. "At least I can help you with a little part of it."

"I appreciate that, but—"

"As we're sitting here," Laudie Kate interrupted, continuing on. "Evie is in Holt's room, the door is locked and braced. She's fixing up a bed for the dog and sitting in a rocking chair with her brother's sawed-off shotgun in her lap."

Orion's eyes widened ever so slightly.

"Marshal Baxter Hollings might be a bit naïve," she continued, intensity in her voice. "But, he is a *good* man. Don't judge that book by its cover. His job here is made tougher by a sheriff who is never around. If anything, Marshal Hollings is doing two jobs. There is no way he is a part of…whatever this might be. Maybe your meeting with the marshal was overheard. Or, you weren't as incognito as you thought you were."

Orion nodded along with her explanation. "Very interestin'.."

"But that doesn't remove any of your other who and why questions about the sheriff or the Viklunds."

"Wish you hadn't set right down on that specifically." Orion frowned. "Tyin' them together like that."

"Mr. Ranger Orion Higbee, I play cards. I can read a situation," Laudie Kate's eyes held the lawman's gaze with intensity. "That's the reason Evie is guarding your friend. Stebbins isn't known for taking potshots at Rangers. It's best to be careful."

"Miss Laudie, you've been *very* helpful," Orion said, scraping his chair back to stand. "Thank you for openin' my eyes. I been feelin' on edge about it." He tipped his hat slightly. "Tag an' I will take it from here."

"Still think I'm not trustworthy?" she said with a smile as he stood.

From his waistband, Orion pulled Laudie Kate's pocket gun and placed it on the table next to her. "It's still loaded," he said. "You helped us, better watch out for yourself."

CHAPTER SEVEN

Upstairs in the small Stebbins hotel room, an unconscious Holt Corrigan faced a tormented fight to remain in the world of the living. The injured Ranger's dreams were vivid. Chaotic. An unsettling and provoking journey.

Getting shot was a nightmare that repeated in Holt's fevered stupor, swirling continually around his senses, making him relive the terrible moment over and over and over...a gun flashing from his right...a sharp concussion against his head...followed by more shots...from somewhere else...was it three shots or four? More? The reports from the guns rang out relentlessly, booming like echoes in a cave.

He felt the first bullet furrow just above his ear, its impact spinning him, his head suddenly filled with the buzzing of hundreds of bee hives. Then, his shoulder burned with a slash of fire. Suddenly, a searing punch stabbed at his thigh. An invader dwelled there now. He was driven to the floor, thick with pain. And fear. As he toppled completely over, a demon flew out of nowhere to bite him above his hip.

In this lurid world, it wasn't the floor that caught Holt. Instead, he fell into a murky, red lake. His head, pounding sharp and heavy, could barely be kept above its depths. Blackness began to descend and envelop him in a deadly, silky blanket, leaving him unable to do anything but lie there in an inky abyss. Before he could be completely swallowed up, he suddenly found himself standing once more at the doors of the Blue Sky Inn. There was nothing he could do but barge through them afresh and face an unceasing horror.

The shots rang out, and he fell into the sea of shadowy crimson yet again. Ahead of darkness taking over, the smell of the dusty floor invaded his every breath. Sawdust, adhered by blood, crawled on his skin and clothes like insects wriggling across his skin…

Suddenly he jerked awake.

The real world came crashing through his psyche and the dusty planked floor became a bed. The darkness disappeared as though a vast raven's wing waved across the landscape, giving rise to light and form.

Disoriented, Holt had no idea where he was, or what day it was, or what was going on. He felt disconnected from his body. Through his spinning vision, he became aware that he only wore undergarments. The rest of him felt tressed up, bandaged tightly.

And on fire.

He felt his medicine pouch on his chest and clutched it tightly. "Four Shields…" he cried out. "I can't hear the spirits! Can they hear me?"

Before he received an answer, Holt Corrigan was unconscious again.

Intense, bizarre dreams surrounded him once more. In the murkiness shrouding him, the bullets flew again. This time, his hat went flying from his head and took off in the shape of a bright red cardinal. A large, unseen raven had spooked the beautiful red bird.

"*Kraa! Kraa!*"

A throaty and hoarse croak rose in pitch and came from the back of the big bird's throat.

"*Kraa! Kraa!*" It was harsher this time.

The raven's screeches were painfully loud.

Holt became aware this winged black specter was taking him to a torturous world of macabre conflicts and strange presentations of people known and unknown.

Shards of memory glittered in his visions. Holt's brothers, Blue and Deed, meandered through his nightmares, like a creek not sure of its banks. They did not seem to even see him.

———

Holt's own name was Holton Jefferson Corrigan, named after their mother's father. Dedrick William Corrigan was his youngest brother's full name, but everyone called him Deed, except their mother. Blue's birth name was Bluemont Wade Corrigan, a combination of the names of their father and paternal grandfather. The name Bluemont had brought more than enough fistfights in school, but his brothers had always been willing to step in and help turn things around.

All three brothers looked a lot alike, even down to their once-broken noses, courtesy of each other. Deed was eight years younger than Blue, an inch taller, fifteen pounds heavier, and definitely wilder. Holt was two years younger than Blue and two inches shorter. Deed and Holt resembled each other the most in looks and temperament, even down to their long hair and mustaches. Their older brother, Blue, kept his face clean-shaven and hair clipped short.

Both of their parents had died when the boys were young. Their mother and sister succumbed to pneumonia when Blue was eighteen; Holt, sixteen; and Deed, ten. Their father had died six months before their mother from a broken neck when he was thrown from a horse. The boys—and their ranch—were saved by the appearance of Nakashima Silka, a former samurai, who took them under his wing. The Corrigans grew to look upon Silka as their godfather.

Three years later, Blue and Holt left to fight for the Confederacy while the much younger Deed stayed with Silka to keep the ranch afloat. While the older brothers were gone, Silka honed Deed's fighting skills. Blue returned from the war with his left arm missing. Holt rode the outlaw trail after the surrender and came home only after Blue convinced him the war was truly over.

———

"*Kraa! Kraa!*"

Holt floated through his hellish dreamscape, not sure of where he was. The raven stopped its cries momentarily, but he could feel its presence nearby. Holt now found himself cradled in a stand of lush, flowing grass, just up the hill from a familiar ranch house. He laid there, looking up through the limbs of an old oak tree, sun cascading through the leaves.

Three boisterous boys suddenly ran by him. As if

from nowhere, a joyously smiling mother appeared, sitting near him on a blanket, watching the roughhouse game of tag the boys invented. A taciturn father sat nearby, smiling dutifully, yet lovingly, at a little girl who was offering a large handful of wildflowers for him to sniff.

The family picnicked around him, oblivious of the wounded man lying there. He watched them, mesmerized. Holt realized this was him and his family, in a world so very long ago. He looked fondly at a sister he barely knew and was fascinated to be reminded of a time when his brother Blue had both of his arms.

"*Kraa! Kraa!*"

Suddenly, the sun was blocked, the repeated shrieks of the raven shattered the tranquility and fun. Holt was now aware he looked on from above, color draining from the scene like chalk being rinsed from a board. The boys ran off. The parents and the little girl faded from view.

Three lonesome, somber tombstones grew from the land like gloomy, gray weeds. Holt turned away. He knew what names were on the stones.

Following that piece of yesterday, he was yanked to another dreamscape, the raven and its shrieks leading the way.

"*Kraa! Kraa!*"

Another hill of flowing grass rose to meet his body, but the world this knoll resided in was filled with hostility and danger. The smell of acrid smoke invaded Holt's nose. The raven's screeches dissolved into a din of explosions and shouts that attacked his ears. It was like half-seeing, half-sensing a horrible and grotesque panorama through brief flashes of lightning. Sabers clanged around him. Wounded men and horses screamed. Dirt flew. The earth shuddered.

Abruptly, Holt was on a horse at the head of Rebel cavalry. He, his brother Blue, and their company swung their sweating horses to charge an entrenched Yankee force. In an instant, a wall of flame erupted near him. The force of the explosion blew Holt from his horse in a storm of wreckage and dust. The world went out like a lantern in the wind. The silence hurt his ears.

Suddenly, the raven screamed louder than ever, and blue-clad figures burst through the haze. Holt's pistols were suddenly in his hands, spitting fire and lead at the dangerous shapes, making them vanish.

Stumbling through the maelstrom, Holt discovered a gray-clad shape lying in the debris. The body focused into view as his brother Blue, his butternut tunic shredded. Holt recoiled at the sight of his brother's battered and blasted body. The throbbing of the ragged, bloody stump where Blue's left arm used to be pulsed like the drumming in Holt's head.

In his nightmarish vision, Holt found the rest of Blue's missing arm and reached for it. To his horror, the arm writhed away from him, forcing Holt to chase it through the eddying smoke.

The next thing he knew, Holt was carrying his severely wounded brother, weaving his way through constant bursts of flame and debris. He lugged Blue's bloody appendage with him as well.

For what seemed like miles, he waded through a turbulent world seething with fury. Finally, he came upon a gruesome hospital tent emanating the coppery smell of blood and the horrid odor of infected, rotting flesh. Holt stood there, surveying what seemed to be an unending collection of similarly mangled and maimed bodies. He yelled in frustration for doctors who never appeared. Blue's severed arm raised and tried to punch him, scurrying away never to be found again.

"*Kraa! Kraa!*"

The cries of the wounded turned into the awful screams of the raven which tugged Holt from the vileness of the field hospital to a familiar restaurant—the Cedar Bluff Hotel in his hometown of Wilkon. Ghastly bedsheets covered in gore swirled into crisp, white cloths covering neat tables set for dinner.

Holt found himself standing by one of the tables. Sitting there was a priest and a half-breed Kiowa outlaw. Father Miguel Beltran and Neemo, the two prisoners who were lynched in Sweetclover. Here they were, now laughing and leering at him. At their feet were gruesomely murdered bodies—Holt's godfather, Nakashima Silka, and Judge Oscar Pence, the man who pardoned Holt and gave him his life back—were among them. The evil priest gestured to Holt, who was suddenly aware he had become their waiter. From a new bottle, Holt refilled their glasses with rich red wine. The two toasted themselves and threw back their heads in laughter, revealing deep, sickening ligature wounds along their necks that had been left by the nooses that took their lives. They sneered at Holt and drank deeply, the wine changing before his very eyes into bright crimson blood.

Their laughter accompanied the gurgling croak of the raven as Holt realized three more people were seated at a nearby table, chatting and smiling. The rich Wilkon attorney and justice of the peace, Meden Taliff, along with his assassin, Kane Barlow, laughed sinisterly along with The Angel. The three were blood brothers in every sense of the words. Seated at the table, looking frightened was Claire Baldwin, the Wilkon schoolteacher.

At one time, all Holt could think about was a future with Claire. She seemed to have cared for him as well, but often chose to be with Taliff instead. Holt had tired of her games and had even burned sage to cleanse his jail of evil spirits and thoughts of her. Claire had been caught in the middle of Taliff's travesty of a gubernatorial campaign. Taliff had been taken down in a hail of bullets. Barlow had been killed by Holt's brother, Deed, with his bare hands.

Taliff, in his morning suit riddled with bullet holes, suddenly stood and with one sweep cleared the table of its contents and their companions. Barlow, with most of his throat ripped away, lifted Claire from her chair and threw her on the table. Taliff reached down, his hands tearing open the front of her gingham dress, exposing her nearly naked body as he moved on top of her. Before Holt could fight for her honor...

"Kraa! Kraa!"

Hatred and blackness began to descend upon Holt once more. The raspy cry of the raven transported him once again to the entrance of the Blue Sky Inn, his guns readied. He hurtled through the doors and the bullets flew...

"Kraa! Kraa! Kraa! Kraa!"

———

From his hotel bed, Holt yelled out, "Nooo! You bastards! Noooo!!"

At the sound of Holt's hollering, Orion sat up from the rocking chair with a start. He strode across the small room to the bed and felt his partner's forehead. It was hot to the touch, his skin flushed and dry. A hard fever was challenging the young Ranger's life.

Laudie Kate had heard the shouting and rushed to Holt's room.

Orion answered the locked door, still in his clothes and wearing his guns, weariness covering his face.

"Hi, Miss Laudie. He's burnin' up with fever."

"Oh no…"

"Shot up like this an' leakin' like he did, I expected it."

"Should I get Dr. Vaughn…"

"Not much the doc can do. If this don't break by mornin', then we'll fetch 'im."

"But…"

"I'm gonna do what the doc would tell us to do. Can you get some broth?"

"Is that all?"

"Yeah, just the broth for now."

Laudie Kate hurried away to retrieve a bowl of broth for Holt. Before long, she returned.

"Thank you, Miss Laudie."

"Is there anything else…"

"No, get yourself some rest."

"Are you sure?"

"I've done this before," Orion said in a gentle voice. "Too many times…durin' the war." His calm smile convinced her.

She reluctantly padded back to her room. Her face wore a look of concern.

Orion took the pistol Holt had cried out for and put it on the nightstand. He then placed a cold wet cloth on Holt's chest. Under Tag's watchful gaze, the older

Ranger sat on a small, straight-backed chair by the bed and dripped spoonsful of the broth onto Holt's tongue, gently closing his mouth each time to encourage swallowing.

"C'mon, Holt, this is good for you," he said with a soothing tone. "Keep fightin', you hear me, peckerhead?"

He managed to get most of the bowl of broth into the young Ranger. He repeated the same technique with a mug full of water.

Before he took another cool rag and placed it on Holt's forehead, Orion looked skyward and quietly said, "If there are spirits watchin' over this man like I think there are, I'm askin' you to help him fight. Help bring him back." He then re-wetted the cloth for Holt's chest. The young Ranger was still too hot, but he seemed calmer now.

"All right, Tag, let's get some rest. Okay, buddy?" He coaxed the dog off of the bed and into his coffee box with a small piece of jerky. The older Ranger sat tiredly and closed his eyes, trying to follow his own advice.

Again, in the night, Orion repeated dripping spoonsful of water into Holt's mouth. The rags on the young Ranger's chest and head were replenished with cool water. Orion tore a bandanna in half, soaking each piece in the basin and wrapping them around Holt's wrists.

Just before dawn, Orion awakened. He felt his partner's head and face. He let out a huge exhale. Holt's fever had broken. He stood over the young man and held his fingers near Holt's nose just to make certain he was breathing.

Orion's smile was as big as Christmas.

Satisfied, the older Ranger pulled the now-warm

cloths from Holt's chest and forehead and went over to the dresser where the water pitcher sat next to a big bowl. He poured a little into the bowl and re-wetted the cloths before putting them both back in place. From the pitcher, Orion filled the coffee mug on the nightstand. As he had done throughout the night, he sat in a chair by the bed, holding open Holt's lips, gently trickling drops onto the unconscious man's tongue, then pushing his mouth closed. Orion repeated this until the mug was empty.

"All right, Holt," the older Ranger said softly. "Find your way back now."

Tag laid by his master's side, as if knowing care and comfort was needed. Orion fell asleep right there in the small, straight-backed chair.

———

The nightmare of Holt's dreamworld disappeared like snuffed candlelight. He was aware that fighting off the tortuous visions that tormented him caused him to sweat through his bedclothes and sheets. He felt his dreams had not totally ended because he was aware of the presence of bear spirits that were there with him. They had brought a friend who spoke in a familiar, soothing voice and offered him life-giving water. Together, they all helped guide Holt on the journey to find his way back.

Tag Along was there too. The dog's soft licks on his master's hand moved his arm toward his medicine pouch.

Holt found the sacred elk skin and calm returned.

CHAPTER EIGHT

Two days ride from Stebbins, in the town of Wilkon, County Sheriff James Hannah was finishing breakfast with his wife, Rebecca, and reading the latest edition of the *Wilkon Epitaph*, just out that morning. The town newspaper came out once a week, sometimes twice. Although Hannah had already received a rundown from his good friend Holt, he read the article about the takedown of Meden Taliff and Kane Barlow.

A large headline bannered across the front page of the *Epitaph*: "Campaign of Horror Ends." Information about the shootout in Modlin had come easily, Hannah's own wife was an unwilling witness, a hostage taken by Taliff and Barlow.

This new edition included quite a few details, but not all. The *Epitaph's* new reporter had decided to leave out the gruesomeness of Deed Corrigan ripping the throat from Kane Barlow. But the article detailed the hard work and bravery of Wilkon's heroes, Ranger Holt Corrigan and his brother, Deed, as well as lawmen

Bradley Cooke and Lear Freeburg. The exploits of townsman, Jimmy Todd, who died in the raid, was also commemorated.

Hannah read the story and exhaled slowly, knowing from experience the dangers facing down a killer; difficulties you could not just put into words. He had spent the final showdown recuperating from the knifing he received from Barlow. Even that tidbit was included in the paper's account as well as a separate announcement of his retiring as county sheriff with a special election for his replacement to held in the fall.

Hannah sipped his coffee and flipped to the inner part of the newspaper. Several items were pieces of news from neighboring towns, some a distance away. While the Epitaph editor, Leroy Gillespie, recuperated from being attacked in Taliff and Barlow's violent rampage, an editor from a nearby town as well as two Wilkon citizens helped keep the local paper afloat.

It appeared this new editor and his cohorts were exchanging stories over the telegraph wire. Clever idea, Hannah thought, make the *Epitaph* even better by helping connect the region, not to mention a good opportunity to keep the lies and propaganda out of the news. One could hope, he noted.

He read a brief article about trouble in cattle country, somewhere up in St. Clair County. It vaguely reported the arrest of a notorious gunman after a shooting that involved Texas Rangers.

The article held few details, so Hannah started perusing a dry goods ad, but his attention was drawn back to the short account from St. Clair County. He readjusted his eyeglasses and read again, "*A Ranger had been wounded in the fight.*" No other information was noted, but the item struck an odd chord in his mind. He drove the thought away.

Holt and Orion were ordered to go to Stebbins, Hannah remembered. But there were several Rangers assigned on this mission. That's what Holt had said. Where is Stebbins located, he wondered to himself. Is that in St. Clair?

Rebecca noticed the look on her husband's face. "What's wrong, James?"

"Nothing. Just 'crap in the paper,' as Holt would say." He half-smiled. But the sentence about a Ranger stuck with him. The timing reported in the article and the printing of this edition of the *Epitaph* meant the incident had recently occurred.

They finished their meal and kissed, both heading off to their days.

Hannah went through his morning routine. Although he had tendered his resignation as county sheriff pending the election of a new lawman, he still felt responsible for upholding the duties of the badge. He checked in on the jail, made rounds through town, and visited with business owners and their customers. Even in quiet times, citizens liked to see that a badge was nearby.

But there was something about that article he could not shake. He needed to address this unsettled feeling.

Hannah fired off telegrams to Ranger Holt Corrigan and Ranger Orion Higbee in care of several town marshals, including the one in Stebbins. Just checking in, a status report of progress, his wires inquired.

"Mr. Hayes, what county is the town of Stebbins located in?"

The meticulous telegraph office proprietor replied, "St. Clair. Cattle country."

"Okay, thanks," Hannah responded, a grim expression matched his thoughts.

He stopped at the general store and chatted with the couple who ran the shop and the usual group of men who held court around the stove there. They asked him about how construction on his new saloon was going. It was their way of asking about a new sheriff without really asking. Hannah talked about how lucky Wilkon was to have dedicated lawmen like Logan Wheeler, Bradley Cooke, and Lear Freeburg.

Afternoon arrived and Hannah was back at the Howard's Real Estate, Insurance & Telegraph Office. He had already checked in there several times since sending his earlier telegrams. This time, Mr. Hayes handed him three wire messages. "They've just come in," Mr. Hayes informed the sheriff.

Hannah shuffled through the small stack of papers. The first one was from Lodgepole. No word or sign of any Rangers since they came through a few months earlier. The second message was from Scheible, with a similar "nothing to report" note. It was the third wire message, from a Marshal Baxter Hollings in Stebbins, that caused Hannah to adjust his spectacles and exhale sharply. "Thank you, Mr. Hayes," Hannah said politely and quickly strode out of the office.

In the middle of town, the oldest and youngest Corrigan brothers, Blue and Deed, stepped out of the Wilkon dry goods store. Blue hefted a small keg of nails on his shoulder, holding it in place with his one good arm. Deed was toting large bags of sugar and flour.

Following them, were their wives Bina and Atlee, and their children, all of them holding various sized bags and boxes of provisions, except for Atlee. This was her first outing since being attacked by Meden Taliff's henchman, Kane Barlow. The sunshine and fresh air was doing wonders for her strength and spirit. Despite her protestations, Deed did not want his wife carrying anything, keeping her exertion down and energy up. He helped her into the seat, then began stacking the heavy bags and boxes in the bed of the wagon. Finished, he joined Atlee on the wagon seat, keeping the horses controlled with the reins in his lap. Leaning over in the driver's seat, arms propped on his knees, he opened the latest edition of the *Epitaph*.

Blue watched the children load the reminder of the purchases into the wagon as Deed came to the same article that had caught Hannah's eye. He scanned through it quickly, reading out loud the interesting parts, "Dustup in St. Claire County…Wanted gunman…Ranger wounded."

Hannah walked up just as Deed was reading the last part.

"Dangerous business…" Blue commented and looked over at Hannah to include him in their conversation, "for anyone who straps on a gun and badge."

The three men could relate. Each of them had been in the line of fire and knew the risks.

"Rangers go after the worst of the worst," Deed said. "Day's work for most of 'em."

"I hope Holt is being careful, wherever he is," Atlee noted, smiling at her husband. Deed's smile said, *me too*.

"Mornin' ladies," Hannah greeted them all warmly. "Tell me, Jeremy, is there any peppermint in there?" he said, tousling the boy's hair.

"Yessir, want one?" Jeremy answered.

"Sure!" Hannah smiled a preoccupied grin. He did

not wait for the boy to find the candy and walked to the front of the wagon team.

"Blue, a moment?" He eyed Deed as well, who jumped down to join them.

Out of earshot, Hannah spoke in a lowered voice. "I just got a telegram from the marshal in Stebbins…"

"Deed was just reading us the article about a Ranger getting wounded in a dustup somewhere over in cattle country," Blue said.

Hannah did not hesitate in delivering his news. "Blue…Deed…the Ranger in the article is Holt," he reported, handing the telegram to Blue.

The oldest Corrigan's face was granite as he read the message. "When did this arrive?" he looked at Hannah and gave the note to Deed.

"Within the hour. I came straight here from Mr. Hayes's office. I set out to find you boys right away."

"Not much here. Could be nothing. Could be bad," Deed said, eyeing Blue with concern. "At least it only says 'shot' and not—"

"We need to know more," Blue interrupted, nodding to his brother.

He walked around the hitched team to the seat where Bina was supervising the final loading of children into the wagon. As Deed climbed back aboard and took the reins, Blue quietly told the women what had happened. They did not believe in keeping bad news from the children, but until there was more information only the adults would know about this.

Blue hugged his wife and helped her up onto the seat, then said, "Deed, you see everyone home, okay? I'll get a message to Ranger Higbee and find out exactly what's going on."

The three adults made the ride to their Rafter C ranch, hushed in their discussion of what to do. Deed and the women readily determined that Holt needed to be brought home as soon as he could travel.

"He needs to be here, so we can take care of him," Atlee said, for the moment forgetting her own recuperation. "No better place to heal than at home." She put her arm around Deed, concerned about how her husband was doing as well as worrying about Holt.

The thought of bringing Holt home to bury him never crossed any of their minds.

A few hours later, Blue returned to the Rafter C ranch and tied his horse out front. After wading through the boisterous greetings of children playing on the porch, he stepped into the ranch's big kitchen. Deed and their wives were seated around the large table in front of the great stone fireplace. Coffee in their mugs had gone cold as they wondered about Holt and talked about the trip to go get him.

It was mere months ago, they had all gathered around this very table as Holt told Captain Laird McCoy that he would wear a Texas Ranger badge and go after The Angel, vowing vengeance on the man who was responsible for killing their beloved godfather, Silka.

———

Silka had been cut down in a running gun battle with The Angel and his henchmen. The evil priest had been exposed as a killer during the funeral of Felix Sanchez, the Lazy S patriarch who the preacher had also murdered. The Angel and his men shot their way out of the funeral and the town in their escape.

In the aftermath, Silka was laid out on the bed in his old room of the Corrigan's Rafter C main house. The ranch had a separate wing where Deed and Silka had lived independently from Blue and his family before the two moved over to the Bar 3. Washed and prepared for his funeral, the former samurai looked peaceful, like he had just laid down for a nap. The serenity belied the blood-soaked violence that ripped him from this world. His weapons had been cleaned and were laid out next to his body.

Alone with the man they cherished so much, the three brothers stood in silent contemplation. Deed smiled through the pain and the tears welling in his eyes. "The first time we met him he said, 'I am Nakashima Silka. I am Samurai.' Put his right fist against his heart and declared, 'Warrior. In Japan. I lived *Bushido*...way of the warrior. None dare challenge me.'" Deed touched a brass circle at his neck. The older Japanese man had instilled *Bushido* in each of them, the "way of the warrior"—a life built on honor, inner strength, determination, freedom from fear of death, and directed action. Deed was too young to fight in the war, so he had worked the most and hardest with Silka. His ability to fight with his hands and feet a testament to Silka's teaching. The brass circle at Deed's neck, a gift from Silka, was engraved with a symbol of *Bushido*.

Holt exhaled deeply. "Silka. Our warrior."

"Hard to think where'd we be if he hadn't come along," Blue said, bowing his head.

Holt pulled the tobacco pouch from his pocket and sprinkled some around the unmoving body. "Wherever the Great Spirit takes you, may you be protected in all directions," he began. "Thank you, my friend...for everything…you've done. We…we…w-were…you s-saved m-my b-broth…us." Sorrow and anger swelled inside him and came out in the form of hot tears. And venomous words.

"Where are You now, God!?" Holt shouted at the heavens. "Where? I've tried hard to believe in You. You know damn well I have. And what have You done? You unleashed those unholy *bastards!* They killed the judge! They killed Felix! *They killed Silka!*" He had not been filled with this much hate and anger and sadness in a long time. A clenched rage like he had not felt since…since the surrender. But this…this was worse.

He turned from the body. A ferocity burned in his eyes that was savage; a cornered, angry panther about to attack. Very few men had ever seen this look on Holt's face. Even fewer were still alive. Raw fury rose and swelled within him, intensifying like a raging storm.

"I'm going after them." Holt's voice was a feral growl. "Wherever they are, I'm going to find them." He slammed his fists on a bedstand. "If it's the last thing I do in this world, I will find The Angel and the sonofabitches with him." His voice was thick with vehemence. *"And I will kill them all."*

Blue silently put his arm on Holt's back and guided him toward the big ranch kitchen. Seated around the large table in front of the big stone fireplace, talking quietly and drinking coffee were Bina and Atlee. And Texas Ranger Captain Laird McCoy.

McCoy had stood, looking directly at Holt. "I am very sor—"

"Captain," Holt interrupted. "I'm going after that priest or whatever the hell he is. Silka and Felix and probably the judge are dead because of that bastard. I'll take that badge now."

Deed joined in, "So will I."

"Swear us all in," Blue had added.

Bina and Atlee said nothing, but both of their faces tightened like someone had slapped them. Hard.

Holt reacted brusquely. "No! That's not going to happen. You're not going! Neither of you. The family needs you here. It's nearing spring. Both ranches need squaring away. And protected. The Sanchezes need looking after too."

"I'm..." Deed tried to start.

Holt held up his hand toward Deed's face, the forefinger extended upward. Their no-nonsense father used to do this many years ago, a silent—and obeyed—gesture to be quiet. Now.

Holt's eyes blazed from Deed to Blue. He meant this. *No!*

Blue tried to speak. "You can't do this alone—"

"There are lots of ways to fight, you said it yourself, Blue. In El Paso. Remember?" Holt interrupted, calmer now. He looked from Blue to Deed and back. "Building a ranch is a fight." Then he smiled softly toward Bina and Atlee, "Raising a family is worth fighting for too."

"Holt..." Blue tried again. Holt's scorching glare returned and seared into Blue's eyes. Intensity like Blue had never seen in his younger brother stopped him from saying anything more.

Holt stepped close to his older brother, his voice quiet. "It was no accident we met in El Paso. The spirits wanted us to cross paths. Your words brought me home," he acknowledged. "I need to do this. This is what I can do for us." His words were guttural from deep within.

"You know my spirit demands that I fight. That's what I am, what I've always been."

Blue knew better than to argue with his brother. "Take Travis, then."

Deed nodded. "He's a good hand. Knows how to handle himself."

"You're a Ranger now," McCoy had interjected. "You'll have a partner. Two Rangers will be enough."

———

The three were broken out of their reverie by the sound of Blue arriving home. His boots clomping on the wooden floors.

"The wounded Ranger is definitely Holt," Blue said.

CHAPTER NINE

Blue now looked at his youngest brother and their wives, placing a telegram message on the kitchen table. "According to Holt's Ranger partner, Orion Higbee, Holt got shot about three days ago while they were arresting a gunman. Orion said Holt was hit four times. Three cut him pretty hard, above his ear, across a shoulder and on his side. The only bullet that stuck was dug out of his thigh. He lost a lot of blood, which is the concern. As of this afternoon, Orion said Holt hasn't fully wakened, just in and out of consciousness. He said Holt spiked a fever but thinks it has broken. So far though, no infection."

"Damn..." murmured Deed.

"Orion reports that Stebbins has a good doctor there," Blue continued. "Orion also said he knows Holt will pull through. Won't contemplate otherwise."

"I like the way this Orion thinks," Deed acknowledged.

"Not awakened yet..." Bina noted, deep in concerned thought. "He still is traveling in the world of darkness." A full-blooded Mescalero Apache, her upbringing taught her much about the connection between men and the spirit world. "He is a shadow right now, drifting between worlds. Before he can come back, his spirit must decide which path to take. This is a dangerous time; one we must be careful to not speak too much of."

Her statement was met with concerned silence.

"Well, we need to go get him," Blue finally declared. The other three exchanged glances at the recognition of the decision they made hours ago.

Suddenly, a voice from the outer room behind them asked, "How's Tag?"

They all turned. Standing there was Deed and Atlee's boy, Benjamin, eyes full of worry. "If Uncle Holt is hurt, where is Tag? Is he okay?"

Deed stood immediately and walked over to his stepson, putting an arm around him. "I'm sure he's okay, Benj."

Blue looked at the twelve-year-old and said, "Benjamin, you only heard the first part about Uncle Holt." He held up the telegraph paper. "Mr. Higbee, Uncle Holt's partner, said right here at the end that Tag was okay, that he was with him. Apparently, Tag has a bed in Uncle Holt's room."

"Uncle Holt and Tag have been through a lot together." Deed smiled at Benjamin and pulled him into a hug. "I'm sure they'll be fine." Then he looked at the boy, a calm seriousness in his voice. "Now you know what we know."

"Are you worried about Uncle Holt?" the boy asked.

"I'm concerned, Benj. He's been hurt bad, but I believe right here that he's going to be all right," Deed said, tapping his heart. "You know, if you feel like crying, it's okay."

"Naw, I'm fine," the boy said, swiping at his nose. "What's gonna happen?"

Deed kneeled in front of the boy, hands gently, but firmly, on Benjamin's shoulders. "Your uncle Blue and I, we're going to go get Uncle Holt and bring him home so your mother, Aunt Bina, the girls, and all of us can take care of him. Sound good?"

The boy nodded his head vigorously. "Can I go with you?"

"If your uncle Blue and I go get Uncle Holt, who will be here to watch over things?"

"Ma will be in charge. She always is. Aunt Bina too."

Deed smiled. "I'm going to need a young man here to make sure his mother and aunt are okay. Understand?"

Benjamin's nod was not nearly as vigorous.

"Now, I want you to hold all of this close until we get things planned," Deed said. "We'll tell the little kids tonight. Can you do that for me?"

"Yeah. I can."

"Good. Now, how about taking care of Uncle Blue's horse and getting it squared away?"

The boy's eyes lit up and he sprang from the room.

Deed stood. He took and released a deep breath.

Blue grimly nodded. "We leave tomorrow to go get Holt."

"Okay, big brother, I'm with you."

The children were understandably upset about their uncle Holt, but their parents, putting on a confident front, eased the worst of the fears among the young ones. After an early supper, Deed and his family said their goodbyes to head back to their Bar 3 ranch. With the two brothers leaving tomorrow to retrieve Holt, Deed had preparations to make.

Shortly after his youngest brother's departure, Blue and Bina put their children to bed. He was now alone with her in their bedroom. She sat on their bed, her lustrous black hair hanging down loosely, her deep brown eyes observing Blue roll up extra clothes for his saddle-bags. It did not cross her awareness that he did this one-handed.

"Holt will complete his journey back to the living," she declared. "I feel this."

"My prayers tell me not to worry as well," Blue added.

"Once back on the living trail, he must come home where we can care for him," she said softly.

"Yes."

"He is to be an uncle again."

Blue finished stuffing a rolled shirt into one side of his bags. A took a moment for Bina's words to sink in...

He looked up into Bina's smiling face and spluttered, "You...mean...you're...?"

"Yes. I am."

He bounded to her, joy filling his eyes. He lifted her with his one good arm into the hugest of hugs, but immediately realized he probably should take greater care of her condition.

"You have been tired lately," he said. "I should have known."

"It is well," she replied, looking at her not-quite-yet-showing belly and moving a hand down there to hold it.

"The spirit is strong with this one. He will be kicking soon."

"He?" Blue didn't finish, just smiled. He caressed her face. It was her turn to take him in a long embrace. Kissing was not something Apaches did, but she took to it enthusiastically on occasion. This was one of them.

"This…is wonderful!" Blue gushed. "Oh Bina, I love you."

"I love you, Blue," she beamed in return. "My heart sings. I have felt…something…lately…a presence…this was it."

They kissed again. Blue pulled away suddenly.

"I have to stay," he blurted. "I can't go to Stebbins. It's not good, both of us leaving you and Atlee. Especially now."

"We can manage—"

"I know you can, but there is so much to do. You shouldn't be overdoing things. Neither should Atlee."

"But, Holt needs—"

"It sounds like Holt only needs time. Deed can bring him home. We'll all care for him when he gets here."

"What about Deed? You shouldn't change plans."

"He will more than understand. Trust me," Blue said. "But I need to tell him…"

"Not now," she cautioned. "There is too much darkness prowling in the night."

CHAPTER TEN

The next morning, just before false dawn, a horseless buckboard sat forlornly in the yard of the Bar 3 ranch house outside the town of Wilkon. Two matching bays would soon be hitched to the wagon by Deed Corrigan and his stepson, Benjamin.

Deed stood outside on the front porch, dressed for the trail. Tan leather cuffs covered the ends of his favorite riding shirt, a faded red wing-tip. A once-blue, now near-gray, neckerchief hung loosely around his neck. Worn denim trousers were shoved into knee-high boots with Mexican-styled spurs. The bullet belt around his waist held a heavy Remington revolver with its long barrel extending past the holster's open end. His long brown hair brushed past his collar as he loaded the wagon with gear. His straight-sided, flat-brimmed hat sat on the wagon seat. Its open crown was now dented and ill-shaped, due to many, many days out in the elements. The fur-felt hat had kept a lot of rain from his neck and helped water more than a few horses and cattle.

Their dog Cooper's barks alerted of an approaching rider. A clip-clop of horse hooves followed soon after.

The voice of Blue called through the diffused light, "Good morning, little brother!"

"You're earlier than I expected," Deed called back. "Didn't think you'd be here till after breakfast."

Blue trotted through the ranch yard and tied up on the side of the house. He climbed down and explained the situation to his brother.

"Of course, you need to stay here, *Dad*," Deed said, happily slapping his brother on the back. "You give Bina my love."

"Thanks for understanding, Deed."

"Understanding? Hell, if Atlee found out you left after Bina told you she was pregnant *and I knew about it too?* She'd chew on the both of us and spit us out." Deed smiled at the fact this wasn't really a joke. "Stebbins isn't far. I'll get our brother home."

"No, it's not a long trek, but you shouldn't go alone," Blue cautioned.

"I already got a plan. I had news for you when you showed up. I asked Benj to go along. Instead of the three of us, it'll be two."

"Sounds good. Sorry to miss out on that adventure. Wait…Atlee's okay with this? Benjamin going along?"

"Touch and go. She changed her mind twice last night. But she helped him pack this morning." Deed chuckled.

Just then, Benjamin approached them from the barn, leading two bays. The horses were a wedding gift to Deed and Atlee from their friends and neighbors, the Sanchezes. Felix Sanchez had personally selected these two from his remuda, training them for driving as well as riding. The Corrigans and Sanchezes had become close, fighting for each other when Agon Bordner had tried to overrun both of their ranches and again when Meden Taliff had Felix murdered in an attempt to seize the Sanchez Lazy S.

Benjamin had already shown a knack for handling horses at his mother's stage relay station and eagerly took on the chore of readying the wagon.

Atlee appeared at the front door, her long, wavy brown locks swept up in a loose bun. She had heard Blue's voice and brought two mugs of coffee for the men.

Blue stepped onto the porch and quietly told her about the situation.

"Here, I don't want to spill these," she said, quickly handing the two cups to Blue for him to hold in his one hand. Then she did exactly that, spilling coffee over the both of them as she gave Blue a big, enthusiastic hug. They both laughed at the news and the empty mugs.

"You *should* be staying home," she said, stepping back and admonishing Blue with a smile. "You never would have heard the end of it from me."

"Thank you, Atlee." Blue chuckled in return, wiping at his now wet vest and shirt. "I'll tell Bina how happy you are."

After double-checking the wagon's harnesses and securing the gear in the back of the wagon, Deed nodded to Benjamin. Time to go.

The two stepped up to the porch to say their good-byes. Benjamin hugged his pal Cooper and quietly led him inside. The dog was not making the trip and would follow the wagon if he wasn't tucked away. They boy returned quickly, eager to get started.

"You got some good words for us, brother?" Deed asked.

"You bet," Blue said, putting his arm around Benjamin's shoulder. "God, You have promised love and faith to see us through tough times. And the courage to meet every day. Guide these two toward our brother, Holt, and protect them with Your strength. May God watch over you and bring you all back safely. Amen."

"Amen." Atlee nodded.

Deed smiled and Benjamin mumbled an Amen.

"Go get that ornery cuss," Blue said, giving his brother a quick hug. Their locked eyes said more.

"We'll be back soon." Deed smiled.

"Take care of your dad, Mr. Benjamin," Blue said, then jumped down from the porch to retrieve his horse. "I'll check in with you tomorrow, Atlee, make sure everything's okay."

"No need. We'll be okay here. Give Bina a hug from me," Atlee called out as Blue clicked his horse to a trot.

"Thanks for the coffee!" He laughed.

The brief joke only kept Atlee's concern away for little more than an instant. She looked at Deed, tears beginning to well up as she gathered Benjamin into her arms.

Deed tried to ease his wife's worries. "Everything will be all right, honey. We'll be back with Holt before you know it," he said soothingly, but her hold on Benjamin was more mama bear than a mere cuddle. "But." He smiled. "We can't get back until we actually go."

Atlee was losing her battle to keep from crying. Her deep green eyes leaked hot strings of worry down her cheeks. She hugged her son so closely he complained.

Her first born, Benjamin's young life had seen his real father killed by Comanches in front of his very eyes and the addition of a stepfather when she remarried Deed. The experiences had not been easy for any of them. The twelve-year-old was like most boys that age, growing like summer grass and getting a mind of his own. Even before he knew about Blue's decision to not travel because of Bina's pregnancy, it made sense to Deed that his stepson, Benjamin, should go along to help bring Holt home. The boy's excitement could barely be contained.

Adding to his joy, Benjamin had been given one of Deed's own hats, an older broad-brimmed, open-crowned fedora. The boy tried to remain poised, but this was his first real "man" hat. And Deed had given it to him.

"It'll take two, maybe three, days to get there, a day to collect Holt, and two or three days back," Deed continued. "We'll be spending three of those nights in a town. It'll be good experience for Benj, get him ready for when he goes on trail drives."

The words meant to comfort Atlee only seemed to pour kerosene on the fire. She renewed her goodbye attention to her son, hugging him once more and kissing him on the head.

"How about a hug for me?" Deed smiled at his wife. She laughed through the tears and reached for her husband. Benjamin used the opportunity to duck away from his mother and head toward the wagon in the yard.

Deed wiped her tears and she held him tight, saying, "You come back to me too." Deep kisses to remind him of home followed.

"You're making it hard to leave," he said, his eyes

glowing deep into hers. The spark was returned in her gaze. They embraced and kissed again.

Their daughter, Elizabeth, who was only seven, thought the two guys were only heading into town and wondered why she couldn't go along. The fact her mother was crying kindled tears in the little girl.

Deed kneeled down and gently dried the tears from his stepdaughter's cheeks. "I need you to take care of your mother…and Jessica too." He smiled and patted the doll Elizabeth clutched tightly in her arms. "We'll have a pancake party for Uncle Holt when we bring him back, does that sound good?"

"Okay." The little girl suddenly brightened. "I'll take care of Cooper too!"

"All right, sweetheart. Be sure to tell Cooper that his buddy, Tag, is also coming home with us."

She nodded and ran back into the house singing a new song about Cooper, Tag, and pancakes.

He stood and put his arm around Atlee's waist one more time. "We'll be fine. I promise."

"I love you, Deed."

"I love you, Atlee."

Benjamin was already seated on the wagon when Deed climbed aboard and grabbed up the reins. "We'll be home soon!" he called out, snapping the horses to movement.

CHAPTER ELEVEN

For the wounded Holt Corrigan, the small Stebbins, Texas hotel room he lay in was a chamber of shadowy illusion. He slipped into a realm where his mind wandered the trails of awareness and oblivion. Indistinguishable between the two worlds, he experienced hallucinations that were a mixture of familiar scenes and those known only in his imagination.

In his waking life, he had come to strongly believe in the supernatural force of the spirit world as well as rebirth within the circle of life. Growing up, he had felt for a long time that his regular dreams were actually glimpses of his previous lives. The idea would certainly explain the fierce nightmares he had long experienced of fighters like pumas, mammoth hunters, gladiators, knights, lancers, archers, and soldiers.

Near the end of the war, in a fit of rage over his army's impending surrender, he had tried to get killed by rushing an entrenched Yankee patrol. He ended up killing them all. The rush of adrenaline and shock of reality afterward brought a powerful vision that he had lived this scenario before, many times, an eternal warrior fighting the same battle through the ages.

Even now through the haze of fever and pain, it came to him clearly enough that he was now traveling through a mystical world, led by the Creator and the ancestors who guided men and nature. They saw everything and had a view to the other side of the sky.

During the war, Holt had heard the actions in one life had a direct effect on the next. A person must be reborn endless times until he found the purpose God had for him. If so, he often wondered, what was his purpose?

He was now aware that the raven had returned to his dream state. Still unseen, its screeches were frighteningly loud. He knew again that this winged black specter was taking him on another journey.

"*Kraa! Kraa!*"

He found himself set down near a dark stream, wide and deep. A single tree lay across the murky torrent. If only to rid himself of the raven's incessant cries, he felt compelled to cross over. Without hesitation, he stepped among the tree's branches and traversed above the churning rapids. Reaching the other bank safely placed him in a peaceful glade.

The screams of the raven persisted, but the sounds of the stream helped to diminish them. Something about the clearing made him feel safe. Knots of thick fog took shape beneath the rocks that encircled above him. Guardian trees surrounded the clearing and held everything close. He tried to peer into the hazy landscape but could see nothing.

Above it all, a voice called out. It resonated, though, as a multitude—male and female, young and old. This ethereal sound was at once beautiful and yet terrifying in its harmony, timeless and ageless in its message.

The ancient ones? The Creator? Whatever it was, Holt could clearly hear what was being spoken.

"The next part of your journey will require great caution," the voice intoned. "For the path is fraught with peril. Only you can deem yourself worthy of continuing. Only the faithful and courageous will make their way to the inner circle. Keep your eyes and ears open, but most of all, keep your heart and mind open."

The voice stilled. The fog slowly swirled away. Holt ventured through the glade, eventually coming to a place where a mulberry tree grew next to a cave. The tree itself not only was alive, but also seemed to be an incarnation, a lone sentinel for the mysterious hole in the rock.

"I have been granted a journey," Holt said assuredly. The mulberry folded its branches back and allowed Holt passage inside.

Within the cave, the path descended. Indistinguishable spirits lingered in the darkness. As he worked his way along the trail, Holt thought he caught glimpses of them. Dim, shadowy figures of a Roman legionnaire, an English knight, a Carthaginian gladiator, a cavalry lancer, a Greek archer, an armed dragoon and an Indian dog soldier were some of the souls that seemed to be observing him. Judgment drifted in their whispers.

Soon, the path leveled. Holt found himself on a confined passage that led westward, through a canyon. The surroundings became progressively lighter, although no sun or light source could be seen.

The trail became extremely narrow at a point where an enormous panther sat on a rock ledge, guarding the passageway. Supernaturally large, the huge cat exuded palpable energy, force and strength. Its eyes, meant to mesmerize and terrify, glowed an intense golden-green. Holt felt as though he was in the presence of an ancient spirit. Not as elemental as a stone-being, but one that had been around for a very long time. When the animal blinked, Holt blinked. When it moved, Holt felt his muscles stir.

As he approached the creature, it stood up on four legs and growled, a powerful rumble coming from deep within its breast. Holt felt it in his own chest as well. He knew, in that moment, this was his panther spirit, what the holy man Four Shields called his *ndołkah*; the one that accompanied him through great turmoil and strife; the force that gave him skill, cunning and strength.

He raised his arm in tribute to the creature and said, "You are what I am, what I've always been."

When Holt showed no fear, the panther let him pass. It joined him, walking on his right side, the side of action and strength. Holt could feel this spirit filling his soul with warrior song, an energy that was at once life-giving and inspiring. His eyes and ears were fully open.

Dim shadowy figures continued to cling to the pockets of darkness on the periphery of his awareness, still observing him. Their whispered judgments fainter now.

At a later, wider part of the passage, two grizzly bears stood in Holt's way. Like the panther, these creatures were unusually large. Unlike the panther though, these seemed to be newer spirits. Holt knew in a moment that these were protector spirits; Four Shields called them his *tsét'soyé*, the souls of those who had looked upon him highly in their living forms. His heart told him he had known these spirits at one time as his godfather Nakashima Silka and good friend Judge Oscar Pence.

Holt raised his arm in tribute to the creatures and said, "My *ndołkah* helps me fight, but you, my *tsét'soyé*, help me fight for what is good and true."

When he spoke to them with courage, they let him pass. They joined in the journey, walking on Holt's left side, the one closest to his heart. Holt could feel his soul fill with friendship and warmth. His heart and mind were fully open.

Soon, he found himself on a trail that seemed familiar. His movements suddenly felt like he was on his horse. The animal spirits had disappeared from his sight, only their essence remained.

He came upon an elevated piece of ground, the advent to a thicker stand of cottonwoods and oaks. The rise up ahead gave a commanding view of the ground that stretched around it. The boulders on one side, trees on the other, looked promising. The cottonwoods and faint animal trails signaled to him that there should be some life-giving water there.

A feeling of comfort came to his senses as he discovered a small spring that greeted him as it meandered haphazardly.

Had he been here before? Without knowing why, his dream compelled him to make camp here. Every part of his being told him this was a place of strong medicine. A place where the spirits watched from the shadows, their approval carried in the winds.

Stepping down, this world instantly changed from day to night. Bright moonlight gave birth to friendly shadows around him.

He was comfortable here. He felt at home. He *had* been here before.

Soon, a feeling embraced Holt that he was not alone. It was an inner sensation of awareness with which he was familiar.

The multitudinous voice called out again. The dream-world and everything in it bent down to listen.

"It is well you have made it to this place," the mysterious voice spoke slowly, almost reverently. "You listen well. You have seen many yesterdays and learned lessons from those who came before. It takes someone who truly cares in order to hear what they are saying."

"*Kraa! Kraa!*"

The otherworldly words began to be drowned out and Holt could hear very little. The pounding in his head returned, along with the squawking of the raven, the one that drove him through all his nightmares. The creature was now perched on his head. Its talons sunk into his scalp and its screeching stabbed sharp torment through to his very core.

"You have heard these words before, but it is you who must find the beauty that lives in each day and every living thing," the voice from beyond announced, loud enough to be heard over the raven's racket. It seemed to lean in closer to Holt as it intoned, "That lesson comes with its very own spirit."

Through the raven's torture, Holt recognized the near-silent sound of the swift *whuff-whuff-whuff* of an owl's wings. Although some people, including his sister-in-law Bina and counselor Four Shields, feared the owl, considering it to be an augury of death, others looked upon the animal as a protector or messenger. Holt believed this bird of the night brought wisdom and understanding and something more…

As the owl's hoots got louder, he felt his mother's presence but could not see her. The manifestation of this harbinger brought an embracing warmth that started in his heart and spread throughout his soul. Deep, soft, yet insistent coos with a stuttering rhythm sang out, forcing the raven to fly away. The owl alighted on Holt's left shoulder, occasionally barking and snapping its bill at the darkness to keep something away.

Holt's head stopped drumming. The pain was no longer there. An overwhelming sense of love came over him. This had to be the spirit of his mother.

He became aware that his bed was now settled into the cottonwoods, the meandering spring to its side. The voices from above were singing, although Holt could not understand what they were saying. He felt as though people he knew were joining in.

As the other voices kept singing, words unspoken were reaching into his mind, "Your *ndołkah*, your panther spirit, and your *tsét'soyé*, your bear spirits, brought you here, so that you may be heard. This is where healing is found. This is where you ask to return."

Holt began speaking in barely a whisper, "Listen to my heart, Great Spirit. Send my voice to those who may guide my return. Allow me a sense of purpose, and to continue the path set by my Bear uncles. May you all help me to be true and return to a world of blue skies." Even in his dream, Holt was exhausted.

The unspoken words reached him once more. "It is well. Your difficult journey from the realm of darkness to the world of light is at its end. Your eyes and ears have been reopened. Rest easy. You will be guided—if you listen."

With that, the cottonwoods vanished, as did the faint animal trails, and the new spring that surrounded him. The owl ascended from view as well. A hotel room formed around Holt's blurry, blinking vision. He realized his good hand was gripping the medicine pouch around his chest.

He had a sense that a panther, not the spirit, but perhaps a real one, was a gentle warmth next to him. It spoke in a voice he had heard before but couldn't quite place how or where.

"It's all right, Holt," this panther spoke in a soothing, confident voice. "You're all right."

CHAPTER TWELVE

"It's all right, Holt," Laudie Kate Hart cooed in a comforting voice. "You're all right."

Holt's eyes opened completely. The sensation of the panther next to him was gone. Instead, the face of a woman was positioned above him. She sat on the bed, gently holding him down, her bright blue eyes looking deeply into his.

He blinked. "Wh-Who are you?"

"I'm Laudie Kate. Welcome back, Holt Corrigan."

The panther voice!

"Wh-what...h-how...where?" He tried to get up, but her hold remained tender, but firm.

"Relax. You were shot," she said. "Dr. Vaughn said you might struggle around. Just lie quietly. You don't want to undo his good work."

Holt's brain labored frantically trying to make sense of everything. This was the world in which he lived. The dreams he experienced had only been in his mind. Or had they? The fog of recovery was confusing him. Being out of control made him a little panicky. He took several deep breaths.

"You need to take things easy," she said, getting up but still keeping a light hand on his shoulder.

He tried to sit up, but his head swam with a force that knocked him down and wanted to send him back to the darkness.

"I told you, Holt Corrigan…" She smiled with a *tsk tsk* of her head. "Tag Along is here. Orion is nearby. It is well."

It is well. Like a spirit from…from his dreams, Holt thought. He blinked and touched her arm to make sure she was real.

Tag hopped up on the bed between them, looking for nuzzles.

"Hi boy, sure glad to see you," Holt smiled weakly, voice croaky. He tried reaching for the dog, but realized one of his arms was bandaged and in a sling. He instead gave Tag a one-armed hug and vigorous rubs along the dog's floppy ears.

A loud growl of Holt's stomach startled even the dog.

"Could I get…" he started to say.

"Some broth and maybe a biscuit?" Laudie Kate chuckled. "I'll get you some. I'll tell Orion you're back too. Turns out he's a pretty good nurse."

"Coffee too?" he called out as he watched her leave and lock the room behind her. He breathed deep, noticing her scent of soap and lavender.

Just then, he realized the mountain lion claw from his pants pocket was in his hand bound by the sling, gripped there tightly for who knows how long. The claw was a gift from his mother when he was a boy. He carefully stared at it and said a silent "thank you" to his mother and the spirits.

This was real. He *was* back. Back in the world of blue skies.

offered it and said sweetly, "Thank you," to his mother
and the spirits.

This was real. He was back. Back in the world of our
story.

CHAPTER THIRTEEN

The food Laudie Kate brought him had tasted good. Holt asked for another biscuit.

"Careful, it's been a while, you shouldn't eat too much. You'll get a stomach ache," she said sweetly.

The hunger gnawing in his belly had subsided and he started to feel drowsy. A tired kind of sleepy, not pain- or fever-induced.

"I-I'm sorry, wh-who are you again?"

"I'm Laudie Kate."

"I-I am very h-happy…to m-meet you, Laudie Kate. Th-Thank you." He barely finished before his eyes closed again.

She smiled and left the extra biscuit on his night-stand. It would be there when he woke up or maybe Tag would sneak it. He was good at that, she thought.

Holt came-to again. He was not sure how long he had been asleep. The sun was still shining. Tag was curled up by his feet. He looked down at himself and, in his mind, replayed getting shot—thinking through the actual event, not the images from his horrific nightmares. He was comforted again to find that he was wearing his medicine pouch. One of the first things he remembered discovering was that he had been clutching his mountain lion claw. He considered whether he should include it in his medicine pouch with his sacred stone. He wondered about the whereabouts of his small bag of tobacco. He often offered shreds of tobacco as tributes to the spirits, an Indian ritual he admired and used for himself.

"How long have I been here?" he murmured. Only Tag heard him.

The door to his room was slightly ajar and he heard voices coming from the hallway. Dr. Vaughn had come by to check on Holt. He, Orion, and Laudie Kate were talking just outside Holt's door.

"I heard he was burnin' up there for a bit. You should've called me."

"Yeah, Doc, he was," Orion responded. "It was middle of the night though. He's a tough man. I figured I could get him through. Had a bit of experience doin' that durin' the war."

Laudie Kate chimed in, "I think he's through the worst. He needs to sleep now. To rest."

"We owe both of you, an' Evie, a lot," Orion said. "I thank you."

A loud thud stopped the conversation. It came from Holt's room.

All three hurried into the room and discovered Holt lying on the floor by the dresser. He had thrown off the sling holding his injured arm and managed to stand. He was trying to put a second leg into his pants before his head had spun in wild dizziness. He was passed out on the floor.

The next thing Holt knew, it was nighttime. He awoke to discover he was wearing clean, new long johns and tucked into bed again. He saw Laudie Kate moving around his room. She was gathering his torn and bloodied shirt and pants.

"I'm getting these out of here," she fussed. "They're beyond cleaning or repairing. We'll get you some new ones when you're ready to be up and around. That ought to keep you from trying to get dressed again." She was warm-faced with sparkling blue eyes. "If you promise not to get up, maybe I'll bring up some bowls of stew for you all."

He was watching her appreciatively, enjoying the sound of her voice. He realized she had said something to him and he needed to respond.

"Y-Yes, Laudie Kate…you're…uh…that would be mighty fine," Holt stammered.

"I won't be long. You stay put, you hear?" Her smile was soft music to Holt as she walked through the door, locking it behind her.

"She's somethin' else, ain't she?" Orion's voice startled Holt out of his Laudie Kate daydream. He hadn't noticed the older Ranger sitting in the rocking chair by the window, a station he had manned while Holt burned with fever.

"She's very nice," Holt responded. "Great name." He tried rolling up onto his good elbow which would allow him to sit up. A wave of dizziness signaled its displeasure at this maneuver. Holt fought through the wooziness and inched his way to a sitting position against his pillows. The effort left him weary and out of breath. At the foot of the bed, an asleep Tag grumbled at the motion, as if adding his own "don't move" admonishment.

"Oh, is that all you noticed?" Orion snickered.

Holt, still gathering himself from the exertion, had no answer. He rubbed at the bandage around his head and asked, "What the hell happened to me, Orion?"

"You were shot, my friend. You busted through those front doors, announced your intentions, an' boom."

"Damn...my dreams have been replaying everything over and over. I'm not sure what's real and what's..."

"One bullet creased your head, over your ear. That's the bandage aroun' your noggin," Orion replied, gesturing at Holt's various body parts as he ran through the list. "Your upper arm got a deep furrow. A slug lodged in your thigh. An' another bullet cut along your side, above your hip."

"I guess nothing important was hit."

"Besides the one on your head?" Orion chuckled. "No, nothin' important. You may not feel like it, but you got lucky."

More movement was not a good idea, but Holt decided he was at least going to take off the sling. Even that took some effort and left him drained.

"Doc did good work," Orion continued. "Got the bullet out of your leg an' patched you up. Stopped your leakin'. The rest was up to you, I suppose."

"It's good to see you and Tag and the pretty lady. Everybody. That fever caused some wild-ass dreams. Scary stuff."

"Not surprised. You lost a *lotta* blood, partner. Enough to not make it back. Gonna be awhile before you feel yourself again."

"Did we...did you...get Longley?"

"Sure did. He's locked up."

"Did you get the guy who shot me?"

"Well…now…that's another story."

"Did he get away? It's okay, Longley was the target."

"Not exactly. We know who shot you, leastwise, we know *one* of the persons who shot you."

"It wasn't Longley, I know that. I'm pretty sure I was looking right at him when I was first hit."

Orion was quiet.

"What's going on? C'mon, tell me."

Just then, a smiling Laudie Kate appeared at the door, a tray with three bowls of stew and a basket of biscuits in her hands. The sight of Holt sitting up brought a stern look to her face and almost caused her to drop the meal. "Holt Corrigan! Do you not listen? I've a right mind to…"

"I-I'm sorry, L-Laudie Kate. I'm j-just t-trying to get better."

"We were just piecin' together what happened that day," Orion added quietly.

"Oh." Her stern countenance softened. "Have you gotten to the part where…"

"Not yet." Orion cocked his wryly.

Holt was confused. "What part? What the hell… what's going on?"

"We didn't get the guy who shot you, Holt," Orion interrupted. "Because, it wasn't *a guy*."

Holt's face was a mask of confusion.

"Miss Laudie, you wanna serve your patient there an' tell 'im how you shot him?"

Holt looked up at Laudie Kate. Her bright eyes were filled with concern, regret, and a little embarrassment.

She was one of the most beautiful things he had ever seen.

"I'll leave you two Rangers to eat," Laudie Kate said matter-of-factly, setting a bowl on the floor for Tag.

"No. P-Please stay," Holt reacted.

"Look, Mr. Corrigan—"

"Holt."

"Look, Mr. Holt, I am very sorry for what happened. But you have to understand, it was not an accident. I *meant* to shoot you." She paused briefly to catch any reaction from Holt. "I thought you were here to rob the place. I didn't think, I just did it. I'd do it again." She watched again for his response.

Holt was staring at her. He had never seen a woman so captivating without making any attempt to be. The take-charge authority in her voice and manner. Her simple beauty. He was smitten.

Her look, though, made Holt realize it was his turn to talk. "Uh.. I...uh...L-Laudie Kate..." he tried to start. He felt his face turning red with her attention. This wasn't the fog of his injuries getting in the way, he had always struggled talking to women. For a man who had faced all kinds of challenges and danger, it was unexpected that he would act so uncomfortable around them. He finally croaked out a response, "Y-You don't need to a-apologize, I understand."

Laudie Kate's face was impassive. She nodded with a scrunched-up half-smile and that was the end of the conversation. She left the room, leaving the Rangers to their talk and their meal.

Holt was upset with himself that he didn't joke to her that this would make a good story for their children.

After that, Holt and Orion quietly ate the stew, chatting only for a few brief moments afterward because Holt started to nod off. A full belly and sitting up had drained his energy.

"What direction is that?" Holt asked, gesturing towards the window near the foot of the bed.

"More or less south, why?"

"Just making sure," Holt answered, voice thick with drowsiness. Orion chuckled slightly, even shot up like this, his partner was mindful of his superstition about sleeping with his head facing north.

"Can you do me another favor, Orion?" Holt asked before he went to sleep. "Ride my horses some, will you? Or get someone to work 'em a little. Take Tag out with you too."

"Can do. Ol' Tag's been stuck to you like glue, but the hotel owner here has taken to bringin' him along when he runs errands. It usually ends with Tag gettin' a bone from the meat locker," Orion mused. "In fact, ol' Tag has actually been lettin' people be nice to him. They're treatin' him like royalty an' he's lovin' it."

"He's good at that." Holt smiled groggily as he drifted off.

Laudie Kate came to retrieve the empty stew bowls in the morning. All three had been licked clean. She was certain the Rangers had not finished off their stew in that manner. Tag Along was the likely culprit, finishing every last morsel.

Orion excused himself and left Laudie Kate alone with Holt. She was pleased to discover him sleeping easily. Her gaze lingered on the young lawman, his hard face softened in sleep. Laudie Kate had to admit he was ruggedly handsome. High cheekbones, trim mustache, muscular frame. It had only been a few days and he was unconscious most of that time, but it was easy to sense the intense energy coiled within him. Yet even in his repose, there seemed to be a hidden gentleness that was difficult to not be drawn to.

She shoved those thoughts aside and returned to her chore of straightening the room. Orion had spent the night, on guard as usual. Two men and a dog have a way of untidying the tidiest of rooms, she smirked. She folded Orion's blanket and arranged it across the rocking chair. She tried to quietly open up a window to allow a little fresh air inside.

Tag Along roused at the creak of the window sash. Holt reacted to the movement near him. The open window brought the smell of lavender to his senses.

Laudie Kate.

He blinked his eyes to wake and focus. His gaze settled on her. Those bright sky-blue eyes…easy smile… *A sight I could wake up to forever*, he reckoned.

Morning light streaming through the window touched her face. The breeze from the open window hurried to caress a stray lock of hair that had escaped from her upswept bun and lay down across her sun-kissed cheek. He realized for the first time there was a long scar there.

Just then, she looked back. Holt was watching. He smiled and she returned the intimacy. Their eyes played briefly before she reached to pick up the tray of bowls and left the room.

Holt was disappointed in himself that he did not manage to even say "hi" to Laudie Kate. He closed his eyes to mull over what he should have said and done. He drifted off to sleep with thoughts of Laudie Kate settling softly in his mind and didn't even notice when Evie took Orion's place on the rocker.

CHAPTER FOURTEEN

T wo days after leaving their Bar 3 ranch, Deed pulled their buckboard next to the Hanson Livery in Stebbins. Benjamin hopped down from the seat, taking in the strange, new sights. Both now stood in the early afternoon sunshine, stretching and stomping life back into their legs and feet.

They had spent a night in the little town of Overfield and one night out along the trail. Their journey had been peaceful and uneventful, giving time for Deed to get to know his stepson a little better. It dawned on him during this ride that he himself had lost both his parents at about the same age as Benjamin had lost his father.

He also had time to finally contemplate on what they might find when they reached Holt. Along with those thoughts, memories of his family had come.

Elements of their mother's approach to life could be found within each of the three Corrigan brothers. Deed cared about all wild things, from snakes to birds to deer. Holt had her fascination with superstition and reincarnation, believing he had lived several lifetimes. Blue's beliefs were more devout. In fact, he served the Wilkon church as a part-time minister.

They had a sister, Calliope Rose. They called her Poppy. She and their mother died of pneumonia within a day of each other. Poppy was only seven. At ten years, Deed was closest in age to her and often wondered what she would be like now.

The brothers' perseverance and aggressive instincts came from their father. He believed in the need for righteous behavior, but also in never backing down. With that, Holt and Deed had developed well-known reputations as fighters. News stories as well as rumors that recounted clashes and brawls involving one brother or the other had spread throughout the region, marking them as men not to be crossed.

Deed had been thirteen when Blue and Holt left for the war, too young, really, to fully understand the danger facing his older brothers. Blue had come back missing an arm, but he had come back. Holt had finally come home as well, but only after Blue got him to realize riding the outlaw trail in the name of the Confederacy was not a path Holt should be on.

———

The ride here had given Deed time to reflect on what had happened to his brother. The question ground on his mind like a corn-sheller.

He now wondered how Holt, who had seen more action than any ten men, had come to this, fighting for his life. His brother was one of the heroes of Sabine Pass, cutting down a patrol of Yankees with his rifle and handguns, and taking out several more with just the butt of his empty carbine. He had been fighting Comanches, Kiowas, Apaches, rustlers, and robbers since he was old enough to carry a gun. As a Texas Ranger, he and his partner had hunted and captured The Angel, decimating the evil priest's gang in the process. And they had just taken down the wicked attorney Meden Taliff and his pack of killers, hard.

A warrior like that doesn't just get shot, he declared to himself as he and Benjamin settled up with the livery operator.

"Stebbins is a bit bigger than Wilkon, what do you think?" Deed said, throwing an arm around Benjamin.

"Busier too," Benjamin replied, taking it all in.

The livery had an area in back where they were allowed to store their wagon. Deed paid the man a few more coins to give their two horses some extra grain. Benjamin held a small war bag filled with their spare clothes and Deed had his own saddlebags slung over a shoulder as they made their way back out to the thoroughfare.

"You best keep your eyes peeled out here in the street, your mother expects me to bring you back in one piece," Deed teased.

People scurried along the sidewalks and across the rutted street, intent on their day's business. A freighter wagon rattled past Deed, and the driver gave him a nod, which he returned. A patrol of soldiers followed a few moments later. The ten-man detachment eyed everyone suspiciously and expected to be given a respectful, wide berth. From their air of superiority and loud talking, it was apparent these troopers enjoyed wearing blue in what used to be Confederate country. An eleventh rider, a lanky, black-suited man rode self-importantly at the front of the squad. Thin as a scarecrow, to Deed, this man looked to be more like a menacing preacher than an Army officer.

"Are those the same men we saw in Overfield?" Benjamin asked quietly. "The ones everyone said were going after the Comanches?" The boy watched the cavalrymen ride by, his free hand shielding his eyes from the sun. One of the soldiers absentmindedly spit a stream of tobacco. Benjamin jumped quickly out of the way to avoid being hit.

"Looks like it," Deed said, his eyebrows tightening as his anger flared. "I hope I'm wrong, but that group doesn't look ready to secure a parade route, much less take on a screaming war party."

Three women were forced to hurry their crossing because the patrol did not stop or slow down. The startled females exclaimed their alarm as they ran to get out of the way. Safely gathered on the other side of the street, the women shared whispered imprecations and threw hateful scowls at the passing unit.

"Let's go find your uncle," Deed said, keeping his arm around the boy, his glare still following the patrol. "Ranger Higbee's telegram said Holt's in a place called the Blue Sky Inn."

The Blue Sky Inn was one of the bigger buildings in the middle of town and its blue-lettered nameplate stood out among the regular black and gray painted signs up and down the street.

They were met in the lobby by a woman with a scar down her right cheek. Deed removed his hat in her presence. Benjamin gave him a sidelong glance and quickly did the same.

"Ah, miss, we're looking for an injured Texas Ranger, name of—"

"Holt Corrigan," she interrupted with a wide grin. She took in Deed's handsome face and long, dark hair. "You must be a brother. Blue or Deed?"

"Why, yes'm," Deed replied, completely taken by surprise. "I'm Deed Corrigan. This is my boy, Benjamin."

"You had to be a Corrigan, you look so much alike. It wasn't a lucky guess; your names have been mentioned a lot." She stuck out her hand. "I'm Laudie Kate Hart."

"Pleased to meet you, Miss Hart." Deed smiled as he shook her hand. "That's a name I recognize from Ranger Higbee's telegrams."

"Hopefully he mentioned me for my nursing skills and not the other..." Her voice trailed off a bit.

"Other?"

"Did Ranger Higbee not tell you I was the one who shot your brother? Well, one of them anyway."

"You?"

"The way he burst in, I thought he was set to rob the place."

"So, an accident then."

"Oh, it was no accident, I meant to shoot him. Call it a *misunderstanding*." She smiled, affably but assertively.

Deed did not quite know how to respond to this alluring woman's revelation. She had gone on to help save his brother's life and Ranger Higbee hadn't arrested her, so he had to assume she was no threat. Her easy smile and sincere confidence quickly assuaged any of Deed's misgivings.

"I think Ranger Higbee has stepped out. Probably for some lunch and checking in at the jail."

"What about Tag?" Benjamin blurted.

Laudie Kate beamed at the boy. "Tag is on his afternoon rounds with my boss, Mr. Navarro. They've become a real pair those two. They'll be back soon as well." She paused a moment, then spoke with a gesture toward the stairs with her head. "You didn't come all this way to talk to me. Your brother's up in room six. Evie's in there. Knock and tell her who you are."

"Thank you, miss." Deed nodded. He and Benjamin hurried up the stairs and knocked on the door.

"Who is it?" a gruff voice responded from inside.

"Uh, we're looking for Ranger Holt Corrigan," Deed stammered. "I'm sorry if we got the wrong room."

He heard the muffled sound of something heavy being moved and the door to room six opened just a crack. A shock of red hair and a deep, green eye told Deed this was a woman, but the boot down at the floor wedging the door from opening any further was a man's riding boot—a bit more rounded than military boots and worn by someone accustomed to being on horseback.

"Are you Evie? I'm Deed Corrigan. Laudie Kate sent us up. We're here to see Holt."

"Why di'nt ya say?"

A scrape of furniture was followed by the door opening slowly to reveal Evie O'Neill, Laudie Kate's friend. In her hand was a wadded up bedsheet. Wrapped inside the sheet, Evie had her fist tightly gripping a sawed-off double-barreled shotgun.

She opened the door all the way and stepped aside so Deed and Benjamin could enter. "Deed Corrigan." She smiled. "Heard that name a few times." She turned and nodded toward a sleeping Holt. She went about straightening up the room, opening a window, and retrieving a meal tray.

Deed half-smiled at the woman's careful greeting and weapon in her hand. He noticed a dresser by the door that had helped to barricade it.

"He's sleepin' again," Evie said, looking over at Holt. "It's good for 'im. He's had a busy day already. Dr. Vaughn checked 'is wounds an' re-did 'is bandages. He's been up on 'is feet a few times th' past coupla days. Even came downstairs to eat a lil' breakfast this mornin'.""

Deed did not know how to react to the news about his brother being so...so...helpless. It was hard to picture him that way.

"He di'nt eat much, but I think he enjoyed gettin' ta hang onta Laudie Kate an' her latchin' onta him." She winked.

"We're mighty obliged to all of you, Miss...Evie..."

"Evie O'Neill. I work down in th' bar for Laudie Kate an' Mr. Navarro."

"Thank you, Miss O'Neill. My brother Blue and I can't thank you enough."

"Call me Evie." She smiled. "A Ranger was hurt in our saloon. We feel responsible, I guess."

"Well, I'm much obliged to everyone. We're here to bring him home, let the Corrigan women take it from here, although I'm not sure the level of care will be the same." He grinned broadly. "Do you know when the doctor is coming back? I'd like to thank him and see if it's all right for Holt to travel."

"I don't rightly know when Dr. Vaughn said he'd return. We can sure get 'im back here though." Her face was earnest. "Holt's dog is out with Mr. Navarro, th' boss. They pick up mail an' visit th' butcher shop together. Mr. Navarro will be right upset when Tag Along goes home." She laughed at the thought. "He was dead-set against a dog stayin' here at first, but Ranger Higbee an' Laudie Kate convinced 'im otherwise, in no uncertain terms. Now they's regular pals. Tag's bed is right here, although he sleeps up with 'is master most've th' time... jus' don't tell Dr. Vaughn."

Deed nodded at her gun and indicated the dresser by the door. "Are you...are you expecting trouble?"

"Trouble? Jus' stayin' cautious, me bein' a wee wall-flower an' all." She half-smiled. "My boyfriend always tells me ta take precautions. I think he's jus' jealous. That's a handsome man lyin' there."

They both chuckled. "Well, me and Benjamin here need to grab a bite to eat," Deed said. "How long do you think he'll be out like that?" He gestured toward his brother.

"Coupla hours, I'd guess." Evie smiled. "He's gettin' better, lots stronger, but he's still really weak. He spilled a whole lotta blood, so it'll...take...time." The last words came out before she realized that Benjamin maybe didn't need to hear such details.

Deed smiled and gave some good natured thumps to Benjamin's back. "Okay, Miss Evie, we're glad Holt's been in such good hands. We'll leave our bags here and be right downstairs."

They looked for a table out of the way, but the Blue Sky's saloon was filling up, the advent of a brisk after-noon of business. Six boisterous cavalry troopers had barged in and had started heartily quenching their thirst with beer and bottom shelf whiskey. Handfuls of drovers, gamblers, and assorted businessmen with loud, arrogant voices and raucous laughter filled most corners of the big room.

Deed read the situation and decided the equation of liquored-up men was not conducive to a peaceful meal with his young son. He got Laudie Kate's attention. "We're going to try somewhere quiet, with a little less... devilment?"

She looked around the increasingly noisy bar. "I understand." She smiled and looked at Benjamin, appreciating Deed's reasoning. "Try the El Matador. It's usually pretty quiet. Good food."

"Again, thank you, Laudie Kate," Deed said. He leaned over to his son to be heard over the growing din. "Hey Benj, run up and tell Miss Evie we'll be right back." He watched the boy rush up the stairs.

"How long are you planning on staying?" she asked.

"If the doctor says it's okay, we'll head out in the morning."

She just nodded at the news.

Benjamin returned as quickly as he left. Deed smiled at Laudie Kate. "We'll be back after we eat."

CHAPTER FIFTEEN

Traffic on the Stebbins thoroughfare had picked up since Deed and Benjamin first visited the hotel. Laudie Kate's recommendation, the El Matador, was situated near the edge of town, at the opposite end from the livery.

Deed and Benjamin walked in the door of the adobe-walled restaurant. Stoneware jars dangling from an overhead beam clinked their welcome. A young Mexican boy, not quite Benjamin's age, sat cross-legged inside the door, braiding a small rawhide quirt, and softly singing an old song. A barefoot girl with large brown eyes stood next to the boy, waiting to seat customers. A large red dog curled beside them, sleeping through the hubbub around it.

The barefoot girl acted as hostess, greeting them with, "*Bienvenido al matador,*" and earnestly leading them across the recently scrubbed earthen floor. Deed indicated a table over by the kitchen entrance would be fine. Out of habit, he had chosen the spot based on the fact it would give him a wide view of the restaurant with no one directly behind him. Nodding, she led the pair in that direction.

Along the way, they passed a table of four men, three of them cavalry troopers. The three had dour looks on their faces as they watched Deed walk by. Noticing the epaulets and stripes, Deed figured this was the leadership of the patrol in the Blue Sky's saloon and the one that insolently paraded through town. He nodded at the scruffy-looking man with them. He was the only one not wearing blue and not drinking whiskey. Wearing a faded gray shirt and dirty buckskin jacket, Deed figured him as the scout for the detachment.

Upon reaching their own table, Deed said, "*Gracias, señorita.*" The girl gave him a smile that stretched across her face, appreciating being referred to as a young woman.

Deed shook off his long coat. Dust whispered around him for an instant before he draped it over the top rail of the chair he sat on. He placed his hat on one of the empty chairs and Benjamin followed suit.

"Those are the same soldiers we saw in Overfield. I remember the man in the fringed jacket," Benjamin stated quietly as he leaned over.

"Good eyes, Benj," Deed said, his eyes taking in the four men. "Looks like these are the *leaders* of the detachment. I doubt most of them have ever faced down a war party…except maybe the scout in the jacket. If they knew better, they wouldn't be letting their men find courage in a bottle."

An older Mexican woman in a loose smock and layered skirt approached the table. In halting English, she reported that the kitchen had run out of eggs, but they had steak and *barbacoa*, and plenty of beans, tortillas, fried potatoes, and radishes, or squash.

"What do you think, Benjamin?"

"What's bar-barba...?"

"*Barbacoa* is usually lamb or goat." Deed smiled and looked at the woman.

"*Si*, goat. Very good. Spicy." She smiled in return.

"How about a couple of steaks, beans and tortillas, and potatoes," Deed said, looking at Benjamin. "Want some squash or radishes?" Benjamin scrunched his nose and vigorously shook his head no.

Deed laughed and said, "How about some lemonade if they've got it?"

The woman nodded. "Fresh."

"Okay," Deed said. "And coffee, *por favor*."

The woman glided away to the kitchen and the Corrigans' attention was pulled to the Mexican boy's large dog which had meandered into the restaurant, waving its tail, and searching for something to eat.

"I miss Cooper," Benjamin chirped. "I bet he misses us. And Tag too."

"It'll be good to get everyone back home, won't it?" Deed replied.

The young boy's hound stopped at the table with the soldiers and sat on its hind legs. The largest of the four men, a dark-headed sergeant with a bushy mustache, set down his glass of whiskey with a loud curse and kicked the dog in its chest.

Knocked to the ground by the blow, the dog whimpered, but then hopped back on its legs and growled at his attacker. The sergeant's hand fumbled to his flapped holster. Just a few steps away, the Mexican boy yelled frantically for his dog to return. The terrified lad ran and stepped in front of his dog, apologizing loudly and profusely in Spanish. The sergeant stopped his reach for the gun and instead delivered a savage slap across the boy's face. The force of the blow staggered the youth and he fell in a heap like a rag doll beside his dog. The bare-footed girl screamed and ran to the boy, who was wiping away a hint of blood that was trickling from his mouth.

"Git that mangy beast away from our table," the sergeant sneered. "You're lucky I didn't shoot it." He shoved the heel of his open palm into the girl's chest, knocking her over the boy and dog.

"The four-legged or two-legged ones?" joked the chunky corporal sitting next to him. The duo's cruel laughter brought a similar response from the lieutenant seated with them. The rumpled-looking scout did not join in their mirth. He observed the troopers stony-eyed and started to leave his chair.

"Sit down, Decker," the lieutenant ordered, his voice lowered. "Leave it be."

Watching the cruel treatment of the Mexican children, Deed instinctively touched the small Oriental-looking brass circle on a rawhide thong worn around his neck. A gift from his godfather, Silka, the disk was engraved with a symbol of *Bushido*.

"Touch *Bushido*...for better luck," Silka had taught him. They both had worn similar disks, except Deed's was connected to a sheathed throwing knife carried under his shirt and down his back.

The man in charge of the patrol, a bespectacled lieu-tenant, wore an air of authority that only went as far as the epaulets on his shoulders. He announced loudly, "Dirty little Mexicans. Where's the owner of this filthy place anyway? We shouldn't have to put up with this crap. I don't think we'll pay." Pleased with himself, he looked around the room. Most of the customers did not meet his eyes, turning uncomfortably back to their tables.

Deed was already in motion before Benjamin realized his stepfather had even stood. "Don't move," he cautioned his son over his shoulder. "Stay right here."

In a flash, Deed was helping the stunned girl and boy to their feet. He spoke quietly to both of them in Spanish and the youngsters nodded their understanding that they would be safe. Deed asked if the boy was all right and he nodded affirmatively, wiping blood from his lip. He told both youngsters to take the dog and return to their spot at the door. After a soft "*Gracias,*" they returned to the entryway.

Behind them, the large sergeant growled, "Leave those Mex kids alone, friend. This is Army business." He smoothed his bushy mustache. Pleased with himself, he folded his arms and eyed his associates for approval.

The chunky corporal, wearing a gold-buttoned short-coat too small for him, whispered something just the table could hear. They all chuckled, except for the scout.

Satisfied the boy and girl were out of harm's way, Deed spun and stepped toward the table. Anger was flaring within him, igniting a raging storm that at one time was reckless and raw. Only with Silka's considerable training had he been taught to channel that fury into deliberate and relentless action.

"Army business?" Deed smirked. "Beating up on children is Army business? I guess that seems about right, the only chore a bottom-feeder like you could handle."

A look of derision on the sergeant's face preceded his standing up to confront Deed. "What's your story, mister?" the sergeant taunted. Taller than Deed, the burly man was used to bullying his way through life. "Are you a Mex lover?"

"You owe those kids an apology," Deed spoke calmly, yet inside, every fiber of his being was roiling and building like a tempest about to be unleashed. "In fact, I demand it."

"And if I don't?"

Deed's cat-quick slap across the sergeant's face was delivered with the full force of a roundhouse punch and his backhanded return blow was equally vicious. The man's face walloped side-to-side. The unexpected double-jolt drove the trooper backward against his chair and he crashed to the floor.

The sudden disturbance snuffed the restaurant to silence. The commotion caught the particular attention of a solitary customer sitting out in the veranda area of the café. The lanky, salt-and-pepper-haired man carefully folded the newspaper he had been reading and quietly set it down, his eyes riveted on the table inside. He did a double-take upon seeing Deed. "I'll be damned," the tall man mumbled to himself.

Across the room, Benjamin stared wide-eyed from his chair. He hadn't noticed a tall glass of lemonade had been set in front of him. He sat transfixed, watching his stepfather with new eyes.

Staring at the soldier sprawled on the floor, Deed hissed, "It hurts, don't it?"

Eyes tearing up from pain, the dark-headed sergeant felt his jaw and saw the red blood filtering through his mustache onto his fingers. His face darkened and his bloody hand went to the holstered gun at his waist.

"You've already made one mistake today. Your next

one's going to hurt a lot worse." Deed's words and eyes made the sergeant move his hand slowly away from the holster.

Leaning over in his chair, the chunky corporal held out a hand to help the sergeant stand.

"If he stands up, I'll put him on the floor again," Deed warned. "That's where cowards who hit children and dogs belong. Feel like joining him?"

The corporal withdrew his hand like it had touched open fire.

Deed's glare returned to the sergeant. "I said I need to hear you say you're sorry to these children."

From the other side of the table, the spectacled lieutenant announced sanctimoniously, "Stay where you are, Sergeant. You had it coming." He turned toward Deed. "Mister, that's a United States cavalry trooper you just struck."

"The only thing I see is someone who needs a lesson in what it means to be a man."

Clearing his throat nervously, the lieutenant tried to sound more assured than he felt. "He's under my command and will be dealt with accordingly." He noticed the whole restaurant was staring.

"You do what you want, *Lieutenant*," Deed snapped. "I'm still waiting for his apology." He gestured with his head toward the children, briefly taking his eyes from the spectacled officer. But in a blur most did not see, Deed's right hand flew behind his neck, drawing his throwing knife. The thrown blade sunk into the table, trapping the sleeve of the lieutenant who had only started moving toward his holster.

"I guess you like making mistakes too," Deed snarled.

Wide-eyed, the lieutenant quickly eased his free hand from his side to the top of table and clasped it with the trapped hand like he was praying.

The grizzled scout made sure his hands were readily visible atop the table. He gazed up at Deed and spoke. "Quicker'n Hickok with that knife. Are you by chance the one who took down two bank robbers and another one holding a gun in your belly? Austin, I believe it was."

"Something like that," Deed said tersely, locking eyes with the man.

"That would make you Deed Corrigan, right?"

Deed did not respond and started walking over to the children. The scout took the opportunity to shoot a glare at the lieutenant that clearly warned him to not say another word or move another muscle.

Deed reaffirmed that the girl was all right. A quick examination of the boy's cheek and jaw helped him decide the blow's damage was limited to a slightly cut lip and a bruised cheek. He then knelt beside the dog, rubbed its head, and looked at the animal's chest. An abrasion from the kick was likely, but it was definitely only a surface injury. The hound licked Deed's hand in response to his care.

"Don't get up, soldier. I said I want to hear an apology. To the dog too." Deed issued the challenge without turning around from examining the dog. "It can end here. If you're smart."

From the floor came the sergeant's hesitant response, "I-I'm…sorry."

"What was that?" Deed patted the dog.

"I'm sorry." The sergeant swallowed a little blood as he spoke again, loudly this time.

"For what?" Deed stood and walked back to the table.

"F-For hitting...children."

"And?"

"And f-for...kicking a dog."

"Good, you can get up now."

The corporal rose to help the sergeant stand.

Just then, an angular man with a gaunt face and precise muttonchop sideburns strode into the restaurant. His chin was raised as he looked down his prominent hawk nose at everyone and everything. His coal-dark hair matched his outfit as well as the long, lit cigar clenched in the corner of his mouth. A large, gleaming badge was pinned to his fine black suit. He carried a black ebony cane with a polished silver ball handle.

Deed knew instantly he had seen this man before.

"Just a moment, mister," County Sheriff Linus Carmichael said through gritted teeth holding the cigar in place. As though he held a rapier, Carmichael pointed his cane at Deed and declared, "We'll have no troublemakers bothering good peoples' lives, especially our boys in uniform."

Deed eyed the shiny badge displayed prominently on the sheriff's lapel and made no further moves. He had defined this man correctly when he first laid eyes on him —scarecrow tall, dark, and forbidding. Like a preacher from hell.

"I need your hands up where everyone can see them," Sheriff Carmichael continued, an upward flick of his cane punctuating his order. "Perhaps some time cooling off behind bars is what you need?"

A clear, assertive voice rang out from the veranda. "I'm gonna have to stop you right there, Sheriff," the lanky, salt-and-pepper-haired man called out as he stood, slowly putting on his flat-brimmed hat. As he strode into the main room, his boots and spurs made imposing *klud-ching, klud-ching, klud-ching, klud-ching* sounds in the deathly silence. A Ranger badge was prominently pinned to his black, buttoned vest. "You've got the wrong idea on who caused all this trouble."

"Who might you be?" Sheriff Carmichael inquired haughtily.

The lanky man stepped closer and drew himself to his full, taller-than-the-sheriff height and announced, "Orion Higbee. Texas Ranger." He now stood halfway between the sheriff and Deed. "An' before that, if it matters, Captain Higbee, Federal Navy." He folded his arms, but one hand rested on the butt of his shoulder-holstered Navy Colt.

"I see." The sheriff took a step back, eyeing the Ranger, then Deed, then looking back to Orion. "You saw everything that happened here?"

"That I did, Sheriff," Orion said. "These troopers here started the ruckus. Slapped a coupla children. Kicked their dog. For no real reason."

The sheriff lowered his silver-topped cane down to the floor.

"Apparently, those pretty blue uniforms ain't filled with the same quality these days," Orion continued.

The sheriff glared at the lieutenant, who sat motionless in his chair, his sleeve still trapped to the table by Deed's knife. "Well, then, Ranger. I'll leave this mess to you." Returning his gaze to Deed and Orion, he said, "As you all were." His cane dotted the floor sharply as he spun and left as quickly as he arrived.

"Pleasant sort, wasn't he?" Orion said, turning and grinning at Deed. "Uhh, were you finished?"

Deed returned Orion's grin with a short, solemn nod and stepped to the soldiers' table. "As you leave, and that would be now," he began. "You're going to pay for your meals and each of you are going to leave an extra coin for that girl and boy." Deed looked directly at the sergeant being steadied by the corporal. "If I ever hear about you bothering these youngsters in any way, I'll find you and finish this. Do you understand, Sergeant?"

The trooper nodded without looking at Deed.

"I didn't hear you."

"I...understand."

Deed turned to the lieutenant. "And *you*. Surely the Army's *finest* knows better." He bent over and retrieved his knife stuck into the table through the officer's sleeve. "You left a knot of men over at the Blue Sky. We'll assume they're as *well trained* as you, so, before they make similar mistakes, you're going to gather them and move on. Is that clear?"

The lieutenant looked up at Deed; the soldier's forehead furrowed in concern about what this stranger might do next. He slowly reached into his pocket and pulled a few gold coins to drop on the table. "All right, mister. We're going. We're going." But he couldn't resist adding under his breath, "We'll meet again, Corrigan."

"I'll hand you some good advice," Deed said with a menacing smile. "Don't try it."

"Is that a threat?"

"I don't make threats. Just a helpful projection of what life holds for you."

"Shut up, Richardson. Just shut up," the scruffy scout said. He had watched the whole encounter with interest and disgust. He stood now, threw some coins on the table, and nodded once each to Deed and to Orion, before heading toward the door.

After satisfying himself the troopers had also left money for the boy, Deed was deftly returning his throwing knife to its hidden sheath when the corporal hollered, "Don't! That's Deed Corrigan for god's sake!"

The sergeant had suddenly broke free from the corporal and charged. In one swift, smooth motion, Deed executed a half-turn crouch and stepped into the sergeant, driving his left elbow deep into the man's midsection, doubling the man over. He followed by detonating a vicious right uppercut that jolted the soldier's head back. The sergeant dropped like a heavy sack of potatoes.

Deed stepped toward the corporal, grabbing his lapel.

"Wait a minute, wait a minute," the chunky man cried. "I didn't do anything."

"That's right. You didn't," Deed responded and delivered a short, sharp jab to the man's face, letting him join his associate on the floor.

"Damn, this sure ain't your day," Orion quipped, looking down at the fallen troopers.

"Now," Deed thundered at the lieutenant. "I'm through teaching manners. Get out of here before I lose my temper!" Deed's hard voice made even Orion wince.

The lieutenant ordered the scout to help the two men get on their feet. The grizzled man in the grubby gray shirt and dirty buckskin jacket was already near the door. He waved a hand dismissively and stepped out onto the bright main street, ignoring the officer.

Orion moved forward. "Lieutenant, don't make this worse than it is. Gather your men from the hotel an' carry on with your mission." He was fully positioned now between the troopers and Deed. "Comanches, is it?"

"Yes."

"We ran into a passel of them a few months ago. Glad to be standin' here to talk about it." He absentmindedly rubbed the side of his face where a heavy scratch had healed, an all-too-close remnant of that skirmish.

"We'll be ready."

"Good luck with that. It appears you'll need plenty of it."

Orion watched the lieutenant struggle to get his two men to their feet. The scene reminded him of a greenhorn trying to wrangle a couple of disorderly calves and he fought to hold back a chuckle. "Let's go find the rest of your men, shall we?" he said, following a few paces behind as the troopers clomped and weaved their way out of the café.

Deed returned to Benjamin. He mumbled an apology to his stepson about not liking bullies, especially ones who went after children and those with different colored skin.

"I-I remember the day the Comanches came and killed my father…and seeing you fight them…b-but there were stories we-we heard…like the one in Austin…Ma wouldn't let me talk about it…the knife…you…" Benjamin couldn't get his words out quick enough, his eyes bright with wonder. "The 'Deed Corrigan' who did all that…is…is…you?"

"I doubt there are many with the same name," Deed said with a sly smile, but then turned serious. "Yes, Benjamin, the Austin story is true. But you have to know that I was defending myself against outlaws, some very bad men." His eyes bored into Benjamin's, searching for, and receiving understanding. "A man should never go looking for trouble."

"C-Can you teach m-me? *That*?"

"I will teach you how to defend yourself, how to be a man. Just like your uncle Silka taught me."

Benjamin's mind was filled with a hundred questions at once. How could Deed fight four men at once? How could he move so quickly? He wanted to know more about the knife that appeared out of nowhere. But just then, they both looked up to see the lanky Ranger approaching them.

"Got them troopers all reunited an' fixin' to move on outta town," the tall man enthused. "Don't know if you remember, I'm Higbee. Orion Higbee. Your brother is my partner."

"I thought so," Deed said with a broad smile, standing and shaking the lawman's hand. "Modlin was a bit of a blur."

When Holt and Orion went after Meden Taliff and Kane Barlow, who were holed up in the town of Modlin, Deed had originally stayed behind to be with his wounded wife. She recovered enough to tell him to go after the man who attacked her. After Barlow survived the Modlin shootout, Deed caught the wicked murderer, killing the evil man in a vicious hand-to-hand battle.

"I'm happy to see you again, Orion," Deed continued. "This is my son, Benjamin. Join us."

"Pleased to meet you, young man," Orion said, extending his hand to the boy as he sat with them. "I gotta say, when all that fracas started," he said, acknowledging both Corrigans, "I did a double-take when I saw you scrappin' there. You're a little younger, an' more clean-shaven, but ho-lee damn, you're a ringer for Holt."

"We're here to take him home. Let the Corrigan women dote on him, heal him up."

Orion nodded. "All he needs now is time to heal. Wouldn't contemplate any other way for my partner."

"I thought he wouldn't be a Ranger now, being wounded and all."

"He might not be a Ranger, but he'll always be my partner. He an' that dog of his saved my life."

"They're a pair to draw to, for sure. You hungry?"

"I was about ready to order, but that was before some scrapper decided to take on the 4th Cavalry." Orion laughed.

Soon, all three were diving into plates heaping with steak, beans, tortillas, and fried potatoes. They enjoyed the meal in silence as was customary. Orion asked for a side of the *barbacoa*. Benjamin gamely tried a piece, but immediately slugged down a big gulp of lemonade, hoping to cool the spicy burn. Deed and Orion grinned at each other.

As they waited for apple pie dessert, Deed spoke up. "I'm much obliged to you for stepping in back there when you did. Who the hell was that character with the cane?"

"From descriptions, that's County Sheriff Linus Carmichael. Cuts a wide swath aroun' here. Mighty flexible 'bout which side of the law he favors too. In all the time we've been here, this was the first time I've even seen the apple knocker. Kind've a scary pecker, if you ask me."

Benjamin worked hard to stifle a snicker.

"This isn't the first time we've seen him," Deed noted. "I doubt he'd recognize us, but we saw him riding with that very same cavalry patrol."

"You don't say?" Orion drew closer with interest.

"I don't know where they came from, but we crossed paths in Overfield. Now here."

"This patrol with the manners, eh? An' the sheriff was with 'em?"

"At the head of the patrol. Both times," Deed declared. Benjamin nodded his head in agreement at his father's statement.

"Now that's damn interestin'," Orion said, sitting back, seriously pondering the news. He continued quietly. "Carmichael seems to be connected to the Viklund rustlin' operation we were assigned to break up. But I'm not certain how he fits in. We sure as hell didn't know about him when Cap'n McCoy sent Holt an' me here. Didn't count on Holt gettin' shot neither."

"By that pretty lady in the saloon."

"Yeah, by Miss Laudie," Orion acknowledged. "She drew an' shot Holt sure as I'm standin' here." He paused a moment. "I can kid a little 'bout it now." He paused again, then joked, "You know, her an' Holt would make quite a pair."

"That'd be some love story," Deed acknowledged with a chuckle of his own. "My brother's not known for being silver-tongued around women."

"I'm just funnin' with that. She's good stock, had a rough life though," Orion reflected as he drained his coffee mug.

"She mentioned something about not being the only one to shoot Holt. Anything to that?"

Orion looked Deed square in the eye. "That's a gotdam puzzle, Deed. Keeps me awake thinkin' on it. Laudie Kate told me she only fired twice. I checked her gun. She was tellin' the truth." He paused and leaned closer so he could lower his voice even more. "But Holt was hit four times. The slug Doc took outta your brother's thigh was a .45. Laudie's gun is a .31. No one claims to have seen anyone else shoot. I sure didn't see it happen."

"Pretty dangerous puzzle," Deed noted.

"I don' know how or who, but somethin' keeps chewin' on me that the extra shots that hit your brother are all tied into this Viklund bunch." Then he gestured with his eyes and head, "An' maybe that scary-damn sheriff." He paused. "We been lockin' Holt's door ever since. Takin' turns stayin' in there. We're not sure if someone'll come an' try to finish the job."

"That explains Evie and her sawed-off shotgun," Deed bobbed his head in realization. "I didn't know. She said it was just her boyfriend saying to be careful. We wouldn't have…"

"Don't worry, Deed," Orion said. "Those two women? Miss Laudie an' Miss Evie? Let me just say I don't wanna be aroun' if they ever got mad." He chortled at the thought.

"Well, Blue and I thank you, Orion. All the more reason to get him back home. And for me and Benjamin to get back to his room."

"So, when do you think you're gonna head back?"

"If the doctor okays it, we'll leave in the morning."

Orion gave Benjamin a quick sidelong glance but made his statement anyway. "Best be keepin' your eyes peeled on that road home. More'n Comanches may be out there."

CHAPTER SIXTEEN

"Evie, it's Deed Corrigan…"

The door opened quicker this time after Deed's knock. No brace or lock. Deed was met by a cheerful Laudie Kate. At the foot of Holt's bed, Evie was readjusting the blankets and sheets. Dr. Vaughn turned from Holt's bed, adjusted his eyeglasses, and stepped aside. Holt was awake and sitting up, looking toward the door, a rumpled-looking smile on his face.

"Well, look who decided to join us," Deed said with a grin so wide it hurt his face. "How're you doing, Sunshine?"

"Felt like a mountain dropped on me, then got lifted," Holt responded quietly. "I wondered when I'd see you, little brother. All these three can talk about is the wildcat who chased the cavalry out of town."

"Just a lesson in simple manners. You'd have done the same." He and Benjamin moved into the room.

Holt started a story for the women and the doctor. "When I saw my older brother Blue for the first time after the war, last summer in El Paso, he told me a crazy tale about our grown-up little brother taking down some bank robbers with his bare hands. I asked him then if you were nuts." Holt grinned at Deed. "He said, 'No, just good. Very good.'"

"You're one to talk, big brother," Deed said. "Don't get me started." He moved close to the bed. "It sure is good to see you, Holt," Deed added, putting his hand affectionately on his brother's shoulder. "I thought Silka taught you how to duck. You can't go scaring us like this anymore."

Good natured laughter swept the room.

"Deed, who is this stringbean with you?" Holt smiled. "I don't believe we've met."

"Hi, Uncle Holt, it's Benjamin," the young man replied shyly.

"You can't be Benjamin. You've grown a foot since I left. I haven't been gone *that* long, have I?"

Dr. Vaughn stepped in. "Deed Corrigan? I'm Dr. Sherrell Vaughn. I heard you were here to take my patient home, so I came to look him over one last time."

"I can't thank you enough, Dr. Vaughn. Orion said you're one of the best he's seen. So, how is he? Can we take him home?"

"I don't think he should be in a saddle or fightin' snakes or anything, but he can be up and around as much as he feels like. It's the only way he'll get his strength back. Just be sure to change those bandages every few days."

"Will do, Dr. Vaughn," Deed said, shaking the doctor's hand. "I'll come by in a little bit to settle up his bill."

The two women started to drift out of the room. Holt savored every move Laudie Kate made.

"I'll look in later, to check on you," Laudie Kate said matter-of-factly. Holt's blue eyes fixed on hers and to him, she was suddenly the only thing near. She leaned over and cleared the nightstand of a dirty mug and plate. He inhaled her brief closeness, nodding at her words without really hearing them.

"Thank you, Laudie Kate," Holt called out. She smiled and left the room. He remembered Deed and Benjamin were there.

"I'm not sure if Bina or Atlee or the girls can stand up to the attention Laudie Kate and Evie have given you," Deed teased.

"They've been right nice, for sure," Holt said, propping himself up with his good elbow. At least his head had stopped swimming when he did that now. "I didn't mean to sleep that long. Guess I slept through a couple of days and nights."

"Slept? Try again, big brother. You were unconscious. For nearly a week. You only came to when your dreams forced you into this world or when that pretty lady fed you something."

"A week? Can't be."

"Can be—and was."

Just then, hotel owner Miguel Navarro knocked from the hallway. The door had not closed completely, so Tag Along pushed on it, forcing it to swing open. The dog swept inside and happily bounded up on the bed, right into the middle of them.

Benjamin grabbed on to Tag with a big hug. The dog's tail wagged excitedly.

Holt laughed. No doubt about it now, he was back and it felt good.

"You heard him, Dr. Vaughn says you can travel if

you take it easy," Deed said. "I say we plan on leaving at first light."

"That suits me fine," Holt nodded. "Where'd Orion get off to?"

"He's out poking around, making sure those troopers actually moved on," Deed said, throwing an arm around his son's shoulder. "When he gets back Benj and I will go pick up some supplies, then square your bill here at the hotel and with the doctor. At the livery too. We'll have 'em make sure all our horses are ready."

"Be good to ride again," Holt acknowledged.

"The only thing your butt is sitting on, big brother, is that wagon, next to me. Doctor's orders. Benj can ride your horses. It'll be useful for him and them."

"If you say so."

"Get some good rest now. We'll take care of everything."

"Thank you, little brother."

———

At dinnertime, Holt dressed himself in new trousers and a shirt. Laudie Kate had thrown away the old ones. They were too torn and bloodied to salvage. His coat and vest had been cleaned of the residues of his being shot as well. Two ragged tears—in the coat's arm and the side of the vest—had been neatly repaired. Holt left them folded on his bed.

He asked Benjamin to stay near him as he walked down the stairs to eat. "I've got to do this myself," Holt whispered to his nephew. "You catch me if it gets ugly, okay?" Holt figured the lad could help steady him if need be and, more importantly, would not lecture him for doing too much on his own. He had to keep pushing himself. Like the doctor said, how else was he going to get better? Holt took care to start down the stairs with his right leg, not because his left one had been shot, but because he had heard it was good luck to do so.

Benjamin was only too happy to help. He sat by his uncle at dinner, eager to regale him on everything he and Deed had done on the trip. To the boy it had been a grand adventure.

After dinner, Holt saw Laudie Kate heading toward the stairs. He quickly finished his glass of whiskey and pushed himself up from his chair.

"I'll be okay," he said to Deed who was raising himself up to help his brother.

Deed shook his head and grinned as he watched Holt carefully make his way in the direction of Laudie Kate.

She saw him out of the corner of her eye and hurried over. "Holt Corrigan! What are you trying to do?"

"Oh, I-I...th-thought maybe...I'd-I'd hurt myself all over again, just so you...and Evie...would keep up all that attention."

She laughed, but he was only half-joking.

They climbed the stairs to the top together, Holt relishing the feeling of her arm around him.

Reaching the door, he touched her arm with his hand, but not because he needed the support. "Laudie Kate, I...I...d-don't know how to thank you. I'm not sure I could have...I just wanted to t-tell you..."

"You wouldn't be here if it wasn't for me," she teased.

"Well, there is that." He wanted to tell the joke about how this would be a story to tell their kids, but his nerves got in the way again.

Silence awkwardly pushed its way between them. Her femininity climbed all over his senses. His body tensed and tingled in a way he knew would probably surprise her. How could she possibly care for someone like him? Who was he? Just some lawman who managed to get himself shot in her bar.

"Th-Thank you, Laudie Kate. I-I'll see you again real soon, I hope," was all he could manage to sputter out.

"Good night, Holt Corrigan," she nodded and turned to step into the hallway. With a final smile, she said, "Take care of yourself," and pulled the door closed behind her.

As the door clicked shut, Holt's heart scolded him that he should have told her how he felt.

CHAPTER SEVENTEEN

F alse dawn was ushering in a new day. Deed and Benjamin were repacking the wagon, arranging new supplies around their laid out bedrolls. Holt could grab a nap there when his energy waned. Benjamin was excited to get the opportunity to ride one of his uncle's horses. Holt had suggested that he ride the buckskin first. Deed agreed. The other one, a dun, might be more animal than the boy was ready to manage.

"Mornin' boys! Fancy some company?"

The two looked up, surprised to see Orion Higbee leading his horses, a powerfully built bay and a dun that looked like it could eat a cougar for breakfast.

"Cap'n agrees with me that the sheriff mixin' with those troopers is somethin' that don't sit true. Gonna backtrack their trail to where you saw 'em in Overfield, see what turns up."

"It'll be good to have the company and another set of eyes." Deed smiled. "Maybe we can clear up any tales my brother may have told you." He laughed.

The small group moved through the mostly empty street, back to the Blue Sky Inn. Deed tried to help his brother down the stairs from his room, but Holt was insistent on doing as much on his own as possible. "I'm sure you'd rather hang on to Laudie Kate or Evie for this trip." Deed smirked.

"Well, they both smell a heck of a lot sweeter than you." Holt looked back over his shoulder at the closed door to Laudie Kate's room. It was way too early. He couldn't wake her and try saying goodbye again. He took a deep breath, disappointed at himself.

When they reached the boardwalk, Holt stopped. "Wait a minute, little brother." He stood straight and reached into his coat pocket for the small leather pouch of tobacco. Spreading a small handful of shreds in all directions, Holt silently thanked the spirits for helping him and asked for their guidance. He placed the bag back into his coat and looked at Deed. "Things could've ended here. Thankful they didn't."

The small caravan started out from Stebbins. Holt sat next to Deed on the wagon seat with Tag nestled between them. Orion rode out to the side on his bay, ponying the dun. Benjamin was beyond happy, sitting aboard his uncle's buckskin; Holt's other horse, a bay, was tied contentedly to the back of the wagon. Everyone was quietly getting used to the day's trail.

Thirty minutes outside town, Holt blurted, "Dammit! Stupid bandage." He was feeling the top of his head. A cool morning breeze made him realize he was not wearing his hat. "All this dressing...I thought my head was covered. I left my hat somewhere."

"Can you manage?" Deed deadpanned. "We sure as hell aren't going back for it." Everyone, including Holt, got a good laugh and kept riding. Joke aside, Holt realized that he hadn't even seen his hat since being shot.

The sun took control of the sky as the hours burned toward midday. The earlier light wind was not going to push away the coming afternoon heat.

The small Corrigan group continued its southward trek from Stebbins to Overfield. The dog had moved to the back of the wagon and was now curled up napping on a bedroll. Sleep was flirting with Holt as well. He had caught himself dozing off several times.

"We need to be thinking about what we're going to do about moving cattle next year," Deed said, obviously pondering about home. "Maybe just a short drive, over into New Mexico."

Holt perked up at Deed's statement, saying, "That's worth studying. Orion knows the coast down south. Maybe Galveston would be a good place to deliver our herd. It's not too far either."

"Good beef is always needed down there," Orion responded. "They can load 'em onto boats, ship 'em to New Orleans or Mobile. It'd be worth y'all checkin' into."

"I hadn't thought about south. We'll get Blue's thoughts when we get home," Deed acknowledged.

The land ahead looked flat, but was broken by hills, canyons, and sudden arroyos. White and gray rock decorated most of the ridges. Prickly pear and mesquite added their own character.

They decided it was time to give both the two-legged and four-legged creatures a rest. The horses were eased down a draw bordered by brush and mesquite on both sides. Not far was a muddy stream edged by a few pecan, live oak and cottonwood trees.

Orion made a quick survey of the surroundings before returning.

Deed helped Holt climb from the wagon but stepped back allowing his brother to find his balance and steady his legs on his own. He had noticed Holt nodding off a few times. It would take time for him to regain all his strength. But now, he had something important to discuss with Holt and Orion.

"How long have we been crossing those unshod pony tracks?" Holt asked before Deed could bring it up.

"Coupla miles," Orion said. "The tracks aren't new, but they ain't wild. Those horses are bein' guided."

"I was thinking they're a day ahead of us, maybe two if we're lucky," Deed added, just a little surprised his brother had noticed, but glad he did. That meant he was closer to being his old self.

Benjamin had been helping Orion check the horses. His eyes were now saucer-wide.

"We keep movin', an' keep our eyes open. 'Bout all we can do," Orion said. "Holt, this just might be part of that Comanche band we tangled with."

"I was wondering that too," Holt said, renewed energy in his voice. "How about I ride wide left and Orion take wide right? Holler if we spot dust or something we shouldn't?"

"Good plan," Deed answered. "But Benj will join you in the wagon. I'll swing wide left. Doctor's orders remember?"

"Yes, dear," Holt smirked. "Ride my bay, you'll like his fire. And toss me my Winchester."

Deed replaced Holt's Winchester with his own Spencer in the bay's saddle scabbard. He tucked a few extra loading tubes into the sheath as well. He also reached back into the wagon and retrieved an extra gun belt and rifle.

"Benj, put this on," Deed said, handing the holstered pistol to Benjamin. "Keep the Winchester close. I don't know what's ahead, but we need to be ready. All of us. Understand?"

Benjamin nodded and swallowed hard. He strapped on the gun belt and carefully drew the pistol to check its rounds and followed up by ensuring the rifle was loaded. Holt and Deed watched all of this quietly and looked at each other with brief, knowing nods.

The small group mounted up. Deed and Orion took wide, not quite out of sight positions on either side of the wagon.

The hours and miles passed. The bright sun heated the rough, broken land. Out to their left by Deed was a cluster of arroyos mixed with small canyons and a long finger of cliffs that barely cleared the horizon. They rode through two dry streambeds, bands of prickly pear and huddled mesquite.

Holt had not seen any sign for quite a while.

Deed trotted back to the wagon. A few moments later, Orion joined them.

"No pony tracks in a long time," Deed reported.

"No dust either. Anywhere," Orion noted. "Good time to rest these horses, have a bite."

The group stopped and let their mounts blow. Benjamin handed out a hunk of jerky and a couple of hard biscuits to each of the men, making sure to toss Tag some morsels as well. They all ate in silence, lost in their own thoughts, never taking their eyes off the trail ahead and behind.

Holt spoke first, grabbing a water bag from the

wagon. "Doff your hats, boys. I think they've cooled enough. Let's water these guys and get moving."

The horses and the dog each got good hatsful of water. Their mounts rested, the group pushed on with Deed and Orion resuming their flank positions. They rode spread out that way for the remainder of the day, seeing no more signs of the unshod ponies. As the sun dipped below the horizon, they reconnoitered to discuss their plan.

"It'd be good to find water for the night, if it's secure," Deed observed. He thought his brother looked worn out, but did not say anything.

The group rode a little further and stopped at dusk by a small pond. The little pool looked in need of a restorative rain, but it held enough good water for their needs.

"Can you see to the wagon hitch, Mr. Benjamin?" Holt asked quietly, setting the brake on the wagon. He then stepped down from the seat and went to untie his buckskin from the back of the wagon.

"You and Benj see to the wagon team as well as the extra mounts," Deed said, stopping Holt from going any further.

"I was going—"

"You were going to pop those wounds loose or pass out or something," Deed admonished. "I'll scout around with Orion."

Holt shook his head and helped Benjamin lead the animals to a stand of grama grass to graze on while they checked their legs and hooves.

It was not long before Deed and Orion returned. "No sign of anything we didn't want to see," Deed declared as they rode up. "The only recent tracks were deer and smaller creatures. Be a good spot to hunt if we were going to be out longer."

"No place out here is completely safe. We'll do all right here, I figure," Orion added. "No need announcin' our presence though. Holt'll have to do without coffee on the bed like he's used to."

"Not the kind of room service I ever want to need again," Holt said reflectively.

"I didn't hear you complain about Miss Laudie's fussin' over you," Orion retorted.

With the horses cooled, Orion and Benjamin led them to the small pool for long drinks. Holt and Deed rummaged through the wagon and assembled a cold, fireless dinner. Jerked beef, corn dodgers, raw potatoes and apples made for a spartan, but filling, trail buffet.

After dinner, they all set about securing the camp and settling in for the night. Holt resumed his old daily routine—cleaning his two pistols and his rifle. The ritual was always precise, wiping down the weapons and ending with touching each gun with the cardinal feather from his hat. He scrunched up his face as he remembered his forgotten hat back in Stebbins. The cardinal feather would be with it. He dug in his trouser pocket and pulled out the mountain lion claw his mother had given him. It would have to do until the hat and feather returned to his head, he thought.

As Holt worked on his guns, he quietly apologized to his partner, "I feel like I'm leaving you with a big job and not enough hands to complete it. I don't like leaving things undone, Orion. I hate quitting."

"Ho-lee damn, Holt, you ain't quittin'. You got shot. You almost..." Orion caught himself. "You almost checked out on me." He paused again. "Look, we got

Moose and Dal posin' as Viklund drovers. The Cap'n is workin' on his end. Now, there's this damn sheriff an' we got no idea how that apple knocker fits in. You gettin' shot can't be coincidence either." He looked at Holt for agreement. "There's plenty to do on this one. We'll still be workin' this when you're ready to come back."

Holt nodded, still frustrated, but feeling relieved Orion considered his role in the mission not finished.

Deed stepped over to the two Rangers. "Benjamin and I will take first watch," he offered.

"Wake me for second watch," Orion chimed in.

"That leaves me the dawn patrol," Holt said. Then he quietly spoke to Orion, "Don't coddle me and take both watches. I'm all right. You hear me, peckerhead?"

Orion chuckled in agreement. "Okay, Gen'rul."

CHAPTER EIGHTEEN

A match snapped to life in the inky darkness. The tiny inferno was brought near the angular face of a man with a hawk-like nose and prominent sideburns. Cupping the flame with his other hand, he lit a long cigar. A deep puff of smoke was exhaled and with it the beacon was extinguished.

In this country, even just a few miles outside of Stebbins as he was, giving away your presence in that manner could be an invitation to trouble. In this instance, it was a signal. A clear invitation of his location.

County Sheriff Linus Carmichael was afraid of very little. He exuded confidence, but most people would describe him as vain, cold, and unforgiving. In addition to wearing the badge of county sheriff, Carmichael was a lawyer, with a very exclusive clientele. After recent events, the sheriff's main client had demanded this hastily arranged meeting.

He had been out here to the Viklund's Windmill V ranch before and was familiar with the terrain. Getting here unseen was always a priority. As usual,

Carmichael's moves were furtive and shadowy. He did not care that he had this elusive reputation.

He sat astride a handsome black gelding that was equally sure of the situation, standing quietly in the darkness. Exhaled breath smoke from man and horse created by the cold air mingled in rhythmic bursts.

This night, Carmichael was dressed in his customary tailored black broadcloth suitcoat, a spotless black trail coat layered over it to ward off the chill of this fall night; an ivory-handled, short-barreled Smith & Wesson sat snugly in a fitted holster at his waist. His black ebony cane topped with a polished silver ball rested in a special saddle scabbard where a rifle typically sat.

A thin whisper of white smoke curled around the sheriff's flat-brimmed, dark-gray hat. He took another pull on the cigar, letting the exhaled cloud blend with his visible breath to chase the first puff away.

His eyes, already adjusted to the near pitch-dark night, drifted easily to a ghostly figure which was drawing nearer, moving slowly into focus. The soft creak of tack leather and quiet hoof plods of a single horse came to his ears.

Lars Viklund wore a full beard and spoke in a loud, gruff Swedish accent that intimidated most people. His reddish beard and thick, dirty blonde hair salted with gray bespoke of a man suited for the outdoors. He was as strongly muscled as the powerful chestnut-colored Morgan he rode. A heavy buffalo coat was belted to the back of the horse's saddle and a Henry rifle was cradled easily across Viklund's rugged arms.

It only appeared he rode alone. The sheriff knew at least one of Viklund's two sons, Baldur or Christer, were close by, out of sight, taking up a precautionary position.

A stray breeze, sharp and cool, gusted out of nowhere. It crossed Linus's mind that the chilly wind accompanied the arrival of Lars Viklund.

A clear voice broke through the darkness. "*God kväll,* Carmichael. *Good evening*!"

"Nice to see you, Lars. Has the day been to your liking?" Carmichael had always felt a bit demeaned with the fact the Swede never addressed him as "Sheriff" or "Linus" or even "Mr. Carmichael."

"I first should hear what you have to say," Viklund replied, his thick accent revealing his Scandinavian ancestry.

Carmichael reached behind him and untied a set of saddlebags. "With the Sergeant's compliments," he said, handing them to Lars. "These are from that scabby settlement next to the fort. The forgeries did not fool the Army, but these counterfeit bills they confiscated will serve your purpose well."

Lars silently draped the bags across the buffalo coat in back of his saddle and continued his sharp gaze onto the sheriff.

"A deposit to your account from the last batch of cattle delivered to McKavett has quietly been made. One hundred ninety-seven steer made it to the fort. The deposit was for nine hundred eighty five dollars."

"Five dollars a head that is," Lars noted. "Seven or more we have been receiving. The reason for this? Someone is taking a cut it seems."

"That's the price paid by the Army. No choice," Carmichael answered.

"Expect your fee to be reduced then," Lars said, his midnight blue eyes glared like an angry sea. "No choice."

"Well...uh...right then," the sheriff continued,

uncomfortably clearing his throat. "The sergeant wants the next herd taken to New Braunfels. Not the fort."

"Very well. This we figured," Lars said, pausing before continuing. "You have more to reveal?"

Carmichael removed the cigar from his mouth and took a deep breath. "The past few days have not gone quite as planned, Lars. But you already know that."

"So, maybe you tell me what happened, yah?"

The sheriff stared off into the night, knowing the large Swede was waiting for his version of the Blue Sky Inn shootout. "As you know, Longley was arrested. Only one of the Rangers…was wounded."

Silence gripped the night.

"A rider of mine was killed."

"Yes, that was one of the unfortunate outcomes of the day," Carmichael responded.

"Unfortunate? A good man was lost."

"Yes, he…"

"By your own deputy," Lars interrupted, but in an uncharacteristically soft voice. "How did this come to happen?"

"Your rider Deke protested when he was rousted by that tall Ranger. Deputy Mercer thought your man was about to proclaim his innocence by pointing out it was the deputy who shot at the wounded Ranger, not him. It absolutely couldn't be known that my deputy was mixed up in any of this. So, he felt it necessary to ensure your man's silence."

"I see…and your deputy's only option was this?"

"Deputy Mercer claimed to everyone that your rider had made a move for his gun. The tall Ranger did not question it."

"The fullness of this story was not shared by my son,

Christer. Upset he was at the loss of his friend and the taking away of his guns."

Carmichael knew to wait for the remainder of the interrogation.

"You alerted me to the arrival of the Rangers. It was your deputy who saw them speaking with the marshal, yah?"

Carmichael listened, clearing his throat again.

"Remind me of your plan, Carmichael. Your deputy, along with Mr. Longley, Christer and Deke were to dispatch the Rangers. *Lätt som en plätt.* '*A piece of cake,*' you said."

"We didn't expect the bar manager to defend her saloon. She shot the other Ranger as soon as he came through the door. No one knew that would happen. They brought the marshal too. Before our men could react, the marshal's shotgun was pointed at Longley and everyone with him, including your son."

"An excuse this sounds like."

Carmichael took another long drag from his cigar prior to responding. "Many times, while serving with General Hood, we had to alter our plans due to unforeseen circumstances. The weather, the ground, our opponents, or other sudden changes conspired against the best preparations. We had to adjust and adapt and deal with it. This is no different."

"*Tusan också!*" the Swedish rancher's voice boomed into the night. "*Damn it*, Carmichael! I do not want to hear of your Confederate *skitsnack*! You Rebels and your 'reverence' for John Bell Hood is utter *bullshit*. A rash and reckless man he was. One who destroyed his army with carelessness. His own stupidity cost him his arm and leg." Viklund's voice was quieter now. "If I to be you, I keep away from copying your general and his... *dåraktighet*."

Carmichael looked at Viklund, a question on his face.

"*Foolishness*, Carmichael. Your precious General Hood was foolish. Such lack of judgment *I* will *not* permit. Do you follow my words?"

Carmichael squirmed slightly in his saddle. The black gelding stamped a foot impatiently. Viklund knew not to hold his associate's feet to the fire any longer.

"The Ranger, Corrigan? Has survived, yah?" Viklund asked.

"Yes. He left town this morning. The other Ranger too."

"Well, gone they are and with it the chance to remove the nuisance."

"We can still get him, Lars. The tall Ranger too. They were locked up in that hotel, but they're out in the open now, headed south."

"A decision your General Hood would have made, Carmichael. Do you not listen? Only disaster follows such a path," Lars scoffed, shaking his head disgustedly. "One Ranger wounded? Draws concern. The same Rangers ending up murdered? Draws *attention*. This you do not see?"

"Being wounded, Corrigan is no longer a Ranger."

"A notable name that be, yah? Was Corrigan also not one of your *Confederate heroes*?" Lars's voice dripped with derision. "This foolishness you must forget. Leave them be. I cannot insist this strongly enough. More important matters we have now. Are you most clear on that?"

The sheriff exhaled deeply. "We'll leave them be."

"A wise decision, Carmichael. Better you to be

figuring out the plan to return my foreman, Mr. Longley, to his duties. I have cattle and business that require attention. Needed he be. Rangers can wait. Agree?"

"Agreed."

"Now, ride with me. There are things you need to see this night."

CHAPTER NINETEEN

Windmill V rancher Lars Viklund and County Sheriff Linus Carmichael trotted their horses through the silence of the night. A quarter moon, veiled by wispy clouds, rose and gave the surroundings an unearthly appearance. The two traveled far enough for Carmichael's cigar to play out to a tiny stub that he tossed aside.

They cleared the top of a ridge and pointed their horses in the direction of a flat, open spoon of pasture. Even in the darkness, it was obvious the land should be teeming with the brown shapes and commotion of cattle. Instead, scattered below them was only a fraction of the beef normally grazing there.

The two men sat quietly atop their horses, observing the pastureland below when, from the bottom of the meadow, a rider and horse bounded in easy strides up the bank to where they were waiting.

"Pappa! Mr. Carmichael! Fancy meetin' you out here," the rider said with a wide, toothy grin.

"Carmichael," Lars spoke up. "You know my son, Baldur, yah?"

"Of course," the sheriff acknowledged, nodding toward the young man. Another slight by the elder Swede, Carmichael noted. He had been doing business with Lars—and his sons—for quite a while now.

Baldur was tall and handsome with long, sandy-colored hair and a thick, slightly darker beard. With his lean, hard physique, he looked every bit like the Norse god he was named after. He was the middle child of Lars and Margareta, born after the two arrived in America. An older sister, Kierstin, made the journey to this country as a toddler on the boat with her parents. Baldur spent his infancy in Chicago when Lars worked in the stockyards there. The younger brother, Christer, had been born after the family moved to Texas. Although the sons favored their father's Scandinavian genes and appearance, their speech and mannerisms had been influenced by their Texas upbringing.

"What's this for a situation?" Lars asked his son.

"W Bar L grazing land, Pappa," Baldur replied, gesturing with a wide sweep of his hand. "'Bout three hundred head out there now. Just gettin' settled back in."

The W Bar L ranch was one of several small spreads in the region. Lillian Whitman, the widow who owned the W Bar L, was barely keeping her ranch alive after her husband, Leonardo, had died. She and her riders had managed to stave off any rustling.

Until tonight.

"This herd is what we're leaving behind. We led them on a loop through the valley to the east," Baldur continued. "It should have created a confusing set of tracks."

"A good plan that is," Lars acknowledged. "And the rest?"

"The cattle we have acquired are on their way to the southern pasture of the Half Moon 6 through the scrub land. There shouldn't be much, if any, of a trail to follow."

Stebbins and St. Clair County were squarely within cattle country. The region was home to several spreads of assorted sizes and had experienced its share of rustling problems through the generations.

But for a year now, the ranch owners had been at odds with each other. The conflict, ignited by disputes over water and grazing rights, pitted the spreads against each other. Exacerbating the disagreements, rustling activity had increased. Most of the ranches were experiencing losses of varying degrees, but the smaller operations were complaining of losing significant numbers of cattle.

It was the war that changed Lars Viklund's outlook. His unwavering loyalty to his adopted country stood out among the Confederate sympathizers in the territory. In addition to—and maybe because of—his Yankee leanings, Viklund never felt he and his immigrant family were completely accepted by the town.

Even though the war had ended in Virginia, he and his home became a target. His first ranch was burned to the ground. His wife and daughter were brutally raped and murdered in the raid. Lars believed that many in the attack were ranchers with land that surrounded his ever-growing operation. In truth, the assault was staged by roving bushwhackers posing as Rebels who were only interested in looting and pillaging.

As Lars stood over the graves of his beloved

Margareta, and daughter Kierstin, he vowed to rebuild and take revenge. The seeds of his plan formed before his tears had dried. Like the thunder and lightning brought by his beloved Norse gods, Lars would not only drive out those so-called neighbors, he would also crush their very spirits. He would dominate this whole region.

The aspiration of it drove him daily.

The regeneration of his ranch began with the construction of a new house and outbuildings. Baldur and Christer were now old enough to ride and be in on their father's plan. Two years ago, Lars fired his foreman and let go all of his old cowhands. New riders who were prepared to follow the Swede's ruthless orders were hired. Now that it was time for his vengeance to go full-scale, Lars brought in gunman Casper Longley and his outlaw band to join the operation.

Action against the small ranches had been carried out with smooth precision, according to Lars's wishes. Rustling of the region's herds became a steady, albeit escalating, problem. Mexican bandits were getting the blame, or the ranchers themselves were accused of looking for excuses for poor management of their lands.

The vital part of Viklund's cold-blooded chess game was the disputes over water and grazing rights, disputes he quietly generated among his fellow ranchers. Disagreements over land filings was a secret storm brewed by Sheriff Carmichael's legal manipulations. False—but damaging—rumors about various cattlemen slithered around Stebbins and the region. The tales were well placed and well timed. Visits by Lars, his sons and his employees to the Stebbins bank, general store, and various restaurants and saloons in town provided fertile grounds to plant and spread gossip. Rerouting one of the water sources away from the northern spreads intensified the conflict.

The overall result of this nefarious campaign was a collection of landowners who not only did not trust one another, but also did not communicate among themselves except to argue and complain. Hardship befalling any one ranch was good fodder for town chatter, but was not met with sympathy, much less any support or assistance.

Watching gleefully over this county-sized chessboard was Lars Viklund. The deadly game, even with the stain of the blunder at the Blue Sky Inn, was playing out exactly as planned.

———

Nearly half of the stolen W Bar L herd, about three hundred head, was on its way to a ranch no one outside the Viklund clan knew was under their control.

"As the W Bar L beef is being moved, our new riders, Frantze and the one they call Moose, are keeping watch for the calves that haven't been weaned," Baldur explained. "They'll make sure those young ones don't get separated from their mamas. The other riders will peel off the steers that we can drive to New Braunfels. That is where we are going, am I correct, Mr. Carmichael?"

The sheriff grunted an affirmative, "Yes."

"So more work there be to be done this night, yah?" Lars asked.

"Yes, Pappa. There is a crew standing by at the box canyon near the Half Moon 6, with fires and running irons. The boys can easily turn the W Bar L brand into other marks. The two hundred head making the New Braunfels trip will be stamped with a new Double-

Diamond Heart. The hundred left behind will get the Half Moon 6 mark."

"Driving to New Braunfels is not a problem?" the sheriff wondered.

"No, not at all. We'll start at night. I will lead, taking three riders," Baldur said. "Pappa, I want the new man, Frantze, to go with me. I like him. He might be better than Longley."

"You still to be thinking Mr. Longley *utbytbar*... *replaceable*?"

"Yes, I still think so, Pappa," Baldur replied. "Attention he draws," he continued with a broad grin that teased his father's way of speaking. "Frantze is more like us. Ruthless, but purposeful and thorough."

"Not like a certain General Hood?"

"Pappa?" Baldur did not follow his father's mocking comment.

"*Glöm det*, my son. *Never mind*." Lars chuckled and threw a sideways glance at the sheriff.

Ignoring the jibe, Sheriff Carmichael chimed in, "You've done a good job of making all these *acquisitions* look like the work of Mexican rustlers."

"*Si, cuando cabalgamos hablamos en su idioma*." Baldur chuckled. "*When we ride, we speak their language*, Sheriff. Anyone who might come upon us thinks we are them. Anyone who lives, that is. Dropping an occasional *espuela* or sombrero completes the trick."

"To spread around town the idea that Mexicans be the *skurkars*, the *scoundrels*, doing such, has been of good help," Lars added. "Before long, evidence of these border villains we shall have, yah?"

"Yes, Pappa. We'll make that Mexican bandit connection even stronger when Christer, along with our other new man, Moose, and Longley, assuming he's freed, will cross the border, and purchase a small herd. They'll return and report they reclaimed our beef. Running irons will make it look like our brand was attempted to be altered by Mexican bandits."

"That ought to remove all doubt anyone has about across-the-border thieves," the sheriff acknowledged.

"We'll wait to make that move until the successful conclusion of this New Braunfels drive," Baldur confirmed. "Weather permitting too, fall is approaching."

"This bundle is to be used to obtain such a herd," Lars said, tossing the saddlebags filled with counterfeit money to Baldur.

"It'll hornswoggle them for sure." Baldur chuckled. "Proof! Mexicans did it!"

"Speaking of proof, Carmichael," Lars continued. "The ownership papers for two hundred head of Double-Diamond Heart cattle we will be needing, to present in New Braunfels."

"And a Double-Diamond Heart brand registration," added Baldur.

"Visiting town for our pantry stock-up we will be doing day after next," Lars said. "You will see to it that we can gather my foreman from jail at that time. You will have our paperwork prepared then as well, yah?"

"I will have the papers waiting for you in my office and Longley will have his release," the sheriff answered.

"*Tack själv*, Carmichael. *Thank you*."

CHAPTER TWENTY

I n the little Corrigan camp halfway between Stebbins and Overfield, even those not on guard slept with a gun nearby and an ear open for trouble. Time passed slowly, but night sounds stayed close and comforting.

In the small hours before false dawn, Orion neared the end of his watch. He had taken station with the horses, reasoning that night thieves like Comanches would target these fine-looking mounts. Tiredness seeped into his body as he silently approached the blanketed figure, also positioned near their picket line.

He looked at his friend, Holt, sleeping peacefully, obviously worn out. The young Ranger slept with a pistol in his hand and his dog, Tag, curled against his legs. For a moment, the older Ranger though about letting Holt get more rest and taking his watch as well, but knew his partner did not want to be coddled.

He also did not want to be shot waking a man with a gun in his hand.

"Hey, Tag, boy," he whispered lightly patting his thigh. The dog stirred and stood, then trotted eagerly to the tall Ranger. The movement awakened Holt, who sat up immediately alert.

"What is it, Tag?" he said in a low voice.

"It's just me peckerhead. It's Orion," he whispered in reply. "Your turn for watch. I let Tag do the waking, didn't want to get shot." He grinned. "Unless you wanna keep sleepin'."

"I'm okay," Holt replied softly. "Besides, you could use some beauty sleep."

Taking care to have laid down in a north and south direction, with his head to the north, Holt propped himself up on his good arm, trying to take advantage of moving before his body fully woke up. He had heard that it was healthier and luckier to position your head toward the north at night.

Sleeping fully clothed in case nighttime action was warranted, the young Ranger tried to faintly stamp some warmth and wakefulness into his feet. He arranged his shoulder rig and checked his Russian Smith & Wessons for dust and dryness before holstering them. The same followed with his Winchester.

"Good night, peckerhead," he whispered to Orion.

A near-asleep mumble was the reply.

Holt made his way to the horses by taking a wide, cautious loop around their camp. Arriving at the picket line, he checked the security of their lead ropes and observed their forage supply. There appeared to be plenty of grama grass, goosegrass, and arrowroot, even some amaranth. Enough to last the remainder of the night.

Tag returned from his morning rounds and relief.

"That's a good idea, boy. Keep your eyes open for me." Holt smiled, setting his Winchester against a nearby tree and stepping to a far enough away boulder to relieve himself. In this somewhat compromised position, he kept a sharp eye on Tag, knowing the dog would alert him to anything threatening or unwanted.

As Orion did, he took his watch station by the horses. A retrieved canteen and a few pieces of jerky provided a wakeup treat for both he and the dog.

Dawn finally came with everyone tired yet pleased to see the welcoming fingers of light that morning brought. The first chilly fingers of an early fall settled around them.

"Coffee sure would taste good wouldn't it?" Orion said, stretching his back. "We did good with a quiet night."

"Yeah, no need for smoke and smells," Holt agreed. "How's little buddy this morning?" He grinned at his nephew.

Benjamin looked as though he could stand a few more hours in his bedroll but was busy putting together their cold camp breakfast. "I'm all right, Uncle Holt," he yawned. "Didn't get cold till I got up."

Deed smiled. "A couple more weeks and we'd be greeted by frost."

"And in a couple hours, we'll be sweating through everything." Holt smirked. He was happy. Being on the trail like this made him feel alive, the aches and pains from his wounds less noticeable.

Holt, Deed, and Benjamin each gobbled a few biscuits, a piece of jerky and an apple as they readied the wagon and mounts. Orion contented himself with a raw potato. Tag did not care much for his piece of apple but relished another small chunk of jerky Benjamin tossed to him. The prospect of reaching Overfield by afternoon moved their preparations at a good pace.

At mid-morning, the day was growing hotter. They stopped to give the horses a breather and hatfuls from their water bags.

As they rested and chewed on corn dodgers, Orion observed, "I haven't seen any trail sign, but that ain't mornin' haze up ahead." He punctuated his statement by pointing at the trail in front of them and raising his naval spyglass for a closer look.

Holt examined the horizon, agreeing with Orion's assessment, "Dust. Far off. But we aren't close enough for that to be Overfield traffic though."

Deed looked at Benjamin and nodded once at the boy. "Ride ready, son. Keep your eyes open." Benjamin somberly nodded his head.

Deed and Orion took the position once again out on their flanks, only not as distanced from the wagon. Rifles were readied across their saddles. Benjamin held his Winchester while his uncle drove the wagon. Tag was on the seat with them. All four of their heads were on swivels, keeping keen eyes on what was around them. They checked their back trail often, not wanting to get caught in a crossfire trap.

They rode steadily forward. The dust ahead seemed to be settling with no more being raised. But the horses' growing tenseness told them there was something ahead.

Suddenly, a dark shape lurched into view from within an approaching ravine.

A horse!

The caravan came to a sudden stop and four rifles were swiftly raised.

Holt calmly and quietly told Benjamin, "Whatever happens, just keep steady, okay Benj? If it happens, you fight to win. You fight to live. You hear me?" His eyes sought the youngster's, wanting to prepare the lad but not frighten him. "The key is to just breathe. Steady and sure. Don't tense up. Use that front sight, squeeze the trigger. Don't think, just do it, okay? If things get real hot, you can lay in the back of the wagon and fire from there. All right, little buddy? I'm going to be right here with you."

Benjamin swallowed hard and nodded. His heart was racing, but his uncle's calm demeanor helped the boy compose himself as best as possible.

From their right, Orion cautiously approached the ravine and the lone animal. Deed advanced from the left. Both had rifles levered and ready. Holt kept the wagon reined in, centered between the flankers.

Orion raised his right arm and waved in big circles.

"In my old Reb unit, that meant 'rally.' To come here," Holt said to Benjamin. "Hope that's what it means in 'Yankee.' Keep your rifle ready though." Holt set his own rifle down and warily edged the wagon team forward. He brought the wagon close enough to view the horror laid out in front of them, but not so close they couldn't cut and run if need be. The wagon team did not like the ghastliness they smelled. Holt set the brake to keep them in check.

Deed was already off his horse, peering down into the ravine. Orion remained on his mount, examining the scene carefully.

"Ambush. Comanches. No one made it," Orion declared.

The stripped and scalped bodies of cavalry troopers were scattered around the small basin. Dead horses lay in dark lumps. Pony tracks, arrows, a broken lance, and strewn Army gear were an easy-to-read, mute story of the attack. Three vultures had found the horrific scene, already scavenging on lifeless bodies.

These were no doubt the troopers they encountered in Stebbins. Now, they lay dead, annihilated by the war party they bragged they would finish handily.

"No Indian bodies," Deed observed.

Holt surveyed the carnage. "If the troopers got any of them, their warriors would've carried them off."

"I didn't think these boys were ready. Ho-lee damn," Orion noted.

Benjamin abruptly retched and threw up over the side of the wagon, reacting involuntarily to the ghastly scene. Holt did not say anything, he just put a hand gently on his nephew's shoulder. The boy wiped his mouth and watched silently.

The horse they first observed, a cavalry mount, slowly approached and stood among them. A simple McClellan saddle hung loose under its belly. It appeared to be the only Army creature to survive the attack.

Deed reached over and undid the cinch, letting the saddle fall. The exhausted and lathered horse calmly stepped away from the burden and shook itself.

"Wonder why the Comanches didn't take him," Deed said.

"Had to catch him first," Orion stated. "He's been runnin' hard, prob'ly in circles. Bet they just gave up tryin'."

"Hope so," Holt added. "Or they're watching us gather him like a stray."

"Benjamin, walk this guy on an easy loop. Cool him down," Deed called out. "Check him for wounds or anything. Then see if he'll drink a little water from your hat."

"Tag, you stay right here," Holt said quietly, pulling a small piece of jerky from his coat to help keep the dog preoccupied.

Another horse just down the rise had a badly broken leg and was trying its frantic best to stand. Its whinnies and snorts were of a shocked animal, not comprehending what had happened to it. Deed walked up to the injured horse, talking softly. Mercifully, he helped it lay back on the ground. The shot that ended its suffering echoed around the ravine. Deed laid a hand on the animal's head and said a silent prayer. Holt touched his medicine pouch.

The shot triggered motion and a faint sound among the bodies. From under a lifeless horse, an arm feebly raised and fell. Muffled moans followed. Holt checked the brake on the wagon and eased himself to the ground. "Give me your mounts," he said to Deed and Orion. "Go see to him."

"Big brother, throw me the saddlebags from the wagon," Deed called to Holt. "There're bandages in them." He caught the loaded bags, touched the *Bushido* medallion at his neck and moved toward the injured man. Orion swung down, handed his reins to Holt, and followed Deed. Holt tied their horses to the wagon and picked up his Winchester, continuing to scan the area all around.

With great effort and much screaming from the wounded man, the two managed to pull him from under the dead animal. It was the scout, his fringed buckskin jacket covered in mud and blood.

"They hit us...outta nowhere..." the scout groaned, as Orion started looking him over. "They jus'...they jus'...came outta th' earth...I warned...th' lieutenant... sign was...everywhere...stupid bastard."

Shock had taken over the man. His wounds were many. He had been partially scalped, his head a gruesome mess. The top of his shoulder had been hacked by a tomahawk. A long knife wound sliced deep along the same arm. He had been shot twice by arrows, one in his already injured arm, the other was driven into his thigh. The shafts had broken off, the points remaining inside his body. It was not clear if the horse falling on him had caused any damage.

"Lotta doctorin' needed here," Orion said to Deed quietly. Their eyes locked, a silent acknowledgment that this man probably was not going to make it.

"Get something over his head to stop that bleeding. Those gashes on his shoulder and arm too," Deed said. "Let me look at these arrow wounds."

"If it's...still there...get th'...lieutenant's pouch," the man uttered. "Important messages...get it..." There was no strength left and he passed out.

While Orion was binding the deep cut on the scout's arm, Deed moved his attention to the arrow in the man's thigh. Fortunately, the arrow had not gone very deep. Deed drew his knife from behind his neck and cut the man's pant leg. A stub of embedded arrow shaft protruded from the thigh. Deed made four cuts around the arrow to hopefully allow for easy withdrawal.

The arrowhead came free, bringing fresh blood. He cleaned and bound the wound, then sought to remove the arrow from the scout's arm. The arrowhead had been driven through his arm. Deed cut off the point, removed the piece of shaft, and cleaned and dressed the gory puncture. He was thankful the man had passed out.

"That's about all we can do here," Deed said, wiping his hands. "See if we can find what's left of this lieutenant and his pouch."

"Doubt it's still here. Hangin' aroun' some warrior's neck now," Orion said, beginning to wander through the carnage.

"Hey! I think this is him," Deed called out, standing near a downed form. The bloodied and rent body still had most of a jacket on it. The sleeve and epaulet of an officer's jacket on one arm identified it as the lieutenant. "No pouch, but there's a stack of papers folded in a pocket."

"Bring it, we'll go through 'em later."

Just then, Holt appeared at the edge of the basin and hollered down. "We got the wagon ready for your patient. We need to get moving before they decide to come back!"

Using a torn blanket they found, Deed and Orion stretchered the injured scout up to the wagon. Holt had redistributed the supplies and gear, spreading a tarp over the bedrolls that had been laid out for him. The surviving horse was tied to the back of the wagon next to Holt's buckskin. Orion would continue ponying his dun.

"Let's get out of here," Deed said. "The sooner we get to Overfield, the better. Keep your eyes peeled!"

Holt snapped the wagon team into movement. At his side, holding both their rifles, Benjamin quietly asked, "Aren't we going to bury them?"

"No, we aren't, Benjamin," Holt said matter-of-factly. "There's no time. We don't know how many of those Comanches are still around or if they'll come back. Hell, they could be watching us right now."

Benjamin looked back at the scene solemnly.

"When we get to Overfield, we'll notify their post. Tell them where they are." Holt said, looking at his nephew. "Best we can do, little buddy. Sometimes it has to be that way."

The trail followed the slope of an uneven hillside. They dipped into a long, narrow draw which left them all on heightened alert not knowing who or what may be peering down at them. They crossed an erstwhile stream and headed across broken land mixed with rock, mesquite, prickly pear and a line of cottonwoods and willows.

The injured scout remained mostly unconscious, sporadically hollering out fevered jibberish. Tag was not comfortable with the noises and rode up on the seat. Benjamin reached back and laid a wet bandanna across the man's brow and occasionally dripped sips of water into his mouth with it.

"That's about all we can do for him, till we find a real doctor," Holt said to Benjamin, eyeing the scout.

Deed loped over to check on their patient. And Benjamin.

"That scout's pretty bad off," Holt offered in a soft voice. "He's got some blood on his lips. I think that horse falling on him did damage we can't see. If he makes it to Overfield, I don't think he'll last the night." He looked over at Benjamin, then back to his brother. "Benj is doing all right, keeping a good eye on him."

They rode on in silence. After a few more hours, the trail turned into a primitive road. It dipped into a shallow draw which they followed. They crossed a dried creek bed and stopped on the frown of a hillside.

The small settlement of Overfield lay in front of them.

The only street in the tiny village was not busy. Holt let Tag down to stretch his legs, cautioning him to stay close.

Upon reaching town, Orion affixed his Ranger badge to his coat and called out to a merchant on the boardwalk, "Y'all gotta doctor's office here?"

The man pointed to a storefront that advertised baths, shaves, dentistry, and drugs.

Reining up outside the shop, Orion jumped down. His heavy bootsteps on the walkway brought out a rumpled-looking man in a dirty shirt and unbuttoned vest.

"You the doc?" Orion said. "Texas Ranger Orion Higbee. We gotta cavalry scout, been set to by Comanches. He's bad off."

"Yes, yes, I'm the doctor," the man said, at first wide-eyed, then remembering his place. "By all means, bring him in."

Deed and Benjamin hoisted the man out of the wagon, using the tarp as a stretcher. The man moaned incoherently.

"I've got wires to send," Orion said to Holt. "To the Cap'n an' the fort."

"We'll get the horses squared away," Holt replied. "I'll take care of yours."

"Good deal. Meet you at the hotel."

Deed and Benjamin reappeared. "Well, that scout can get some better attention now," Deed remarked.

"Maybe *full-time* attention, I don't know about *better*," Holt responded. "Let's get the horses bunked. Orion's gone to the telegraph office. We'll meet him at the hotel."

The Corrigans led their mounts and the wagon to the livery. They were met by the operator, a bald man wearing a bandanna around his head like a pirate. He stood beaming in the wide open, sliding-door entry. He did a quick double-take, not sure if he could believe his eyes.

"Lawdamighty! *Holt Corrigan!*" he exclaimed. "I'd've knowd you anywhere. 'El Jaguar' hisself. It's 'n honor to meet ya. Mr. Corrigan. Folks call me Griff." The stringbean of a man took Holt's hand and shook it vigorously. "I fought wit' ya near th' end. In Tennessee. I knowd a few of th' boys ya rode with, ya know, a'fer th' war. Dixie's in yer debt. Forever."

"Well, Griff, it's good to see you," Holt said with a wry grin. He had not heard his old nickname in a long time. When he was riding the outlaw trail hoping to extend the war, a newspaperman had heard about the panther design on his gun grips and gave him the nickname, *el Jaguar*. "We all did what we thought was right," Holt said. "War's over now. Time to move on."

"Yes, indeed," Griff continued. "I think I heared ya was a Ranger now. I'll be danged."

Holt did not correct the man. "Been wearing a badge for a while now," he said. "You got room for seven horses and a wagon?"

Griff chuckled. "I gots a lot o' room."

Benjamin led in Orion's mounts and the surviving army horse.

"I don't recanize th' big bay an' that mean-lookin' dun, but that gray...the one all wore out...it belongs to one o' them troopers thet comes through here a lot." He stopped and spat. "Never pay their bills. 'Ceptin' for their scout. He's th' only one ta ev'r pay. Them no-good cal-vry bluebellies…"

"The scout's across the street at the doctor's," Holt interrupted. "I don't think he's going to make it."

Griff swallowed the rest of his words.

Deed added, "Comanches. Wiped out the whole patrol. Except for the scout."

"I'll be goddammed," Griff said quietly. "An' thet creepy scarecrow who rides wit' 'em?"

"No," answered Deed. "Just the troopers. Their post is being notified as we speak."

The men were silent as all of their animals got settled into stalls.

"Those four will be leaving at first light," Deed said, pointing to Holt's horses and his own wagon team. "I'll let Ranger Higbee tell you about the others."

Holt arranged for two rooms at the Overfield Hotel, one for Orion and a larger two-bed space for the Corrigans. He did not say anything about Tag staying with them and the clerk did not ask.

Everyone unloaded their gear, washed up and met downstairs for dinner. They were seated around a big table in a corner of the hotel's tavern.

"Benj, little buddy, you're about to experience the best thing about trail food," Holt grinned. The boy gave his uncle a quizzical look.

"Yessir, Mr. Benjamin," Orion said with a twinkle in his eye. "The best thing about eatin' on the trail, is not eatin' on the trail."

Chuckles surrounded the table. In addition to ordering their meals, Holt asked the waiter for a bowl of stew for the Ranger dog dining with them.

Soon, plates heaping with steaks, cornbread with

gravy, fried potatoes and onions, and baked beans were set in front of the hungry foursome. A bowl of steak scraps and gravy was brought for Tag. Lots of coffee and huge slices of pecan pie accompanied their feast.

"I got room for one glass of good Irish whiskey," Holt declared. Deed and Orion agreed. Benjamin thought he had room for another small slice of pie.

"I'm gonna stay here, prob'ly for another day," Orion announced. "See if that scout makes it an' can answer some questions. Telegrams from Cap'n McCoy an' Fort McKavett need to find me here too."

"Soon as I get healed up, I'll be tracking you down," Holt vowed. "Help with the Viklunds if you need it. But I'll be heading back to Stebbins for sure. I'm going to find the bastard who shot me."

"You hadn't mentioned that second shooter," Orion said. "I wondered if that part of the story sunk in."

"It did. I'll get him. Unlike Laudie Kate's, those bullets weren't an accident."

"An' headin' back has nothin' to do with lookin' in on her?" Orion winked at Deed who got a good laugh. Holt just shook his head.

They finished their whiskeys.

"You look wrung out, gen-rul," Orion said. "Mr. Benjamin, you need to get your uncle tucked into bed."

"I'm going, I'm going," Holt agreed. "It's been a long day. Time to pack it in."

———

First light was welcoming an overcast day. Before dawn, clouds had built and delivered a brief downpour. As fast as it had come, the rain decided to go elsewhere, leaving only a gray mist and equally gray day.

At the livery, Holt, Deed, and Benjamin were readying their horses. The steady jabbering of liveryman Griff provided a backdrop to their preparations.

"You sure you wanna take that dog with you?" Orion called out cheerfully as he approached the stable yard. "Y'all will be home tonight, won't you?"

"Should be there by suppertime." Holt smiled. "And yes, Tag is headed home too. He's got a buddy, Cooper, who's been wondering where he disappeared to." The two men stood over the gray and brown dog and took turns giving him pats on its head.

"It don't look good for that Army scout," Orion informed Holt. "He made it through the night, but the doc said he's real busted up inside. Like a gut shot you can't see."

"I wondered if that horse falling on him had done more damage than the Comanches," Holt said. "Dammit. I wish he could tell us about that patrol. And about that sheriff."

"Yeah, me too. I'm gonna go back, sit with him. Dyin' men sometimes like to talk," Orion added. "Maybe the folks at Fort McKavett can shed some light too. Especially why Sheriff Carmichael was ridin' with 'em. Gotta tread lightly 'round that subject, I expect."

Deed walked over. "We're all squared away. Benj is going to ride your buckskin to start." He turned to Orion. "I reckon our paths will cross again, Orion. Until then, thanks for looking out for my brother. Blue and I appreciate it very much."

Orion smiled and shook Deed's hand. "He'd have done the same," he said, nodding toward Holt. "So long, young man," the tall Ranger said, giving a friendly thump on Benjamin's shoulder. "Take care of these two."

It was Holt's turn. "I don't have the words. Thank you, my friend," he said to Orion. They shook hands. Holt briefly gripped his other hand on Orion's shoulder, then gave it a quick thump. "Ride careful, Orion Higbee."

"You too, partner. An' take care of my buddy, Tag."

CHAPTER TWENTY-ONE

The Corrigans were only a few miles into the last leg of their journey home when splatters of cold rain returned and began drumming against the land. The three stopped briefly to don their slickers.

Holt manned the wagon by himself with Tag huddled next to him. An oilskin tarp had been spread across the opening of the wagon in an attempt to keep their gear and food dry. The covering extended up onto the seat, which Holt arranged into a makeshift shelter for the dog to settle under. Benjamin was riding close to the wagon on his uncle's buckskin. Deed had been riding out on the flanks, keeping an eye on both sides. Coming across yesterday's Comanche attack weighed heavily on everyone's mind.

Nearly an hour into the heavier rain, Deed quickly trotted back to the wagon.

"Rain coming hard now," Holt noted with concern. "That's going to wash away any signs if that Comanche war party is on the move."

"Keep any dust down too," Deed added. "No sense in fanning out. I'll ride closer to the wagon."

Ominous clouds bubbled. Like the hungry stomach of huge sky being, thunder grumbled in the distance.

The weather was a gloomy companion to Holt's thoughts. The conditions exacerbated his aches and pains. He also was upset with himself, believing that he should have expressed his true feelings to Laudie Kate before he left. He also reckoned that he was departing Stebbins in defeat. He and Orion had arrived with orders to help break up the Viklund rustling ring. Not only was he now riding away with the Viklunds still in operation, but he also had been wounded in the process and was no longer a Ranger. Dejection rode squarely and heavily on his mind.

He had never been beaten like this before. Not personally anyway. The war was a completely different story, one that had taken him a long time to accept. He had lost fistfights growing up, but not many. If an older boy or group of boys had whipped him, he thought of nothing else until he could return the favor. He told himself, even then, that they were from a previous life and that he had been victorious over them in that earlier time.

As they moved further away from Stebbins, he also grinded on the fact that someone else besides Laudie Kate had shot him. Her action was a misunderstanding, basically self-defense. But someone in that room knew who he was, why he was there, and had tried to end him. That knowledge, plus his disappointing departure from Laudie Kate and leaving Stebbins in defeat, was draining. The rain only made his weariness eat at him further.

During a break for the horses, Benjamin rummaged

under the wagon tarp for a snack. Deed sensed his brother's mood and figured to break the glum silence. "Not the best circumstance, bringing his wounded uncle home, but I think this trip has been good for Benj," he offered quietly.

The words roused Holt from his doldrums, but he didn't quite hear what was said. "Wh-what?" he startled to attention. "Is little buddy all right?" He grasped the butt of one of his pistols, now fully alert.

"Easy, just making conversation." Deed half-chuckled. "I said, it's been good to get Benj out on the trail, start picking up on things like we did at his age."

"You thought about how to tell his mother about all the things he's 'picked up on'?" Holt full-chuckled a response.

Deed just looked at his brother.

"I'm sure it's been a helluva adventure for a twelve-year-old," Holt continued with a grin. "He shot guns, watched his new dad beat up some soldiers, and witnessed a Comanche massacre. You're gonna have to be mighty careful explaining that to Atlee."

"I don't know if I'd put it that way…wait, how'd you know about the guns…"

"He told me you let him get some practice shots on your way to Stebbins. Ah hell, I'm just poking you, little brother. Atlee will understand. Benjamin's a great kid. He's a lot like us, you know, losing his father and all." Holt paused before continuing. "You…me…Blue…we're his Silkas now."

Deed nodded. After a moment, he smiled and said, "Silka would say 'That is most good.'" He thumped his chest the way the barrel-chested Samurai often did.

"Aiee, it is so," Holt responded, echoing another

favorite Silka phrase. The memory brought a smile to his face, maybe the first time since his murder that recollections of their godfather brought him happy thoughts.

The heavy clouds began to lighten. It still left the sky overcast, which matched his thoughts, but Holt was encouraged to see them pushing on to relieve themselves on distant land.

The weather made his wounds ache and his mind drowsy. Holt sat on the wagon seat and forced himself to pay attention. This was not land to take for granted, lots of ravines and washes could easily hide trouble. But his attention gradually drifted to reflections of his mother and father, Blue and Bina, Deed and Atlee, even his good friend James Hannah and his wife Rebecca. The spirits had seen to it that each of those people found someone with which to make a life. Holt wondered when, or if, this good fortune would come to him.

Laudie Kate drew closer in his thoughts. Her smile, her smell, her presence. She would be someone worthy to have beside him on the trail of life. She would make all things good.

As they drew closer to Wilkon and home, the overcast was burning off. A timid sun was trying show who was boss.

Although thoughts of Laudie Kate had buoyed Holt's spirits, he was kept from falling into dreamy bliss by the fact that she had no idea how he truly felt. He broke the silence, calling out to Deed, "I want to ride to the ranch. Not on this. Nothing wrong with a wagon, but I need to ride."

"What did the doctor say about—" Deed answered.

"He isn't here and I'm not askin'," Holt interrupted.

"All right, big brother, but if you bust something

open and arrive bleeding, I'll hear about it from Blue, not to mention Atlee and Bina."

"I'll be okay. Blue will understand."

"I'm not worried about him."

At first, Benjamin reluctantly agreed to the switch, but the boy's disappointment changed when Deed told him that he could drive the wagon all by himself.

Holt was going to take careful precaution climbing aboard his bay. He found a small boulder to stand on to help reduce the distance from his wounded left leg to the stirrup. Bending the leg to get a foothold in the stirrup was a new adventure in pain. The hole where the doctor had dug out the bullet made its presence known with a sharp ache of agony. Holt held this position for only a moment, burying his face into the bay's shoulder so his brother would not see any grimacing. Then, concentrating all his effort to keep the pull and pressure on his wounds to minimum, he bounced hard with his right leg and swung it over the top of the saddle.

Seated squarely in the saddle, the effort had caused sweat to break out along his brow. He sat there, trying to hide his heavy breathing and took mental stock of the condition of each wound. The last thing he needed right now was to pop one of them open, triggering noticeable bleeding. He knew he absolutely could not afford to lose any more blood. More important to him at the moment, he wanted to avoid any potential scolding from Deed.

He had to smirk in spite of himself. Climbing onto a horse was normally second nature to him. Not today.

The gashes would be screaming painfully at him if any had broken open. He inhaled a big sigh of relief. He was in the saddle. So far, so good.

Tight, dormant muscles searched for familiarity and

found bolts of agony, branching across his body like lightning. A slight wooziness flitted through his head and went away. Holt's mind felt better even if his body did not. This might not be a good idea to most, but to him it was essential. He had to fight this, to get better.

From atop Holt's other horse, Deed watched his brother with careful eyes. People worried this man was at death's door—rightfully so—not all that many days ago.

Out of habit, Holt reached for his hat and the familiar good luck cardinal feather. His face wrinkled in frustration at the reminder his hat was somewhere back in Stebbins. He looked over and saw his brother watching him.

"What?" Holt tried to grin through his predicament. "Can't a guy miss his hat?"

"Don't you dare start bleeding," Deed admonished.

Holt smirked. "All holes still plugged." Deed just shook his head at his brother's weak joke.

Tag sensed the novelty of his master finally riding atop a horse and wanted to be up in the saddle with him. Holt coaxed the dog over to some boulders to his right. From there, he could easily step onto Holt's good leg and join him on the saddle where he had ridden many times before.

Holt found the bay's walking rhythm and before long most of his tight, unused muscles relaxed. The places where he had been shot still sent jolting reminders of pain, but Holt felt good about riding again. He placed a hand inside his shirt to grasp the medicine pouch and thanked the spirits for opportunity. Holt then leaned forward to give Tag a one-armed hug. This was good medicine too.

The ground around them became more familiar. They passed landmarks the brothers knew by heart.

"Let's take the old campfire trail," Holt said. "I'm not ready for town."

Deed smiled his agreement.

Benjamin followed Deed and Holt, steering the wagon past a line of cottonwoods and down a brush-guarded wash. Just before the creek played out, the small group eased out of the wash, across a long grassy draw and past an undercut bank. Safely above the bank, the hidden remains of an old campfire ring lay, like a shrine from yesteryear. The ring, encircled by weathered and blackened rocks, sat atop a solid bank that, depending on how much rain had come through, overlooked a creek, a roaring stream or a dry wadi. A legion of pecan, mesquite and ash trees stood sentinel, along with thick brush and scattered boulders.

This encampment was hallowed ground for the three Corrigan brothers. It was here in this protected, sacred place that they had used as a hiding spot, a fort, a castle stronghold, an army bivouac, and many other glorious realms their childhood imaginations had concocted.

A startled doe and its little one bounded away from the brush surrounding the ring, disappearing over the rolling hill. An owl glided overhead on a rare daylight hunt and hooted a loud welcome.

"Hello Mother," Holt said softly, looking up at the large bird. "You knew this was where we always disappeared to, didn't you?"

He reached into a pocket and pulled out his small bag of tobacco. The spirits were standing with him, the owl made him feel his mother's presence. He tossed some shreds in all four directions as tribute.

"What'd you say?" Deed asked, seeing his brother's

silent ceremony but not acknowledging it, letting it remain private.

"I said, the three of us need to bring the boys here before too long."

"I like that idea. When they're older, the girls can come along as well."

Benjamin did not really know what they were talking about, but he smiled because it sounded wonderful.

Turning sharply out of the draw, they picked up the trail that led in the direction of Wilkon and, after a half mile, turned to the right, across flat grasslands toward their Rafter C ranch. The sky was clear and shining bright.

"We turn the other way and can head straight to the stage station," Holt said. "Should we do that? I bet you can't wait to see Atlee."

"That's right, there's a pretty lady waiting for me," Deed acknowledged. "I have a feeling, though, everyone's together…waiting for you."

Holt smiled. The blue sky and the thought of coming home lifted his mood.

They passed a gentle slope that ended in a shelf of rock. The shelf reminded him of his first journey with Orion. The two were only a couple of days into joining forces to track The Angel. A shelf rock like this housed them during one of those early nights on the trail. Orion had given Holt a glimpse into his war background, his starting as a cavalryman, then turning into a naval officer and, finally, becoming a privateer. Holt had shared thoughts about his days riding the outlaw trail, refusing to believe the South had lost as well as the challenges he and his brothers had faced as youngsters. They had quickly formed a warrior bound that resulted in their successful hunting down of the evil killer and his wicked boss.

Upon seeing this ledge of rock, Holt knew the spirits were showing him that he would get the chance to finish the current business he and Orion started...to find the man who shot him and to bring down the Viklunds.

His thoughts returned to the trail. Craggy sandstone hills lay ahead and to their right, fronted by a lonely mesa. Holt guessed the caprock had marked this trail for centuries.

They eased their one-wagon caravan down a channel guarded on both sides by overgrown brush. Not far was a muddy stream lined with pecan, live oak and cottonwood trees. They stayed parallel near its banks on a faint, but sturdy trail. Before long, the muddy creek got deeper and ran smoother and cleaner.

"I know we're getting closer, but this is a good spot to give the horses a breather," Deed said. "I'm guessing you could use a break too, big brother."

"A good stretch would be welcome," Holt agreed.

He looked for an uneven patch of ground or rock that he could cozy his horse up against. By doing so, there would be not as much space before he touched the ground when he swung down from the saddle. Again, trying to keep the pull and pressure from his bandaged wounds was the goal. He found a perfect natural mounting block by situating the bay on a downhill position next to a rock outcropping. When the horse stood on this lower spot, the small ridge was almost the height of his stirrup. Swinging out of the saddle used to be almost as easy as getting out of a chair. Used to be. Pain seared with the movement. He sucked in a deep breath and took a mental inventory of his wounds. No leaks, at least none that would be noticeable. The soreness ebbed like the slow-moving creek.

Holt was light-headed but knew he was stronger than he felt. He walked around his horse, out of sight from his brother, using his good hand and arm to balance his movements until the wave of weakness passed. The bay did not mind, not knowing it was helping keep its rider upright.

Holt let the gentle breeze waft across the soggy bandage on his head. He hoped the dampness was from the earlier rain. If it was blood, he figured Deed would have seen it and raised hell.

They led the horses to the trickling water and let the animals nuzzle the creek's coolness. Like the clouds, Holt's light-headedness passed.

"Maybe you take the wagon the rest of the way in," Deed added. "Don't push things. That leg of yours has to be barking."

Holt smiled through the lingering pain and weariness. "I've got to push it. It's the only way to get better, to get past it. Didn't Silka teach us stuff like that?"

Deed's silence was not necessarily agreement, just an acknowledgment of his brother's stubbornness.

Benjamin tossed them all, including Tag, a piece of jerky. They took drinks from the stream as well, enjoying the refreshing coolness.

"Tag, you want to show us the rest of the way?" Holt said, scratching the dog's ears. "Let's ride." He led his bay back to the rock shelf he used to dismount and carefully swung onto the horse and slowly sank into the saddle. His thigh was painful and stiff, but Holt did not care. Riding a horse was a part of feeling at home too.

Tag was content to trot ahead of the group as advance scout.

Soon, they were into broken country that became rolling plains. Cattle country. This wasn't Rafter C land yet; it was pasture filed on by the Lazy S, owned by the Sanchezes who were neighbors and good friends of the Corrigans.

Finally, they curled off into a wide spoon of land that was the beginning of Rafter C pasture. Small clusters of grazing cattle were scattered before them. Tag woofed at their presence.

"It's okay, Tag," Holt called out. "They're home. So are you."

Before long, Holt, Deed, and Benjamin rode into the Rafter C ranch yard, happy and relieved. They passed familiar, sturdy buildings—a large barn which now held their best horses and four milk cows as well as serving as the storage area for feed. There used to be two barns. Meden Taliff's attack dog, Kane Barlow had set fire to their largest barn and ambushed Rafter C men rushing to fight the blaze. The skeleton framework of a new barn was just starting to take shape.

Outside the barn area stood an equipment hut. Up the hill from these outbuildings was a bunkhouse and a well that provided water year-round. The property surrounding the main house also featured two corrals, a foreman's cabin, and a small cooling shed for meat and butter.

The Rafter C homestead was a well-built two-floor structure with a big porch and second-story balcony. This main house had a separate wing built where Deed and Silka had once lived. Holt's bedroom had always been kept for him, waiting his return from the war. Deed now lived with his family on the Bar 3 spread, which sat adjoining the Rafter C and Lazy S.

As the small group rode in, Deed and Atlee's dog, Cooper, was the first to see their arrival and barked an alert. Tag returned the call and dashed to greet his buddy. The pair ran and jumped and woofed and chased each other around the yard, delighted to be reunited.

"Hello the house!" Deed called. Hurrying from somewhere inside, Blue's kids Matthew, Mary Jo, and Jeremy burst onto the porch, followed by Deed's stepdaughter, Elizabeth. They all were squealing peals of happiness and laughter, creating one solid hullabaloo of joy as they ran into the yard.

Atlee and Bina followed the children, standing on the porch with beaming grins.

Benjamin guided the wagon team into the front yard and set the brake. Deed swung down from his horse and moved to help his son secure the wagon team to the hitch rack. Holt reined in by the water trough and carefully used it to dismount.

Calls of "Uncle Holt!" and "Uncle Deed!" and "Daddy!" and "Benji!" bobbed up and down as the kids swirled around the returning heroes.

Holt smiled through a grimace as Matthew latched onto his wounded thigh in a welcome home hug.

"Careful kids!" Deed called out. "Be careful with Uncle Holt!"

"Yeah, be careful with Uncle Holt," a voice from behind the chaos hollered out. "The fool clearly forgot to duck."

Holt turned and saw the smiling face of his brother Blue. Alongside Blue was the Rafter C's foreman, Harmon Payne.

Blue swung from his horse and hurried to his brother. They hugged and thumped each other on the back. Wisps of trail dust escaped from their coats.

"Oh...I should watch that," Blue caught himself. "You're wounded, bandaged everywhere."

"It's all right, big brother," Holt smiled. "It hurts, but it feels better to be home."

Relieved he had not caused any damage to his younger brother, Blue shook his head, "Damn it, Holt, you had me worried." The rare curse escaping from Blue's lips betrayed his anxious relief that his brother was finally home. "I'm mighty glad to see you. The Lord was watching out for you."

"It's good to see you too, Blue," Holt smiled. "I know the spirits were watching over me." He gestured at the activity swirling around him. "This is quite the welcoming committee."

"The kids have been wound up for two days wondering when you all would be home." Blue laughed.

"Hey, let me in on some of that!" Deed called out. He wrapped his two brothers up in a large bear hug and the three of them laughed.

Harmon walked over and spoke up. "It's good to have you home, Holt. You all go on in, I'll see to the horses."

"Let me help you, Harmon," Holt said.

"You need to get inside so everyone can start taking care of you." Deed laughed as he headed to the house.

"I think you got a couple more hugs coming too," Blue added, motioning his head toward Bina and Atlee.

Deed arrived at the porch first. He said a quick hello to Bina, then scooped Atlee up in big hug. "I told you we'd be right home." He smiled.

She hugged him back, then took his face into both her hands, smothering him in kisses. "I missed you."

The bootsteps behind them were Holt's.

Bina was beaming and held out her arms. "I am glad your journey brought you back," she said knowingly, gathering him into an embrace. "The spirits listened to your heart, did they not?"

"Yes, Bina, they did. In a way, I figured you would know this. Someday, we must talk, I learned so much, but understood very little."

"We shall, but care must be taken. Speaking directly of such things is not wise."

"One journey like that is enough," Holt smiled. "I'm glad to be back."

Atlee was next. "It's so good to see you, Holt. You had us all very worried," she said, giving him a welcome home hug as well.

"I've had a lot a people looking after me," Holt said with a big grin. "I'm a lucky man." He cocked his head slightly, his voice turning softer, "I hope you're okay too." Atlee had been badly wounded in an attack on her relay station during Kane Barlow's violent rampage ordered by Meden Taliff. This last-ditch message of diabolical retribution by the disgraced attorney was directed at the Corrigans and their friends, an attempt to cast them all asunder for easy pickings. The fiendish plan had not worked, the Corrigans and their allies were all stronger, even when apart.

"Everything's healing, no more bandages." She nodded.

"Not all wounds can be seen," he said, concern in his eyes. "Are you sleeping okay?"

She smiled back at Holt and spread her arms to

gesture around her. "Having everyone here, together, is the best medicine."

"I've noticed that too." He grinned.

As everyone poured into the house, including Tag and Cooper, Holt held back, standing out on the porch. He once again pulled the small sack of tobacco from his coat pocket. Taking a handful of shreds, he scattered them in the four directions. Holding his medicine pouch over his heart, he thanked the Creator and the spirits for bringing him all the way back.

Home.

Eventually, everyone settled down around the kitchen table. Harmon joined in as well, at the brothers' insistence. Bina and Atlee served a supper of thick beef sandwiches, bowls of pickles, baked beans and scalloped corn. Atlee made sure to declare that the official welcome home feast would actually be tomorrow morning with a breakfast pancake party, hosted by Elizabeth, Deed and Atlee's young daughter.

"Cooper's helping too!" Elizabeth added.

As the meal finished, table talk continued all around. Holt excused himself quietly, "I'm going to go square my gear."

Blue followed him to his room and handed him an envelope. "Harmon got this in town earlier today." A telegram was enclosed:

HOLT CORRIGAN:

    HOPE THE RETURN HOME WAS SMOOTH.

    P. HEAD YOU FORGOT TO LEAVE LIEUT'S PAPERS.

    READ & REPORT WHAT THEY SAY.

    SCOUT SAID THE PATROL WAS ASSIGNED

    TO GUARD SHERIFF & MONEY HE CARRIED.

HE DIDN'T MAKE IT.

GAVE THE CAVALRY HORSE TO YOUR LIVERY PAL,
GRIFF.

HIGBEE

"Ah hell, we forgot to give him those damn papers,"
Holt said. "Deed has 'em."

"I'll tell Deed and come back for you when the
cobbler's ready," Blue said.

Thirty minutes later, Blue and Deed returned to
Holt's room to gather him for dessert. Deed had the pack
of papers from the dead lieutenant as well. They eased
into the room. Holt was fast asleep, having gotten only
his boots and spurs off. Tag lay curled tight against his
master.

"Let him sleep," Deed whispered. "He won't admit it,
but he's nowhere near back to being Holt yet."

Blue nodded. "I'm just glad he's home. We'll bring
the rest of him back."

CHAPTER TWENTY-TWO

The same day Holt, Deed, and Benjamin arrived home in Wilkon, back in Stebbins the town was abuzz with news of the considerable amount of rustling that had occurred at the W Bar L ranch.

The day had started with the widow Lillian Whitman and her foreman paying a visit to the jail to report the loss of about three hundred head of cattle. They went to the jail because Sheriff Carmichael was not in his office and nowhere to be found. They brought with them a torn sombrero one of their W Bar L riders had found when making the discovery. Their gloomy news was spread across town as they made other stops at the general store and bank.

Just before lunch, the Viklunds had breezed into town and called on the same spots visited by Lillian Whitman, loudly reminding people that Windmill V riders had brought in the bodies of three Mexican men to town earlier this year. Viklund claimed then and now that they were rustlers shot on his property.

"They had at least a hundred head of our beef

rounded up before we caught 'em. You remember, right?" Baldur recounted for those outside the bank who would listen—and there were many. "Caught 'em red-handed. Brought their bodies here to the sheriff's office."

"Certain it is Mexican bandits made off with W Bar L beef," Lars said in front of more than one group of town folk. "Of that there can be no doubt. A torn sombrero from the bandits they brought to the marshal."

Coming from the Viklunds, most figured, the tale had to be true.

Christer Viklund had stopped at the jail to give the rustling report to the marshal and an interested prisoner, Casper Longley.

"Those Mex bastards are at it again," Christer informed both men. "They need to be hunted down."

Taking the cue, Longley grumbled, "Goddam, did we get hit again?"

"Are ya positive yer missin' beef?" the marshal asked. "Yer shure they di'nt jus' wander off? Cattle like ta do that, ya know."

Before Christer could answer, Sheriff Carmichael had strutted into the jail. "Marshal, there is no evidence these out-of-jurisdiction warrants for Casper Longley are valid," he announced icily. "The Rangers were sloppy. This prisoner is to be released immediately." Carmichael handed an official-looking document to the marshal and left as abruptly as he had arrived.

"I wondered when this was a-comin'," Marshal Hollings said, reading the paper and shaking his head resignedly. "I guess Lars be needin' ya back at th' ranch." He stood and slowly made his way to the cell where Longley was held.

The door groaned as it opened and the marshal let the

scruffy-looking man step out. The gunman's dirty trousers and faded work shirt hadn't gotten any cleaner. Longley adjusted his eyepatch and beat-up brown sack coat. His one good eye glared at the marshal. "Where're my guns, Hollings?" he demanded.

"Jus' hold yer horses, Longley," the marshal said with exasperation. Handing over the outlaw's gun belt, he turned and spoke to the youngest Viklund son. "Y'all ain't bin hit this time. Are ya gonna be helpin' th' W Bar L riders?"

"Huh?" Christer blurted, caught off-guard.

"Seein's how Missuz Whitman an' th' W Bar L lost a sizable number uv beeves, an' y'all dun fought them Mex bandits b'fore, I jus' figgered ya'd want ta help out," the marshal continued.

"Uh...uh...I-I d-don't know about that," Christer stammered. "Th-That'll be my father's or brother's decis—"

"Does Lars think it's the same cross-the-border outfit as before?" Longley interrupted calmly, as he strapped on the guns around his waist. It helped change the line of questioning.

"Looks that way. Heard that the widow's foreman said the tracks appeared to be heading toward the border," Christer replied, relieved to share different, rehearsed details.

"That'd make for some happy hunting," Longley said with a wolfish grin.

In front of the general store, Lars and Baldur held court by their wagon filled with ranch supplies. They had two mounts ready for Christer and Longley. Tucked safely inside Baldur's coat pocket was fresh, crisp paperwork picked up from Sheriff Carmichael's office—a filing document verifying two hundred head of Double-Diamond Heart cattle and a new brand registration.

Christer reported what Marshal Hollings had asked, about the Windmill V helping the W Bar L go after the Mexican rustlers.

"Perhaps such an offer should be made," Baldur mused.

"Tell people we did, but our help the widow didn't want," Lars responded.

"Most of these coffee boilers won't care after today." Longley chuckled to his boss. "I didn't thank the sheriff, Lars. He disappeared before I got the chance. So I'll thank you."

"Not to worry," Lars assured his foreman. "Done well was his job today. A great deal of work is ahead of us now."

———

It wasn't so much the cattle and their value that Lars Viklund was after. He didn't need it. His own herd was several thousand head.

The stolen herds were taken to create financial strain on the small victim ranches. A brutal attempt to force them out. Viklund did not give a second thought to the hardship he caused these ranch owners. He believed it was the price they must pay for their crimes against his family.

Two ranchers in particular—the owners of the Half Moon 6 and River D—complained that rustlers had stripped their spreads beyond the ability to operate. Very

few people in town paid much attention to their griev-
ances. If their trouble ever was discussed, the problems
were chalked up to rustlers from across the border or just
poor ranching.

Most importantly for Viklund, hardly anyone noticed
the owners' absence. They each had sold out and left in
the past eight months.

The sales of the Half Moon 6 and River D ranches
had been accelerated by encouragement that no one knew
about. After his men decimated their herds, Lars Viklund
unleashed Casper Longley and his gang. Longley made it
clear in no uncertain terms that he and his men would
eliminate the ranchers' families if they didn't sell.

After selling, the owners of the Half Moon 6—the
Mason family—were ambushed on their way to Califor-
nia. That attack got Lars his money back from his
purchase of the ranch. Riders from the Viklund Windmill
V had waited to pounce until the Masons reached the
New Mexico Territory so that news of their deaths would
never make it back to Stebbins. All information identi-
fying the family was destroyed as well.

A few months later, rustlers struck Micah Dailey of
the River D ranch. He had resorted to hiring a so-called
gunman to help protect his ranch crew and modest-sized
cattle herd. Dailey had been checking on his small herd
after dark when Baldur and Windmill V riders, dressed as
Mexican bandits, attacked the River D, and ran off most
of the herd. In the chaos, the hired gunman was killed.
Somehow, Micah Dailey escaped the wrath of Baldur and
the disguised Windmill V riders, but he had heard them
curse at him Spanish. He then told everyone who would
listen that it was Mexicans who stole his beef. His plight

was duly noted around town, but not acted upon. He sold out soon after.

Dailey and his wife were on their trek back to Missouri when they were hit by Viklund riders. As soon as they crossed from Texas into Arkansas, a fate similar to the Masons befell them. No one finding the gruesome scene could tell who these unfortunate settlers were or where they were headed. The money they were carrying from the sale of the River D was returned to Lars.

No one in town except County Sheriff Linus Carmichael and Bank President Ames Wooster was yet aware that the Half Moon 6 and River D properties were now secretly deeded over to the Väderkvarn Cattle Company. "Väderkvarn" was the Swedish translation for "Windmill." The company was owned by Lars Viklund.

Like a simple chore list, Viklund was methodically making his way through the roll of ranches within the county, prioritizing action against them by purported weakness. With the two smallest ranches now his, the next move was to go after the widow who owned the W Bar L. The money generated from the sale of beef stolen from her would be a nice addition to Lars's bank account, but the real benefit of this latest effort was the effect the loss of cattle would have on Lillian Whitman and her ranch. By his calculations, she would be barely able to hold out much longer. The thought of her financial struggle and the inherent anxiety it brought satisfaction to the big Swede.

The next largest spreads in St. Clair County, the Triple S and Flying G, had yet to be targeted by Viklund's rustling and scare tactics. They would offer greater, but not insurmountable, obstacles. The biggest target—and the largest prize—on the list, the huge 5 Star ranch, would present an entirely different challenge for Lars. But, no matter the size, these larger operations would be dealt with in time. Getting his hands on them was the only way Viklund could accumulate the entirety of the county land along with all its accompanying resources as well as his ultimate goal—power.

————

The fact that the Windmill V had not officially reported any loss due to cattle theft did not raise any suspicion: To a casual observer, the number of riders Viklund had hired to protect his land was thought to be deterrent enough for the Mexican rustlers to leave them alone, preferring the easier pickings of the small ranches. Also deflecting attention was the memory from earlier this year when Lars and his son, Christer, brought three bodies of Mexican men into town, claiming they were rustlers shot on Viklund property. Even Sheriff Carmichael did not know that they were just three itinerant Mexican workers who had been murdered by Windmill V riders.

Most of the rustled stock Viklund acquired was not assimilated into the main Windmill V herd. The majority of the stolen beef was quickly moved out of the region. However, driving these smaller stolen herds to the border was too obvious, and it was much too far to take such a small herd to meet up with the railroad in Kansas. Instead, with the assistance of Sheriff Carmichael, Lars had found an ambitious and unscrupulous broker down south in New Braunfels who would buy all of the live-stock the Viklunds could provide.

Using these tactics, Lars Viklund was in his element:

another step in his plan, another move in the game. Before long, not only would thousands of acres of good cattle land and a massive herd of cattle be his, but also the people who butchered his family would have finally paid their massive debt.

CHAPTER TWENTY-THREE

T he days turned into weeks and summer began to give way to fall. Outside Wilkon, at the Corrigan Rafter C ranch, time passed easily, but Holt was growing restless. He felt his recovery was not moving quickly enough. Every day he sought ways to challenge and push himself to get stronger. Cold, blustery days made him feel even more like he was caged, a wild animal penned against his will.

He no longer wore any of the bandages. Those had been cast aside weeks ago. The wounds weren't in danger of opening up any more and had stayed free of infection. It was Blue's wife Bina who, right away, had suggested removing the dressing from around his head and cutting his hair short to help the heavy laceration on his scalp mend. She even offered to do the barbering. Holt was concerned when she chopped off more than he thought necessary, but did not complain. In fact, as long as he was home at the Rafter C, he thought the short hair suited his sojourn and had Bina cut it regularly.

He also had not shaved since he and Orion had

started their journey to Stebbins. At first, he avoided picking up a razor because he did not want to see himself in a mirror, all beat up. But then it became a chore he figured he could do without. Time that could be spent getting healthy again.

Bina had also given him a jar filled with healing salve for his wounds. He tried coaxing the recipe from her but could not get her to reveal the ointment's ingredients.

"My father was a healer, what you might call a holy man," she related to Holt. "I do not use his name any more. I only speak of him now to help you understand. He is *yah-ik-tee*." She gathered herself momentarily. "He is not *present*. And to repeat the healing words he gave me is a memory I must not relive."

Holt realized at once that Bina's father must have passed away and that he also could never fully grasp her Apache way of believing. He was not one of them. But he understood enough to respect her reluctance to talk about her family.

As he rubbed the salve onto his wounds, his nose helped him guess there was tulle pollen, arnica, and piñon in it, and likely some crushed mescal leaves. There was no doubt the concoction worked and it sure smelled better than the tin of Navajo medicine rub he carried in his saddlebags.

She was even less obliging when Holt tried to question her about the spirits he encountered along his otherworldly journey. He wondered how they worked and why they had chosen him.

Her reaction was guarded, almost fearful. "It is best not to ask and risk offending powers such as these," she cautioned. "They are not *present*, they have gone on. If they speak, you should listen wisely to their counsel lest you insult them. Respect they must be given." As she spoke, Bina was looking directly at the area under Holt's shirt where his medicine pouch lay. Like Four Shields, she seemed to know exactly what was there.

He started to tell her about the eerie holy man who had come out of nowhere and given it to him. She refused to let the words come out of his mouth. "Whether he selected you or you found him, just be grateful. As long as he walks along with you, choose your trail wisely. Guard well this honor." With that, she would speak no more of Holt's journey. He realized he could not broach this subject any further.

In his daily routines, Holt took every opportunity to work the soreness and stiffness from his wounds. Although the bullet had not lodged in his shoulder, it had gashed a deep furrow across the muscled part of his upper right arm. From his godfather Silka's teachings, he prided himself in being able to fight and shoot skillfully with either hand, but his right one was more dominant. Holt needed that arm to bounce back, fully and quickly.

It was his stamina that had been the slowest to return. When he was shot, he had not stayed conscious to be aware of it, but he had been told by everyone from Orion to the doctor to Laudie Kate, that he had lost a lot of blood. That, more than the bullet wounds themselves, was what nearly took his life and was the toughest part of his recovery. When he first came home, he often found himself needing to sit or even lay down. Even though Tag approved of taking lots of naps with his master, Holt grew impatient.

His exercise had steadily grown from short walks to the barn and back, to more strenuous tasks like helping the ranch foreman Harmon and the Rafter C riders with the mucking of stalls, loading hay, and helping build the new barn as well as adding to the rock barriers and fences around the property. The work exhausted him at first, but he understood its value. He tried to do something more, something harder each day.

Soon, helping curry and brush their horses turned into throwing saddles on them himself and taking forays across the huge Rafter C yard. Eventually, he was taking longer treks, first with Blue and then alone, across the entire ranch property. He also ventured over to the Bar 3 and helped his brother Deed with winter chores there.

So they would not be alarmed at the sounds, he told Blue and Harmon that he would be using these Rafter C outings to get reacquainted with firing his guns.

In a far corner of the property, three large vegetable cans were filled with holes from his pistols. The quickness he had on the draw had not yet returned to his liking and there were a few too many misses for his satisfaction, but he could tell his hand coordination and aim were slowly coming back.

His eye with a rifle was returning more quickly. A couple of those trips resulted in his shooting a deer and an antelope for the cooling house. They could use the food, but Holt was gratified that he had bagged the two animals with one rifle shot apiece. He also was able to field dress and maneuver the carcasses by himself. He was most pleased that all those activities hadn't completely exhausted him either.

Two things were never far from Holt's mind: the question of who else had wanted him dead, and Laudie Kate. He could not stop thinking about her, especially her eyes. They were so beautiful, so confident, like a bold blue sky stretching on to forever. Silka had often told the brothers to not believe what a woman with fancied-up eyes had to say. "If she not want you to see her real eyes, she not be telling truth either."

Holt smiled at the thought of Laudie Kate's natural beauty. Gazing into her eyes was something he felt he would never grow tired of doing. He had to return to see them again.

Wondering who shot him was decidedly less pleasant. He searched his memories for this faceless gunman. Was the shooter connected to Longley? The Viklunds? Did that peculiar sheriff fit into any of this?

Holt had looked through the dead lieutenant's papers. It was a wad of twelve, mostly blank, pages. Only one had anything on it—brief hand-written directions and crude map of a trail from Fort McKavett to a cattle corral operation in New Braunfels. No other explanation. No other meaning. He had telegraphed Orion with the information but hung on to the papers. He would give them to his partner when he saw him again.

CHAPTER TWENTY-FOUR

Summer was losing its steam. Fall was in its early whispers, pecking at the sizzling grasp the season had on the land. Holt felt he had been cooped up long enough and decided he needed to venture into town. He knew he was not quite at full strength, but felt the trip would be a gauge to just how far along he had progressed. He had not visited there nor seen his friend James Hannah since his return. In the aftermath of bringing down Meden Taliff and Taliff's kidnapping of Hannah's wife, James had turned in his resignation as county sheriff.

Besides, Holt needed to find a hat. The old woolen Kerry cap that had been his father's was fine to borrow as he healed. But now that he was spending more and more time outdoors—where he belonged—it was time to buy a hat that matched or was similar to the one he left behind in Stebbins.

After the usual early ranch breakfast, he helped with morning chores at the barns, then saddled his bay. He left

Tag behind to play with Blue's kids and set off for his day trip.

As he reached the outskirts of Wilkon, sights and sounds of the day greeted him. He noticed a handful of new storefronts and buildings had sprung up or were being built. The water well was now completed. Its new pump creaked and groaned before releasing its liquid. The fire station that disgraced Justice of the Peace Meden Taliff had promised was under construction right next to the well. Funds from the evil attorney's account had been adjudicated to pay for the completion of this and other Taliff-begun projects.

Taliff's grand-looking new saloon was awaiting finishing touches. With the help of Mayor Cooke and his lumberyard as well as the Wilkon bank, James Hannah had come forward to take over construction and ownership of the large tavern. The election for Hannah's replacement as county sheriff was mere weeks away. Holt's friend was looking forward to the transition from wearing a badge to being a businessman.

As Holt entered town, he observed that wooden skeletons of four bungalows and three large, shop-sized structures had sprouted. Holt guessed it was Mayor Cooke's lumberyard employees crawling all over the new buildings, making a racket with their sawing and hammering. Somewhere, someone playing a tinny piano was trying hard to brighten the morning.

The town itself seemed busier too, with lots of horse and wagon traffic on the main street as well as folks scurrying back and forth in between.

Holt was hoping he could go about his visit unrecognized. He caught a glimpse of himself in a store window as he rode by. Another barbering from Bina had left his hair even shorter than his brother Blue's, and months of no shaving resulted in a full bushy beard to go with his mustache. Holt deemed the reflected image he saw in a store window looked pretty much like the same old Holt Corrigan. So much for blending in, he thought.

Suddenly, three shots from a cantina across the street from him blistered into the thoroughfare, one shattering the store window he had been watching. Instinctively, he jumped down from his horse, drawing one of his Smith & Wesson revolvers in the movement. Using his bay as moving cover, he hustled to a support beam holding up the store's overhang. In between more firing from the cantina, he hurried to the relative safety around the corner of the building and tied his horse there.

Pausing, safe from the line of fire, dizziness from all the sudden, unanticipated movement tried to grab Holt, but he shook his head. Not now.

Without thinking, he reached up to touch the cardinal feather in his hatband—an action he had done hundreds, if not thousands, of times—for luck. His bare head was an instant reminder that his hat lay somewhere in Stebbins. He then touched the medicine pouch that lay hidden under his shirt. Clutching the sacred bag against his chest, he asked for strength and guidance.

Two men, in a heated argument, spilled onto the street. They struggled and tugged at each other as they rolled in the dust, hollering insults, their pistols still drawn. They separated, one hiding in back of the front water trough, the other holing up behind a stack of pallets standing next to the tavern. The two continued to take sporadic, inaccurate potshots at each other.

Marshal Logan Wheeler and Deputy Bradley Cooke came running from the jail. Marshal Wheeler, a tall man with a pointed nose and firm chin, and Deputy Cooke, a young man barely twenty-two years old with long blonde hair and lightning-quick with a gun, were seasoned professionals at their jobs. They both were sworn in when Holt became a Texas Ranger and James Hannah was elevated to county sheriff. Both played key roles in bringing down Meden Taliff and his attack dog, Kane Barlow. A second deputy, Lear Freeburg, was off duty, spending a day with his family.

The two lawmen quickly assessed this situation and fanned out, trying their best to advance yet not be targets.

"Stop th' crap an' drop yer weapons!" Marshal Wheeler hollered from behind a freight wagon, his Winchester levered for business. Deputy Cooke continued moving in a crouch down the street and took cover behind a trough directly across from the cantina, not far from Holt's hiding place.

As Holt watched all of this unfold, the thought occurred to him that the two yahoos from the bar were not really mad at each other. The "combatants" were even allowing themselves time to reload.

A voice behind Holt came low, but firm. "Are you a part of this or did you just want a better look?"

Holt turned his head and looked into the smiling face of his friend, acting Sheriff James Hannah.

"I came to buy a hat." Holt grinned in return. "But it seems law and order in this town has disappeared in my absence."

"Damn, it's good to see you, Holt."

"You too, my friend."

"What do you think?" Hannah motioned with a flick of his head. "These two fools can't be blowing off steam."

"No. A Ranger friend of mine would declare, 'There's shenanigans afoot.'"

"The bank's two doors down. I think that's where the real action is. Let's take the alley."

"Right behind you," Holt said.

Hannah got Deputy Cooke's attention and motioned that he would be taking station next to the bank. The deputy nodded, slowly catching on to what might be happening here.

Just then, a bedraggled teller stumbled onto the boardwalk from inside the bank. His coat and shirt were ripped and his hands were tied. "They're robbing the bank! They're robbing the bank!" he screamed. A shot from within tore across the man's leg, knocking him down. His falling caused another shot to miss him entirely. He lay motionless for a few moments before staggering to his feet and limping awkwardly to the safety of the hotel next door.

With the appearance of the teller, the arguing men from the bar suddenly wheeled and began firing at the marshal and deputy. A third outlaw appeared from the cantina's alleyway and joined in the barrage.

Four shots spit at Marshal Wheeler as he crouched behind the wagon; one creased across his lower left leg, dropping him to a knee. From behind a wagon wheel, Wheeler shoved aside the pain and aimed his rifle at boots visible behind the water trough. He squeezed the trigger. The outlaw screamed and rolled sideways, grabbing for his wounded leg. Wheeler's second and third shots hurled the outlaw backward like a door slamming.

At that moment, two masked bandits made a break from the bank, bundles of stolen loot in their hands. From their hidden positions, Hannah's double-barreled shotgun exploded and Holt's handgun fired six times almost simultaneously. Both thieves were cut down before even clearing the boardwalk.

From their vantage point in the alleyway, the two outlaws still standing near the saloon watched the destruction of their plan. Five horses were tied up behind them, the animals now frantic to get away from the chaos. One gunman fired covering shots, while the other scampered to get their mounts. Deputy Cooke left his cover to stand and fire his Navy Colt at the first bandit. His first two shots hit the man belly-high, his third left a large hole in the crook's cheek. The remaining outlaw came charging out into the street aboard a horse, pistols blazing in his hands. The deputy unloaded his Colt at the same time Hannah's shotgun detonated and Holt's pistol blasted. The bandit and his horse dropped immediately into an unmoving heap.

The three Wilkon lawmen and Holt slowly and carefully emerged, eyes scanning everywhere for possible hidden assailants.

From the hotel on the other side of the bank, a thin-faced man with sad-dog eyes behind wire-framed spectacles emerged out onto the street.

Acrid gun smoke still wafted around. Holt quickly shoved cartridges into his empty guns. "What a waste of a good horse," he grumbled looking down at the unmoving animal.

"Thanks for your help, Ranger Corrigan." Hannah grinned.

"Not a Ranger at the moment," Holt acknowledged. "The state of Texas thinks bullet wounds and badges don't mix."

"Holt? Holt Corrigan?" the thin-faced man chirped.

"Is that…my god, it is! I didn't recognize you!" Leroy Gillespie, the owner, editor, and chief reporter for the *Wilkon Epitaph* newspaper adjusted his eyeglasses, not sure of what he was seeing. The thin man bounced out onto the street, notepad at the ready. He poised himself beside Holt, unleashing a torrent of questions. "We heard you were shot. Is that true? What happened? Are you okay? Did you get the shooter who did it? Oh my heavens…What ab—"

An irritated Sheriff Hannah shook his head and yelled, "Gillespie, you gotta be kidding me! Can't you see what's going on? Gawdalmighty!"

Holt growled at the little reporter without looking at him. "If I were you, I'd get back inside. This ain't over, and bullets don't care what they hit."

Gillespie stopped and glanced around, pursing his lips. He had only recently recovered from his own wounding at the hands of Taliff and Barlow. He readjusted his glasses, thought better of his decision to wander into this mess, then walked hurriedly back inside the hotel.

Hannah walked over to Holt, breaking open the shotgun to replace the loads. "Actually, I think it is over," he said quietly, chuckling.

"I know, I just can't stand that little gnat. I was sorry he got hurt in that Barlow rampage, but, damn, he can be a real busybody."

Deputy Cooke reloaded his pistol and checked on Marshal Wheeler. "I'm all right, Bradley," the marshal said. "Justa nasty scratch. Can ya get th' undertaker out here? We got trash that needs cleanin' up. An' someone needs ta get that poor hoss moved."

"Will do, Logan, and I'll fetch the doc for you." The young deputy hurried away.

"Check on that bank teller too," Holt called out. "He's in the hotel."

Hannah finished the reloading of his gun. He studied and assessed the scene.

Holt untied his horse and approached the marshal. "You sure you're okay, Logan?" he said with an easy smile.

"Hannah always said bein' aroun' Holt Corrigan was no picnic," Wheeler answered, getting used to walking with the burning crease along his lower leg. "Still, it's good ta see ya, Holt."

"You too, Logan." Holt smiled.

"C'mon, I'll buy you both a cup of coffee," Hannah said, joining them. "Or something stronger."

"A banner day in Wilkon," Holt grinned. "James Hannah is buying."

"Buying hell," Hannah snorted, "We're headed to the jail. We'll drink whatever's there."

Even Marshal Wheeler laughed through his discomfort.

The three reached the jail. Holt looked around inside. The outer office had a sparse, yet familiar and comfortable feel to it. He had spent a considerable amount of time in here. Decorating one wall was a framed photo of Sam Houston. Judge Oscar Pence's robe hung ceremoniously on another. Holt sat next to the desk, his own healing leg propped on a stool. Marshal Wheeler shuffled back to the empty cells and plopped down on one of the bunks and started taking off the boot on his injured leg. Hannah coaxed the fire in the stove, where a half pot of coffee was still warm on top.

"Coffee, Holt? Logan?"

"If that's all you got," Holt said.

"Whiskey's in th' bottom drawer," Logan answered. "No coffee fer me, justa shot o' that."

The gunplay had been over for about twenty minutes, but sitting there, Holt realized that his heart was still racing. He wiped beads of sweat from his brow. He knew he would be feeling the jump from his horse later on. All that exerted stress was more than he had faced since charging through the doors of the Blue Sky Inn. It was good to feel like that again though. Combat always made him feel that way. Alive.

As Holt unwound, the mere thought of that day in Stebbins flooded his mind with vivid, detailed images. In the rush brought on by today's skirmish rush, Holt suddenly envisioned clear pictures of those moments before he was shot...the table in the Blue Sky...locking his eyes onto Casper Longley...then...

Gunfire.

In the split-second before his leg was hit and he went down, Holt now recalled seeing Longley glance over at a man standing at the end of the bar with a gun. In this vision, Holt's eyes could follow Longley's movement. Like clouds parting, the face of the man who shot him came into view.

Hannah broke Holt's contemplation, handing him a mug of hot coffee laced with whiskey. "So, when did you turn into a Yankee general?"

Holt took the mug, still in the fog of his vision, concentrating on memorizing the face that just flashed through his mind.

"The West Point hair...and this..." Hannah continued, making a comical circling gesture around his own face. "Is this beard a Ranger thing or did all those bullets make you forget how to shave?"

Holt's attention returned to the jail and his friend. He rubbed at his bushy face and chuckled. "Been too busy healing."

"Not a bad look," Hannah continued. "I'd recognize you anywhere, but I imagine most wouldn't."

"Something to be said about time saved not scraping your face with a sharp blade." Holt smiled.

"So, are you all right now?" Hannah turned serious. "I got that first telegram from Stebbins. The Stebbins marshal said you were shot. Your brothers put on a good face, but they were scared to death. Rebecca and I were too."

"It happened quickly. I wasn't aware of much, afterward. I guess it was touch and go. A good doctor and the spirits decided I should stick around."

"I thought you were looking into a rustling operation, in St. Clair County."

"Captain McCoy's orders were help break up a rustling operation. But, going in, we didn't know much about the setup," Holt sipped at the coffee and whiskey, savoring the flavor. "You ever heard of Casper Longley? Orion and I dropped into a hotel saloon there to arrest him. Four bullets caught me out of nowhere."

"Longley? Yeah, heard of him. Crazy as a cut snake. One of those Rebs who didn't really fight the war. A bushwhacker. Just liked killing." Hannah paused. "Sorry. You know what I mean."

Holt shook off the comment. "Never heard of him until we got there. Turns out, he's the foreman for the ringleader. Our very first move was going to be to arrest him. As Orion says, 'Things went sideways.'"

"What are you going to do now? You're not a Ranger at the moment, are you? They're known for leaving a man when he can't…"

"I heal up. That's what. Then I'll get my badge back and go finish what I set out to do."

"Just like that, eh?" Hannah questioned.

"Well…" Holt hesitated and started to blush. "There's some other unfinished business in Stebbins—"

"You met a girl," Hannah interrupted, a wide smile on his face. "Look at you getting all red-faced. I know you. You met a girl."

Holt grinned and took a sip from his mug.

"Does she know, this girl, that you've set your cap to her?" Hannah smirked. "You're not exactly mellifluous around women."

"She's the one who shot me."

At those words, Hannah slapped his thigh and broke instantly into hard, deep laughter. Logan, listening from the bunk, joined in the mirth with his own cackles. Hannah carried on until he realized Holt was not joking. "Oh…wait…hoooo boy," he stopped, took off his eyeglasses and wiped wetness from his eyes, still giggling. "Seriously? You fell for…a woman who shot you?"

"Well, she was one of the shooters. The one we know about. It was a misunderstanding."

"A misunderstanding? I'd say so. Damn."

"Laudie Kate works at the hotel. She thought I was busting in to rob the place. She didn't hear the 'Hands up, I'm a Ranger' part."

Hannah nodded. "So she pulled a gun and drilled you."

"Twice."

Hannah stifled more laughter that wanted to bust out.

Holt continued. "Yep, just as calm as can be. Two of the shots were hers. Someone else fired twice, trying to kill me. I don't know who or why yet, but I've got his face."

"So you're going to go back and find this bastard…"

"After I pick up my Ranger orders…and…tell Laudie Kate how I feel. *Mellifluously*."

"Laudie Kate, is it?" Hannah said. "I hope she's good enough for my good friend."

"It's me who needs to be good enough."

"I hope she sees that. No man will have better than a woman who stands beside him."

"How is Rebecca?" Holt asked. "Is she okay, after… the…" He left the remainder unsaid. She had been kidnapped by Taliff as he tried to run away. Although she was returned unharmed, the trauma if it all had shaken Hannah to his core, leading to his resignation. "When I left, you had resigned as sheriff and were talking about whether to build a house and start a family."

"You probably saw our bungalow on your ride in. Mayor Cooke's crew is putting it up for us. We're working on the other part." Hannah smiled.

"Work? Maybe you're doing it wrong," Holt teased.

"Hey, that's my wife we're talking about."

They snickered easily. "My brother Blue would say 'All in God's time.'" Holt smiled.

They finished their mugs of coffee and whiskey in comfortable silence.

"All right," Holt said, carefully standing, testing the stiffness that was starting to tighten the muscles throughout his body. "Enough adventure for one day. I need to find a hat before heading home."

"You weren't kidding about the hat thing." Hannah chortled.

Holt just shrugged and pointed at his bare head.

At that moment, Deputy Bradley Cooke breezed through the door after fetching the undertaker and doctor. "Holt!" the young man called out.

"Hey Bradley, good to see you." They shook hands. The young man had shown his mettle and played a key role in finishing off the man who had been behind the horrible Angel murders. Holt smiled and gave Bradley a thump on his shoulder. "You handled yourself well out there. You're good at this badge-wearing business."

"It seems to fit."

Holt greeted Dr. Sandor as well. "He's back there, Doc," he said, motioning to the cell where Logan sat.

"So, it's true," Bradley continued. "Holt Corrigan *is* back."

"It must've been Gillespie spilling the beans about your visit to town, Holt," Hannah chimed in. "No one else would recognize your General Grant getup." He paused. "You'll have to excuse Mr. Ranger, Bradley, he's on his way to buy a hat."

"What a day. Bank robbery. Yankee insults. Logan getting winged again. Let's do this again soon." Holt laughed sarcastically. "Bye James. My best to Rebecca."

"Dinner and stories soon, my friend," Hannah answered.

CHAPTER TWENTY-FIVE

H olt rode home knowing weariness was soaking into his body. He refused to acknowledge any aches from the old wounds that tried to prod their way into his awareness. All he concentrated on was the face of the man who shot him—the image abruptly coming to him in the jail. Holt had thanked the spirits for the waking dream they sent him, offering a tobacco tribute before he rode out of town.

The vision of seeing the shooter was a revelation. He would never forget that sneering expression as the man pulled his trigger. That bastard would pay.

He was also encouraged by the way he handled the shootout in Wilkon. He was not one to look for trouble and never relished having to take someone's life, but he and his friends had been given no choice. They all, at one time, had each sworn to uphold the law. He, instead, was focused on how sharp his reactions had been. Jumping from the horse had been done without thinking, just instinct. And handling his gun…Target practice was one thing, throwing lead at someone who was aiming to kill you was another. He was feeling the aftermath, though, and rubbed at the soreness in his thigh. "The one time I wished you weren't so damned long-legged." He smiled, patting his horse's neck. All in all, he was satisfied. His body reacted better than he expected. Pretty much like before he was shot.

The new hat felt funny on Holt's head. The longer he wore it, the more the hat just did not feel the way it should. The fedora looked fairly similar, narrow-brimmed the way he liked, but it just was not the same as his old one. He rearranged the hat to sit differently. Still no. The weight was off. It wasn't loose, it wasn't tight. It just wasn't right. He wasn't sure about the hatband either. Would it hold a cardinal feather?

Suddenly, thoughts freight-trained through Holt. Cardinal feather…hat…left behind…Stebbins…the man who shot him…

Go get him.

Go get Laudie Kate.

Now.

It wasn't the hat that was bothersome. It was him. His spirit was restless. He knew without a doubt it was time. Time to return to the Rangers. Time to return to Stebbins. Time to return to the Blue Sky.

He kicked the bay into an easy lope, eager to get back to the Rafter C.

After dinner, Holt stood on the porch with Blue. Breath smoke circled them in dusk as the waning summer day surrendered to a robust fall night.

His older brother was initially concerned when he heard Holt give his account of the day's events. But he saw the spark in his brother's eyes, a determination in his attitude and knew the worry was misplaced.

"Blue, it's time. I'm going back to Stebbins."

"I wondered what was up with you. You've been like a caged panther."

"I've got to go back, to finish what I started."

"I've been around you all your life. I know I can't stop you once you set your mind."

"You've stopped me before."

"That was when we were young and I'd slug you. It always meant you'd slug me back. I'm not doing that anymore," Blue laughed.

"I'm not talking about that. You stopped me from fighting a used-up war. Remember El Paso? Your words brought me home, Blue. I'll be forever grateful."

Blue stared at his brother and nodded.

"You know my spirit demands that I fight," Holt said. "That's what I am, what I've always been."

"I know. Bina noticed an urgency about you when you got home today. She's always believed spirits were strong with you. She said that they were all around you tonight. She thought they were preparing you for your next journey."

"Thank you, Blue." He paused. "I'm not leaving just yet. I've got some telegrams to send. A little matter of getting reinstated and finding out where Orion is now. I'll need to code those messages a little bit, keep 'em from prying eyes, you know. Wish I had more to tell them about those empty lieutenant papers too—"

"Code 'em..." Blue interrupted, something Holt said caught his attention.

"Huh? Yeah, you know, code words..."

"Blank paper..." Blue continued, gathering an idea.

"I need to keep things secret..."

"Wait!" Blue held up his forefinger, like their father used to when they were boys and he wanted quiet.

"So bad guys don't—"

"I know that, *Holton*, just hobble your lip a moment!"

Holt laughed at his brother's use of his actual name, but realized he was serious.

"Pretty much all of those papers from the dead lieutenant were blank, right?"

Holt nodded. "Yeah, one sheet had a scribbly map for a trail from Fort McKavett to New Braunfels. The rest were all blank. Odd."

"Remember when General Lee ordered our officers to avoid sending telegrams?"

"Yeah, direct dispatches. Cost us time and men."

"Some of those messages back then were invisible, Holt."

Holt watched his brother in silence.

"Did any of those papers smell?" Blue asked. "Like lemon? Or onion?"

They both immediately hurried inside to Holt's room. From one of his saddlebags, Holt pulled out a thin, plain parfleche. He carefully opened the pouch.

"It's vellum paper," Blue said, peering at the contents. "That's the kind you need."

Holt spread out the pack of papers on the dresser top.

"You write with a toothpick or quill dipped in lemon juice or onion juice. Do those papers smell?"

Holt sniffed at the stack of blank sheets. "Smells like leather and tobacco, maybe the back end of something."

"Light that candle," Blue instructed. "The heat from the flame will reveal anything written."

Holt positioned the first sheet near the flame and squinted at the paper.

"Careful you don't burn it," Blue said, looking over his brother's shoulder.

"Remember when you said something about me slugging you?"

Blue chuckled.

The first few pages were still blank over the candlelight. A sheet near the middle of the stack slowly revealed smudgy brown words.

Holt read the message written there and muttered, "I'll be damned."

CHAPTER TWENTY-SIX

Two days later, Holt walked out of the Howard's Real Estate, Insurance, & Telegraph Office in Wilkon. He was so engrossed in reading the note in his hand that he did not pay much attention to the two riders who reined up in front of him.

"So, it's true," one rider said.

"Yep, looks like they'll consider letting just about anybody be a Ranger these days," the other joined in.

Holt looked up. "Hey! It's my two favorite brothers!" he exclaimed, a huge grin on his face.

Blue and Deed swung down from their horses to join their brother.

"Well, what's it say?" Blue asked, gesturing at the message. "It's from your captain, isn't it?"

"Wait a minute, let me read it again," Holt said. "This time though, I'll put my badge on." He fished the shiny circled star out of his vest pocket. "Now, it's not just a note from Captain McCoy. It's orders." He beamed, then paused as the meaning sunk in. "I'm sorry, Blue...

Deed...I hate leaving you in the lurch like this. With a little luck I can be back, maybe not for roundup, but to help—"

"It's all right, little brother. I know you want to finish the job." Blue smiled.

"The Sanchezes have a contact over in New Mexico," Deed said. "We might throw in with them. Take a small herd from our two spreads. It's not as far as Kansas, but the money should be right."

"I heard that Oliver Loving died on a drive into New Mexico not long ago. Attacked by Indians. Look into that before you decide."

"We will, Holt. Nothing's been determined."

Deed pointed at Holt's badge good-naturedly. "That jewelry looks good on you." He grinned. "You go find the bastard who shot you. Take down those rustlers. Then bring Laudie Kate home so we can tell her the truth about you."

They all smirked knowing Deed wasn't kidding.

"So, now what?" Blue asked.

"Well, I've got to go to the Jorgensens' store...pick up some ammo and supplies for the trail...maybe a couple bolts of fabric. Tag and I will head out in the morning. The captain says to meet up with Orion back in Stebbins as soon as I can get there."

"Don't forget dinner tonight on your list. Everyone'll want to say goodbye," Blue added. "Maybe Bina will give you another haircut before you go."

"Wait...fabric?" Deed winked.

"Yeah, for Laudie Kate and Evie. I think I ruined their dresses when they helped the doc...when I...you know."

"Don't let Atlee or Bina hear that," Deed continued, laughing. "If it means new dresses, they might decide to shoot you too."

Holt joined in the laughter.

CHAPTER TWENTY-SEVEN

Autumn was on the doorstep of the town of Stebbins. Soon, ranches all over cattle country would be conducting their fall roundups.

Roundups often brought neighboring ranches together to pool their riders and resources. Fear and mistrust among the Stebbins-area ranches had made this an unworkable venture. The only thing most Stebbins residents now agreed upon was that the rustling activity was the product of Mexican outlaws.

Little more than a month ago, Lars Viklund had stormed into town, angrily reporting that rustlers had hit his Windmill V ranch.

"Two hundred head of beef they took, those Mexicans did," he roared in front of the general store at a gathered crowd. "Get away with it, they will not."

About two weeks later, Windmill V riders led by Christer Viklund and Casper Longley appeared on the outskirts of Stebbins with nearly two hundred head of cattle. As the herd made its way back to the Windmill V ranch, Christer had orders to make a big show of this movement of beef. He and the rest of the riders made sure the herd was driven slowly, within sight of town.

One of the riders on this drive was Texas Ranger Moose Elkins, still posing as a Viklund cowhand.

Lars Viklund just happened to be visiting the bank, general store and the Blue Sky Inn that same afternoon. As the dust settled from the passing herd, he told anyone and everyone that his riders had tracked down the stolen beef across the border.

"Stole our own beeves back, we did," Lars had claimed loudly to eager audiences. "From thieving Mexican bandits across the border."

Satisfied that the seeds of misinformation had been planted, Lars retreated back to the Windmill V to put his next moves into motion.

Behind him, disgruntlement and blame spread easily. Marshal Baxter Hollings was the only visible lawman in Stebbins and he heard—or at least felt—the brunt of the finger-pointing. His daily rounds became more uncomfortable as whispers of his failings grew in number and voice. It did not matter that rustling and ranch affairs was county business and therefore under Sheriff Carmichael's jurisdiction, Hollings became the unjustified scapegoat.

Not too long after Viklund's big show, Marshal Hollings visited the Blue Sky Inn. As he was leaving the hotel owner's office, the marshal ambled through the saloon.

He walked by a group of drovers drinking around a table. Three of them rode for the large 5 Star spread. The fourth cowboy, a huge man, rode for Viklund's Windmill V.

One of the 5 Star riders, not knowing the marshal was walking by, said in a loud voice over the saloon noise,

"Whattaya make of all of this stolen cattle across the valley? Don't it make ya wonder how good the law is around here?"

Another 5 Star rider chimed in, "Yeah, we haven't been hit that I know of, but it shore does seem the law ain't doin' much for those who have. I hear some of them small ranches're gettin' hit hard by these Mexes."

The large Windmill V rider said, "Don't go tellin' my boss, but things ain't always what they appear. It's real easy ta point fingers. Somethin' else is goin' on. Mark it."

The first rider reacted with derision. "Maybe so, but you'd think the law around here would do *something* about it."

Marshal Hollings heard this and could not help responding. He stopped and addressed the men around the table, "Gentlemen, I'm Baxter Hollings. *Marshal* Baxter Hollings. Lemme tell ya, th' rustlin' problems ain't mine ta fix. If ya *really* are concerned, git th' sheriff y'all elected involved. Rustlin' trubble at th' ranches is a county problem. That's Sheriff Carmichael's bailiwick. Y'all oughta be talkin' ta im." He eyed each man carefully before striding out onto the street.

The drovers sat in brief silence. The large Viklund rider finished his whiskey. "Y'all ride careful, now. I gots ta get back b'fore they miss me," Moose Elkins said as he set down his glass and stood. He knew exactly what was going on out at the Windmill V. He needed to make a report to his fellow Rangers, but his buddy Orion Higbee was nowhere to be found.

CHAPTER TWENTY-EIGHT

Two days after leaving Wilkon, Holt Corrigan and his dog Tag Along arrived in Stebbins. Holt was pleased to have made good time. His strength and energy held up too. Here, he would be the only one who knew he might not be all the way back to his intimidating self.

The end of day traffic on the main street was busy enough that people would not take notice of a trail-worn rider with a plain-looking, big-eared dog. For some reason, a feeling he had, Holt had decided not to affix his badge to his coat when reaching the outskirts of town.

He reined up in front of the Blue Sky Inn, taking care to not to hitch his horses in the same spot where he had tied up...*before*. That would invite bad luck. He even switched the order in which his mounts stood at the hitching post.

When Holt first became a Ranger, he had a lot of territory to cross and had to be able to move without delay. Alternating between horses helped him keep both mounts healthy and fresh enough to cover ground in time he did not have. Speed and distance were not an issue on this ride, but he had grown to appreciate the idea of having a back-up mount. For his return to Stebbins, he had ridden his big bay and ponied the buckskin just as he had done previously. It helped that neither horse minded when Holt would place Tag on its back.

Through the Blue Sky's open doorway he could hear a piano player performing a satisfactory version of "La Paloma," followed by, "Beautiful Dreamer." Holt chortled to himself that those sweet-sounding tunes were an interesting accompaniment to the hubbub of drinking and gambling going on inside.

A shout of betting achievement perked up the ears of Tag and the horses tied up along the hitching post. An inebriated townsman dressed in a wrinkled frock coat stood just outside the entrance and watched Holt tend to his horses with boozy fascination. Holt felt the man's eyes on him and looked up. The man raised his glass of beer in tribute, belched loudly, then lurched and sat down hard on the planked sidewalk. He looked around to see who or what yanked him. Seeing no one, he took a big guzzle of his mug from his new sitting position.

Holt tossed a piece of jerky to Tag and quietly told the dog to stay put on the boardwalk. He passed the seated townsman and said, "Evening, friend."

The drunk reached up to tip a hat that was no longer there. He went through with the gesture anyway and called out to Holt, "Elop!"

Holt snorted a brief laugh, figuring the nonsensical word meant something to the man. He nodded and continued on into the saloon. It took a moment for his eyes to adjust to the duskiness of the large room. Daylight waned, no longer pouring through the front windows. Its reach did not extend very far inside. Wall-mounted oil lamps struggled mightily to illuminate the shadowy, smoky space.

He took a position just inside the door at the end of the bar. The hard-working bartender looked at Holt and raised his eyebrows in a silent "What'll you have?" expression.

Holt smiled and said, "Irish," and laid a coin on the countertop. His eyes searched the room looking for Laudie Kate. Loud guffaws from a table of merchants in the center of the room caught his attention. Evie O'Neill stood there with an empty tray, good-naturedly, but firmly admonishing the men to keep their hands to themselves. Although several females worked there as waitresses, like Evie, they were not "sporting" women. Miguel Navarro, the owner, would not allow the practice. The Blue Sky had a reputation as a respectable establishment, doing plenty of business in alcohol, food, and games of chance without such carnal dealings.

Holt spotted Laudie Kate in the back of the saloon—right where Casper Longley was sitting the day Holt was shot. She stood watching a table that had a serious card game in progress. She wore a white Louisa blouse with billowy sleeves and a tan skirt that flared wide at her knees. It was hard not to notice her proud figure. She was every inch a woman.

For Holt, she became the only person in the room, an irresistible force.

The wall lamps along the back highlighted her high cheekbones and facial scar. Her face glowed with a hard work freshness. Holt thought her smile was the most wonderful thing he had ever seen. Her blue eyes sparkled happily like a forever blue sky.

She wove her way through the crowd, heading back to the bar. She joined Evie there, both of them preoccupied with pouring drinks. The two laughed and chatted with each other as they were loading trays with tumblers and mugs filled with whiskey and beer.

Suddenly, two men erupted into a heated brawl at the billiards table. No one knew exactly what touched off the animosity between the pair. They had spent most of the game trading angry remarks, the tension rising. The two propelled themselves at each other like enraged billy goats, thrashing and wrestling furiously. They only separated when they crashed into a table and knocked over chairs.

An instinctual wariness, like a panther ready to pounce, tingled through Holt's body as he watched the fight unfold.

One of the combatants, a tall clerk wearing suspenders, picked up a cue stick and swung it, breaking it over the back of the other fighter, a burly drover with a handlebar mustache. The drover, unfazed, reacted by throwing a billiard ball. The tall man ducked and the ball flew across the room, crashing into a shelf of bottles behind the bar just to the right of the two women. Evie screamed in reaction.

When the glass exploded, Holt moved swiftly from his vantage point and sprinted behind the bar toward Laudie Kate as the fighters abruptly squared off. They each went for their guns and the sudden sound of gunfire shattered the early evening calm.

Holt wrapped Laudie Kate in bear hug and brought her to the floor with him, holding her tightly. From the safety of the floor, he reached up and yanked Evie down next to them as stray bullets peppered the area where the women had just been standing.

A haze of smoke blanketed the saloon. From behind the bar they could hear, but not see, the unfolding chaos. Sounds of someone praying mixed with a few frightened gasps rushed to fill the void of sound between shots.

In the melee, the tall clerk tried to hide behind the pool table, with the burly drover diving to safety behind some chairs. From the floor, the drover shot through the opening under the table and hit the tall man twice in the stomach. The clerk fell forward, his face slamming against the floor planks like a dull axe. A friend of the fallen man took up his cause and began firing at the combatant who was still on the floor hiding behind some chairs. Both fired at each other, wildly, not hitting their targets, but causing damage to walls and lamps. Two bystanders were hit by errant rounds.

Even with the bedlam ensuing on the other side of the bar, it was difficult for Holt to concentrate. Holding Laudie Kate in a protective hug, the scent of her surrounded him. He was in intoxicating heaven and wished he had cleaned off some of his own trail dust.

Boom!

Abruptly, the roar of a shotgun detonated from the front of the saloon.

"Drop them guns!" came a shout from the doorway. "Drop 'em, I say, or I'll kill ya all dead," Marshal Baxter Hollings yelled. "Ya hear me? Drop 'em now, gotdammit!" He quickly ejected two spent shells and replaced them smoothly with new loads.

The silence in the room indicated that everyone understood the law had arrived and that the fireworks were over.

"You can let go of me anytime now, mister," Laudie Kate said, squirming in Holt's protective embrace.

"Wait…" he cautioned.

Laudie Kate was a strong woman. "I said, *let go*…" she sternly admonished and turned forcefully, breaking out of the hold she had been in. Grim-faced, she faced the man who had pulled her from the line of fire. "Thank you for pulling me to safety, but you just can't…" Her bold blue eyes went from stormy and wild to sunny and warm. Her face softened as this stranger became a familiar face.

"Wait…Holt?" she said, incredulously. "Holt Corrigan, is that you?"

He gave her an adoring smile. "Hi Laudie Kate. It's me."

Their eyes met and danced briefly.

Evie, on the floor next to them, broke their intimacy, exclaiming, "Holt Corrigan! I swear, lookit that beard… you cut yer hair…I almost di'nt recognize you!"

Laudie Kate was still absorbing the sudden appearance of the Ranger she had helped nurse back to life, who now was in front of her, very much alive…*and close*. "Hello, Holt," was all she could manage. Her hand reflexively went to adjust her hair. Their eyes had settled on each other, and they weren't looking away.

"Th' men…th' guns…ya saved us, Holt," Evie spluttered.

Laudie Kate's sparkling gaze was thanks enough for Holt. His fleeting closeness with her, thrown together by danger, was over with the fight's end.

That the two women didn't immediately recognize him caught Holt's attention. Inspiration flashed through his brain.

Like the first bubble in a kettle of water just beginning to boil, an idea began to surface in his mind. Another bubble followed, a bigger one this time, and then another. The details of a plan roiled within him.

"Laudie Kate, is the sheriff in town?" he asked.

"He's gone," Evie spoke up. "My beau, Moose, was here yesterday an' said he watched 'im ride outta town a few days ago."

"Yeah, just Marshal Hollings, as usual," Laudie Kate added, gesturing toward the saloon where the marshal was sorting through the aftermath.

"Any of the Viklunds around?"

"Not that I'm aware of," she said. "They usually stop in here. They haven't been around, well, I guess since the sheriff left."

"Okay. Good," Holt said, gathering his thoughts.

The women tried to stand and get back to work. Holt gently, but firmly, took hold of their arms and kept them down with him.

"Look, I'm back...with the Rangers," Holt began. "Arresting Longley was only the beginning of our assignment. I'm healed up now and need to finish the mission I came here for." He paused a moment. "You two saw me the most...*back then*, yet you didn't recognize me right away just now."

Laudie Kate and Evie eyed each other, not sure what was coming next.

"I can use that to an advantage," he explained. "First of all, don't tell *anyone* I'm back or that you've even seen me. Okay?"

They agreed.

"Do either of you know where I might stay for a day or two and not be seen much...or at all?" His awkwardness talking to women was forgotten. He was operating in combat mode now, and they were his co-conspirators.

"Th' bungalow where I'm livin'," Evie chimed in. "I'm th' only one rentin' a room in there right now. Th' other girl left town."

"It's on the opposite end of town from the jail," Laudie Kate added.

"Do you think…do you mind…if Tag and I holed up in there?" He looked at both women for approval. "Orion will be here in a day or so and we'll move on with our mission."

Laudie Kate just shrugged and nodded consent. Evie confirmed her support as well.

"I know you have to get back to work," he continued. "Is there somewhere I can go, *now*, out of sight, until Evie can show me this bungalow?"

Laudie Kate pointed to the end of the bar where Holt had been sitting. "Right there, in the corner," she said. "See that door? It opens to a storeroom behind the bar. No one'll see you in there. At the other end of the store-room is another door that opens into the private back hallway. That corridor is where Señor Navarro's office is." She took Holt's hand. "Here's the key to the office. Wait there." She knew Navarro might really frown at this, but she was caught up in the moment. Besides, if you can't trust a Ranger—especially this one—who can you trust?

At first, Holt was focused on how soft her hand felt, but he quickly realized what she had done and focused on the key. "Thank you, ladies," Holt said as Evie was already standing up. "It's good to see you, Laudie Kate." He grinned.

She threw him a quick smile in return.

The fight and its aftermath were still occupying the attention of everyone in the bar. Holt used the commotion to slip unseen into the pantry. He easily found his way to the office from there. He knocked on the door. No answer. He held his breath and quickly unlocked the door, glancing inside. To his relief, no one was there. This would work, for now.

He suddenly remembered...Tag! "Ah hell, he's still out there," he murmured to himself. "I hope."

It was dusk, almost dark, so he decided it would be okay to chance retrieving his dog and horses. He snuck through the private hallway to the back door. Once outside, he peeked around the corner of the alleyway toward the street. As he reached the front of the inn, he saw his dog taking a nap on the boardwalk next to the drunk townsman from earlier.

"Tag, pssst, let's go, boy," Holt whispered as he untied his bay and buckskin. The dog awakened, eagerly wagging his tail. "I'm sorry to leave you out here, buddy. Plans changed." Holt looked in all directions, convinced his presence was sufficiently covered by the growing darkness. He took great care to lead his horses back to the alleyway, with him walking between them, shielded from view.

He returned to the shadows in the rear of the hotel. He tied up the horses in the alley and retreated inside, accompanied by Tag. Under his arms were two packages from his saddlebags.

CHAPTER TWENTY-NINE

T he rest of the night passed slowly. Although Holt did not want to admit it, the travel to Stebbins and the anxiety of the barfight were catching up to him. With only a small lamp providing a shadowy glow, the dim office and its relative quiet tempted him into drowsiness. He sat in an overstuffed chair and began to doze.

The door opened with a rush of light. Holt startled awake, ready to apologize to Señor Navarro.

The light from the hallway silhouetted the shape of Laudie Kate. Holt would recognize that figure anywhere.

"Holt?"

He stood in the muted light, almost losing his balance. "Y-Yeah...right...right here, Laudie Kate." Being alone with her, his awkwardness had returned. Dammit!

She crossed into the office and struck a match. The soft flame from a large table lamp illuminated the room. She had placed a small tray and bowl on the desk.

"As I recall, you and Orion loved our stew. I brought

you some." She smiled, but then noticed Tag wagging his tail in greeting. "I forgot your assistant there. I'll get him some too."

"Th-Thank you, Laudie Kate. That's…uh…v-very nice. Thanks."

She turned and left. He rolled his eyes at his clumsiness. Thank god James Hannah isn't here, he thought. He'd never let me forget.

Laudie Kate returned in a matter of minutes. "There you go, Mr. Tag Along," she said, setting down a bowl and talking to the floppy-eared dog. "It looks like you took good care of your master."

"I -I didn't have…there wasn't…much choice." Holt tried to chuckle. "Blue and Deed…their wives were pretty…insistent that I give myself time to heal."

"Rough duty having pretty women take care of you," she teased. "Maybe someday you could have one of your very own."

Her eyes and grin kidded him. His wry smile and lifted brow indicated this would be a wish come true. He caught himself and thought out loud, "Ah, what was I saying?"

She laughed at the handsome man so surprisingly shy.

"Oh…right…" he recalled. He turned around and reached down for a package wrapped in plain paper and twine. She watched him, fascinated, not sure what was going on. He stood back up and bashfully held it out for her. "This is…for you."

Laudie Kate stood next to him and took the package. She untied the string carefully. Opening the paper revealed a bolt of calico inside, sky blue. She looked at the fabric, then at Holt, in delight.

"I hoped it would match your eyes," he blurted, surprising himself.

"This is wonderful, Holt. You didn't…"

"I bled all over the nice dress you were wearing…that day. I want you to have a new one."

She ran her hand over the soft cotton.

"There's one here…for Evie…green," he stammered.

"Oh, Holt, you shouldn't have!" She leaned over on tiptoes and gave him a quick peck on the cheek.

Without realizing, he reached up and held his hand to the spot she kissed. "I also want to…apologize…for leaving without saying thank you or goodbye," he said, finding his nerve.

"But you did…say thank you and goodbye."

"Not the way I wanted to."

She smiled and the dimples on her cheeks appeared even deeper than the last time he saw her. Even the cheek decorated with a scar. The usual tight bun of her brown hair was end-of-the-night undone, strands of it embracing her shoulders. Her simple blouse and plain skirt could just have easily been a sparkling gown.

"Why, Holt Corrigan, whatever do you mean?"

"Oh, no, I didn't…I just…well, I would really… but…" He stopped and laughed at himself. "Ah hell, you make a guy have trouble with his tongue."

She giggled and touched his arm. "I'm sorry, did I…"

"Oh no…Laudie Kate…you're…just…real fine." He felt a redness dawning from his shirt collar.

He wanted to say, "I'm trying to say you're beautiful. You make me feel good just to look at you. You're all I can think about. And I have completely, hopelessly, allowed myself to fall in love with you."

But he didn't.

Just then, Evie breezed in with a tray of coffee and whiskey. "I figgered you might be thirsty, so I brought some of both," she declared.

Their moment broken, Holt and Laudie Kate looked at each other shyly and moved slightly apart, toward Evie.

"I remembered how much you love coffee," Evie continued.

"Uh...yeah...it was mighty scarce...for us...during the war," Holt said, gathering himself. He was a little relieved, but mostly disappointed that his connection with Laudie Kate had been interrupted, again. "Damn Union blockades. And I refused to drink any traded-for coffee. Beans taken from a dead Yank or prisoner were another matter..." He caught himself. Women don't want to hear that stuff. *Shut up.* "Our coffee was mostly cornmeal or rye, sweet potatoes or rice. Acorns. Chicory, if we could find it. It was just brown liquid. Tasted awful."

There was a moment of silence before he continued. "Thank you, Evie. This tastes good. Uh, I have...something for you."

Evie wiped a little tear from her eye when she saw the new fabric. She nearly knocked Holt over with a sudden hug. "Thank ya, Holt!"

"I hope your man won't mind. Like I told Laudie Kate, I kind of bled all over one of your other dresses."

"Aww, he won't mind. Besides, a lil' jealousy might do 'im good."

Although he had not met Moose Elkins, Orion had given Holt a description of the huge Ranger. "I heard he was a big guy." Holt chuckled to Evie. "Let's not make him too jealous, okay?" The women laughed with him.

They sat around Navarro's desk. He was away

visiting family for a few days and had left Laudie Kate in charge. The women sipped whiskey while Holt finished his bowl of stew and a couple mugs of coffee. Tag dozed at their feet.

"After that fracas earlier, business slowed down a mite," Evie said. "Laudie here told me I could go. She an' th' others are goin' to close up for th' night. Are you ready fer me ta show ya th' bungalow?"

"Um…uh…sure, Evie. If you're ready to go…" Holt said, taking a quick glance at Laudie Kate.

"There's not much more but some clean up to be done tonight." Laudie Kate nodded. "It's been a big day, what with the return of Mr. Corrigan and him saving our lives." She smiled slyly at him. "Will I see you tomorrow?"

"I hope so." He grinned.

CHAPTER THIRTY

The next morning, Laudie Kate sat at her boss's desk in the back office. A big mug of coffee steamed next to her free hand. In between smoothing imaginary stray hairs back into the tightly swept back bun on her head, she would reach for a drink. Uninhibited and unladylike, she slurped loudly at the hot brew. Her attention was focused on jotting notes for her boss, Miguel Navarro, about the events from yesterday as well as the day's financial report. She had written a report like this each morning for the past few days while he was away. Laudie Kate knew he would appreciate the information and respect the attention to detail.

As she wrote, she also reminisced on the other happenings from the day before. Her thoughts this morning often wandered to Holt Corrigan. He had returned to Stebbins yesterday and re-entered her mind. And would not leave.

Laudie Kate scolded herself.

Men.

Her father was a stubborn man. A good man, but

obstinate and narrow-minded. Her husband, Lucas, had promised her a wonderful life of adventure and travel. She didn't know he was a cheat and a liar. The only thing he said that came true was travel—she had needed to keep moving to stay ahead of that wanted poster on which they both appeared.

Now, Holt Corrigan.

A man like him was always attracting danger. Such a man could be killed at any time. Someone had already attempted to end his life in her saloon. God knows how many others had tried. How could she think of being with someone like him?

The thought of Holt Corrigan being killed made her cringe. She shut her eyes tightly to rid herself of that awful image. Seeing him lying wounded was bad enough.

Although she had work to do, she found herself hoping he would walk back in.

She refocused on her paperwork. Miguel did not give her the combination for the safe he kept near the bookcase. Rather, he instructed her to place the money in the large lockable drawer in the desk while he was away. His apparent lack of sureness about her was not mistrust and did not bother her. It was more about him keeping control of his own personal business. She would do the same if the roles were reversed.

Laudie Kate was well aware of the fact that a skeleton key for the door and another simple lock on a desk drawer was not the most secure situation. Since being hired by Navarro to help run his hotel, she had taken protecting the Blue Sky very seriously, as though it was hers. It was what caused her to shoot Holt that day he burst through the doors.

Holt.

His grin, charming and disarming all at once. She had not noticed how solid his chest was or how muscular his arms were until yesterday. Even in the midst of yesterday's shootout chaos, the way he wrapped her in his heady, protective embrace was exhilarating and fiery. She nearly forgot they were in danger.

She shook her head to chase away the stirring daydream. Where was she? Yes, the task of accounting of yesterday's money.

In Laudie Kate's view, Navarro's hiding place for the Blue Sky cash was too obvious. Instead, she kept the hotel's money from the past few days in a lockable walnut box, which now sat securely under the floorboards in her room upstairs. She had discovered the loose flooring under her bed when she first moved in. The small chest sat in its dark hiding place next to a velvet bag that held a few pieces of her mother's and grandmother's jewelry. The pieces that had not been stolen by her husband. A small throw rug covered the loose boards and her chamber pot guarded the rug.

She pictured the whole process of securing the money and hiding the box in her mind. That side of her bed faced her dresser. On the dresser sat a low-crowned black hat with a damaged cardinal feather in the hatband.

Holt's.

Images from last night glided back and took control. Holt had given her a bolt of beautiful fabric to make a dress, replacing one he thought he had ruined. A wave of warmth rushed to her cheeks as she remembered peeking at the way his trousers fit his tight hips and trim legs when he turned around and bent over to pick up the package.

"That's enough," she said out loud to herself, driving away all provocative thoughts. She shook her head. Her mind scolded. *You cannot allow yourself to feel that way. No man will ever have control over you like that again. Give him his hat back and be done.* She cleared her throat, took a big slug of coffee, and pushed at her hair to ensure the bun was still in its ordered place.

Just then, she heard a slight rustle at the not-quite-closed office door. She glanced over to see it swing open as Tag Along trotted into the room, tail wagging furiously.

"Well, hello there, Tag!" she beamed, putting down her pencil. The dog trotted to her and put his front paws on her knees. "I'm sorry Miguel isn't here or he'd probably have a bone for you!"

Holt trailed the dog a few steps. "Mind some company?" he said, his smiling face peered around the doorframe.

"Not at all, come on in," Laudie Kate said, standing to smooth her dress and check her hair once again.

Holt stood there, captivated by her manner and simple beauty. She gazed at him, her blue eyes investigating his ruggedly handsome face. He suddenly realized just standing there was awkward.

"Tag, uh, decided it was time…to take me for a walk."

"Oh, really?" she said, reaching over to scratch the dog's ears with both hands.

"It's hard to sit around…keep out of sight. Finally, a couple of big freight wagons arrived in town," Holt said, finding it easier to talk to her. "All the unloading was creating lots of noise and clatter. I figured we could slide down the alley unobserved." He shifted his new, uncomfortable hat in his hands and briefly stared at his feet.

"Well, sit down, sit down. I'm finishing paperwork for Señor Navarro. Do you want some coffee?"

"That would be wonderful. Thank you."

She left to get them both some coffee. He looked around the office. "'Wonderful?' Who *talks* like that?" he scolded himself.

Laudie Kate soon returned with a tray filled with an urn of coffee, a mug, and a bowl of water for Tag. She set the bowl down for the dog and poured coffee for Holt and warmed up her mug.

Holt noticed that even the strong brew could not drown out her lavender scent. "Don't let me take you from what you need to do," he said.

"It shouldn't be much longer." She smiled.

Laudie Kate resumed her attention on the papers at the desk. Occasionally, she would reach for her mug and slurp at the hot brew. As he did back when he was bedridden, he watched her in fascination. He had never seen a woman so captivating without making any attempt to be.

The recent issue of the Stebbins newspaper sat on an end table. He reached for it and began reading.

Even in the silence, they both were content with each other's presence. Occasionally, their eyes would meet, dance together for a moment, then dart away for other things to look at.

After a while, Tag started sniffing around the office, nosing into the strange shapes and smells. "C'mon, boy, I think you need to visit the alley." He carefully checked out the private hallway and cautiously opened the back door, making sure there weren't any prying eyes.

When they returned, Laudie Kate was straightening up Navarro's desk and putting things away. "Are you hungry? How about some lunch?"

"That would be wonderful," Holt said brightly, then looked away as she left. Shaking his head slightly, he chastised himself. *Stop saying that!*

They ate across from each other at the desk. Over plates of ham steak, fried potatoes, and corn, they talked more than most people did during a meal. Tag was hunkered down among their legs, enjoying his own pieces of ham.

Their lunch lasted more than an hour. Holt was surprised, yet pleased, that words were just jumping from his mouth. They shared highlights of their respective childhoods, but little of their recent pasts. Her eyes connected with his and time was forgotten.

Holt started talking about the current situation. "I don't know exactly when Orion will get here. Given that I'm holing up until he does..."

"Do you think you're still a target?"

"I don't know...doesn't matter really. I'm not hiding from that."

"I figured as much. You're not the type."

"I just want the people we're after to not get jumpy. One Ranger could just be passing through. Two Rangers..."

"Gets bad guys like the Viklunds and the sheriff jumpy."

He looked at her for moment, wishing she hadn't come to that particular conclusion. "You shouldn't—"

"Christer Viklund was eating with Casper Longley the day you...the day Longley was arrested. Longley, a Viklund employee, gets released on the 'legal say-so' of

Sheriff Carmichael. Then, the Viklunds show up with a herd they 'stole back' from Mexican bandits. And you asked about both the sheriff's and the Viklunds' whereabouts last night. Doesn't take much of a poker player to read all that out."

"Fair enough," Holt said, shaking his head. "Wait, what happened? Something about a herd they stole back?"

Laudie Kate apprised him of the ostentatious appearance of a cattle drive with two hundred head that the Viklunds claimed was once theirs, retrieved from Mexican bandits who had stolen them and fled across the border.

"Awful quick and easy to make all that happen," she continued. "Moose was part of the crew and didn't want to tell Evie too much about it. To me, the whole situation felt like the Viklunds were running a big bluff."

"Well, you may be right, just keep those particular cards to yourself." He smiled, but wanted to change the subject. "You know, I'm kind of useless just sitting here. Feeling a bit caged up…"

"That's a thought, you being…my prisoner." She grinned slyly in return, eyes twinkling. "It's better than when you were my patient."

Uncomfortableness suddenly rose inside Holt and redness crept up his neck. He wasn't sure how to react. His awkwardness returned. "Do you…need any help? Is there anything…I can do…around here?"

"As a matter of fact," she said, patting the top of his hand. "Yes. I think I could find some chores that'll keep you busy."

"And out of sight," he reminded.

That afternoon, Holt spent a few hours re-stacking

kegs and boxes in the storeroom behind the bar. More deliveries were coming soon, so the created space was needed. Laudie Kate took time from her duties supervising the saloon and restaurant to look in on him. He was too busy concentrating on the task at hand to notice her admiring his sweaty, shirtless frame.

The bar wasn't busy yet, so Evie strolled over to her friend to see what Laudie Kate was so absorbed with. "So, Miss Hart, what's got yer attent…oh my. He's… very…*shirtless*, ain't he?"

"I hadn't noticed," Laudie Kate laughed.

"There's a lot ta look at, isn't there?" Evie said, not taking her eyes off Holt. "I mean, we helped th' doctor with 'im an' all, but now, he's…he's…"

"Moving about."

"Yeah, *movin'*."

"We should leave him be," Laudie Kate said, closing the door, but re-opening it briefly to get a last peek. Finally closing the door, she shook her head. *No. Stop this, Laudie Kate Hart. Not him.*

The remainder of the day and again next morning, Holt carefully followed Laudie Kate like a lovesick puppy, just wanting to be near her as often as he could. The pantry in the kitchen got organized and cleaned like it hadn't been in a long time. Holt even learned how to make beds under her patient tutelage.

Lunch found the two in Navarro's office once again. They sat quietly, enjoying each other's company over fried chicken and mashed potatoes.

Once they finished, Laudie Kate needed to get back out to the main room. They stood loading their dishes and utensils onto a tray. "Someday, I'd like to have a meal with you that isn't me trying to recuperate. Or hide," Holt said, sharing the thought that had been on his mind.

"I need to thank you, Holt, for all of the work you've been doing. He won't know who did it, but Miguel will notice what's been done."

"Señor Navarro has been very gracious to me and Tag. It's the least I could do."

"I appreciate it too, very much."

"Thanks for putting up with me. For *hiding* me." He smiled.

"It's been nice having you around."

"I'd spend as much time…with you…as you'd let me…"

That statement and any response was overtaken by Evie bursting into the office.

"Ranger Orion's here," she exclaimed. "He jus' ordered a beer an' a steak."

Holt stared down at his feet in exasperation at once again being interrupted just when things were getting interesting with Laudie Kate. He gathered himself and looked up. Laudie Kate had already moved away and was picking up their lunch tray. "Send him back here, Evie," he said. "Tell him Laudie Kate needs to talk, but don't tell him I'm here."

CHAPTER THIRTY-ONE

Evie brought a beer to the lanky man with a full shock of salt-and-pepper hair. His flat-brimmed hat, pushed up in front lay on the table.

"Thank you, Miss Evie," he smiled broadly.

She leaned over and quietly said, "Laudie Kate is back in Señor Navarro's office. Can you talk to her for a moment?"

"Why, sure. Everythin' all right?"

Evie just shrugged and said, "I'll go check on that steak."

Shortly, there was a knock at the office door. "Miss Laudie? You in there? It's Orion Higbee."

Laudie Kate answered from the desk. "Come on in!"

Orion stepped inside. "Miss Evie said you wanted to see me. Is everythin' all right?" His voice was filled with the soft lilt of Texas. Not a drawl really, just warm syrup.

At the familiar sound of Orion's voice, Tag—no longer able to be held quiet—sprang from under the desk and bounded to the tall Ranger.

"Hey! I know this guy!" Orion knelt to embrace the

happy dog. "That must mean…" he looked around the office.

Stepping from the shadows, Holt said quietly, "It means she'll let just about anybody in this place."

"Ahh ha!" Orion laughed his exclamation. "Look at you!" He stood and stuck out his hand. "I'm Orion. Orion Higbee. Welcome back to th' Rangers!"

"Call me, General William Tecumseh Peckerhead."

The two men laughed hard and shook hands, then hugged each other with heavy thumps on their backs.

"Ho-lee damn, Holt, that's your bad arm. I'm sorry."

"Nah, don't worry. Didn't hurt. I had a special Apache healer see to it that I'm all better."

"Ahh yes, your brother's wife. Blouse an' bloomers, those Corrigan ladies sure took good care of you."

"I got pretty special care here too," Holt said, smiling at Laudie Kate. "But I'd say that Bina and Atlee were more forceful about it."

"Well, I'm damn glad to see you. That *is* you, right? Short hair an' a beard ain't a look I've seen you sportin' before. Come on, lemme buy you a steak an' a beer."

"Hold on, Orion. This look gave me an idea. The people here in Stebbins who saw me the most were Laudie Kate and Evie. They really didn't recognize me at first. I thought it seemed like a good idea if no one knows I'm around. That's why I was tucked away in here."

Laudie Kate spoke up. "I'm going to leave you gentlemen to your business. Ranger Orion, I'll tell Evie to bring your steak back here. I need to go to the general store and see if they've got any lamps to replace some shot-up ones."

She left the two in the office. Holt's eyes followed her all the way out.

"Shot up?" Orion asked. "Anythin' to be concerned about?"

"Naw. Two yahoos got angry over billiards the other day. Cue sticks and pool balls weren't enough, so they drew pistols. One of them got killed. Two bystanders hurt. Some lamps got taken out. Laudie Kate and Evie were about to be right in the middle of it, so I pulled them down to the floor behind the bar, out of range."

"Sounds right cozy."

"When neither one recognized me right away, it gave me the idea. Been hiding out ever since, waiting for you. Couple of days."

"Good place to hide, what with the scenery an' all," Orion said, gesturing with his head at the door where Laudie Kate just left.

A bit of redness shot up Holt's neck. "Laudie Kate? She's…she's…"

"A widow." Orion playfully grinned.

"I was going to say, real pretty," Holt said, not playing along. "I wondered if there was someone in her life. Wait…did she shoot her husband too?"

"No." Orion laughed. "Someone else did. He was a real sonuvabitch."

"Hmmm."

"You mean to tell me you been hangin' aroun' her for all this time an' you didn't know that?"

"Well, I already found out she can handle a gun. I know she's from Westport, Missouri. Spent some time after the war in Denver. She's not much for singing or dancing. Hates riding sidesaddle. She had a dog named Penny when she was little. She's never baked a pie. She likes an honest game of poker, but won't touch faro,"

Holt bantered. "And her eyes can go from flashing like a stormy sky to sparkling like a summer day."

Orion was tilting his head, listening to his partner swoon, a widening grin crossing his face.

A knock at the door announced Evie's arrival with Orion's steak, along with beans and tortillas and two fresh mugs of beer.

"Thanks again, Miss Evie," Orion smiled. "Can I ask how your beau is? Moose, I think it was."

She blushed and said, "Oh my. Yes, Moose is good. I haven't seen 'im fer a coupla days, but he's real good. I 'xpect he'll be in town in th' next day or so."

"Nice fella. Tell him Ranger Higbee said hey."

The two Rangers sat down and Orion dug into his steak. "This sure beats a corn dodger an' a hunka jerky," he said between bites.

"Orion…I've got to tell you…I've been searching my memory to try and recall who shot me."

"I guess you remember Miss Blue Eyes shot you, right?"

"Of course, but someone else did too."

"Yeah. An' I've played that day over an' over," Orion said. "For the life of me, Holt, I dunno who did it."

"That's what I'm trying to tell you. At first, I thought it was just part of my nightmares, but I *knew* I had seen who did it. Then it came to me, in a vision, clear as daylight. I saw him, Orion! I saw the no-good bastard."

Orion quietly sipped his beer and listened to his partner.

"Dark hair, maybe black," Holt continued. "Cut short, like mine is now. No mustache or beard, but not freshly shaved."

"That don't narrow it down much."

"Medium height, maybe my size."

"So was most every man in there that day."

Holt took a deep breath, searching the image he had memorized. He snapped his fingers. "A vest! The sonofabitch wore a vest. One of those fancy cowhide ones, light with brown spots. Fancy buttons but unbuttoned."

Orion's brow furrowed and he slammed his mug down with a bang, some of the golden brew launching out over the top. "Fancy vest?" His jaws clenched. His eyes blazed up like lit torches. "That no-good, mud-crawlin' ferret…"

"You know who I'm talking about?"

"Sheriff Carmichael's deputy. Mercer's his name. That apple-knockin'…"

"So you *do* know. We shouldn't be sitting here. Let's go!"

Orion did not acknowledge Holt. Eyes slightly closed, his mind was traveling back in time. He began recalling one of the incidents of that messy, troubled day. "Marshal Hollings pointed out Mercer as a deputy…I ragged his ass for not helpin'…claimed he was a *county* deputy and was off duty…then…he shot…that Viklund rider…who…who was professin' to be innocent. The rider had started…to raise his arm…an' point. He was startin' to say somethin' important…an' Mercer shot him!" Orion opened his eyes, but his mind was still in the past. "Mercer shot him. Claimed the rider was tryin' to draw, so he shot him. Ho-lee damn! Mercer shot that guy because he thought the rider was gonna peach on him 'bout shootin' you!" He looked at Holt, fully in the present now. "It didn't seem top rail then. Makes sense now."

"All right, let's go get that miserable—"

"No, Holt, wait!"

"What the hell for? That bastard needs to be ended."

"Holt, this is hard to say an' gonna be harder to hear but calm down. This ain't the time."

Holt folded his arms and glowered at Orion, waiting for an explanation.

"You dunno what a great move you made by stayin' outta sight an' all. We always wondered if Viklund an' Carmichael were in cahoots, right? Your rememberin' about the deputy is important, Holt, real important."

"How's that?"

"It's pretty clear now, we walked into an ambush that day. Longley wasn't alone at that back table. Viklund's son Christer an' the Windmill rider who got shot were with him. Nearby was that skunk-assed deputy. They *knew* we were comin', Holt. They were set to kill us. All four of 'em."

"So, either the marshal told them or someone saw us arrive in town."

"It wasn't the marshal. He's solid. I'm guessin' it was Carmichael's deputy skulkin' around in the dark an' saw us visit the jail the night we arrived."

Holt's face darkened at the revealment of the plot. "That no-good sonofabitch…"

"Don't forget he's only a pawn. We're after the king. If we jump on that deputy now…"

"Viklund and Carmichael could climb into their holes."

"Or send more than four after us."

They both sat in silence, contemplating this information.

"In a strange way." Orion finally spoke up. "Laudie Kate shootin' first probly saved both of us. No disrespect to your sufferin'."

"Thanks for that."

"Listen…her firin' took 'em by surprise. When you… fell…I had Longley an' his table covered by Marshal Hollings's shotgun before they could react. Of course, the deputy managed to squeeze off those two shots that hit you." He paused. "But he wasn't sittin' at the table, which is why he was able to get away with it! Ho-lee damn."

"So, why didn't they try to finish the job and come after me in the hotel?"

"You weren't aware, but your door was secured an' someone armed was with you all the time, includin' an' 'specially Miss Evie." Orion nodded with a smile at the memory.

"But what about you? They could've got you any time you weren't tucked away in my room."

"Maybe they were scared to tangle with me," he mused. "I'm guessin' that when the ambush failed an' Longley was actually arrested, Viklund or the sheriff called things off. One Ranger gettin' wounded is merely concernin'. Two Rangers killed gets lots of attention an' draws more Rangers."

"This *is* serious. How are…" Holt lowered his voice. "Is it Moose and Dal? Are they still riding for Viklund? Are they on sound footing?"

"Yeah, still there," Orion responded quietly as well. "They're in good stead. To hear Moose tell it, the oldest Viklund son, Baldur, wants Dal to take Longley's place."

"I'd say that's good."

"There's a lot in play now. I'll have to catch you up," Orion said, finishing what remained of his beer while Holt got up to check the door and peek outside for any eavesdroppers. "Remember that scout we found near-dead? Before he died, he told me that the patrol wasn't huntin' Comanche, they were ridin' protection for Sheriff Carmichael. He was carryin' loads of money. The scout said they did it often."

"They weren't Comanche fighters, that's for sure," Holt noted.

"The patrol was handpicked. They never had to do basic assignments, just guard duty for Carmichael. When your brother saw him with the patrol in Overfield, the sheriff was bringin' back two sets of saddlebags with him. The scout said it was all loot from Fort McKavett."

"Money from the Army?"

"Yes, one of them bags was filled with real treasury notes. Payment for a small herd of stolen cattle," Orion continued. "The other set of bags was crammed with counterfeit currency."

"Counterfeit?"

Orion acknowledged Holt's question with a bit of a snicker. "Yeah, that got me wonderin' if that scout wasn't just babblin' on his deathbed."

"Kind of specific for dying words," Holt noted.

"That's where I was leanin' too," Orion acknowledged. "Then I remembered there's a settlement around McKavett that's chock-full of saloons, gamblin' halls, whorehouses an' opium dens. Nothin' but evil an' depravity. That's exactly where the fake money was gathered… or confiscated. A real hell on earth."

"All that near an Army fort?"

"The Army is why the hellhole exists! Don' tell me your Reb army read Bibles an' cleaned halos when you was off-duty."

Holt snorted a laugh. "I lost my halo at Sabine."

Orion smiled and continued. "I'm guessin' that the real money went into the sheriff's and Viklund's bank accounts an' the phony stuff was used to buy a small herd of beef somewhere, maybe even in Mexico. Just so the Viklunds could claim it was Mexicans who stole it in the first place."

"You know this for sure?"

"Naw, that part's just an educated guess right now. Anyway, Moose an' Dal's next report oughta be good. Moose was part of the crew that supposedly retrieved their herd from the Mexicans. Hope it's soon, the Cap'n will be waitin'. That's why I told Miss Evie to tell her beau, Moose, hello. He'll know I'm back."

"Interesting you connected the money to the Army," Holt said. "When was the last time you heard from Captain McCoy?"

"A week, give or take a coupla days, why?"

"He needs to poke around McKavett, into their chain of command."

Orion's intense gaze let Holt finish.

"Remember those papers we took from what was left of the lieutenant? There were messages written on them in disappearing ink."

"Disappearing...I'll be damned..."

"Wait," Holt urged. "The messages connect everything you just told me. Sheriff Carmichael's brother is an Army quartermaster..."

"At McKavett."

"Yeah, at McKavett." Holt nodded. "That's why we

need to get the captain looking into whether this is just a couple of idiot brothers or if there's some bigger brass involved."

"Ho-lee damn, Holt. What have we dug ourselves into?"

CHAPTER THIRTY-TWO

Orion was having breakfast at the El Matador. He liked eating out on the café's veranda, where he got the best of being outdoors and eating someone else's cooking. He was savoring a last biscuit with honied butter when an older man, about Orion's height and age, approached his table.

"Ranger Higbee," the lanky man in a crisp white shirt and gray vest said quietly. "I am sorry to interrupt, but Marshal Hollings needs to speak with you, in the jail." The badge on his vest told Orion that this was the town deputy who shouldered all of the Stebbins law responsibilities with the marshal.

"We haven't had occasion to meet yet," Orion answered. "You must be Marshal Hollings's hard-workin' deputy."

"Gus Brooks. Glad to know you."

Orion was fascinated, but not surprised, that he had been tracked down here. He had not checked in at the jail nor worn his Ranger badge since arriving back in town, choosing to keep a lower profile. Not hidden like his just-reinstated partner, just unassuming and quiet. He had not seen Linus Carmichael, but he had to presume that the crooked sheriff also knew he had returned, which meant the Viklunds were aware as well. For that reason, he had stayed away from seeing Holt.

Orion had instead spent time these past couple of days riding a little bit of the wide-ranging ranch lands surrounding the town. Just getting the lay of the land, trying to see if he could work out how cattle could be moved and not be discovered.

Holt did not go with Orion on these informal tours of the county. Orion had not seen evidence his forays were being tracked, but it would be foolish to assume he rode unnoticed. In fact, the two Rangers had kept their time together to a bare minimum, passing messages back and forth through Laudie Kate. It was best that Holt remain concealed, a weapon to be drawn against the Viklunds when the time was right.

Not that hiding was easy for Holt and Tag. They stayed close to the bungalow. Evie brought home food for the pair in case sneaking to the Blue Sky wasn't prudent. Of course, Holt still found ways to slip over and steal every moment he could to be in the presence of Laudie Kate.

After leaving the El Matador, Orion followed Gus to the jail. The deputy waved Orion on inside, choosing to stay out on the walkway. "I'm going to make sure Mercer or any of the other Carmichael lackeys aren't nosing around," he explained. "I can't stand any of those sons-abitches."

Orion nodded and stepped inside to greet Marshal Hollings.

"Sorry ta root ya out, Orion, an' disturb yer meal," the marshal said. "Figgered ya been busy."

"Not a worry, marshal. Been keepin' to myself these past coupla days."

"We got rough news firs' thing t'day 'bout th' widow who owns th' W Bar L."

"I don't know the lady, is she okay?"

"Well, yeah. I guess. Her foreman, Big Jeff, rode in ta report th' W Bar L herd was jus' 'bout cleaned out a coupla nights or so ago," Marshal Hollings quietly informed Orion.

"Cleaned out?"

"Lillian, Mizzuz Whitman, has had a hard fight ta keep her ranch goin'. She lost nearly half her herd ta thieves a few months back. Fer awhile, she an' her riders had managed ta hold off any more rustlin'. Till now."

"Is that foreman still around?"

"Naw, said he needed ta get back, ta keep an eye on th' ranch an' Mizzuz Whitman. He's awful worried 'bout her. Not sure what she's gonna do now."

"He's sure it's rustlers? Not just beef gettin' spooked or decidin' to wander off?"

"Big Jeff's a good cow man, one o' th' bes' there is. Those beeves di'nt wander off."

Orion's brow furrowed as Marshal Hollings continued.

"Ol' Jeff also had some purty interestin' news 'bout Viklund an' Carmichael. Said they've threatened Mizzuz Whitman."

"Threatened?"

"Yeah, bullyin' her ta sell an' move on. Said they'd kill her if she tol' anyone," the marshal said. He rubbed his grizzled chin, trying to hold down his anger. "I always guessed th' sheriff was a damn criminal. Lars too. This 'bout ceements it." He paused. "Figgered ya'd want ta know rightaways."

Orion stood and adjusted his gun belt. "Marshal, I need you an' your deputy to stay quiet with this, 'specially that bit about them threatenin' the widow. It's best if those owlhoots don't know that we know. Understand? No one."

"We'll follow yer play, Orion."

"Good," he said, tugging down on his hat. "Big Jeff, you say? Does he look like his name?"

"Cain't miss 'im." The marshal half-chuckled. "Big ol' bright red hair an' beard, like th' biggest damn elf ya ev'r saw."

"Hmm, I should meet this Big Jeff an' have a chat with Missus Whitman," Orion said. "It'd be good to have a familiar face with me. Wanna come along?"

"Can do. Mizzuz Whitman needs ta know we's worried 'bout 'er too."

"Get your horse. I'll be back in fifteen."

Before leaving, Orion stopped in at the Blue Sky. It was a good bet Holt was around there, and Orion wanted to let his partner know about this latest incident.

"I haven't seen him yet today," Laudie Kate said smiling, making sure no one was near enough to overhear. "I imagine he's still at the bungalow. He probably wasn't comfortable venturing out."

"Thank you, Miss Laudie. I'm certain there are people markin' my whereabouts, so I best not go visitin' there. If he sneaks in, let him know I'm takin' a ride out to the W Bar L with the marshal."

"Will do. Watch yourself," she warned.

"Careful is my middle name."

As he untied his horse outside, Orion overheard the youngest Viklund, Christer, holding court on the boardwalk, a small group of townsmen circling him, intent on listening.

"At least two hundred head, maybe three, gone, just like that from the Whitman's W Bar L," Christer spouted off loudly. "I don't know if it's the same Mexican bandits who made off with our beef, but it sure is a tragedy for Lillian Whitman. I'll bet the marshal isn't doing a thing to help the widow."

Orion did not stick around to hear the murmurings of agreement.

———

At a trot, the lanky Ranger and doughy marshal reached the widow's ranch in little more than an hour. They were met at the border of the ranch by W Bar L two riders. Unlike in town, Orion had made sure his Ranger badge was now plainly seen on his coat.

Just to make sure these visitors were peaceable, the riders followed the two lawmen to the ranch house. From a distance, Orion could see a massive form pacing the front porch of the handsome home. The figure appeared to be wearing a large, fuzzy red woolen cap.

"G'mornin', Marshal." Big Jeff nodded as the two rode up, a Henry rifle cradled easily in his arms. The big man had a smile on his face, but his eyes were carefully inspecting the stranger who rode next to Hollings.

Orion stifled a wry grin with a disguised clearing of his throat. It wasn't a woolen cap he had seen from a distance, it was Big Jeff's unruly mane of hair. The Ranger could not help but remember the marshal's description of the man. Although the mop of red hair and bright, red beard was elf-like, this enormous man was no pixie. Orion truly wondered if this man could, maybe, be even bigger than Ranger Moose Elkins. The Henry rifle Big Jeff carried looked like a toy against his massive frame.

"Big Jeff? I'm Orion. Orion Higbee, Texas Ranger. Baxter here's been tellin' me about what's happened. Mind if I get down an' talk to you a bit? Maybe meet Missus Whitman?"

"We's in big need'uv help, Ranger. Climb on down." The big man waved to his riders that everything was okay, and they left to resume their guard patrol.

Big Jeff gave the same report he had made earlier that morning to Marshal Hollings. Back in the fall, nearly three hundred head of their beef vanished. Almost half the W Bar L herd. Then, three nights ago another three hundred head disappeared. He and the Whitman riders combed the property and surrounding land trying to track the stolen stock, but the trail was disordered and faded into scrub land.

"They was headed in th' gen'rul di-rection of th' border," Big Jeff shook his head. "I dunno, mebbe ev'ry-one's right an' it is them dam Mexes stealin' beef, but I jus' caint' see it."

"Kind of a long way for them to come, don't you think?" Orion said. "Lotsa places to hit nearer the big river."

"See? Thass' what I bin sayin'!" The huge red-haired man swung a heavy arm in an exaggerated gesture. "Somethin' don' seem ta fit right 'bout that notion o' Mexes. Injun sense tells me them thieves is nigher ta home."

"How's Mizzuz Whitman?" the marshal asked.

"She's b'side herself," Big Jeff said, working a meaty hand through his wild mop of hair in frustration. "Not sure what ta do. Th' lady don' have much in th' way o' family. Purty much just us riders," Big Jeff said, quickly swiping at his nose. "Hatin' ta see her troubled so."

Just then, a woman stepped through the front door onto the porch. Lillian Whitman was taller than average and square-shouldered, holding herself proudly. Smoky silver hair was pulled back into a long, broad braid. Orion guessed she was about his age, maybe even older, it was hard to tell. As he took in her whole frame covered by a plain linsey-woolsey shirt and worn denim trousers tucked into beat-up, mule-ear boots, this was not who Orion pictured as "Widow Whitman." From her attire, she was no stranger to ranch work. From her ability to keep a ranch afloat and the .32 Smith & Wesson at her hip and short-barreled carbine in her hand, this was no helpless damsel either. Not to mention, she was a strikingly handsome woman.

But, this morning, her light brown eyes, normally gleaming with energy, were sad and tired-looking. It was obvious she had been crying.

"Jeffrey, I heard voices, do we have visitors?" Lillian spoke in a trying-to-be-strong voice. "Oh, hello, Marshal Hollings."

"Howdy, ma'am," Baxter said, tugging off his hat.

Orion's hat was already in his hand. "Missus Whitman, my name is Orion. Orion Higbee, Texas Ranger. I am pleased to meet you, but I am sorry for the circumstances."

"I'm pleased to meet you as well, Ranger Higbee."

"I've heard most've what's happened from Big Jeff

here, so I won't bother you with repeatin', but I'd like to hear about your dealin's with Lars Viklund an' Sheriff Carmichael. If you feel like talkin' about it, that is."

"I can't tell you one thing without you first hearing about the other," Lillian began. The widow explained that this latest rustling had nearly cleaned out her entire herd. All cattle ranches counted on money raised from drives to keep operating. Her W Bar L was no different.

"My husband, Leonardo, bless his soul, was a prince, but he did not have princely wealth," she weakly jested. The loss of beef earlier in the year was a blow, she explained, but not necessarily a fatal one. Now, she doesn't know what to do. "Everything in me wants to fight. I can't quit, but I don't know the way forward." She was on the verge of breaking down into tears but would not allow herself to do so in front of the lawmen.

Orion offered for her to sit down on the chairs arranged along the porch. The widow shook her head no. "Let's walk," she said. "I think better that way." They left the porch, Orion walking next to her, the marshal and Big Jeff following behind.

She began again, explaining that Sheriff Carmichael paid a visit a couple months ago, shortly after the first theft. He had offered his legal skills to help negotiate a settlement with the bank to sell the ranch. He even proposed a more personal arrangement, suggesting the two become a couple. "I believe I told him, 'If you lie down with dogs, you will get up with fleas.'" she said. Although the story had humor, she shook her head, wanting to rid her mind of the encounter.

"Can I ask what happened next?" Orion asked, concerned etched across his face.

"The sheriff got angry and said, with me or without

me, he was going to enjoy living here. Since he wouldn't leave, I drew my gun and fired twice in the air, spurring his horse away for him." The widow smiled slightly at this memory.

"An' Viklund?" Orion continued.

"Lars Viklund and some filthy man came by recently and made more menacing threats."

"This 'filthy man' have an eyepatch?"

"Yes. Yes he did."

Casper Longley, Orion noted to himself.

"Viklund was pleasant at first. He offered to pay what *he* claimed was a good price for my land and house. I told him I wasn't interested in even hearing numbers and ordered him off my property. With that, his tone changed. He said they could not promise safe conduct for me or my men. He laughed when he said that he would certainly hate to see anything happen to me. Laughed." She swallowed and breathed deep to compose herself. "He rode away, but that filthy man lingered and told me he'd...he'd enjoy...'*having his way*'...with me..." She stopped and cleared the retching bile that rose in her throat. "I will not repeat his exact words."

"No, please don't, Missus Whitman," Orion broke in. "I am sorry." Silence stood between them for a moment until he spoke again, "When was this last visit?"

"The day before Jeffrey discovered our southern pastureland was practically empty." She paused. "I don't have many riders left. Jeffrey and those who've stayed can't be everywhere at once."

"Interestin', mighty interestin'." He paused and rubbed at his chin. "Have any of you spoken to anyone outside the ranch about this latest thievery? I mean, besides the marshal here?" Orion asked both the widow and her foreman.

"I only tol' th' marshal this mornin'," Big Jeff spoke up. "Mizz Lillian ain't even left th' property, right? She's tol' no one. Our men have all stayed hyar, standin' guard. I kin vouch fer that."

"I was th' only one 'round when Big Jeff came in," Marshal Hollings said. "My deputy hadn't reported yet. An' Carmichael's lackey wasn't 'round neither."

"No, I've spoken to no one," Lillian answered, regaining her normal composure. "We mostly keep to ourselves. Rumors around town say it's Mexican bandits. I don't think Jeffrey believes that's true though."

Orion spoke up. "This mornin', right before I rode out here, I heard Christer Viklund bad-mouthin' the marshal to a bunch of townsfolk. He was sayin' that nothin' was bein' done about the rustlin' that happened out at the W Bar L a few nights ago."

"What!"

Lillian and her foreman both exclaimed.

"Ask yourselves, how'd Viklund know about all that?" Orion finished his point.

Big Jeff thundered, "That lousy son of a motherless goat! I'm gonna…" He stopped and looked at his boss, deciding to choose his next words carefully. "I'm gonna stomp that lil' *gombeen* inta a furry lil' ball!" he roared.

"Hang on, Jeffrey. Hang on," Orion began again. "You're gonna get your chance. But right now, you're overmatched an' outgunned." He paused, looking at him and then Lillian for agreement. An idea, a wild one, was forming in his head. "The fact that the Viklunds don't know what you know can be powerful. Understand? We're gonna use it against them."

Lillian Whitman drew herself up to her full height and eyed the lanky Ranger. "What do you have in mind, Orion Higbee?"

"Do you have confidence in the Rangers?" Orion asked calmly. "Will you trust me?"

Big Jeff took a deep breath and looked at his boss. She nodded grimly.

"Okay." Orion nodded in return. "How many riders you got left?"

CHAPTER THIRTY-THREE

"I still haven't seen him," Laudie Kate talked directly into Orion's ear on his return to town. "But…" she gestured around at a very crowded and very noisy Blue Sky bar, "he could be hanging from a chandelier right above me and might not get noticed." She looked down to concentrate on the tray of drinks she was pouring, then spoke again in his ear so only he would hear. "You're welcome to go check Señor Navarro's office. He might've snuck over from the bungalow."

Orion waded through the crowd of milling drinkers and jammed card tables toward the back of the saloon. He gave a quick wave at Evie from across the smoke-filled room. A brief smile was all she could muster as she hurriedly served drinks and took orders.

He finally reached the dark, quiet sanctuary of the private back hallway. At the closed office door, he knocked, not expecting a response, but he soon heard the door unlocking, then slowly opening. Holt's eye and Tag's nose peeked out through the crack.

"Is there a secret password I should know?" Orion

teased. The door opened and Tag did happy figure-eights around the lanky Ranger's legs as he stepped inside. To Orion's surprise, his friend Moose Elkins was seated in the office with Holt.

"Well, look who's here!" Orion grinned. "Moose, how'd you get through the crowd an' past Miss Evie without bein' seen? An' Holt, how'd you know who this big galoot was?"

"There ain't no sneakin' past Evie," Moose responded. "So, I greeted her first. Holt here must've saw me stealin' a kiss from her an' figgered who I was. I usually come an' go through th' back anyway, so when I was leavin', I hearda voice call my name from th' dark hallway. I'd hoped ta git a chance ta meet th' Ranger I'd heard so much 'bout. An' here he be."

Holt and Orion chuckled at the good-hearted big man.

"Look," Moose added. "I might not have lotsa time b'fore I have ta skedaddle, an' there's lots ya need ta hear."

The other two Rangers nodded. Holt got Tag to settle down so everyone could hear and concentrate.

"First, like we suspected, them Viklunds are totally an' completely behin' ALL th' rustlin' that's been goin' on here. Me an' Dal seen nearly every bit've it. But, they only take small pieces o' herds at a time. That way, it's easier ta ree-locate 'em. It also don' take long ta change brands an' ya don' need as many men to move 'em from place ta place…usually jus' four riders. Quick an' easy."

Holt started to ask a question, but Moose stopped him.

"In case I gotta stop an' get outta here, lemme get everythin' out first." He paused. "These small herds are taken ta Fort McKavett or New Braunfels nearby. We got 'em all ta pieces on that fer sure. Dal hisself has been on two o' them short drives an' is leavin' soon on 'nother. That's testifiable."

Holt and Orion quickly looked at each other in acknowledgment.

"Here's th' trick: Lars ain't rustlin' for th' cattle or th' money, he's doin' it ta go after th' small ranches, for their land. Stealin' their beef puts 'em in a bind an' Viklund gets 'em ta sell out. An' if th' rustlin' ain't enuf ta convince 'em, that evil Swede sends Casper Longley to pro-vide 'xtra motivation ta get 'em ta move on."

"What ranches besides the W Bar L has Lars targeted?" Holt interrupted, asking a question anyway.

"This was all happenin' b'fore Dal an' I was bein' hired. Prob'bly why they needed 'xtra hands. But since we've been workin' at th' Windmill V, Viklund dun run off th' folks who owned th' Half Moon 6 an' River D. Viklund owns 'em now, I'm guessin' under a different name. Carmichael or th' bank would know fer sure, they handle all Lars's bizness. Th' stolen W Bar L beeves have been tucked away at th' Half Moon 6 since they was stole. There's no one there who'll complain, it's all Viklund folk. Like I said, that herd'll move out from there real soon."

"An' the Mexican rustlers?" Orion chimed in.

"'Bout as real as Sanny Claus," Moose responded. "That noisy ol' herd th' Viklunds paraded aroun' a coupla weeks ago, claimin' they stole it back? They bought it from a Mexican rancher, usin' phony money. I was part o' th' crew that acquired 'em an' brought 'em back. They altered brands with a runnin' iron every night ta get 'em changed b'fore arrivin' in town."

"We knew about the counterfeit money." Orion

nodded. "We only suspected the Viklunds bought a herd with it, sayin' they stole it back."

"They shore 'nuff did," Moose acknowledged. "Tol' anyone who'd listen 'twas Mexicans who thieved 'em."

"New Braunfels. Do you know why they take the stolen beef there?" Holt asked.

"Whoever th' Viklund's agent is, an' I dunno who that is, has 'em go there occasionally. Baldur sells th' herd an' th' broker ships them beeves by boat down th' Guadalupe ta Matagordo. Dunno much more 'bout that part o' th' equation though. Rest o' th' time th' cattle jus' goes ta Fort McKavett."

"Have you or Dal heard who's behin' this operation at the fort or in New Braunfels?" Orion asked.

"No, cain't say we've heard. It don' matter if'n it's the fort or New Braunfels, it's th' same broker though," Moose acknowledged. "I think Carmichael knows 'im."

"How about mules? Have you seen the Viklunds involved in rustling or selling mules?" Holt continued.

"Naw, ain't heard nothin' 'bout any damn mules," Moose answered. "Thank gawd. Hate them damned things." The thought shivered his enormous body.

"That's a whole lot, Moose. Good stuff. Let us share what we've discovered," Orion said. "Pieces of the puzzle are startin' to fit. Besides, we each should know everythin', in case...you know..."

"Moose, remember that cavalry patrol my brother tangled with?" Holt asked.

"'Twas all anyone could talk 'bout for a spell." Moose chortled.

"They were a protection squad for Sheriff Carmichael. He's the Viklund's courier, bringing the money back, whether it's from New Braunfels or the fort. The real money and the fake stuff."

"That figgers," Moose declared. "That's why he's always gone."

"That patrol was wiped out, Moose," Orion added. "Comanches."

"So *that's* why they's addin' two riders fer this next trip," Moose reacted.

Orion continued, "Their scout survived long enough to talk about their mission. That's how we knew about the sheriff an' the counterfeit money."

"The lieutenant in charge of that patrol was carrying a map of the trail from the fort to New Braunfels," Holt said. "He also had secret invisible messages from their broker."

"The broker just happens to be one of the fort's quartermasters," Orion interjected.

"I'll be damned…" was all Moose could utter.

"There's more," Holt continued. "The Fort McKavett quartermaster in question is Sergeant Porter Carmichael."

"Sar-gent *Porter Carmichael* as in 'related ta Sheriff Linus Carmichael?'" Moose asked in stunned disbelief.

"As in '*brothers* Porter an' Linus,'" Orion answered.

"Don't' that beat all." Moose shook his head. "Are ya shure?"

"Unfortunately, yes," Holt said. "Apparently, the Carmichaels had been stealing Army mules and selling them back for a few years. They only recently got involved in cattle when they connected with the Viklunds. Found themselves a more than willing partner in that bastard Swede."

"Lars Viklund wants th' land. The Carmichaels want th' money. They're all no-good thieves," Orion added.

"I'll be damned an' go ta hell…" Moose rubbed his face in amazement. "This ain't nuthin' what we thought we was bitin' off, is it? I ain't never heard of such a thing. Goddam…Wait! Does this stop with th' sergeant or's it go higher up?"

"We're not sure, Moose," Holt said. "The captain's looking into that. Right now, we're going to focus on the sheriff and the Viklunds."

"You said Dal was goin' on another drive," Orion interrupted. "Is that with the W Bar L herd swiped the other night?"

"Yep, shure is."

"An' they're headed to New Braunfels?" Orion continued.

"Yep. In a coupla weeks, af'er things cool down," Moose said. "Baldur's leadin' th' crew. Dal's gonna be ridin' next ta 'im."

"Moose, we need to get all this on paper an' have you sign it," Orion interrupted. "Just in case."

"Sign what?" came a voice from the door.

All three Rangers spun in their chairs toward the sound. Evie O'Neill stood in the doorway, hands on hips.

"Hi, honey," Moose said, standing to face her. "How long ya bin standin' there?"

"Long enough, Michael Patrick Elkins. What th' hell is goin' on? I thought you left."

Holt and Orion looked at each other. Orion mouthed the words, "Michael Patrick?"

"Looks like someone di'nt shut an' *lock th' door*," Moose glared at Orion, then took a deep breath. "Evie, darlin', I…uh…couldn't tell ya b'fore…"

"You're a Ranger," she said calmly.

Moose stood stunned for a moment, then asked, "How'd ya know?"

"I didn't know. At least, I didn't…till now. But seein' you with these two…well…it makes sense."

Moose could only shake his head.

"There's justa way 'bout you," she said. "I grew up on a ranch, with a brother." She paused. "You…You're polite an' know how to use a knife an' fork properly. You're maybe th' best smellin' cowhand I ever met." She half-chuckled. "Even th' ones who try ta spruce up, never quite get there."

"Aw, Evie darlin'…" He started to move in her direction.

"Don't 'Evie darlin' me, mister. You lied to me! You made up this whole 'ranch hand' story! Is Michael Patrick Elkins even your real name? Do you…" She choked on hot tears that exploded as suddenly as her world had just changed. "Do you…even care for me…or was that made up too?" she blubbered.

Holt and Orion looked at each other wide-eyed. Holt gestured toward the door with his head and they both stood slowly to creep out into the shadowy back hallway. A soft snap of fingers got Tag to follow along.

"Of course I care for ya, Evelyn Grace O'Neill. Ya know everthin' 'bout me. I ain't made anythin' up, 'ceptin' where I actually draw my pay. We was sent here ta catch some rustlers, but th' bes' thing I caught was you."

Evie melted further into tears, and Moose handed her a handkerchief. "It's clean."

She laughed through her tears. "Of course it is." She wiped at her face with the cloth. "If you're makin' this up, Moose, I swear, I'm gonna put you down like a fevered cow…"

"I swear, Evie. I had ta pretend that I was jus' some ranch hand. I di'nt pretend anythin' else." He was standing next to her now.

She reached up to take his face into her hands and brought it down to kiss him long and hard.

"Listen, darlin', I gotta ask ya a big favor…an' it'll help ya too," he said. "Ya can't tell anyone who I really am, even yer friend Miss Laudie. If ya love me, ya have ta keep that close."

She looked up, her hands still cradling his face, her eyes searching his.

"Look," he continued, "I bin wantin' ya ta have somethin'." He dug one of his large hands into a coat pocket. "This belonged ta my gramma." He presented her a silver locket on a long silver chain. "Th' photo of her an' grampa fell out. Mebbe someday soon we can make our picture an' put it there."

New tears, these of happiness, ran down her cheeks.

"I love ya, Evie."

"I love you too, Moose. I'll be wearin' this every day."

They hugged each other tightly, not wanting to let go.

As they waited in the dark hallway, Orion peeked into the office. He turned to Holt and whispered, "It's gonna be a few more moments. When they're done, you write out everythin' we just shared an' get Moose to sign it. Then you sign it too."

"Me, write it?"

"Yeah, you." Orion smiled. "I'll sign it later. Right now, I've got a telegram to send to the Cap'n an' some packin' to do."

"So, we're doing this plan of ours?"

"I don't see it any other way." Orion nodded.

CHAPTER THIRTY-FOUR

Morning came on surprisingly strong and hot even for an early fall. Holt and Orion had left town separately, headed for the ranch that neighbored the W Bar L to the west, a huge estate called the 5 Star.

Holt was gone well before daylight, attentive in the precautions he took to ensure his movements weren't seen or tracked. He was waiting for Orion inside the tree line several miles outside of town. "Good morning, Sunshine!" he called cheerily to his partner.

"An' to you too, peckerhead." Orion grinned. "Woulda got here sooner, but I backtracked a coupla times, makin' sure no one was sniffin' my trail."

"Same here. I'm pretty sure we're in the clear."

"Let's go see how Mr. Frederick is this fine day."

"Yeah. I hope he's willing to listen," Holt said.

Harold Frederick, the owner of the 5 Star, possessed or claimed grazing range no one could ride across in one day. The 5 Star was the county's biggest spread by far.

The Rangers were guessing that, for Lars Viklund, this would one day be the prize piece in the deadly game he was playing.

Holt was happy to finally be moving about. Stretching out the stiffness in his healing left leg was welcome. Tag enjoyed the open space as well. Keeping out of sight around town was a good plan, but being cooped up was a limitation to which he would never be accustomed. The only good thing about hiding was returning to the Blue Sky and getting to be near Laudie Kate. The worst part was that he had yet to find a way to tell her about the feelings he had for her. Something or someone always seemed to get in the way.

Fortunately, the 5 Star ranch house was situated upon its huge tract of land so that it was not a long stretch to travel to and from town. There was enough ground to cover, though, that Holt and Orion could discuss, once more, the complexities of the plan they were setting into motion. Successful coordination of all the timing and people—all in different locations—in an orderly fashion would be tricky. Captain McCoy's telegraphed response to Orion last night sternly warned them that the scope of what they were dealing with was immense. He was on-board, but the stakes were high.

As they rode, there also was opportunity for Orion to fill in Holt on what he had learned about the owner of the 5 Star and his ranch.

Harold Frederick was a hard-working and successful man. He and his wife had lost two sons in the war, both on the same day, during the same battle. Frederick had fought alongside them and was wounded in the same action that took his boys. After surviving that ordeal, he walked away from the war to come home and care for the remainder of his family.

Pouring his heartache into his work, Frederick had built the 5 Star into the largest cattle operation surrounding the region. He, his wife, two daughters, and remaining son were well known and respected in Stebbins.

The two Rangers settled into an easy lope across a green Texas valley. Blossoming clusters of blue and white wildflowers stretched from a winter's slumber. Rolling hills held the pastureland in place, helped by a sturdy, gurgling stream. Sentries of blackjack, post oak and juniper were hunkered in groups along the water. Large clusters of brown cattle grazed peacefully, signaling the beginning of 5 Star land.

Tag Along announced the Rangers' arrival at the ranch house by running ahead to bark and play with two dogs that bounded toward them from the huge front porch. Both Holt and Orion had prominently affixed their badges outside their coats.

Although Tag had moved on up to the house with his newfound friends, Holt and Orion stayed on their horses and kept a respectful distance back, waiting for someone to acknowledge their presence.

A youngish man stepped from the front door onto the porch. A rifle was casually held, but easily readied, in his hands. Holt could see shadows of other forms in several upstairs and downstairs windows. Cautious people, he thought, but not surprising out here in open cattle country.

Orion waved in salute, partly to be friendly, partly to show his hands were empty. Holt kept both hands on his reins in plain view, to show similar good intentions.

"Good mornin'! I'm Texas Ranger Orion Higbee," he called out in a loud, friendly manner. "This here's my partner, Texas Ranger Holt Corrigan. I wonder if we could speak with Mr. Frederick?"

"I'm Luke Frederick. Mr. Frederick is my father." The young man gave a welcoming response. "Tie up over there by the trough and come on up."

The Rangers left their horses at the hitch post on the side of the large two-story house. They climbed the porch steps and shook hands with the young man, who still kept the rifle in his left hand.

"Luke? It's nice to meet you," Orion said with a friendly grin.

"Is there trouble, Rangers?"

"I'm afraid so," Holt answered. "But not of your doing. This isn't that kind of visit," he smiled.

"Well, that's good," Luke said. "My father will be here shortly." The young man, in his early twenties, was shorter than the two Rangers, but solidly built. His eyes took in the detail of both their badges. "I see you travel with a scout." He smiled, indicating Tag, who was still bouncing and frolicking with the two 5 Star dogs.

"That's Tag Along," Holt said. "He adopted me awhile back. A good partner to have…besides this guy." He laughed, nodding at Orion.

"Ol' Tag is a Ranger dog, First Class." Orion beamed. "He's saved my life."

"He's also been shot by bank robbers and knifed by a Comanche," Holt added. "But he's still ready to ride at a moment's notice."

"He sounds like a good one to have on your side." A deep voice from the front door sounded.

A short, stocky man with sandy hair and intense

green eyes stood at the entryway, studying the lawmen. His face was tanned from a lifetime of being outside. He wore a crisp, white shirt under a new-looking leather vest. He was a spitting image of the young man, only a couple of decades more weathered. Unarmed, he stepped onto the porch and stuck out his hand, "Harold Frederick, owner of the 5 Star. What can I do for you, Rangers?"

After introducing themselves, Orion casually asked, "There's been a lotta rustlin' in the county. You been havin' any trouble with that here at the 5 Star?"

"We haven't had any rustling problems," the older man said. "Rome keeps a pretty keen watch on our herds and makes sure our riders patrol our land as thoroughly as possible."

"Rome is our foreman," Luke added. "Man could track a whisper in the wind."

Harold continued, "We've heard of some of the other ranches having trouble. I don't know what to think of it. I guess there could be Mexican bandits crossing the Rio Grande, but it seems funny they'd come all this way to plunder and then head all the way back."

"Lotta pickin's a mite closer to the big river," Orion acknowledged.

"Yes, that's exactly why it doesn't make a lot of sense to me," the older rancher said.

"Rome mentioned something about a few ranchers being poor managers of their land, just not keeping good track of their stock. Cattle liking to wander and all," his son offered.

"That's a possibility," Holt said. "But there's too much missing stock." He looked over at Orion, a *Let's find out if he's game* cue in his eyes.

"Mr. Frederick, we're here about the rustlin', but there's more to it than that," Orion said.

"You boys want to come in for some coffee?" the owner asked.

"I'm thinkin' we best stay here," Orion answered, looking Harold in the eyes.

"What we need to talk about needs to be kept real close to the vest," Holt said. "No offense to anyone inside, but you two ought to be the only ones hearing this."

"I think you'll understand once we explain," Orion clarified.

"Well, at least have a seat," Harold said. "Please."

The Rangers began by sharing that they had strong proof that Lars Viklund was behind the rustling operation menacing the entire county. They explained they also had evidence that the Mexican bandit story was conjured by the Viklunds as well. Holt and Orion told the Fredericks that they could not reveal exactly how this information was gathered but assured the two that their information was rock solid.

"That doesn't surprise me much," Harold said. "Lars has always seemed a bit unhinged to me. I know he hates anything and everything related to the Confederacy."

"Rome says Viklund blames Rebels for murdering his wife and daughter," Luke added.

Harold continued, "He once got drunk and blamed me and the men in my unit for his tragedy. Vowed to take revenge." He took a breath and began to explain. "I was with Terry's Rangers, the 8th Cavalry. We were nowhere near here when his family was attacked. We weren't even in Texas, mostly fighting Yankees in Kentucky and

Tennessee." He paused again. "My war ended in Murfreesboro. All that ought to be behind us. There shouldn't be any more 'sides.'"

"Amen." Orion smiled at the older gentleman.

Changing the subject, Harold looked at both Rangers. "So, I reckon Sheriff Carmichael is not around to handle this rustling problem like he should?"

"In a word, yes," Orion said. "I haven't seen him in several days. His office is all closed an' locked up."

"As usual," the rancher responded.

"Well, Mr. Frederick, you should know…" Holt began, then looked at Orion for agreement. Orion nodded slightly. "Sheriff Carmichael is part of the Viklund's scheme. An important part."

"I guess that shouldn't surprise me either," Harold said, disgusted. "I never did like or trust that man."

"There's lots of movin' parts to this," Orion explained.

"What do we do?" Harold asked. "I'm guessing that's why you're here."

"We'd like you to push for a roundup of all the local ranches," Holt began. "I come from Wilkon, south of here. My brothers and I own two ranches there. We always have a spring and fall roundup where all the operations, all the families, pitch in to sort out the roaming stock. I imagine that's the way things used to operate around here."

"Yeah. It sure did." Harold nodded sadly.

"You carry a lot of weight around here, and respect," Holt continued. "Get a pre-roundup meeting scheduled. Invite all the ranches, even the Viklunds. You'll need to be persuasive and, by the calendar, you'll need to do it soon. Real soon."

"We believe this'll draw Viklund out," Orion said. "He'll be tempted to try somethin'. An' he'll ride right into a load of molasses, tar, an' Rangers." He looked both of the Fredericks square in the eye.

"This is why things need to be kept close to your vests. Don't tell anyone else...your family...even your foreman," Holt added.

"Rome," Harold said.

"Even Rome," Orion continued, keeping his grim look on the 5 Star pair. "Lots at stake here."

"I understand. I think I can do that. We can keep it a secret. I can at least get a meeting called," Harold said. "What else do you have in mind?"

"This is a big ask, Mr. Frederick..." Holt hesitated.

"Go ahead, if you think it's important."

"Mrs. Whitman from the W Bar L, and her men, there's five counting her...let them bunk here...until this is over."

Frederick was poker-faced and silent.

"Hear me out," Holt continued. "Right now, Viklund's men have nearly cleaned out her herd. He thinks he's got her beat. Carmichael is ready to confiscate ownership of her land and take it for himself. You know her, she isn't going to quit. Let's make it look like she's given up."

"If that roundup happens, you're gonna be pretty thin here rider-wise at the 5 Star," Orion added. "An' gun-wise."

"The W Bar L crew can help provide protection, plus handle some of your chores while your men are gone," Holt would not let Frederick's eyes wander.

"Okay, I can see the strategy behind that. Anything else?" the 5 Star owner said.

Holt grinned. "If the roundup happens, hire me on as one of your riders. Most people know my name, not what I look like."

"Now there's an interesting hand to be dealt. *Holt Corrigan, 5 Star wrangler*." Harold chuckled. "I've heard about your exploits."

"I can't explain about continuing to fight a war that ended a long time ago in Virginia," Holt continued to lock eyes with Harold.

"No need to," Harold declared. "I'm talking about what the two of you did to bring in that killer priest over in Sweetclover and that corrupt attorney who thought he could be governor."

Holt raised his eyebrows.

"I've read more about that business with The Angel and Meden Taliff than any of the other stuff about you. Figured a lot of that outlaw bunk was pure crap," Harold said. "I'd be proud to have *Texas Ranger* Holt Corrigan ride for me."

"I would take my orders from your foreman, Mr. Frederick. No one will be the wiser that there'll be a Ranger presence in roundup camp," Holt said. "I'll report back here when a roundup date has been set. When I return, you'll know me as Samuel Holton."

"Sounds good, Mr. Holton. And your dog?"

"When he needs an alias, he goes by 'Dog.'" Holt grinned. "He's a handy one to have in camp. A great sentry. Good herder too. He knows that cattle are crazy."

The Rangers thanked the father and son for their help and took their leave from the 5 Star. A few miles away, Holt and Orion stopped where the well-used trail split. Straight ahead led back into Stebbins. The route south forked down toward Overfield—and further on, Fort

McKavett and New Braunfels. The tricky part of their plan, coordinating timing and people, all in different locations, would begin now with the two lawmen splitting up.

"Lotta movin' pieces," Orion said. "Like a coupla chess games goin' at once."

"Good call about chess," Holt responded. "I wonder if Lars Viklund plays."

"Are you feelin' charmed again?"

"Like midnight in Laelia." Holt grinned, referring to the night they crossed the Rio Grande to capture the infamous killer known as The Angel. "That'd be a good song title. Yeah, I think this can work."

"I think so too."

———

As brand new Ranger partners, Holt and Orion had tracked the infamous killer priest known as The Angel to Sweetclover, Texas, a town near the Rio Grande border with Mexico. A chance conversation with a nurse there led them to discover the existence of a large church just across the river in a little town called Laelia.

"The mission at Laelia was run by an old padre," she had told Holt. But suddenly, she said, there were no more messages from Laelia. No more requests from the minister. "There was talk that the church may have been abandoned," she explained to Holt. "Maybe someone else just took over and ran things differently."

Holt had left his conversation with the nurse with a hunch. "I think we need to visit Laelia," he confirmed to the tall Ranger. "You're thinkin' he's there?" "I got a feeling. If I'm wrong, it costs us a day."

Their excursion across the Rio Grande was risky and unauthorized by both country's authorities. The cutthroat priest was too dangerous and had rampaged too long. If he was close, the Rangers were not going to let him get away.

But they had no evidence The Angel was even there.

Sneaking up on Laelia at dusk, the Rangers scanned a position behind the church and cemetery. If they were going to move against whoever was holed up there, that would have to be their post.

"If we're lucky, we can hide behind it," Holt had said.

"Lucky? We're askin' to be downright charmed," Orion had commented. "All this hide-an'-seek don't mean squat if The Angel ain't here."

"Let's say he is," Holt said determinedly.

"I think he's here too."

From their position elevated from the street, they could hear faint clip-clops growing louder. Entering town from the far end, two riders approached, one atop a horse, the other riding a mule.

In the dusk, the lanterns of Laelia helped illuminate two dark-skinned riders. The man on horseback had a heavy mustache and long black hair with familiar thick braids. The rider on the mule had russet-colored skin and thick brown hair greased into place.

"That's The Angel," Holt had said in a dead calm voice.

"You're sure?"

"That's him all right. That braided bastard was with him in Wilkon. He's the one who killed Silka."

"We're charmed indeed. Now we can open the ball," Orion had said.

No strangers to high-stakes risks, Holt and Orion now spoke one last time before springing their latest plan into action. Holt would be headed back to Stebbins. Orion would visit the W Bar L before venturing on to New Braunfels.

"You sure you can talk the widow into abandoning her place and staying at the 5 Star? *And* keep quiet about it? That Big Jeff might be a wild card."

"She's got sand. An' brains," Orion answered. "Big Jeff'll do whatever she orders. So will her riders."

"You got our statement about everything that's gone on here with the Viklunds and Carmichael? Moose Elkins's report too? Did you remember to sign 'em?"

Orion patted his chest, where the signed document was nestled in a coat pocket.

"Same with that dead lieutenant's secret messages. Take care of them. They're a big part of trapping the Carmichaels. I'd hate to see anything happen to that evidence."

"Yessir, Gen'rul Corrigan." Orion grinned.

"You think we've got enough to take care of Baldur and his crew when they arrive in New Braunfels? And the quartermaster?"

"The Cap'n thinks so, which is good enough for me. Don't forget we've got Dal Frantze right in the middle of those thieves. As far as arrivin' in New Braunfels, I can't get there ahead of that stolen herd if you don't let me get goin'."

"Okay, okay." Holt shook his head. "Tag, it's time to let the grouchy man leave."

"*You* keep me an' the Cap'n posted on what's

happenin' here in Stebbins, whether that roundup meetin'
takes place or not. Lots ridin' on that comin' to fruition."

"Mr. Frederick will make it happen."

"I think so too."

"Ride careful, my friend." Holt smiled. "Give my
regards to the captain."

CHAPTER THIRTY-FIVE

The time passed quickly. After the visit from the two Rangers, there was really no doubt that 5 Star rancher Harold Frederick would get a pre-roundup meeting scheduled. But despite Frederick's persuasive powers and universal respect, there was, however, a great deal of uncertainty as to just who would show up.

For more than a year now, the St. Clair County ranches and their owners had been at odds with each other, ignited by disputes over water and grazing rights—disputes deliberately stirred up by Lars Viklund.

To Frederick's—and everyone's—surprise, someone from every ranch in the St. Clair County region attended the meeting. Even the Windmill V was represented. Lars Viklund and Casper Longley dared not miss this show. To keep up appearances, Lars had instructed one of his riders, Moose Elkins, to attend and appear to be the new foreman of the River D. Another Viklund rider showed up posing as the foreman for the Half Moon 6.

No one in town except Sheriff Carmichael and Bank

President Ames Wooster was aware that the Half Moon 6 and River D properties were now secretly deeded over to the Väderkvarn Cattle Company. "Väderkvarn" was the Swedish translation for "Windmill." The company was owned by Lars Viklund.

Thanks to Frederick's leadership and persuasive skills, everyone agreed to put aside differences. With the respect he garnered, the decision to accept his proposal seemed to be easy: There was undisputed agreement to start a roundup right away. A date was set.

This important step meant the group could begin immediate discussion of planning their cowhunt. Before attending to business, Frederick had an announcement. "Given the recent, unfortunate events surrounding the W Bar L, we need to all agree that we will round up and set aside any stray W Bar L beef that we might find." He pulled a telegram from his pocket and read from a message that the nephew of Lillian Whitman would be arriving from San Antonio to help with the roundup and keep an eye on any W Bar L interests, at least until the widow's estate could be sorted out.

"As you know, until we start cutting brush, there's no telling where some of these cows have ended up," Frederick said in his concluding remarks to the assembled ranchers. "Might even turn up some of them that was thought to be rustled."

At this turn of events, Longley shot Lars a look, which the big Swede subtly shrugged off. Lars liked the idea of all the ranches being together because he was suspicious of everyone. Having the widow's nephew along was not an issue that concerned him. Besides, having representatives from all ranches sitting right here in this room was providing kindling to his fiery rage.

Bringing down thunder and lightning on these people—right here, right now—would be a glorious end-game for his plan of domination. His beloved Norse gods would be smiling.

Setting aside his smoldering wrath, he contemplated the cold-blooded chess game of vengeance he had set. This roundup could provide an opportunity he had not counted on.

A plan was forming in his evil mind...

Why not use the roundup as the perfect time to move against the 5 Star and destroy the Frederick family? The thought brought a huge grin to his face.

Around him, the room moved to the next item of business, selecting a roundup boss. The head of the roundup was the on-site overseer of the joint enterprise. This boss required having the faith of the participating cattlemen and be known for sound judgment. It was understood that the overseer's authority during the roundup was all but absolute and his instructions were respectfully followed by all.

Rome Seley, the foreman of the 5 Star ranch, was nominated by Rob Faulkner, the owner of the Triple S, and seconded by Moose Elkins to run the roundup. In what could have been a sticking point, the vote, instead, was unanimous. To some surprise, especially Frederick's, Viklund did not disagree with this selection, even going so far as to volunteer the use of his chuckwagon and cook. Casper Longley even looked agreeable to Seley's election. A smiling Harold Frederick also pledged the use of the 5 Star's chuckwagon and cookie. All of the representatives agreed to split the food costs.

With no further discussion, the meeting adjourned. There was much for each spread to organize in the way of riders, remudas and gear—and in a short amount of time.

Riding home after the meeting, Lars declared to Longley, "Figured I have, that the moment has arrived for a move to be made against the 5 Star."

"I wondered why you were so agreeable in there," the gunman said. "You're not going to wait to pick off more of the smaller ranches or swipe 5 Star beef first?"

"Too much of the time it would take, I now see. Frederick, his son, and the foreman will be right there in roundup camp to be eliminated," the big Swede said impassively. "Vulnerable their ranch will be at the same time, yah? I'm to be thinking that you take care of the 5 Star riders in camp. Another group we send against the house. Only women and not many riders there."

"Your son Baldur, Dal Frantze, and the others will be leaving on the drive to New Braunfels. Won't we be thin as well?"

"Who would be the fool crazy enough to come against me?" Lars laughed. "Talk to Mr. Carmichael, I will. Maybe he could provide a gun or two, yah?"

CHAPTER THIRTY-SIX

It was easy for Holt to glean the surprisingly positive news from the roundup meeting. The news was everywhere in town. He sent carefully worded telegraph messages to Captain McCoy and Orion Higbee, informing them that the roundup was on and confirming the forced sale of the Half Moon 6 and River D ranches to Lars Viklund. Orion sent an immediate return response:

SAMUEL HOLTON:

BRANDING RALLY GOOD NEWS.

SET BAIT CAREFULLY.

TRAP & SNARE EXECUTED HERE.

SUBJECTS SOON WILL BE AS WELL.

RIDE CAREFUL P-HEAD.

HIG

With the roundup starting, it came time for Holt to move out to the 5 Star in preparation for posing as a ranch rider. He decided to gather enough gumption and profess his true feelings to Laudie Kate.

He planned to tell her, then sneak back to the bungalow to collect his things and retrieve Tag before heading out to his new job at the 5 Star. He daydreamed the conversation with Laudie Kate would go well. On one hand, he was soaring with joy at the thought of this beautiful woman professing similar attraction to him and on the other, he carried a leaden sense of doubt that she would never, ever settle for him.

Being mid-morning, he guessed that Laudie Kate would either be in Miguel Navarro's office or the main part of the saloon or maybe upstairs straightening up rooms. As usual, he was able to enter the Blue Sky unseen via the back door. Leaving Tag behind in the bungalow aided his concealed movement. A simple knock at Navarro's locked office went unanswered. A brief, stealthy peek into the saloon revealed the owner regaling two customers finishing a late breakfast at a table. Two drovers stood quietly at the bar.

Holt moved as inconspicuously as possible along the shadows hugging the walls leading to the staircase. He moved quickly and quietly up toward the rooms.

Laudie Kate and Evie were cleaning the very same room he had recuperated in after he was shot. As they changed bedsheets, they were speaking about Laudie Kate's feelings for Holt.

"He's so smitten with ya," Evie said, smiling as she wadded up the old bedclothes.

"It's sweet someone like him could be so…so…shy and tongue-tied," Laudie Kate acknowledged.

"So, why don't *you* tell 'im how ya feel?"

"About the time I think I'm going to have the nerve to say something, I hear my mother…"

"You have those talks with yer mama in yer head too? I think 'bout bringin' Moose ta my parents' house for 'em all ta meet."

"Oh my god, can you imagine? My mama would exclaim…"

Holt heard their voices coming into the hallway from the open room. He crept closer to the door in order to determine a good time to interrupt their conversation. Their quiet conversation suddenly took a turn as they spoke back and forth in mocking voices.

Laudie Kate continued, *"What kind of life could a woman have with a man like Holt Corrigan?"*

Evie chimed in, *"How could you consider such a thing"*

"What kind of life together would there be?"

"He's a man of the gun."

"A man like him is always drawing danger to him."

"Such a man could be killed at any time."

"How could someone ever be with Holt, wasn't he an outlaw?"

"What a silly question to be thinkin'."

They both guffawed at their imaginary parental banter.

Holt wasn't laughing. All he heard were two women talking about why he was unlovable, not two friends joking about broaching the subject with their judgmental mothers. Stinging hurt and resentment rose red hot from his collar. He turned and left the hallway as quickly and quietly as he came.

Laudie Kate spoke, returning to her normal tone of voice. "My mother would say all of that, but I'd be happy to tell her and Daddy it would be easy to be with someone like him…forever."

"He's in a dangerous line o' work. That part's true," Evie countered. "He could find his end in an instant."

"If that's to be, I'd rather spend a short time with him than a lifetime without him."

"I've told Moose pretty much th' same thing." Being best friends, Evie couldn't help herself and had shared the fact that Moose was actually a Ranger with Laudie Kate.

"At first, my head kept telling me to not lose myself in a man again," Laudie Kate said. "Then I thought Holt might get scared and run off. It's what I would have done before meeting him. Now? My heart tells me to hang on to him with all I've got," she said wistfully.

"Is that why ya still have his hat?"

"You're going to laugh, but I wanted to find a new cardinal feather for his hatband. It broke because of me…" Laudie Kate held up her hand and paused. "Wait…" she said, leaning out the door, looking up and down the hallway.

"Didja hear somethin'?"

"I don't know…it just felt…like…someone…was there." She frowned. "Oh well, probably something from downstairs."

Holt had hurried down the stairs and hastily retraced his steps through the edge of the saloon and out the back door. The fresh air did nothing to cool his rising anger. Well, Holt, she made that pretty clear, didn't she? How stupid are you to think a woman like Laudie Kate could love you?

Outrage, grief, shame, pain. Emotions ran through him like the fanning of a pistol. His anger-filled thoughts raged like a forest fire, but anguish grabbed at his heart as if it was torn beating from his chest.

At the bungalow, he hurriedly stuffed the rest of his gear into saddlebags, tossing a piece of jerky to Tag. "Eat up, boy, we're leaving," he advised his companion. "We don't need anybody but us, right? We'll take care of each other." His panther-inlaid Russian Smith & Wessons were carefully stowed away in his saddlebags. He did not want to draw attention as *that* Ranger. He was swiftly transitioning from Holt Corrigan, lawman, into Samuel Holton, wrangler and man with a past. His old Confederate outlaw alias was perfectly aligned with the darkness he was feeling and the job he had ahead of him.

Harold Frederick was supposed to have left a 5 Star mount for his new employee, "Samuel Holton" in the Stebbins livery. Holt headed there now to pick it up. It was time to leave.

"Let's ride, Tag. I'm sure you're the only one they'll miss at the Blue Sky."

CHAPTER THIRTY-SEVEN

Heading west from Stebbins, Holt and Tag made their way to the 5 Star ranch, Holt's "new" employer. He knew the way having ridden this trail recently, with Orion, when they presented the roundup portion of their plan to Harold Frederick.

Overhead, a red hawk watched the rider and dog, sailing on unseen billows of wind. The hooves of his horse made soft pushing sounds in the long grass, almost melodic, if Holt was listening. But he wasn't. The rolling hills that held the pastureland in place were but a backdrop to the heartache relentlessly gnawing at him. His attention was taken away by the thoughts of Laudie Kate that repeated in his head. The scent of her surrounded his mind. Whenever he closed his eyes, she was there. But so was her voice. And the words he heard her say... *"What kind of life could a woman have with a man like Holt Corrigan? What kind of life together would there be? How could someone ever be with Holt..."*

"Stop!" he heard himself holler, trying to chase away the anguish.

Nearby, Tag stopped in his tracks, looking up at Holt in obedience and confusion.

"I'm sorry, boy. Not you." Holt frowned. He rummaged in his coat pocket and tossed the dog a small hunk of jerky. "We don't need her, do we?"

He tugged at a well-worn, wide-brimmed cavalry Stetson that he had found in a closet at the bungalow. An old duster trail coat left at the Blue Sky was rolled up on the back of his saddle. His regular trousers, leather rancher vest and brush jacket completed the outfit. If no one recognized him in short hair and a beard, Holt figured no one would notice his clothes. He wore an old, converted Navy Colt revolver in a simple holster around his waist. A lot of drovers didn't even carry a pistol or use one very well. The riders who did carry guns wore them for protection from things like rattlesnakes or a stampeding cow. Drover alias or not, Holt was not going into this without a pistol or his Winchester, tucking the rifle comfortably into his saddle scabbard. If need be, his Russian Smith & Wessons were hidden in his saddlebags.

The buckskin that Frederick had left at the livery for him listened in to the conversation, waiting for further instruction from his rider. Even with his preoccupation with Laudie Kate's stinging words, he had noticed this horse was spirited, yet responsive. He kicked it into an easy lope, soon reaching the sturdy, gurgling stream that indicated he was drawing nearer to his destination.

"C'mon, boy," he called to Tag, "let's go meet some new friends!"

Before long, Holt, with his new look and old alias, was shaking hands with his temporary boss, Harold Frederick. In addition to a necessary part of his cattle business, Frederick knew this roundup was a high-stakes ploy to lure Lars Viklund into revealing another element of his rustling scheme and helping the Rangers catch him in the act. He was poker-faced about his role in the plan.

Ever since learning about the results of the pre-roundup meeting, Holt had thought Viklund's docile acceptance of every single part of the arrangements felt oddly out of place. "So, Lars didn't speak out against *anything*?" Holt asked Frederick. "He didn't offer one of his sons or even Longley to be in charge?"

"He voted for Rome as roundup boss. Without hesitation. Offered his cook and chuckwagon too."

Holt shook his head. "Awfully cooperative. Something doesn't ring quite right with that. Does it to you?"

"No, it doesn't. Not exactly sure what to think of it though. I wanted to discuss it with you."

"I saw too much of that damn war and fought too many Comanches and Kiowas. I can feel when something's going to spring," Holt said. "Harold, I know you've seen it all too. But Lars is up to something and it might not have anything to do with what's going on at the roundup."

Frederick nodded, a serious look on his face.

"In fact, that's it!" Holt exclaimed, keeping his voice quiet. He pulled Frederick further aside. "The ruse will be there, but the clash will be here. He'll think you're vulnerable."

"That makes sense. We'll stay ready, here, at the house," Frederick agreed. "I can stay behind. Viklund won't expect that."

"Good idea. We faced something similar not too long ago at my family's ranch, the Rafter C," Holt continued. "We found it handy to station a few men with rifles on the roof. Provides a good view and intruders won't suspect it. I imagine if anything is going to happen, Viklund will wait until a couple of days into the roundup."

"You've seen to it we have five extra guns," Frederick said. "Mrs. Whitman and her crew will be good help." Then he turned serious. "I'll be arming my women too."

"Anyone say anything about the W Bar L folks being here?" Holt asked.

"Not that I've heard. My men have all been too busy getting ready for the roundup, plus the widow and her crew have kept a low profile. For all anyone knows, they could be my wife's family on a visit." Frederick reached out and patted Holt's arm. "Come on, Mr. Holton, let me introduce you to who you'll be taking orders from," he said, smiling.

The pair walked through the spacious ranch yard toward an enormous barn. A group of men were clustered near two large corrals, both filled with horses. They were focusing their attention on a stout-looking man with close-cropped black hair and a thick, bushy mustache. His worn, dusty batwing chaps bespoke countless days on the trail and in the brush. His light-blue work shirt was dark with sweat. A beat-up, low-crowned Chinaco sombrero hung along his back by a stampede strap. When he saw Frederick approach, he excused himself from the men and walked to meet his boss.

"Rome, I mentioned adding some more help in time for roundup," Frederick began. "Say hello to Samuel Holton, from down near Cassidy County. He was friends with my boys, Mark and John. I know it's kind of last minute, but I also know you'll need the help out there. Holton here is a good hand."

"Pleasure, Samuel. Name's Rome Seley." The foreman, slightly taller than Holt, stuck out a tanned, calloused hand. The two shook hands and took quick stock of one another. "Were you part of Mark and John's unit with Terry?" the foreman asked.

"Friends, from before the war," Holt answered. He had thought about his story, deciding to reveal bits and pieces of his actual history, like during his bank visit. Silka had always taught them not to lie, it was too hard to remember what you made up. "I was at Sabine."

"I fought with Longstreet," Seley replied.

"Seems like a lifetime ago."

"That it does," Rome nodded. "Is this your partner?" he said, indicating Tag, who was playing with the two 5 Star ranch dogs.

"I hope you don't mind," Holt said earnestly. "Knows his place around cattle. Helpful at rooting out the young ones that don't want to come out of the brush. And he's a helluva night watchman too."

"He sounds right handy to have in camp."

"I understand if you don't want him around," Holt said. "Don't let my relationship with Mr. Frederick color how you treat me. My orders will come from you."

"'Preciate that. What's he go by?"

"He answers to 'Dog' mostly."

Rome nodded with a smile before changing the subject. "We got a lot of work ahead of us. If Mr. Frederick says you'll do, that's good 'nough for me. 'Dog' too. C'mon, I'll introduce you to our wrangler, Purd. Get you set up with a string."

Purd Libby was a compact man whose face looked to

be a map of wrinkles and cigar smoke. His spare, slender body and bow-legged stance was honed by a lifetime spent in the saddle. Just how long that lifetime had been was anybody's guess. The 5 Star wrangler had forgotten more about horses than most men even knew. Holt would hear the other riders joke that there wasn't an animal on earth that Purd couldn't throw a saddle on and ride.

"Holton," Purd said through eyes perpetually squinted by the sun and an ever-present cigar. "Mr. Frederick said you'd be joinin' us today. Said you were from Cassidy County. A ranchin' family."

Holt chuckled. "You got me pegged, Mr. Libby."

"Mr. Libby, hell, you call me 'Purd' or 'sonuvabitch.'" He took the cigar out of his mouth and spit. "*Mister* Libby. Hah! Whattaya like to ride, Holton?"

"I like a steady attitude. Good belly. Strong, muscled. One that's intelligent, thinks first, then reacts. Quickly. Doesn't waste energy."

The wrangler eyed Holt with an appreciative gleam and said, "Let's find you five or six you might like."

The two worked their way through the larger of the two corrals, each man with rope in his hands. When Holt saw a horse he was interested in, he looked into its eyes, making sure they were bright and clear and alert; then he checked out the health of its hooves and cleanliness of its legs, no lumps, bumps or heat. His attention to detail did not go unnoticed by Purd. It took a while, but Holt selected two bays and a couple of duns, which they put lead ropes on and led them to the second corral.

"That buckskin I rode in on should go too," Holt added. "I like his stamina. And fire."

"Fire, eh?" Purd said, his eyes opening ever so widely. "I got the best ropin' an' cuttin' horse here." He pointed at a grulla standing near a couple of paint mustangs.

"If he's all that, why hasn't he been added to someone's string already?" Holt wondered.

"Well, Holton, there are some who say he's mean," the wrangler said with a grin.

"Mean? That's not a good quality for a remuda or a herd of dumb cows. Sounds like a bad recipe for getting thrown or starting a stampede."

"Oh, it's a sweetheart to other animals. This one's mean to anyone who tries sittin' on it an' ain't *suitable*."

Holt's expression was unconvinced.

"What I'm sayin' is it don't suffer fools gladly," Purd explained, removing his cigar and spitting again. "Won't let jus' anyone saddle an' ride it. But if'n this one knows you're worthy, *an' he can tell*, it'll do all the work. An absolute darlin'. You jus' sit an' enjoy the scenery. If he's gonna be trubble, I wouldn' recommend 'im. Hell, I wouldn' have it on th' property."

Holt nodded. "I've got a good friend who likes to claim that sometimes you need a horse with a little more fire than might be safe for some," he recalled. "One like that will keep you on your toes. He says it's kind of like women. The good ones should scare the hell outta you sometimes."

At that, Purd howled with laughter, holding his cigar in one hand and slapping his thigh with the other, producing a fair amount of dust from his worn trousers.

Rome watched the interaction between Purd and this new rider with a smile. He knew his boss, Mr. Frederick, wouldn't burden him with a problem, but it was good to get independent confirmation. The old wrangler and his cigar could sniff out a greenhorn or troublemaker a mile away. These two were carrying on as if longtime friends.

"Well, Purd, you sold me," Holt said smiling. "Let's move that grulla over to the holding corral. I'll want to tack 'em all up and ride 'em a little. They need to get a feel for me too."

"Now you're talkin'." The old wrangler grinned.

CHAPTER THIRTY-EIGHT

The morning the roundup began found the main camp forming and organizing quickly, resembling a mobilized army bivouac. As agreed upon in the pre-meeting, the first rally point for everyone was the River D ranch. Its grazing land would be worked first.

St. Clair County was home to seven cattle operations, each spread out around the town of Stebbins. The roundup would systematically comb each of their grazing lands. Lars Viklund had volunteered to have his huge ranch, the Windmill V, be the last property worked.

An oddly magnanimous offer that did not escape the notice of Holt Corrigan.

Starting with the River D, the roundup would work its way counterclockwise through the county. Next would be the Triple S; followed by the Flying G; then the largest operation, the 5 Star; after that the W Bar L; then the Half Moon 6; and ending with the Viklund's Windmill V.

All of the cowboys, assembling in the pale morning light, were a little tentative at first having not worked a cooperative roundup in some time. Ever since tensions had risen and owners became wary of one another, each ranch had held its own separate cow hunts. Care was taken during those times to not trespass across land boundaries. Stray cattle were carefully shooed toward property where they belonged.

With the assured, confident nature of 5 Star's owner, Harold Frederick, persuading his fellow ranchers to come together, this roundup had become a reality. Ranchers knew the benefits of such a cooperative venture and had decided to take a chance. It had worked that way before, when they all had gotten along.

Frederick was in camp to give a friendly welcome to participating ranch owners as well as each ranch's foreman and riders. In his opening greeting, Frederick introduced the assembled cattlemen to Larry Malloy, the nephew of W Bar L owner, widow Lillian Whitman.

According to recent stories, Whitman had suddenly abandoned her ranch. Murmurs throughout the county speculated as to where she had gone; the only fact people knew for sure was that rustlers had appeared to pretty much wipe her out. Frederick reminded everyone that they all had agreed to gather and set aside any stray W Bar L beef that might be found.

The nephew, a thin, bespectacled man with a scrubby goatee, seemed nearer a minister or bookkeeper and thoroughly out of place at this rough cowboy camp. He was there simply to represent his aunt and all W Bar L interests.

Holt, in his Samuel Holton guise, eyed this slender relative of Mrs. Whitman with interest and looked across the camp to give Moose Elkins a barely perceptible nod, which the huge man returned.

"I wish each and every one here a safe and successful roundup," Frederick continued, winding up his welcoming remarks. "I have business that requires me to return to my home, so I now turn everything over to the capable hands of the man you all elected roundup boss, Rome Seley."

Christer Viklund, Lars's youngest son, listened to the introduction and whispered to his father, "What's this all about? Frederick's going home?"

"Relax you should. This changes nothing to our plans," Lars responded quietly. "The W Bar L is in our grasp and soon will the 5 Star be."

Seley, the 5 Star's foreman, took charge.

The chuck wagons had already been set in place with his instruction. Fires were being stoked for cooking, branding, and farrier work. He directed wranglers to an area where long ropes could be tied between trees to hold the ranch remudas not being ridden. A sturdy pole corral was being thrown up to hold any calves and stray stock that were about to be branded. Temporary pens for other cattle were being staked out.

The foreman of the ranch the group would be working on coordinated with Seley on anything riders should know about the land. Things like creeks with quicksand, pitch seeps, big gullies were important to know.

Moose Elkins had been spying on Lars Viklund for several months, infiltrating the ranch as a rider for Viklund's Windmill V ranch. For the roundup, however, he was instructed by Lars to pretend that he was the River D's foreman, keeping up the masquerade that the ranch was independently owned, that Lars hadn't forced out the River D's owners. He had ridden River D land enough that he could provide information to Seley without raising any doubt.

Information in-hand, Seley next sent men out in groups, riders from different ranches mixed together, with orders to cover a general area. The plan was to cover as much ground as possible and to round up every head of beef that did not have a brand or had strayed off its home property.

Soon, cowboys were pushing reluctant cattle out of ravines and brush, and over hills for sorting and branding.

The foreman from the Flying G helped coordinate the branding operation. It was a time to brand and count, readying herds for wintertime. Riders worked hard to bring in the animals. Other sweaty men worked steadily and quickly over hot fires, laying hot iron to unmarked calves and cows. The mothers were allowed to hang around the calf corral as long as they weren't unruly. New calves were branded with the same mark as their mothers. Any unbranded strays were divided evenly among all the ranches.

Holt made sure he was in the small working group with Rome Seley and Frederick's son, Luke. Holt wanted to make sure Seley was comfortable knowing that Mr. Frederick's word about "Samuel Holton" being a good hand was reliable. He also wanted to be around in order to protect Luke and Rome from anything Viklund might try.

The young Ranger and his dog jumped right into the work, combing heavy thickets for cattle embedded in the thick growth. It did not take long for the 5 Star foreman to realize that Samuel Holton and his dog were top hands to have around.

End of day brought tired cowboys and horses to the main camp. They dismounted far from the gathered herds as possible. A horse freed of its rider might shake the saddle and scare the cattle. Wranglers and riders inspected their mounts for any wear and tear.

After carefully checking their ropes and tack, some riders found a nearby creek to soak their feet. Others gathered with friends and new acquaintances to talk horses and boots. Stories were swapped about the day's adventures of wrecks and near-wrecks.

Rome Seley was demonstrating that the choice of him being chosen roundup boss was a good one. He assigned camp and herd watches for the night and announced that the base operation would move tomorrow after breakfast to land closer to the next ranch, the Triple S.

Holt stood off to the side of camp, making sure Tag was free of briars and stickers. He briefly locked eyes with Moose, each giving the other a quick nod of assurance. Holt then looked across the main campfire and spotted the widow's nephew, dirty from head to toe and blowing on a hot mug of coffee. He was as filthy as all the other cowboys were, but he still seemed out of place. Holt had avoided the not-so-quiet jokes about the stranger, but he still had to snicker to himself at the sight of the diminutive man.

———

The first night passed peacefully. The gentle morning breeze would normally bring a wonderful fragrance of spring, but early pre-dawn in roundup camp brought its own pungent aroma as well as activity, dust, and noise. Cattle, horses, and men were pushed together in an organized mass, even if the animals sometimes did not like being pushed or organized.

More likely than as not, a brief morning outburst would occur near a picket line. A horse with a belly full of food and a night of rest might unleash pent-up energy or resist a saddled rider with a buck or crow-hop to punctuate its feelings. Such occasional blow-ups were normal for horses but concerning for anyone trying to keep a large number of cattle quiet and calm. Sudden noise or movement was incredibly upsetting to normally docile cows.

This morning, the W Bar L nephew, Larry Malloy, happened to latch onto a horse that decided now was not the time it wanted to be ridden. The dun gave a half-buck and tried to rear. The scrawny man stayed solid in the saddle.

"Okay, bud." Malloy spoke calmly and firmly, pushing the animal forward using his legs to add pressure and keep the horse's head up. "We're not going to do this. This isn't the place to get silly." The dun started to rear again, then crow-hopped sideways. Malloy encouraged it to walk. The horse hesitated, then started moving. Another attempt to rear and another crow-hop was met with firm handling by the nephew as he guided the dun away from the picket line and holding areas for cattle, and away from further trouble. Gradually, the horse's head dropped, indicating it was comfortable with a man on its back.

"By golly, that's a hossman right there," wrangler Purd Libby exclaimed to Holt.

The young Ranger was gathering his first mount of the day from Purd's picket line. The old wrangler convinced Holt that the grulla he was so proud of was a "morning horse." He chuckled at the grizzled man's reasoning as he led the grulla away from the picket area. He did like this horse, and fortunately, the feelings were mutual.

Holt watched the outburst with Malloy's horse, not liking any flare-up this close to large numbers of cattle. He was relieved at the savvy the nephew of Mrs. Whitman had shown.

"Watch yourself around all these guys bigger'n you," Holt reminded Tag. Most horses did not mind being around a dog, but sometimes could kick at something they did not like or that startled them.

He had just laid a stirrup fender over the saddle seat and was beginning to tighten the grulla's cinch when another rider's horse acted up. The frisky bay actually succeeded in freeing itself from its cowboy and trotted quickly away from its picket line. This second clamor triggered commotion and uneasiness from the nearby cattle herd.

Suddenly, loud scuffling noises, accompanied by louder curses, erupted from the branding fire. An enormous, unbranded young bull got startled by the outburst at the picket line and broke loose from a rope restraint. It was charging wildly, swinging its horns at anything in its way.

The cowhand bringing the huge animal to the fire went flying when the beast spooked and broke free. The bull spun and smashed into another brander who was slow to get out of its way. Unfettered, the longhorn shook its enormous head and stamped and pawed at the ground, then bounded in the direction of Holt and Tag.

"Run, Tag, run!" Holt hollered, forgetting he was not

supposed to call the dog by his usual name. The dog scurried away as Holt drew his Winchester.

The beast was now thundering directly at Holt and closing fast. The grulla was holding steady, not yet startled by the imminent danger.

Holt brought up his Winchester and fired. An instant after his shot a powerful rifle crack came from behind him, followed immediately by another.

The bull grunted and jerked sideways. Holt levered a new cartridge and fired again as the enormous beast continued to rumble toward him. Another shot from behind Holt rang out as well. Now, the enraged animal looked as though an invisible rope stretched taut and abruptly tripped its front legs. It staggered and fell, heaved two big breaths and was still.

Holt took his own deep breath and glanced around. Shaken, alarmed cowboys looked wide-eyed back at him. Holt shook his head in relief. A mad steer like that could trample or gore a man or a horse and do horrible damage. He finally looked behind him. Still in his saddle, with a smoking Henry rifle in his hands, sat Larry Malloy, the nephew who now more than fit in.

"I guess we're having beef tonight," the diminutive man said with a smile. "Courtesy of my aunt."

Word quickly spread throughout the day that the W Bar L nephew could handle a horse and a rifle after all.

CHAPTER THIRTY-NINE

The roundup was progressing successfully, the spooked steer breaking loose the only mar on the operation thus far. Two riders had been bruised by the crazed animal, but neither was hurt seriously. Only one of them needed a day's mending time before being able to continue with his work. Even more importantly, none of the other livestock had reacted negatively to the outbursts.

Everyone had agreed that 5 Star rider Samuel Holton and the W Bar L nephew Larry Malloy had saved a lot of cowboys from getting hurt or worse. They also were very appreciative of the meal their quick thinking and quicker shooting provided. Even on a roundup, fresh beef was not usually on the menu.

During that good-tasting meal, Lars Viklund had approached roundup boss Seley to ask if it was all right if a few of his Windmill V riders took the next day to bring a large group of their rounded-up cattle back to his rangeland.

"Relieve pressure on the corrals by driving our gathered herd home we can," Viklund reasoned. "Less cattle for your camp to shepherd, yah?"

"We're in a good routine, Lars. The cattle hunt's going smoothly, we're moving closer to the third ranch, the Flying G," Seley responded.

"Only a day my men would miss. Back by morning, they'd be. Ready to work again."

Seley was wary of upsetting the big Swede, but the idea of thinning their gathered herd did have some merit, so he agreed to Viklund's request.

The next morning, after the usual pre-dawn breakfast for the entire camp, Lars gathered a small group of his riders that his foreman Casper Longley had handpicked. Most Viklund men working at the Windmill V and now at the Half Moon 6 and River D were not cattle drovers, nearly all were outlaws on wanted posters throughout Texas and the surrounding region. The hardened crew met at the Viklund picket line, away from prying eyes and ears.

"Two of you, Johnny and Smitty, be taking our Windmill cattle back to the ranch. Handle it you can, yah?" Lars began. "The rest, after you're out of sight, across Flying G land you will ride. Carmichael's Deputy Mercer you'll be meeting."

Longley spoke up, "You'll rendezvous with the deputy at the crossroads where the big creek branches north and east. Davy, you know the spot. Meet Mercer there."

Although the men nodded in agreement, one of them asked, "I thought Sheriff Carmichael was going to be part of this."

"Carmichael and I agreed that visible he should be," Lars explained, not entirely appreciative at being questioned. "From his office, handle anything in town he shall. Plus, an obvious alibi he will have for what happens out here."

"There's five of you and the deputy," Longley broke in, changing the subject. "That will be plenty. The 5 Star isn't expecting what's coming."

"Around here, you must look," Lars explained. "Most of their riders are right over there. How many they have left who aren't here, we do not know, but it can't be many," Lars added.

The men listened intently to their boss.

"Put an end to as many of their riders as you can, but with Harold Frederick and his family, you must *döda dem alla*. Understand?"

Not all the riders looked as though they understood.

Longley explained, "There's Frederick, his wife and two daughters at the house. Do what you want with the women first, but make sure that none of the Fredericks survive. *Döda dem alla. Kill 'em all*. Got it?"

Lars nodded at the men. "Sure to be back by morning, all of you, yah?"

CHAPTER FORTY

D usk was turning the surrounding yard of the 5 Star ranch house into a vivid tapestry of earth tones and blue sky hues. This was usually Harold Frederick's favorite time of day. The brilliant color and peacefulness that came from a setting sun brought to his mind the rich fullness of life—the bitter with the sweet—that he appreciated.

Ever since the roundup started and most of his riders left to work the cow hunt, Frederick had not been able to enjoy the beautiful array of colors each evening brought.

He had taken the caution of Holt Corrigan to heart. The young Ranger had an ominous feeling that Lars Viklund would use the roundup as an opportunity to escalate his plan of forceful acquisition of surrounding county ranches. The rancher had to admit that his hackles had been raised as well. No stranger to armed conflict, Frederick shared Holt's gut reaction that an attack was coming.

When the roundup became reality and Viklund went along with everything so agreeably, the certainty of the

Swede's treachery had hit Holt like a lightning bolt—Lars would use the roundup to target the 5 Star. Holt's instincts were put on alert at the inevitability of danger. He believed it was his panther and bear spirits that guided him to hatch a high-stakes plan. Frederick had agreed completely with the strategy.

The tactics began with Lillian Whitman, appearing to abandon her struggling W Bar L ranch. The widow, her foreman, and her remaining three riders secretly moved to Frederick's 5 Star spread. Sending more than half of his own riders to the roundup would have left a very thin line of protection for Frederick. Adding these five guns was a comforting increase of strength.

After he returned from the roundup, Frederick kept one lookout on the roof of the ranch house during the light of day, when an attack was unlikely. Everyone else went about their daily chores heavily armed. At near dusk and through the night until sunrise, however, the protocol changed. Frederick, using his military experience, deployed the 5 Star defenders accordingly. The three W Bar L riders were all stationed on the house rooftop, spread out, covering the entire ranch yard from above. They were instructed to remain vigilant and out of sight.

Only a few days after the start of roundup, a familiar face showed up in the afternoon and hallooed the 5 Star ranch house. The smiling countenance of Texas Ranger Orion Higbee rode into the ranch yard. Riding beside him was another Ranger, Dal Frantze. Both explained that their part of the plan, a reckoning in New Braunfels had ended successfully.

"Mr. Holton suggested you could use an extra coupla guns here," Orion said with a smile. Even though Holt was somewhere out in roundup camp, because others were listening in, Orion took care to not reveal who the new 5 Star rider actually was.

Adding the Rangers to their defense gave everyone at the 5 Star a tremendous boost of confidence. In addition to the W Bar L riders on the rooftop, Orion and Dal now took positions on the first floor with Frederick. Lillian Whitman, along with Frederick's wife and two daughters were placed at second floor windows. Big Jeff, the widow's foreman, would not leave his boss's side, so he posted himself upstairs with her and the other women.

The remaining five 5 Star riders who were not working the roundup, had moved their bunks into the large barn near the ranch house. Their horses were kept saddled night and day, ready to be ridden at a moment's notice. Ever the tactician, Frederick had them standing by as mounted troops. Their orders were to ride hard to the sound of the guns.

Orion and Dal agreed with Frederick that any attack would likely come at first or last light. Now they must wait. For what they could only guess was coming.

The first night and morning with the Rangers present passed nervously, but quietly. Those on all-night watch got rest when they could during the day. Most of the usual ranch chores were accomplished, in case scouting eyes were observing them.

Late afternoon shadows once again crept across the yard. The 5 Star defenders coolly took their positions. It would be completely dark in a couple of hours.

Orion took a deep breath and rolled his shoulders, easing away tension. Something caught his eye. "Hey, there's someone movin' down there by your tree line," he whispered loudly, levering his Henry rifle.

"Yeah, looks like four, maybe five, hard to tell," Dal acknowledged, readying his rifle toward an open window. "Hard to say. They're fanning out now."

"Mr. Frederick," Orion continued. "In case they haven't seen those bastards already, let 'em know upstairs we've got intruders at the front fence. Tell 'em to quietly let the rooftop know."

"An' no one shoots till *we* do down here!" Dal urged.

Frederick alerted Big Jeff and the defenders on the second floor. His low, calm voice instructed them to keep an eye on the flanks and the back of the house.

Unseen by the attackers, the protectors of the Frederick ranch hunkered down and waited, watching in every direction, from all parts of the house.

"Looks like a few wanna closer look," Orion observed as the assailants approached from the front. "There's three at the yard fence."

"When do you want to welcome these lunkheads?" Dal asked.

"Easy now," Orion ordered with a steady voice. "We wait. The closer they get, the bigger the surprise."

"Bigger targets too," Dal chimed in.

"Not too close though," cautioned Frederick. "If they get too near, the guns on the roof can't help."

Suddenly, a line of rifle fire from the Viklund riders exploded from the fence line. Orange flame tore into the silence, roaring in the dusk and peppering the house with lead.

"There's our invitation! Now!" Orion hollered.

Gunshots from the 5 Star snarled back. Silhouettes of the invaders could be seen taking surprised cover.

One figure by the fence moved slower than the others. Fast action from Orion's Henry pumped bullets into the intruder. His body slammed against a stacked-rock fencepost. The man shuddered and slid to the ground in a strange heap.

Another assailant hiding behind the post, was startled by the body slamming into it and showed himself a moment too long. A withering volley from the rooftop caught the attacker all at once, suspending his body momentarily before he jolted backward, riddled with holes.

To left of the house, behind a large post oak, a heavyset Viklund gunman aimed his rifle at the figures on the roof. The return fire from atop the house and its first and second floors was intense, but so far, the tree was protecting him as he shoved new loads into his gun. The outlaw leaned around the tree and squeezed off two shots at a second-floor window. The shattering of glass was followed by a woman's scream.

On the far right, a dark-haired man in a fancy cowhide vest was concentrating shots at the first floor window from where Orion was shooting. Ranger Frantze readjusted his fire and levered three quick shots at the man. Two of the bullets caught the intruder in the chest. The man reacted to the impacts, half-standing from his concealment. One of the shots from the second floor caught him square in the forehead. The fancy-vested outlaw awkwardly jerked his leg straight out in front of him, then fell straight back like he'd been pole-axed, moving no more.

Without warning, mounted 5 Star riders charged from the barn. Two groups split to ride around the house. Three horsemen rode for the front, two circled behind, all with guns drawn.

The 5 Star men racing around the back encountered a

Viklund invader who had slunk his way near the small spring house where meat, butter, and milk were stored. The trespasser tried to force open the door, but was cut down before he could hide inside. One of the 5 Star men emptied his pistol into the unmoving form before riding on.

The heavyset invader hiding behind the tree, turned toward the sound of horses rumbling directly at him and swung his rifle just as two pistol shots caught him in the shoulder and belly. The stocky Viklund gunman was spun forcefully. He groaned and collapsed to the ground. Two of the riders fired additional rounds into his body as they raced by.

The three 5 Star riders completed their charge around the front of the house and united with the two that had ventured out behind. They continued to gallop in a widening circle around the ranch house.

Silence took over. No more shots rang out from invaders. The 5 Star defenders were wary but had no immediate targets.

Orion and Dal shoved new cartridges into their rifles and waited. Frederick, hearing the earlier scream, ran upstairs to check where his wife and daughters were posted.

On the second floor, W Bar L foreman Big Jeff hollered to his riders on the roof, "Stay alert! This ain't over!" He cautioned the women stationed with him to use this quiet time to reload their weapons.

Frederick returned to the first floor, reporting that all was well upstairs. One of his daughters had reacted in fright when a window shattered next to her.

"Cover us," Orion said. "We'll have a look-see." The two Rangers slowly opened the door and crept out onto the front porch, taking cover behind chairs. Frederick posted himself in a window next to the door.

Orion called to the 5 Star mounted riders, "Comb the tree line. They've got horses somewhere, probably with guards. This might not be all of 'em."

Just then, a Viklund killer who had managed to avoid the onslaught of bullets, stirred and stood up. He had crawled close to the house, then watched in horror the carnage of his fellow gang. He sprang from his hiding place and dashed away to the safety of the fence.

"Don't shoot! Let him go!" Frederick hollered.

Orion who had leveled his Henry, responded, "If you don't thin 'em out now, you'll be duckin' their bullets again later."

Three shots from Ranger Frantze's rifle rang out almost as one. Dust flew from the man's coat as bullets blasted into him, sending the outlaw sprawling.

The Rangers held their covered position from the porch, awaiting further attack. The second floor and rooftop guardians stayed alert. Time passed slowly. Shadows deepened into evening. Soon, two of the 5 Star riders rode up from beyond the fence, ponying six horses.

"We found these down by the cottonwoods," one rider hollered at the house. "They're all carrying Windmill V brands. No sign of any other men or mounts."

Soon after, the remaining three 5 Star riders returned from checking the property in back of the ranch house with a report of no other intruders. One of the riders, however, was bent over in the saddle, obviously hurt.

"What happened to him?" Frantze hollered.

"Rattlesnake spooked his horse and threw him. I think he broke his arm," one of the riders answered.

"Viklund sent vipers an' a real snake is the only thing that hurt us," Orion mused.

Almost as soon as it started, the attempted raid was over.

Orion and Dal jumped down from the porch and cautiously approached the downed Viklund outlaws. Frantze pumped an extra shot into each of the bodies, just to make sure.

The last body they approached, the one on the far right with the fancy vest, was rolled over with a flick of Orion's boot.

"This is Sheriff Carmichael's deputy," Orion noted grimly. "The bastard who shot Holt."

"Do you think this is all he sent to take down the Fredericks?" Frantze asked. "Six?"

"I'm not surprised. He's an arrogant bastard," Orion said. "I'd say these bogholes were told it was only Frederick an' his women plus a few riders. Counted on surprisin' Frederick an' scarin' the hell outta everyone. I'm sure they were ordered to kill all of the Fredericks, leavin' the way clear for Lars to grab up the 5 Star for himself."

"That means Luke Frederick, their foreman, and their men back at the roundup are also targets," Frantze noted. "And Holt."

Orion nodded. "He knows."

CHAPTER FORTY-ONE

T he next dawn found tired men at roundup camp already stirring, drinking coffee, and alternately planning and cursing the day. Roundup boss Rome Seley wanted one group to go with him to check the remaining Triple S land for strays prior to moving the entire operation to the Flying G and the outskirts of the 5 Star.

Holt had noticed Lars Viklund's send-off of men the day before. His panther spirit prickled with the sense that Seley, Luke, and the rest of the 5 Star men here in camp were now in danger. Holt suggested that he and Luke Frederick go with Seley this morning, letting the rest of the roundup crew move on. A quick glance from Holt prompted Moose Elkins to volunteer to go with Seley's little group as well. The two disguised Rangers would do what they could to protect these two main 5 Star riders.

Casper Longley immediately liked Seley's idea, especially with Moose going along with them. He spoke up, reporting that he was certain some cattle had worked their way down into a long line of draws on Triple S property to the northeast. He noted that the buffalograss was thick there, with heavy trees and brush too, making it hard to see. Longley said he thought that Seley would find some late-born unbranded calves and their mothers, but also that it made sense for the rest of the roundup to move on.

Rome acknowledged Longley's stated assessment. He announced that his small group would be the one to comb the last of the Triple S land, then handed out the remainder of the rider assignments and gave instructions to the cooks where to set up the new camp for the night.

As Seley finished his business, Longley casually approached his boss, Lars Viklund. He whispered that he knew there would be stray cattle for the 5 Star's foreman and Frederick's son to find because his Windmill V team discovered them yesterday and left them there.

"They'll be preoccupied working those beeves way back in the brush," Longley hissed. "Ambushing them will be a piece of cake."

"While camp is moving, expecting I am to hear from Deputy Mercer that the 5 Star has fallen," Lars noted.

"Thought they'd be back by now," Longley said.

"No worry to be had. The deputy and his group will be back in time to help us take down the remaining 5 Star riders in camp. Wipe them all out we will when you return to camp later today."

"Thanks for not starting without me." Longley grinned evilly.

"First, two men you choose will go with Christer and yourself. Attack the 5 Star foreman and Frederick's son, you will. Our big drover, Moose, will aid you in bringing them down."

"Looking forward to that, Lars." Longley nodded.

"Be sure that 5 Star rider that's always with them goes away too, yah?"

"You do know that rider is Holt Corrigan, don't you?"

"The Ranger? You sure to be of that?"

"Beard or not, I'd recognize that miserable bastard anywhere."

"Ahh, the trickster he trying to be?"

"A dead trickster this time," Longley spat.

"It is of no matter, new ownership the 5 Star will have by nightfall." Lars grinned gleefully.

———

Daybreak haze was being pushed aside by an increasingly confident sun. For the small roundup team —Luke Frederick, Rome Seley and the incognito Rangers Holt Corrigan, and Moose Elkins—the morning flew by in a tangle of brush, brambles and bawling. A herd of fifty-some calves and cows had sprouted from their efforts, the young ones hollering at the unknown and making sure their mamas did not leave them behind.

The team had finished combing the intended land and now took a midday break. Their quick meal was hard biscuits and cold, fried pork belly left over from breakfast, and warm canteen water. Only Holt's dog, Tag, seemed to enjoy the repast.

The men switched to fresh horses brought along for the afternoon's return ride, and pointed their reclaimed herd toward the new camp. The morning's hard work settled onto the men and they drifted into a trail-weary silence, the quiet broken only by the clops of horse hooves and the occasional plaintive cry of a calf or bellowy grunt of a bull or cow.

Holt knew he should be focusing on what lay ahead, but his mind wandered like a stream finding a new course. Laudie Kate's words still stung him. He was disappointed and hurt. Other Rangers were married, some with families. Why not him? Could Laudie Kate not see that? Why wouldn't she want that?

Holt chased the thoughts of her away by stretching his recently healed left arm and right side torso, gauging any lingering tenderness. He alternated dangling his legs from the stirrups to ease building stiffness, especially the left one where the doctor had dug a bullet from his thigh a few months back.

It had to be coming. Viklund's ambush. Soon.

Holt mulled over Viklund sending some of his men away yesterday, supposedly to bring cattle back to his land, relieving the camp of cattle to babysit. Regardless of his stated intentions, Viklund's maneuver had to mean he was unleashing his assault on the 5 Star—just as Holt believed would happen during this roundup. Lars's action yesterday also meant an attack against Frederick's son Luke, and their foreman Rome, as well as the other 5 Star riders—including Holt—was imminent.

But what if he had guessed wrong? What if Lars was content to continue deliberately running off the smaller ranches? The questions ground against his mind.

Lars and Casper had played nice, following the trail boss's orders, and working hard like the rest of the riders. But their treachery and brutality of the past year could not have just disappeared.

No, they are the snakes you watch out for, the ones that hide in plain sight waiting to strike.

Holt tried to stay focused, keeping his eyes on the trail and the ragtag herd in front of them. He held his medicine pouch briefly through his shirt, asking for strength and guidance. The young Ranger squinted against the afternoon sun and concentrated on the terrain surrounding them.

Immediately ahead on their left, an enormous mound loomed that crested into a rock-topped ridge. Lightly elevated at the bottom and sloping steeper at the top, the round hill stood directly in the way of the trail. It appeared as though an earthly giant had plopped a huge scoop of land sprinkled with boulders, buffalograss and scraggly bushes as a prank to travelers just wishing to get from one point to the next. Over time, a route had been worn around the base of this knoll with open land once again expanding beyond.

Off to the right, a long line of post oaks and mesquite were concentrated like a tall, silent brigade creating a thick wall along the well-established trail. The hill and line of trees created an enclosure that gave Holt a sinister, penned-in feeling. His attention darted back and forth from the rock-lined hilltop to the stand of trees.

On the gray ridge up to his left, Holt's practiced eyes caught an eye-blink of movement where there shouldn't have been any.

His panther spirit stirred. What was that up on the ridgeline? His imagination? Did thinking a trap was imminent make him see something that wasn't there? Whatever that movement was did not belong and was no longer around. It wasn't a deer or a bird. No, his instinct told him it was a man.

He became aware that their surroundings had become

quiet. Too quiet. Birds that had gathered in the wall of trees to discuss the afternoon were strangely silent.

Curving trail ahead…good cover…concealment. He would pick this spot too. Just past the big mound.

It would be there. The ambush.

Holt's senses now bristled with a heightened sense of danger. He glanced at the men with him. All seemed to be adrift in their weariness, oblivious to the unease Holt felt.

The 5 Star foreman, Rome Seley, was focused on everything and nothing, likely thinking through the hundred or so details with which a roundup boss must concern himself. Luke Frederick was intently watching a wiggly calf just ahead of him, the young animal barely being kept in line by its mother. Moose had an easy-to-read look of fatigue, lost in the rhythm of his horse's gait.

Deciding what to do came quickly. There weren't many options. This ambush was expected, but as the day progressed the threat had been shoved aside by their hard work. They couldn't turn around and take a different trail. The herd made that a tough proposition. Besides, those bastards could easily find a new spot for their sneak attack. They could gallop by the Viklund bushwhackers in a wild Custer-like cavalry charge, firing as they went, cattle stampeding in front. That would be stupid, Holt surmised. Just like that overblown Yank "boy general." Or they could pull up and dig in. Not a good choice either. How many guns were readied to face them?

No, he knew what he needed to be done. He reached over to touch Rome on the shoulder, getting Moose's attention in the process. They turned their heads to him and Holt whispered, "Don't react, but we've got company ahead. I'm going to try and surprise them." He made a simple, subtle gesture to them all that indicated the trouble was waiting around the curve of the mound.

Rome's eyes widened and Moose's narrowed in determination. Holt motioned for them to keep moving just as they were, but get ready one at a time. They did not want to appear as though they had been alerted. Moose nudged his horse into a faster walk and pulled up alongside the 5 Star owner's son. As they talked quietly, Luke's expression turned from surprise to purposeful.

Silka—and war—had taught Holt the power of patience combined with the added force of surprise. Patience was always vital in a fight. Holt had spent years honing the skill. It was a basic tenet of combat. But there was a point in battle, of any kind, when it was time to move out and meet the fight head on.

His instinctual wariness told him that now was the time to change the situation. It was time to attack. Any sudden movement by them might tip off the ambushers into springing their trap, but Holt thought the risk was worth it. Where he was headed wouldn't be rifle work, so Holt slowly retrieved one of his Russian Smith & Wessons from his saddlebag. An easy look at the cylinder assured him the gun was loaded and he shoved it into his back waistband. He reached again to grab the other panther-inlaid pistol, keeping this one in his hand.

He took the time to hold the medicine pouch underneath his shirt against his heart, asking the spirits to watch over him. He missed having the cardinal feather in his hat to touch, so he moved the mountain lion claw from his trouser pocket to a vest pocket. For luck.

He casually gave the lead rope of his ponied horse to

Rome, then tied together the reins of the horse he was riding and draped them around the saddle horn. Making sure Tag was still preoccupied with the cattle and wouldn't follow him, Holt smoothly slipped down from the saddle, his fellow riders surrounding him and concealing the movement. He gave his horse a reassuring pat on the backside to encourage its continued forward motion and let the small remuda pass him by.

Moose discreetly pulled his rifle loose from its saddle sheath, leaving it there, but quickly drawn and readied. Moments later, Luke calmly followed suit.

In a crouch, Holt used the group as a shield and eased away. When he felt he was clear from anyone viewing from the top of the ridge, he dashed up the far side of the hill, hopefully blind to the waiting attackers. A magpie jabbered its day song and strutted across the rocks in front of him. He grimaced at the magpie crossing. That meant bad luck. Not necessarily for him though, he quickly reminded himself. Swift strides took him near the top, but still below the ridgeline and out of sight from whoever lay behind.

Removing his hat, Holt peered cautiously over the top. Ambushers awaited there all right. Standing protected behind boulders, facing the trail as it rounded the bend. Four of them. Rifles readied. They had not noticed his departure.

Casper Longley was there, as was Christer Viklund, plus two other Windmill V riders. They were talking quietly among themselves, probably determining who would shoot whom. Their conversation stopped as the sounds of the herd grew louder. Below Holt, his friends were just yards away from clearing the mound and riding into gunfire.

He had to move, now. Holt bolted from his hideaway, drawing his pistol.

"Good place for a picnic," he called out, cocking his guns. "If any of you bastards move, you're going to die."

CHAPTER FORTY-TWO

The four would-be attackers turned as one, utter shock and disbelief registered on their faces. The youngest Viklund son, Christer, glanced down at the trail then back at Holt, not believing what was happening.

A fat Windmill V outlaw overcame his initial surprise and spun his rifle toward Holt. The young Ranger fired instantly, pumping two bullets from his pistol into the man's chest. The plump gunman cartwheeled backward down the abrupt slope. Holt wasn't sure if his bullets dispatched the would-be killer, but if not, the fall certainly did.

A short, dark-skinned Viklund rider also tried to squeeze off a round at the young Ranger. Two more shots barked from Holt's gun, turning the outlaw's head into a red pumpkin and driving him into a scraggly bush. Not wanting to remain a target, Holt quickly repositioned himself nearer some boulders.

Just then, Moose came flying around the bend, bolting up the lower part of the hill on his charging horse. His rifle was aimed one-handed and ready to fire.

"Thank god, you're here!" Christer shouted. "Get him, Moose!"

Not slowing his rushing mount, Moose aimed and fired once.

The young Viklund with long blonde hair stumbled. He dropped his rifle in pain. Moose's bullet had driven deep into his shoulder. Christer's face was painted in astonishment at Moose's deed, then his eyes flashed hatred.

"Shoot the bastard, Casper!" Christer roared, holding his bloody shoulder.

"Take 'is advice, Longley, an' all yer gonna git is dead," Moose snarled as he reined up just below the one-eyed outlaw, his Winchester still at the ready. "An' you, ya lil' Viking pissant, I'm a Texas Ranger, so shut yer goddam mouth." The levering of another bullet into his rifle's chamber emphasized Moose's order.

The gunman Casper Longley seethed quietly, not moving throughout any of this. Instead, his one good eye narrowed with fury at the bearded man holding pistols on him.

"Drop the rifle now, Longley," Holt ordered. "It's over."

"I don't know what you're hollering about, *Samuel Holton*," Casper sneered. "We were tracking rustlers when you jumped us."

"I said, drop the gun. Or my next shots go right through that filthy eye patch."

Longley's rifle dropped to the rocks with a loud clatter.

"Now your gun belt," Holt snapped. "Same rule

applies." The clicks of the hammers drawing back on both of Holt's guns punched the air.

The one-eyed outlaw slowly loosened his holster and let the gun belt drop. "You just murdered two of my men, Corrigan," he growled.

"So, you remember me. Congratulations," Holt said. "Now move back from the rocks and step away from those guns."

Longley moved from his guns and out into the open, away from the boulders. His eye seared with rage.

As Moose got down from his horse, Holt continued, "Your rider, Dal Frantze, is a Ranger too. We know everything your no-good family's been up to, Christer."

"Yer family is finished, lil' Viklund," Moose continued. "Yer pappy. Yer brother. An' you."

Lars's youngest son began to shake. The shock of the bullet wound was wearing off and the revelation of the Ranger's words was sinking in. Christer was scared, in pain, and about to vomit.

Right then, Luke and Rome quickly climbed the incline near Holt, guns in-hand. "I found their horses," Luke informed the Rangers, slightly out of breath. Tag followed them in easy bounds. Luke stood near Holt. Rome stayed downhill closer to Moose. The two added their levered rifles to the two prisoners being held by the Rangers.

"Thankfully, the herd didn't seem fazed by the shooting," Rome reported. "Most are grazing not far from where Luke found their horses. Our mounts are with them."

Holt picked up Longley's discarded pistol, adding it to the number of guns pointed at their prisoners. "Christer Viklund, Casper Longley, you're both under arrest for rustling, murder and attempted murder," he declared, his eyes boring into the frightened son's face. "The two of you as well as Lars and Baldur Viklund, and Sheriff Linus Carmichael are all under suspicion for the disappearance of the Mason family at the Half Moon 6 and the Daileys of the River D. You also threatened the lives of Lillian Whitman and her employees. There's more, but that's enough to start."

Casper's sneer turned into a menacing smirk. Christer swallowed even faster to control surging bile.

"Wipe that smile off your face, Longley," Holt barked.

"Go to hell, Corrigan. Viklund riders and Carmichael's deputy hit the 5 Star last night," Longley couldn't help himself, scoffing at his captors. "Frederick, his wife, and his daughters were all slaughtered. All bet those boys all had a grand time with the women before…"

A flash of movement bolted at Longley before he could finish. "You miserable bastard!" Luke Frederick screamed as he smashed his rifle butt into the gunman's midsection, doubling him over and driving him to his knees.

"Don't listen to him, Luke!" Holt implored. "The 5 Star is safe!"

Luke shoved the barrel of his rifle into the stunned outlaw's open mouth and levered a bullet into the breech. The outlaw, struggling to reclaim his breath, could not move for fear of having the back of his head shot off.

"Your family is all right," Holt said steadily. "I'll bet my life on it."

"That's the lives of my family you're talking about!!" the young rancher stormed.

"Luke, listen to me," Holt said calmly. "I know what I'm saying is true."

Luke's face was an anvil of fury and hate.

Holt spoke to Luke in a reassuring voice, "Right now, the W Bar L widow, her foreman and the rest of her crew are guests of your father at the 5 Star. Two Rangers are with them as well. In fact, I'll bet everyone at the ranch, including your entire family, is celebrating the big surprise party they threw at the scum Lars Viklund sent their way."

The 5 Star owner's son seethed; his finger tightened on the rifle's trigger.

"Don't burden your conscience killing this animal. It's not worth it," Holt continued. "Your family is all right. Trust me."

Tense moments that seemed like an eternity passed. Then Luke slowly nodded his acknowledgment. "Okay, Ranger," he finally said, his anger abating. "You better be right." The young rancher settled himself. "This miserable prick can wait to die."

He eased the hammer forward on his Winchester and withdrew the weapon from Longley's mouth. In his not-completely-satisfied rage, he bashed the barrel of his rifle across Longley's cheek, walloping the gunman flat to the ground, out cold.

Christer could not hold back any longer. He retched and threw up all over his boots.

"What party were ya plannin' fer us, lil' Viklund?" Moose asked. "Talk fast, I'd just as soon kill ya right here an' now."

"W-We were s-supposed to shoot Luke here an-and the foreman and Corrigan," Christer struggled to answer, indicating he was talking about the group surrounding him. "Pappa thought you…Moose…w-would pitch in, help take everyone out. The rest of the 5 Star riders are gonna be t-taken care of when we returned." He wiped at his mouth and swallowed rapidly against more bile that wanted to erupt.

"Ya thought I'd help so y'all could laugh over dead 5 Star men," Moose observed. "Start contemplatin' th' hilarity of a rope, ya lil' pissant."

Christer dropped to his knees and vomited the rest of the contents of his stomach.

CHAPTER FORTY-THREE

J ust as he was coming to from being slugged by a rifle barrel across his cheek, Casper Longley found that his hands were tied up and he was being lifted onto his horse where his legs were lashed securely to the stirrups. A nasty purple welt along his cheekbone was already rising.

Christer's hands were tied to his saddle. The young Viklund son had a bandanna stuffed into the hole in his shoulder to slow any more bleeding. The prisoners' horses were lead-roped to Moose's strong grasp. Holt rode just behind the two prisoners, his reloaded pistol kept just out of sight, Longley's gun shoved into his waistband. The bodies of the two dead Viklund riders were strapped across the saddles of their mounts, ponied by Holt.

Rome and Luke kept the small herd they had gathered under control, but kept their rifles drawn. Tag also provided assistance keeping the cattle in line.

The motley group began making its way back to roundup camp. It was too early in the day and too bright for Holt or the other two 5 Star riders to fake being Viklund men. They would need to take control of the camp as soon as they arrived. Moose led the group, followed by the Viklund prisoners, immediately followed by Holt and the dead ambushers. The small herd with Rome and Luke brought up the rear. The hope was to be on top of camp and hail for assistance before anyone could react.

Wood smoke and the aroma of a large band of collected stock signaled their approach to the roundup bivuoac. Christer was half-dozing, the effects of the blood loss from his shoulder wound wearing him out. Longley, head bowed, glimpsed at the scene around him with his one glaring eye.

As they reached camp, most cowboys did not give the group a second look. Rome and Luke had peeled off early, guiding the sixty-plus head of cattle they had gathered in the direction of the pen areas. Two chuck wagons and their cooks were busily going about their chores readying the upcoming evening meal. Riders were still finishing the last of the day's branding, examining the strings of horses, and checking or repairing ropes and gear.

Holt rode directly toward the center of camp. Moose, with the prisoners in tow, pulled toward the 5 Star picket line. Before Holt could call out, Longley suddenly and unexpectedly flailed his arms apart, somehow jerking them free from his constraints. "Lars! We've been played!" the gunman shouted. "Moose Elkins crawfished us, he's a Ranger! It's a trap!"

Moose turned toward the racket behind him, beginning to level his rifle. A bullet from Longley's small hideaway derringer raked across the huge Ranger's arm.

Holt wheeled, one pistol already in-hand, the other drawn quickly afterward. He blasted four quick shots into Longley's torso. The one-eyed outlaw's body stiffened and tried to topple backward. Roped into place, his lifeless body could only lurch forward onto his horse's neck. The leg constraints lashing him to the saddle prevented him from falling to the ground.

A Viklund rider sitting in camp recovered from the surprise and drew a pistol. Moose, gritting through the pain in his injured forearm, winged the shooter with his rifle.

Holt barked at the camp, "5 Star, Triple S, Flying G men grab your guns! Texas Rangers need your help! Everyone else are riders for Viklund! Don't let them get away!"

Drovers were shocked into reacting, not quite believing what was happening. Holt shouted his orders again. "Do it now!" he finished.

The 5 Star cook grabbed a shotgun from his chuck wagon. He pointed it at his Windmill V counterpart preventing the man from reaching to do the same. Rome and Luke ran from the picket line, rifles readied and aiming at any movement. Everywhere in the encampment, guns were drawn in an uneasy standoff.

Reacting to Longley's commotion, Lars had drawn his pistol. The two Viklund riders he was speaking to had pulled their weapons as well. Rattled and agitated by the sudden change of events, Lars frantically pointed his weapon everywhere at everyone, not knowing what to do. His two men looked as though they had grabbed onto a flaming gunny sack of cow manure.

Silence, for the moment, commanded the camp.

Holt knew a scared man with a gun was like a

cornered animal; one never knew when—or if—he might strike. Right now, he was facing three fearful men. Each of his pistols were leveled at the two Viklund drovers as he spoke. "Think very clearly about your next moves," the young Ranger said calmly. "You are *not* in the trouble your boss is. You've got at least a dozen guns pointed at you. This can end with you alive."

The two Windmill V riders looked at each other. One of the drovers dropped his weapon and backed away from his now former boss.

"All right, Lars. Drop the gun," Holt turned his attention to the big Swede. "It's over. You're through. We know about your entire operation."

"What operation?" Viklund's booming voice rang out. "A bluff you are running."

"There is no bluff. You're a rustler and a murderer. You're under arrest."

"Doubting that seriously. My son and my attorney will straighten out all of this. Clear my name they will."

Moose interjected, "Which son? Th' son who danced a mid-air ballet a week ago? Or this one, who can't keep 'is lunch down?" Still on their horses, he poked Christer with his rifle.

A voice called out from near the cook fire.

"It's best you follow the advice and drop your gun, Viklund." The W Bar L nephew, Larry Malloy, stepped out from the chuck wagon, his Henry leveled at the Swede. The nephew advanced, tugging at his lapel. He removed his hand, revealing a bright shiny badge. No longer speaking in the nephew's timid delivery, his strong voice now rang out.

"Allow me to introduce myself. I am Captain Laird

McCoy of the Texas Rangers. Before this roundup, I came from New Braunfels by way of Fort McKavett."

Lars eyed the captain warily, not dropping his gun.

"Lars, stop the charade," the captain said. "Your son Baldur and three of your Windmill riders were captured in New Braunfels for possessing stolen livestock…"

"There is no crew from my ranch in, where is this you said, New…Brownfield?"

"A military tribunal has Sheriff Carmichael's brother in custody," Captain McCoy continued.

"What's that to me?"

"Sheriff Carmichael and his Army quartermaster brother have been the business end of your wicked venture," the captain responded.

Holt joined in. "And that ugly dead guy here was your muscle," he said, pointing at the lifeless Casper Longley flopped forward in the saddle, still securely attached to his horse. The young Ranger quickly reloaded his drawn pistol as he spoke.

"Enough with the lies…" Lars bellowed.

"We have signed and sworn affidavits from two Texas Rangers, Moose Elkins and Dal Frantze, who witnessed close-hand your thievery for many months," Holt added.

"Lars, your son and your three men were caught with stolen beef. You should know they were tried and hung," Captain McCoy stated matter-of-factly. "They're dead. Carmichael's brother will be sentenced by the Army to hang too."

"So drop th' gun, lingonberry. This has gone far enuf'," Moose demanded.

Lars's eyes shot daggers across the camp at Moose.

"Traitor!" the Swede erupted angrily and fired his

weapon at Moose. The bullet struck the huge Ranger's already wounded arm, causing him to drop his gun. Moose dove from his horse and rolled, picking up the gun and beginning to fire.

Shots exploded throughout the camp. Not all of the Viklund riders had been disarmed. Chaos took over. The horse holding the dead Casper Longley bucked and careened frantically through camp, the body tied to it bouncing wildly.

Momentarily distracted by the out of control horse, Luke Frederick did not see a Viklund rider take aim. The son of the 5 Star ranch owner grabbed at his leg and tumbled to the ground.

Holt emptied his pistol, downing two Viklund riders, including the drover who shot Luke. A third Viklund rider flew into one of the campfires after catching one barrel blasted from the 5 Star cook's shotgun.

In the bedlam, Lars ran in a crouched position, dodging the confused medley of gunfire. Reaching a saddled horse, the big Swede rode off in a flurry of pounding hooves.

With Lars gone, the Viklund men were leaderless and outnumbered. One by one, the Swede's henchmen fell or were wounded in hails of bullets. Finally, the shooting dwindled. Holt and the captain got the riders from the ranches not affiliated with Lars to get the drop on the remaining Viklund men.

CHAPTER FORTY-FOUR

I n the ensuing quiet, Holt ran to a wounded Moose, who was sitting behind a large rock, holding his arm.

"How is it, Moose?"

"I'm not carryin' lead, Holt," Moose answered. "Gotdammit these things sting tho."

"I don't think it broke anything either," Holt added, looking at the huge Ranger's forearm. "They got you twice though. Were you trying to swat those bullets away?" he half-chuckled.

"Jus' lucky, I guess. Here's a 'kerchief," Moose said. "Can ya tie it off? Stop some o' this bleedin'."

"There," Holt said, bandaging the rasped furrows of flesh. "You sit still. I'm going to go look at Luke." The big man nodded and shoved cartridges into his rifle.

The captain was already finishing tying a bandanna around the young Frederick's leg. The Ranger stood up and met Holt. "That leg is probably not bad, but bad enough," Captain McCoy reported. "He's leaking a fair amount of blood. We should get him to a doctor right away."

"Yeah, Moose's arm looks uglier than it really is, I think," Holt said, now taking the time to check the loads in both of his pistols. "Still, he needs to have someone look it."

Captain McCoy took command of the situation. He put the roundup boss, Rome Seley, in charge of getting the cowboys in camp to collect the men who supported Viklund and get them tied up and ready to travel into town. The bodies too.

Just then, a familiar voice hollered from beyond the encampment. "A-ho the camp! It's Rangers Orion Higbee an' Dal Frantze! We're comin' in."

Soon, the two Rangers trotted into the middle of the campsite. "We've been lookin' for you fellas," Orion said. "With all the fires an' beeves, you'd think our noses would've told us where camp was. We couldn't find this place till we heard shootin'."

The two Rangers reported the results of the attempted raid on the 5 Star ranch.

"There were only six of those bastards, can you believe it?" Dal stated. "Six! We got 'em all, every last one."

"We got that mother jumpin' deputy for you," Orion nodded at Holt.

"I'll tell you what, Harold Frederick at the 5 Star is a fighter, a good tactician," Dal noted. "Those Viklund scum weren't expecting our fusillade."

"Just like Holt suspected, Cap'n," Orion added. "Lars got greedy. He saw the 5 Star as vulnerable. We arrived from New Braunfels a few nights ago. They tried to hit us last night…"

"Speaking of Lars," Holt interrupted. "He got away. We've got to go after him!"

"You and Orion go," the captain responded. "Bring him down. Hard. Dal, stay with me, help get this mess squared away."

Orion followed Holt to where the young Ranger had tied his horse. "It's good to see you, my friend," Orion said. "Is Lars headed to his ranch or town?"

"Hard to tell until we track that miserable sono-fabitch," Holt answered, pulling on the shoulder holsters from his saddlebags, the loaded Russian Smith & Wessons nestling comfortably into place. The pistol he had been carrying was shoved into his bag. "Let's ride!" he hollered.

Holt and Orion thundered off with Tag on their heels. Just outside camp, the two split up to follow conflicting tracks, but soon came back together. Lars's trail was easy to determine.

"He's headed straight south," Holt confirmed. "Right into Stebbins." They followed the trail left by Lars at a gallop.

Without warning, shots rang out from a ridgeline just ahead of them. The Rangers peeled off, drawing their rifles as they dropped from their horses to seek shelter.

"Where'd those shots come from?" Orion peered into the higher ground.

"Up there in those rocks. It's got to be Lars, with a rifle."

Holt took off his old borrowed hat and stuck it out the side of where he was holed up. Two more shots blistered nearby.

"Buzzard's got us zeroed in all right," Orion said.

The two Rangers waited patiently. A deadly silence descended.

"I think he's gone," Holt finally said, sticking his hat out once more. No shots came in response. Holt suddenly rolled out from his hiding spot to a new set of boulders. He sprang up and quickly fired his Winchester three times at the ridgeline. No response again.

Just then, from behind them, Tag caught up to his master. The noise briefly startled the Rangers. The dog was tongue-dragging wore out, but okay. Holt gave him a quick hatful of water.

"Let's give these horses a little water too," Orion said.

"We gotta keep moving, boy. You ride with me." He set Tag on the saddle in front of him, a familiar spot for the dog.

"Maybe this was a ruse for Lars changin' his path," Orion said.

"I agree," Holt answered. "Let's split up until we know which way he's headed."

It wasn't long before Orion came loping back up to Holt. "My tracks played out. Yours are still headed straight for Stebbins. That's gotta be the Swede."

They pushed their horses and arrived in town. On this hot afternoon the mounts were lathered and worn out.

The Rangers saw several men in front of the Blue Sky Inn hovering over a collapsed horse. One of the men was the hotel's owner, Miguel Navarro. The diminutive man informed the Rangers that Lars and the sheriff had taken Evie hostage.

"He kept shouting sometheeng about her boyfriend being a traitor and that she must pay. Oh my…" Navarro caught his emotions. "Mees Hart tried to hide her friend and they took her too."

"They took my wagon!" one of the men reported. "Lars and the sheriff threw those women in the back and took off."

"Bastards. We gotta keep moving," Holt said.

"Yeah, but not on these horses," Orion acknowledged. "We pushed 'em hard. Can't let 'em end up like this one."

Marshal Baxter Hollings had just walked up to the scene. He heard Orion and gestured toward the jail. "Take our horses, Rangers."

"Much obliged, Marshal," Orion said.

"Miguel, can you take care of Tag Along until I get back?" Holt asked the hotel owner. "He needs some water like those horses do."

"Tag Along?" Navarro said, perking up. "Oh my stars, Holt Corrigan! It ees you! I deedn't recognize...of course I weel look after your dog!"

"Take him inside and keep him distracted or else he'll try to follow."

As the Rangers traded out their rifles from their worn-out horses to the marshal's and his deputy's mounts, Holt exclaimed, "So, they got away and took Evie and Laudie Kate."

"Where're they headed?"

"I'm not entirely sure, but I've got a hunch."

"Gonna be hard to track the roads outta town."

"Is it?" Holt questioned. "Lars isn't going to head home. He's proven that. "

"The sheriff took quite a shine to the W Bar L, didn't he?"

"More than a shine, I'd say. We go there. Now."

"This is just like Laelia, ain't it?"

"Charmed is your middle name, remember?" Holt said. "Let's ride."

CHAPTER FORTY-FIVE

E ven though the sun was beginning its last hours, the afternoon was hot and breezy. The lengthening shadows of a dying afternoon would be a welcome respite. Holt and Orion pushed the horses toward the W Bar L as fast as they dared.

"They're gonna see us comin'," Orion called over to his partner.

Holt's face was dark, set in determination. "Yeah, that's how I figure it."

"You gotta plan in mind?"

"We do what we do best," Holt said grimly.

"I was afraid of that."

The house looked as it did before, except now it had an unoccupied feel to it. The big porch looked empty. No smoke from the chimney. No horses hitched out front. No dogs playing outside.

The Rangers tied their horses by a tree in the yard, using the large trunk as cover. They crept close, rifles readied. Stunted olive trees out front provided more camouflage than cover.

Holt felt his medicine pouch move underneath his shirt. He acknowledged the spirits and reached into his vest pocket to put his hand around the mountain lion claw there. He took a determined breath.

"I don't suppose it's worth tellin' you to calm down," Orion said.

"I *am* calm. You ease around back and come in through there."

"Where'll you be?"

"Going right through the damn front door."

"That didn't work so well before, remember?"

"I'm expecting to get shot at this time."

"Gimme a coupla minutes to get around…"

"Tell the widow I'll buy her a new door," he hollered to Orion as he suddenly took off, rifle in hand. Without breaking stride, he threw his body at the door, slamming his shoulder against the locked entrance. Although shorter than his partner, the young Ranger was deceptively strong, with a solidly built chest, and arms and shoulders that were layered with hard-earned muscle.

Smash!

The impact shattered the simple lock. The door splintered open and he crashed through inside. The borrowed cavalry hat bounced away from his head as he hit the dark ranch floor.

"Ho-lee damn!" Orion exclaimed, taken by surprise at his partner's rashness. He took off running around the side of the ranch house.

Holt laid there a moment, expecting gunfire.

None came. A surprise.

From this prone position, he took stock of his surroundings. The room swirled with intertwined aromas: musty, familiar, and curious. An unearthly quiet draped everywhere. Westerly facing windows presented bright beams that illuminated slowly swirling dust. Heavy shadows started to play in rooms not arrayed with afternoon light.

He retrieved the beat-up hat and stood carefully. As he was getting his bearings, Holt levered his rifle into readiness. The house smelled like it had not been occupied for a while, which made sense; it had been almost two weeks since the widow had moved to the 5 Star ranch. Still, faint odors of a fireplace, saddle soap, cooking grease and other interesting smells lingered.

The ranch house was easy to navigate. The huge one-story structure was a dog-trot design, probably left over from two big log cabins that eventually had a common roof thrown over them. Holt easily made his way through a foyer to the main hallway that led directly to the back door. He noiselessly prowled his way in the stillness to where the back door stood. He grabbed for the handle and yanked it open.

Leaning over, readying to come inside, was Orion. "*Hey-zoos marimba*, Holt!" The lanky Ranger stood up immediately, startled.

"Hello there," Holt said with a deadpan smile.

"Dammit, don't be bustin' my nutcrackers like that! Are you just askin' to get shot?"

"I had to make sure there was no welcoming party out here. We already owe the widow one door."

"What's with the 'we owe'?" Orion said, quickly gathering his wits. "I take it there's no tea on. Missus Whitman would be horrified."

"It's quiet," Holt said. "Too quiet."

"Think we made a mistake?"

"No, they're here. Or have been. I smell lavender."

Whether she wanted him in her life or not, Laudie Kate's scent would be forever imprinted on Holt's mind.

Without warning, a crash and a woman's scream came from the far right side of the house.

The Rangers crouched and spun toward the sounds, guns readied. They spread out and crept quietly toward the danger. This side of the house was blessed to receive morning light; however, this time of day dusky darkness was arriving.

From the hallway, a large doorframe marked the threshold of a sitting room. Holt entered first.

Just inside the parlor, an angular dark shape launched itself from the shadows. Sheriff Linus Carmichael materialized like a haunted scarecrow, a drawn sword from within his silver-tipped cane raised as he rushed at Holt. The shiny blade glinted off the light that dared to reach the room.

At the last second, Holt raised his rifle to parry the sheriff's strike. The force of the chop knocked the gun from his hand. The young Ranger instinctively side-kicked the attacker, delivering a fierce blow that would have made his mentor Silka proud. Carmichael flew backward and grunted as his bony frame thumped heavily against a wall.

"I got this bog-holed ferret," Orion called. "Find the women."

Holt moved into the sitting room. Behind him, the clatter and crunches of a heated brawl continued. He left his rifle on the floor. This was too close a range for a rifle anyway. This was pistol work now. Holt drew one of his Russian Smith & Wessons. A distinctive *click-click* announced the gun's presence as he cocked its hammer into readiness.

Near the back of the room, the wick wheel on a gas lamp was adjusted. The slow-growing radiance chased most of the shadows to the corners and slowly illuminated two dim figures.

"You'll be dropping your gun now, Holt Corrigan. Or I will kill this woman, *yah*?" The hard, accented voice came from the shadows behind the lamp.

Holt glared at the sound, not moving, not dropping his gun.

A large form moved from the gloom. In the diffused light, the hulking physique with a full reddish beard and thick, dirty blonde hair looked like an eerie Norse specter. The strongly muscled Lars Viklund held Evie O'Neill with his left hand as if she were a toy. His right hand brandished an Army Colt.

Holt matched the Swede's fierce glare. Holt's were the eyes of a warrior. Lars's were those of a killer.

"Put down the gun, Corrigan, or shoot her I will," the large man repeated. "She would not be the first woman I have killed, I can assure you."

Holt glanced away for a moment. Laudie Kate was now propping herself up from the floor to a shaky standing position after being thrown off her feet. That was the crash, Holt noted. He returned his stare to Lars.

Everything in Holt wanted to attack, and Viklund knew it.

"Don't. She will die before your first footstep lands." The huge Swede's smile was evil. "I want you to be dropping that gun. Now."

Holt eased the hammer forward and his pistol thudded against the floor. The young Ranger stood with his hands clenched at his sides and snarled, "Don't you dare hurt that woman…"

"Or what?" Lars couldn't hold back a snicker.

"Or you will not have enough bullets to stop me from snapping your neck." Holt challenged.

The Swede's dark-blue eyes sparkled wickedly in response.

At this, Laudie Kate began to sob loudly, holding her hands to her face as she stood there. She then used her left sleeve to wipe her eyes. Her right hand moved smoothly to the pocket of her frock.

Holt knew in an instant what was hidden there. What was she thinking? She could never clear it and fire quick enough. He frowned and started to tell her not to try it.

"Please…" Laudie Kate sobbed. "Please don't hurt her…she didn't know who Moose was. Take me instead. I'm the one who saved this Ranger's life. Take me."

Lars noted this and nodded. In one rapid movement, he shoved Evie away and grabbed Laudie Kate. Her right hand somehow stayed in her pocket as the Swede yanked her to him. It all happened too swiftly for Holt to react.

Lars matched eyes with Holt. "Don't be trying it, Ranger. Good you might be, but not that good."

Holt looked away for a moment at Evie, hoping to buy time, any time.

Pop! Pop! Pop!

Holt swiftly drew the other gun from his shoulder holster.

Bang!

Bang! Bang! Bang!

The huge Swede's eyes widened in shock as his head exploded in a large ball of crimson mist, adding to the blood beginning to drench the entire front of his torso. Smoke from Laudie Kate's hidden pocket pistol surrounded his face.

As soon as Lars had yanked Laudie Kate to him, she had drawn her .31 Colt and jammed it behind her into the Swede's body and fired three times as fast as she could work the trigger action. When the bullets tore into his belly, Lars bent convulsively forward and Laudie Kate spun away from his grasp. The Swede's hand spasmed, firing the pistol, the shot thumping harmlessly into the floor. The final three shots were from Holt's pistol, drilling Viklund in his chest, cheek, and just above his eyebrow, turning the Swede's head into a torrent of gore.

The force of the head shots from Holt's gun propelled the evil cattleman backward like a felled tree. The Swede was dead when his body hit the floor.

Holt rushed to Laudie Kate and grabbed her. "Oh my god, Laudie Kate! Are you all right?"

She was stunned, in shock at what had just happened, unable to speak at first. She started to wipe at her eyes, pistol still in hand, but then stopped. "I...I...don't want this anymore," she said, handing the gun to Holt.

Evie hurried over and the two women clutched each other in a tight, tearful embrace.

A fist of thought hit Holt's mind. He was jolted away from the drama of what just happened to the very real peril of Orion's struggle with the sheriff. He jammed Laudie Kate's gun into his waistband and whirled, his own gun at the ready, determined to see what had happened behind him. He was stunned to find both men lying in the entryway of the sitting room.

"*Orion!...*" He grimaced in horror as he rushed toward the motionless body of his friend.

Sheriff Carmichael stirred slightly and groaned.

In a fury, Holt holstered his pistol and picked up the sheriff. He held Carmichael by the lapel with one hand and began administering a savage beating with his other fist. Holt launched uncounted blows into the man's hawk-like face, delivering punches like pistons on a locomotive as he screamed, "What did...you do...you miserable..." Rage completely took over Holt's body, like a panther tearing its prey to pieces.

"Missus Whitman ain't gonna like all this bleedin' in her house."

Holt stopped. Ragged gasps had claimed his breath. He realized he had been screaming. His throat felt shredded. Hot tears were streaming down his face.

Orion stood there holding his arm, a weak, wry grin on his face. "That stickpin of his slices worse than a damn Ketchum grenade." He lowered his left hand and looked at the nasty slash that ran down the length of his right arm where the sheriff's chop had narrowly missed doing more damage. His shirt was torn and bloody.

Holt looked at his friend, not quite registering the fact Orion was standing there. He wound up to smash the sheriff again.

"No, Holt. He's done."

With an acknowledging nod, Holt exhaled and released Carmichael's coat, letting the sheriff collapse in a dead-weight heap.

"Holy damn, Orion, I thought you were really hurt. Or worse."

"Mother jumpin' frog bangers, this stings like all get out. Doesn't that count?" Orion responded, rolling his eyes.

"You were laying there pretty convincingly, amigo," Holt said, wiping the tears from his face.

"Can't a guy just catch his breath?"

"Help me tie this boghole up. I think I might've busted my hand on his stupid face."

They dragged Carmichael outside and unceremoniously dropped him on the porch.

As they tied his hands behind his back with pigging string, the sheriff groggily came to. They pulled him up to his knees. His face was starting to swell, bruising rapidly taking over his eyes and face, blood streaming from his nose. Two of Carmichael's teeth lay on the floor in the sitting room. Struggling through busted lips, the sheriff started complaining, "Auugghh! My hands! My arm! My nose! You can't do this. A judge will…"

Crash!!

Carmichael's cries were abruptly silenced as he pancaked to the ground. Evie stood behind the sheriff, one handle and the neck of a large urn were still in her hand. The rest of the hefty pot lay in pieces after she shattered it over his head. She dropped the remainder of the container and threw her arms around Holt, tears flowing down her cheeks.

"It's all right, Evie. It's all right," Holt said calmly, eyeing Orion over her shoulder with raised *"What do I do?"* eyebrows. "It's over. You and Laudie Kate are all right. You're all right."

She calmed down and let go of Holt. He noticed she had a welt by her left eye.

"Where did that come from—" he started to ask.

"Lars…after he broke down Laudie Kate's door…he was blamin' Moose…" she explained haltingly.

"Unholy meatball," he growled and thought about giving their prisoner a kick to the ribs. He reached down and yanked the county sheriff badge from the unconscious man's coat instead.

Evie blurted, wiping her face, "Lars doin' all this... does that mean...what happened at th' roundup...where's Moose?"

"Everyone's headed to town," Holt said. "We can..."

She did not wait for the rest of Holt's words, running off the porch and, in one motion, untying the reins to the mouse-gray dun Orion had borrowed from the marshal and climbed into the saddle.

"Evie...wait!" Holt called out, but she was streaking toward town before either Ranger could do anything else.

Holt looked at Orion. Orion shrugged.

Laudie Kate had watched all of this, beginning to move out from underneath the shock of the events. She handed Orion a towel for his bloody arm and said, "There should be horses and a wagon out back or in the barn. It's how they brought us here."

Holt hurriedly retrieved the wagon from the barn. Lars and the sheriff had not bothered to unhitch the animals. With his own hand still stiff and numb and Orion's sliced arm, it took effort to load Lars and the sheriff into the back.

Orion steadied himself after the exertion, exclaiming, "Wooo! These boys are heavy, made me a mite dizzy."

"You've leaked a bit too much there, partner. Get that towel back on it," Holt noted. "I'll take your horse. You sit in the wagon."

Instead of Holt climbing up onto the seat next to her, Laudie Kate was disappointed when Orion stepped aboard the wagon with her but didn't let it show.

"The captain ought to be heading into town," Holt mentioned. "Let's get there. I'll keep an eye on our cargo." He took time to toss some tobacco shreds in grat-

itude to the spirits for finding the women alive and
bringing an end to Lars Viklund and Linus Carmichael.

"You got this?" Orion asked, turning to Laudie Kate.

"Hang on," she said, snapping the reins to the wagon
team as they lurched to a start.

"I'll take that as a yes." He chuckled, holding on to
his hat.

CHAPTER FORTY-SIX

Marshal Baxter Hollings tugged at his ear along the scar where the lobe should be. He did that when he was nervous, as he was now, pacing anxiously on the walkway in front of his Stebbins town jail.

Dusk had brought a strange silence to the town; muffled, subdued, like during a heavy snowfall. Two women taken hostage from the Blue Sky Inn by local rancher Lars Viklund and Sheriff Linus Carmichael muted the usual sounds of music and mirth from the saloons. Everyone seemed to be on edge, not knowing when or where a storm of violence would next erupt.

In the distance, the marshal heard the pounding hoof-beats of a single horse. Running hard. The drumming *thudalup thudalup thudalup thudalup* got louder and drew nearer.

In the dimming light, Marshal Hollings saw a woman, all wild flowing hair and billowing skirt, bolting a horse down the street. Reining up in front of the jail, the horse and rider practically skidded to a stop. Evie O'Neill, face red and puffy from hard riding and tears, jumped from the saddle.

"Whoa there, missy, settle down now," the marshal hollered, grabbing for Evie and the worn-out animal. He threw the horse's reins into a quick tie on the hitching post.

"Where's Moose? Where are the round up riders? What's happened?" she cried out, blurting between gasps and sobs, barely taking a breath.

At the commotion, the marshal's deputy and W Bar L foreman Big Jeff ran outside to see what was happening. Both were armed with shotguns.

"Evie, what th' hell is goin' on?" the marshal exclaimed. "Is you okay? Navarro said you an' Laudie Kate was kidnapped."

She grabbed his arms. "You've gotta tell me where he is! What's happened ta him?"

"Where is who an' what happen'd ta what?" he sputtered. No one could understand what she was saying through her blubbering.

"Set down those scatterguns, boys," the marshal called out. Then he spoke quietly, in a more serious tone to the two men. "Guys, this here's my horse. It's th' one I lent ta Ranger Higbee when he lit outta town. An' now *she's* ridin' it. Whattaya think that means?"

Deputy Brooks gave his boss a hard stare, "I don't know, Marshal. It's a sure bet she knows."

"Take 'er inside. Get 'er calmed down. Find out what's goin' on," the marshal said coolly. "I gotta take care o' this horse rite now. It's almost done in."

Big Jeff was staring down the street in the direction

from where Evie just rode, concern painted across his face. "All right. See to yer hoss," the huge man said. "We'll be ready. Come back when you can. We'll lock th' door behin' us." The enormous W Bar L foreman had come to town yesterday with his boss, Lillian Whitman. The two of them had brought in the 5 Star rider who had broken his arm in the aftermath of the Viklund raid when a rattlesnake spooked his horse. They also had ponied in the dead bodies of the Viklund attackers, including Sheriff Carmichael's deputy.

The marshal stepped down to the street and patted the lathered horse, talking to the worn-out animal in soft, soothing words. Its neck was sopping with frothy wetness. Hollings wiped his hand against the saddle blanket. The mouse-gray dun had been pushed hard, maybe too hard. With a quick yank, he loosened the cinch and pushed the saddle and blanket off its heaving back. He picked up the blanket and wiped at the sweat covering the horse's body. "Hey Gus-Gus," he hollered into the jail at his deputy. "I'm gonna walk 'im aroun' a little, cool 'im down. Then take 'im to th' livery."

Forty-five minutes later, Hollings approached the stables, no longer as worried about his horse. Calming the animal down, letting it walk to cool itself seemed to be working. The dun was bouncing back slowly: worn out, but its legs were sturdy now. Down here at the far end of town, the marshal was the first to see a unique parade emerging from the outskirts.

Leading the procession was Luke Frederick, half-asleep on his horse, his bloody leg hanging down, the foot out of the stirrup.

Immediately following him was a large wagon driven

by a Flying G rider. The buckboard was crammed with the surviving Viklund men, each heavily trussed. Most of them had some sort of bullet wound. Off to one side rode Moose Elkins, his bloody arm tucked into the front of his shirt, acting as a sling, his good hand brandishing a rifle. On the other side of the prisoners was Texas Ranger Dal Frantze, riding with a borrowed shotgun across his saddle, wary for trouble. Three drovers—two from the Triple S and one from the 5 Star—followed immediately behind on horseback, each nursing injuries from the camp fight, but carrying their guns drawn anyway.

Trailing that part of the column, was another 5 Star rider driving a smaller cart. The wagon was stacked with the dead bodies of Viklund men, including Casper Longley.

Bringing up the rear and ponying a long string of several horses, some packing dead bodies slung over saddles, was Captain Laird McCoy.

"I'll be go-ta-hell," Marshal Hollings mumbled. He hurriedly handed over his horse at the livery, giving instructions to the on-duty hand. Running down the street, he caught up to the odd caravan.

"We've come from th' roundup!" Moose hollered. The marshal walked alongside the procession as it entered town. "Lars sent men ta attack th' 5 Star…"

"Way ahead've ya," the marshal responded. "Mizzuz Whitman's here, tol' us all 'bout savin' th' 5 Star. Rangers Corrigan an' Higbee've been here too."

"Holt an' Orion? Here?" Moose asked with surprise, sure in his notion that his Ranger associates had chased the Swede to his ranch.

A few onlookers started to emerge out on the boardwalks, so Hollings spoke in a subdued voice, not wanting to spread rumors or fear. "Lars stormed through here lik'a tornado. He an' Carmichael kidnapped a coupla women from th' Blue Sky…"

"What'd ya say 'bout kidnapped women?" Moose said, alarmed at what he thought he heard.

"Lars an' that evil sheriff grabbed a woman from th' Blue Sky. Miss Evie."

"Oh no…" Moose exclaimed.

"Señor Navarro said Viklund was rantin' 'bout a ranch hand who actually was a Ranger. Blamed 'im for ever'thin'. 'Nother woman, Miss Laudie, fought ta keep it all from happenin', so they took 'er as well." He stopped his story for a moment. "You is Miss Evie's Moose, ain't ya? I guess that wrangler…er…Ranger is you."

Oh shee-it…" Moose blurted out.

"She's back though. Miss Evie. Not ta worry. She rode in 'bout an hour ago, all upset, wonderin' where some guy—prob'bly you—was. Worried ya was hurt."

More patrons from the saloons and restaurants in town began milling out onto the street. Evie joined the growing crowd on the main thoroughfare. Her hand jumped to her mouth to hold in a scream when she caught a glimpse of Moose. She ran toward him, the folds of her skirt gathered up and her hair flying.

"Ranger Elkins," Luke interrupted. "This is Dr. Vaughn's office."

They reined up in front of the building with large painted letters "DRUGS" on the facade. A weathered sign proclaimed "Physician · Surgeon · Apothecary within."

Captain McCoy ordered the wagonload of Viklund men to continue on down the street to the jail. Ranger Frantze and the captain accompanied the captives, the silent column of dead Viklund riders following behind.

A white-haired gentleman in rumpled vest and trousers appeared on the boardwalk in front of the drugstore. "Dr. Vaughn!" Luke called out. "This Ranger's been wounded. He needs your care."

"Ah, Mr. Frederick," the doctor noted soberly. "Looks like that leg of yours needs attention as well."

The marshal helped Luke from his horse and propped him up as the young man limped inside.

Moose tied up his horse in front of the drugstore as well and gingerly climbed down, his wounded arm still tucked into his shirt. He was just reaching the ground when Evie arrived. She threw her arms around the huge Ranger and wept tears of relief.

"Aww, Evie darlin', ya had ta know I'd be alright," Moose soothed, trying to calm Evie's emotions.

Down the street, Captain McCoy arrived at the jail and began taking charge of the distribution of outlaws. Under Ranger Frantze's watchful glare, Christer Viklund and the other surviving Viklund riders were clapped into cells. The restraints were not cut from their wrists until they were securely locked inside a cage. W Bar L foreman Big Jeff chased away the gawkers so the work of sorting through the clutter of bodies and prisoners could be completed. Onlookers who did not disperse were put to work by the big man, helping to lay out dead bodies to the side of the jail, out of the street. Another bystander was sent to fetch the undertaker.

In the midst of this commotion, Holt arrived with

Orion and Laudie Kate. He reported to the captain what had gone on out at the W Bar L.

"Wagon's loaded with Lars an' Sheriff Carmichael," Orion announced.

"Lars is dead," Holt added. "Carmichael didn't feel like cooperating, so he's a little sore from learning manners."

Murmurs of the news ran through those helping around the jail.

"Deputy, give us a hand here!" Orion called out.

Deputy Brooks hustled over to the wagon and started to help Orion from the seat.

"Not me, gotdammit," the lanky Ranger bellowed. "You can help the lady if she wants, but we got fishbait an' a tromped-on toad in the back there."

The deputy hesitated a moment and wiped his hand on his shirt, then offered it to Laudie Kate. She smiled, not needing the assistance, but grabbed his hand anyway and jumped down off the seat. The deputy then climbed his way into the back of the buckboard and found two figures lying there.

"Uuuggh," Deputy Brooks grunted, seeing the gruesome mess of Lars Viklund's head. "Fishbait is right."

The deputy flagged down Big Jeff to help fling the two bodies out of the back. The lifeless body of Lars Viklund landed in the dust with a perfunctory thud. The trussed-up body of Sheriff Carmichael moaned when it hit the ground.

"Ahhh, looks like we'll have enough of Carmichael left to hang," Big Jeff nodded.

"Take him inside. Lock him up," Captain McCoy announced. "We'll get the doctor to look at all these prisoners later, after Luke and Moose and the rest are patched up."

Holt looked around. "Where's Evie?" he asked the deputy. "Did she make it back here?"

"She made it all right, Ranger. She…" The deputy suddenly realized exactly who he was talking with. "Why…Holt! Holt Corrigan…it *is* you! I'll be damned. You're here, you're all better."

Caught up in the commotion, Holt for a moment did not follow what the deputy was saying, but suddenly remembered he had been concealing himself since returning to Stebbins and not everyone knew he was back. "Hello, Deputy Brooks. Yes, I'm all right. In fact, I'm doing real good at the moment. We got those bastards." They both smiled at the statement. "By the way, thanks for the use of your horse."

"Don't mention it. Uh, Evie ran down the street to see her boyfriend, that Moose fella." The deputy paused. "Say…isn't he a Viklund rider? Why…"

"That Moose fella is Texas Ranger Moose Elkins," Holt acknowledged.

"I'll be damned. You Ranger boys had that no-good Swede all figured out." Deputy Brooks scratched his head. "Anyway, it looks like there's a mess of them down at Dr. Vaughn's. The marshal's there too."

With the news, Holt and Orion hurried down to the doctor's place. Laudie Kate overheard the words about her friend and followed along.

The two Rangers were heartened to see the enormous figure of Moose Elkins sitting on a bench outside the drugstore, Evie clinging to his good side. He was savoring something from a small glass bottle as the two smiled and laughed with each other. Laudie Kate hurried ahead of the two Rangers to join her friend. The two women embraced once again, relieved to be free of their kidnapping nightmare.

Reaching the big man, Orion smiled at his longtime friend and declared, "Moose, I swear, even shot up, you manage to find a drink an' a pretty lady."

"Well, yeah," Moose said, as though it was the natural thing to do. He took a quick sip of the amber liquid. "My Evie says that no-good Swede gave 'er that shiner. She also said Holt an' Miss Laudie took that miserable turnip down hard."

"Laudie Kate made that happen." Holt nodded. "She was amazing, very brave."

"Well, thank ya both," Moose said.

Holt stole a quick glance at Laudie Kate and nodded his head with a brief smile.

"The doc's lookin' at Frederick's son," Moose continued. "I'm next, I guess." He held up his bloody arm. "I'm pretty sure I ain't carryin' lead, but it stings sumthin' fierce." He took a quick pull from the bottle. "I hate doctor's offices, so we're jus' waitin' out here." He paused, cocking his head as he looked at his lanky Ranger friend. "Looks like ya need a new shirt an' a bit o' this, my friend," he said, offering the bottle to Orion.

"It's good to see you too, you big lug." Orion smiled, taking the bottle for a short pull.

"Good ta be seen. Ya know I'm too damn mean ta be stopped by a coupla scratches on my arm."

"Did the doctor say anything about Luke?" Holt asked.

"Th' doctor seems ta think Luke's leg'll be fine," Evie said. "Said it was a through-an'-through."

"There ya are." Moose nodded and shook the liquor

bottle. "I'm 'bout out here. Les' go find a real drink." He stood up from the bench.

"Now you're talkin'," Orion chimed in.

"Hold it right there, big 'un," Holt interrupted, stepping up to stop Moose in his tracks. "You too, peckerhead. Where do you think you're going?" The two injured men stood taller than their Ranger buddy, but he stopped them in their tracks. "You and Orion are staying right here until the doc or someone patches you up. No one wants to drink with a couple of bloodied-up yahoos." Laudie Kate and Evie also positioned themselves by Holt to help block Orion and Moose's path to leaving.

"I think you both need to follow this young Ranger's instructions," Lillian Whitman declared from the boardwalk in front of the doctor's office. Hands on her hips, the widow's light-brown eyes held Orion in a nononsense stare. Her smoky silver hair was pulled back in its usual long, broad braid. A borrowed white apron could not hide a holstered pistol at her waist or her statuesque shape.

She had been keeping watch over the injured 5 Star rider who broke his arm when a rattler spooked his horse. With all these new arrivals, she had been pressed into nursing service.

"The only time I'll ever think about wishin' I was hurt…" Holt half-teased his Ranger buddy.

The idea of this strikingly handsome woman tending to him changed Orion's mindset more than anything a bottle could offer. He smiled and ambled toward the doctor's drugstore and Lillian. Moose shuffled along behind, Evie making sure he kept moving in the right direction.

Holt and Laudie Kate caught each other's eyes. She

smiled, her eyes hopeful and warm. She knew he was razor-focused on his job—his very dangerous job—but she was confused that he had not said much to her since they had left the W Bar L.

Holt resumed watching the two injured Rangers enter the doctor's office. "That could've been a lot worse," he said before giving her a quick smile and hurrying to rejoin the business at the jail.

CHAPTER FORTY-SEVEN

Early fingers of false dawn were feeling their way across a sky that had seen a troubled night. The town of Stebbins was absorbing the aftermath of the toppling of Lars Viklund's empire and Sheriff Linus Carmichael's reign. No longer milling about, townspeople had relocated to saloons, restaurants and homes to buzz about what had just happened. Many people had not gone to bed, either too wound up to sleep or too busy with their work. The undertaker and his Chinese helpers had labored through the night, dealing with the amassed collection of dead Windmill V henchmen, from the 5 Star attack and the roundup. Those in the doctor's office had worked all night as well.

Orion stood in the middle of the street outside the jail, conferring with Captain McCoy. The lanky Ranger was wearing a fresh shirt that covered the bandage swaddling his right arm from armpit to wrist. He had balked at receiving the dressing until Lillian Whitman ordered him into an examining room. Once he realized that the handsome widow would be treating his wound, Orion settled in and was a model patient.

"Good work, Orion," the captain said. "I had no idea what a spider web of crap this was. We thought it was just a plain ol' case of rustling."

"The Army has to be likin' our work too. Saved 'em a passel of money, I'm guessin'."

"The fort will have to deal with the scandal. It'll bring a lot of attention and notoriety. It didn't appear that this particular action went further than the sergeant, but there's plenty of shenanigans those boys in blue will have to look into."

"Power comes with temptation." Orion nodded wistfully.

"I've wired the federal magistrate to come here right away. Viklund's son and that Carmichael idiot have to answer for a hell of a lot. There's quite a bit of property that needs to be sorted out too."

"Not to mention the lovely town of Stebbins is gonna need a new county sheriff," Orion added.

Meanwhile, Holt had stepped into the Blue Sky to retrieve his buddy, Tag Along.

"Hees upstairs," the owner of the hotel, Miguel Navarro, said. "He seems to think you might be there."

As Holt climbed the stairs, memories of his shooting and the days spent recovering flooded through his mind. Thoughts of his first awareness of Laudie Kate and her gentle ways were tantalizing, but immediately pushed aside by the hurtful words he heard her speak just days ago... *What kind of life could a woman have with a man like Holt Corrigan?*

The hallway showed signs of the earlier struggle when Viklund and Carmichael stormed through and grabbed the two women. In the hallway, one of the rocking chairs and a side table were strewn about. The marshal had told Navarro not to touch anything until they could get a better look at it.

He reached the room where he had struggled to come back to the world of the living. Just across the hallway was Laudie Kate's room, the door partly ajar, its hinges splintered and handle broken where Lars had busted through in a rage. Holt's anger rose at the image of the two women trying to barricade themselves only to have that bastard Viklund break in and abduct them. Knowing that Lars lay dead provided a measure of solace, but Holt was still incensed by the thought of the terror the Swede had put Laudie Kate and Evie through.

Only then did he notice that Tag was in her room, sniffing around.

He stepped inside to lay Laudie Kate's pocket pistol on her bed. "Hey boy," he said to Tag, patting his thigh. "C'mon. You shouldn't be in here." He was concentrating on getting Tag out of the room when his eyes spotted something on her dresser.

His narrow-brimmed fedora, with the cardinal feather in its band.

Confused, he walked over and looked at the hat. *Why does she have this and never said anything about it?*

His breath caught. The cardinal feather—his lucky cardinal feather—had been broken by something, the bullet's impact or when the hat fell from his head. The shaft had splintered, but it still barely hung together.

"That about figures, doesn't it, Tag?"

He placed the old cavalry Stetson he had been wearing on the dresser and reverently picked up his long-lost hat. He carefully pulled the broken feather from the band and held it gently in his hand, staring at it as though it was an actual deceased bird. Holt tugged the fedora onto his head and called for Tag. As he strode out of the room, he dropped the feather to the floor.

After reaching the street outside, Holt saw Orion and got his attention. "They got you cleaned up and respectable looking again, I see."

"Not sure if it'll work better than that Navajo concoction of yours. It smells a little better though," Orion said. "Hey, we've been invited to a little thank you gatherin'. We're gonna help escort Luke Frederick and Lilly back to the 5 Star."

"The widow?"

"Yeah, she said so when she put all this on me."

"So it's *Lilly* now, huh?" Holt grinned. "You? Mister 'I Don't Need A Doctor' sat still for the pretty widow?"

"Well, yeah." Orion smiled. "I thought it was a good move on my part."

Holt shook his head and laughed.

"You about ready to go?" Orion asked. "I think Luke's all patched up."

"That I am, my friend." Holt nodded. "That I am. Let's go say goodbye."

The 5 Star horses that Holt and Orion rode from the roundup camp were still tied up in front of the Blue Sky, where they had left them hours ago, each standing patiently. The Rangers would pony them back when they escorted Mrs. Whitman and Luke.

As he pulled his saddlebags from the borrowed horse, Holt contemplated the whole ordeal of how this all started. Being shot by Laudie Kate and Carmichael's deputy. His journey through the spirit world of dark and light to come back to living. Going home to heal and finally returning to Stebbins to finish what he started. Holt thanked his bear spirits for watching over him.

His head full of gratitude, he ambled over to the jail, gear in-hand.

Inside, the large front office was filled with laughing men and Evie O'Neill. Whiskey was being poured.

"Holt! Orion! Yer jus' in time fer breakfast!" Marshal Hollings yelled. "We's celebratin' Moose here a-tradin' badges!"

Everyone had congregated around a big desk. Seated behind it was a bandaged Moose Elkins. Evie had fetched him a clean shirt. It was barely big enough for the man's massive frame, but at least it wasn't bloody. Seated above him on the desktop, she beamed at her beloved Moose.

"Les' all raise a glass fer th' new actin' sheriff o' St. Clair County, Moose Elkins!" the marshal said loudly over the group.

Cheers and glass clinks circled the room.

"That badge comes with a right pretty filly," Orion quipped, winking at Evie. "Did you clear all this with her first?"

Good-natured laughter continued around the celebration circle.

"Clear it? She's th' one who suggested it ta me!"

Big whoops of laughter filled the room as another round was poured.

Holt finished his glass and announced that he and Orion were taking off. "We're headed out. Going to accompany Luke Frederick and Mrs. Whitman back to the 5 Star."

Orion nodded in agreement.

"Where ya headed a'fer that?" Marshal Hollings asked.

"Home to Wilkon. Just as soon as I can get there," Holt said, then gestured toward Orion. "Taking this guy along."

Moose held an empty glass in one oversized hand and eyed Holt with a wry grin, "Mighty nice ta finally meetcha, Holt Corrigan. Don' be a stranger." He stuck out a huge paw. "You said g'bye ta Miss Laudie?" he said, shaking Holt's hand.

"No. There's no need. I heard her talking to Evie the other day. She said she could never be with someone like me," Holt said with a shrug. "I can take a hint." Then he patted Moose on the shoulder. "You be careful, big'un. This new job isn't Rangering, but it's not always a picnic either." He smiled and gave Evie a quick hug. "Thank you again, Evie. Take care of this guy."

She smiled and held on to him for a longer embrace. "Thank you, Holt. You know, Laudie—"

"Laudie Kate is a wonderful woman," Holt said, cutting her off. "I heard her talk. She made things clear. Even if I wasn't a Ranger, she said she could never be with a man like me."

"But that's not what she said…or meant," Evie tried to explain. "You got it wrong—"

"You're a good friend." Holt smiled painfully. "Take care of her too."

She was interrupted from saying anything further when Orion stepped over to put his long arms around both her and Moose. "I'm happy for you, my friends. Be good to each other," the lanky Ranger said. "I'll be seein' you."

Orion moved outside and found Captain McCoy enjoying the quiet of the new day with a cigar. Holt was standing with him.

"Captain, I'm headed home," Holt said. "Going to take this guy with me. For some reason, my family wants to meet him."

"Headed home myself. We've earned it," McCoy said. Then he put his hand on Holt's shoulder. "I never did say anything to you directly about all that Angel and Taliff business. That was damn good work, Holt Corrigan. Damn good. Here in Stebbins too. *Both* of you."

"You know where to find us." Holt smiled. "But I hope you won't need to find us for a while."

"Well...until then." The captain shook their hands. "Ride careful, boys."

As they walked to the livery to retrieve their horses, Holt stopped in the center of the Stebbins main street and fished out a small pouch from his coat pocket. From the leather bag, he tossed tobacco shreds in the four directions, thanking the spirits.

"Cap'n had a good-smellin' cigar an' now you're throwin' tobacco. Makes me want one."

Holt reached into another coat pocket. "I hope you have a match, because I don't." He grinned as he held out two cigars. "Thanks, partner. For everything. I hear there's a steak and some Irish waiting for us at the 5 Star. Let's get out of here."

Cinches tightened and cigars lit, the two Rangers trotted from the livery aboard their own horses, leading their backup mounts as well as the 5 Star ponies. Lillian Whitman, her foreman Big Jeff and a bandaged Luke Frederick were waiting for them at the drugstore. They all spurred their horses into the brightening day, Tag trotting happily along next to them.

———

Laudie Kate walked alone up the Stebbins main street. She had stayed through the night to help Dr. Vaughn with the remainder of the roundup patients. The merriment at the jail beckoned for a look-see, but the weight of everything that happened had made her weary and she decided to head to her room at the Blue Sky. Her only wish was to maneuver her way unseen through the lobby saloon and up the stairs.

"Ahh, Mees Hart, it ees sooo good to see you!" Miguel Navarro exclaimed as he waded his way through the early morning crowd and grabbed her in a quick hug. Embarrassed at himself for the unusual, for him, show of emotion, he continued, "Forgive me for…the *familiarity,* but I was so, so worried. For you and Mees Evie. You are both fine, yes?"

"Yes, Miguel. I appreciate your concern. We are, thankfully, fine."

"Sorry I am for the damage to your door. *Una maldición sobre* those evil men. No. *A thousand* curses! I have already made arrangements for a new one. Kept people from upstairs I have. Except for Evie…and Ranger Corrigan…"

"Ranger Corri…Holt?"

"*Si.* He was here earlier. He left Tag Along weeth me when he went…to rescue…you."

Laudie Kate hurried away from the hotel owner and up the stairs.

"Sleep in another room tonight you should!" Navarro called out after her.

She stopped in the doorway to her room. Evie was sitting on the bed but stood when Laudie Kate appeared.

"There you are," Evie said. "You look exhausted…"

Laudie Kate's eyes were immediately drawn to the

broken cardinal feather at her feet. She reached down and carefully picked up the red plume, holding it delicately as though it were a real, injured bird.

Evie told her what Holt had said, what he thought he had heard. "An' he left. Jus' like that," she finished.

Laudie Kate listened as she gently tried to straighten the feather into one piece again. The damaged plume could not hold together any longer and came apart into each of her hands. She struggled not to, but tears came uncontrollably. "Oh, Holt…" She buried her face in her hands and sobbed into the feather.

CHAPTER FORTY-EIGHT

Acting County Sheriff James Hannah returned to the Wilkon jail after morning rounds with Deputies Bradley Cooke and Lear Freeburg. Hannah brought two hot-off-the-press editions of the *Wilkon Epitaph* which he and Marshal Logan Wheeler now sat reading. Wheeler's healing leg was propped up on the desk. Bradley and Lear moved off to a corner to work on cleaning the rifles and shotguns in the jailhouse weapons rack. All were nursing steaming mugs of fresh coffee from the stove.

"Lord a'mighty, this article 'bout th' Fort McKavett quartermaster?" Wheeler blurted out. "An' his brother, th' crooked county sheriff?"

"All tied to a Swedish immigrant rancher knee-deep in rustling," Hannah added, adjusting his eyeglasses.

"Good gravy, whatta mess," Wheeler exclaimed.

"That's what Holt was involved with, wasn't it?" Lear asked, looking up from a broken-open Greener.

Hannah nodded. "The whole deal sounded crazy from Holt's telegrams. Quite the operation. Rustling. Murder.

Counterfeiting. Crooked sheriff. Corrupt Army sergeant. Ranger spies posing as rustlers."

"All that, plus The Angel and Taliff business. He could write a book," Bradley joked.

"Yup, here's his name," Wheeler said, holding up the newspaper. "They dun busted it all up. Says right here, '…Texas Ranger Captain Laird McCoy and Rangers Holt Corrigan, Moose Elkins, Dal Frantze and Orion Higbee battled the rustlers and brought them to justice…' I'll be damned."

"Yeah, our boy Holt keeps getting those plum assignments." Hannah smirked. "You saw, though, it almost cost him big this time."

A hard rap on the main door interrupted their conversation.

"Open up, Texas Ranger!" came a deep, unfamiliar voice.

"What the…" Hannah exclaimed. The two lawmen sat up and put their newspapers on the desk. They were not expecting a visit and had no real reason to be suspicious. However, both Hannah and Wheeler had decided that, with all the previous year's incidents, they would operate the jail more securely than in the past.

Wheeler stood and headed for the door. Hannah slowly drew his pistol. The deputies followed suit, loading shells into the Greeners they were working on.

With Hannah's nod of readiness, Marshal Wheeler opened the secured peep gate on the new jail door and looked outside. He was greeted by a lanky, salt-and-pepper-haired man wearing a serious look. The gray-bearded visitor backed away from the door allowing Wheeler the opportunity to see his Texas Ranger badge and that his hands were empty.

"It's a Ranger all right," Wheeler observed to Hannah as he unlocked the door. "Dunno who though."

A lanky, black-coated Ranger strode inside and tugged at his wide, flat-brimmed hat, "Mornin' boys! I'm lookin' for an owlhoot by the name of James Hannah. He's gotta lot to answer for. Heard he might be hidin' out in this here town."

Tension rose in the large jail office as though all the air was sucked out of it.

"Wait a minute…" Lear said.

Before Lear could finish or anyone else could respond, a floppy-eared, gray and brown dog ran through the open door, passing by the tall Ranger, wagging its tail furiously at the jail occupants.

"Hey! That's Tag Along!" Bradley exclaimed. "That's Holt's dog!"

The charade ruined just as it was starting, Holt stepped into the entryway, a huge grin on his face.

"Hey! It's three of my favorite lawmen…and James Hannah!" he exclaimed.

The jail's tension instantly flew from surprised caution to happy jubilation. Weapons were put away. Hannah shouted, "The hometown hero returns!"

"Don't know about the hero part, but it's good to be home," Holt beamed, coming the rest of the way into the jail.

The four of them met just inside the door laughing, shaking hands, and thumping each other on their backs. Tag wove his way in and out of their legs, eager to be a part of the celebration.

"When'd ya git back, Holt?" Wheeler asked.

"Yesterday. We've been at the Rafter C. The family wanted to meet this guy," Holt gestured to Orion. "Now

it's your turn. Gentlemen, after all this time, let me intro-
duce Orion Higbee. Orion, say hello to James Hannah,
Logan Wheeler, and Bradley Cooke. You remember Lear
Freeburg from the final Taliff shootout in Modlin.
Logan'll soon be our sheriff and Lear will take over as
marshal."

Orion beamed and enthusiastically shook hands with
each man with his left hand. "Movin' a little careful right
now, gotta slash under here," he explained, gesturing
along his right arm. "That scarecrow of a sheriff thought
he could fillet me like a channel cat."

"Finally, a face to go with all the telegrams." Hannah
smiled in return. "It's been a while since those 'owlhoot'
days. You had me going there for a moment."

"It was all this guy's idea." The lanky Ranger
laughed, nodding at Holt.

"Well, I'm glad to know you, Orion," Hannah said.
"Thanks for looking out for this miscreant and seeing
him home safely."

"We both needed some lookin' after." Orion chuckled. "Glad I brung him an' Tag Along though."

"Actually, we never did care for Holt much." Hannah
grinned in response. "We really only like his dog."

"You know," Holt interrupted, "a man could die of
thirst around here before someone offered him a drink."

"Ah hell, Holt, I think I'm dun cleaned out." Wheeler
shrugged. "But ain't it a mite early?"

"Never too early to enjoy a libation with friends, I
always say," Orion declared.

"That's why we get along so well," Holt exclaimed.
"With Hannah around, I'm not surprised you're out,
Logan." He chuckled, pulling a new bottle of fine Irish
whiskey from the saddlebags slung over his shoulder.

"Do you all have glasses or do I have to provide them too?"

"You're whinier than I remember," Hannah remarked.

"Someone else better have matches," Holt continued as he produced a fistful of cigars from the saddlebags.

Soon, drinks were poured and cigars were lit.

"To coming home," Holt toasted.

"An' to new friends," Orion added.

"May both always be there when you need them," Hannah joined in.

Tag felt it was time for another round of welcome home pats as well.

After another toast to the soon-to-be-named new sheriff and marshal of Wilkon, they settled in around the desk to share laughs and stories. The Rangers' recent adventure in Stebbins against the Viklund family took most of the attention.

"Sounds a little like that Bordner pissant who tried to clear you and your family out," Bradley observed. "Where do people get illusions of grandeur like that?"

"Probably from crap in the paper," Holt said, picking up a copy of the Wilkon newspaper and chuckling at Hannah.

"The paper's gotten a little better," Hannah defended quickly.

"Is that possible?" Holt joked.

"Lil' Gillespie, th' reporter, was nice in mentionin' th' job all you Rangers did," Wheeler interjected. "Mentioned ya each by name."

"There just might be a reason for the Epitaph's improvement," Bradley noted. "Go on, tell him the best part, James. Tell Holt why the newspaper is better now."

"Well, Gillespie has a better boss now," Hannah said.

"Ah hell, James." Bradley grimaced.

"I bought the paper." Hannah smiled.

Holt was incredulous. "Wait, you own the *Epitaph* now?"

Hannah just nodded his head and snickered.

"No…" Holt said in disbelief.

"Guilty as charged." Hannah grinned. "I like to think it's *less crappy* now. You might even like it."

"I can't leave you alone, can I?" Holt joked.

"I'll tell you more later," Hannah said. "I needed something to do when I finally turn in this badge."

"I thought your new saloon was going to keep you occupied," Holt noted.

"One's a daytime job. The other's for the nighttime," Hannah said with a wink, then quickly changed the subject. "What happened to that gal, the one who shot you? Thought you'd be bringing her with you."

"Laudie Kate? Let's just say she didn't cotton to the idea of tying down with someone like me."

"That so? She told you that?" Hannah continued.

"I heard her talking with a friend."

"Well…that wasn't what Moose's Evie recalled she said or meant," Orion interjected.

"So, you just left without telling her how you felt?" Hannah questioned. "What happened with telling her '*Mellifluously*?'"

"I *heard* what she said about me. Besides, she was hiding my hat. Who does that?"

"Someone who wants you to come back!" Hannah practically hollered.

"Or stick around," Orion added as he sipped from his glass.

"You aren't helping here," Holt said to his partner. "Why didn't you say something sooner?"

"Hopin' maybe you'd come to your senses. It still ain't too late."

Holt stared quietly into his glass and drained the whiskey from it.

CHAPTER FORTY-NINE

A few days later at dinner, Blue Corrigan set down his eating utensils. "You're a big part of the celebration, little brother!" he said, with exasperation in his voice. "You can't just up and leave, and not show up."

"Ah hell, it's only a party. We'll be on stage, all wrapped up like a package with Orion as the ribbon and me as a bow," Holt groused, then gestured toward his Ranger partner, Orion.

Holt had just mentioned his intention to leave at first light in the morning, to ride back to Stebbins and to Laudie Kate. Blue was astounded at Holt's announcement, not the reasoning behind it, but the timing. The celebration, even if it was only partly for Holt, was tomorrow.

Bina and Orion were sitting with the two brothers at the dinner table.

Orion did his best to keep a knowing smirk hidden, but couldn't help himself. "I've never been a ribbon before," he teased. "Is there a special hat I'm supposed to wear or somethin'?"

Bina kept her counsel to herself, but smiled at Holt for discovering that he had found someone with whom he could share his heart.

Holding a citywide Wilkon celebration had been talked about for a while but had never gotten off the ground. The timing had never been quite right. Even though new buildings had been constructed, not all of the new businesses had opened. There just hadn't been a really good enough reason to throw such an event.

That is, until Wilkon's own hero, Texas Ranger Holt Corrigan, returned—this time coming home healthy. That gave Mayor Cooke and his wife all the inspiration for arranging a celebration. And what a party it would be! Wilkon was growing. A new tavern, new stores, new bungalows, new fire station and new town water well were all to be christened as part of the festivities. All the new projects were possible due to Meden Taliff's philanthropy, but so were the murders and evil that plagued the region. The town needed to move on from all that. The celebration was going to help.

The results from the election for county sheriff would be announced as well, but since Logan Wheeler ran unopposed, the results were not exactly a surprise.

The symbolic guest of honor would be Holt, with a thank you commendation to his Ranger partner Orion Higbee—both men being recognized for their roles in capturing the men responsible for the murders of three of Wilkon's leading citizens.

"The town's fit to bust and give you two a hero's welcome," Blue wound up his admonishment. "A lot of people want to see you and thank you. You can go after Laudie Kate afterward."

———

The next morning dawned bright and early. A happy caravan of Corrigans arrived in town amongst a lot of other traffic. Blue's family were all packed into one wagon with Deed's family arranged in another. Holt and Orion rode their horses alongside. The Corrigan children were eager to partake in the special games and contests being set up for youngsters as well as to sample treats like cake and ice cream.

As soon as he spotted Holt's arrival at the livery barn, Mayor Cooke flashed over to greet him, breathlessly giving the two Rangers the full schedule of the day's events. He excitedly provided a detailed rundown where the two heroes should be at all times.

"That feller's a nervous bundle of energy, ain't he?" Orion grinned as the mayor bustled away.

"Remember the sharp young deputy from the jail? That's his father," Holt responded.

"The young man must take after his mother." Orion chuckled.

Prior to the official speeches and announcements to kick-off the celebration, James Hannah had invited special guests, business owners, reporters, and the town lawmen, including Holt and Orion, to a private opening of his new establishment, the Black Hat Saloon. The Black Hat was one of the new businesses included in the special day's grand openings.

The Black Hat Saloon was originally started as a Meden Taliff project. He first mentioned it to Holt and

Hannah months ago, asking their opinion if such an operation made sense for Wilkon. Hannah thought it fitting
that, after helping to vanquish the crooked attorney and
would-be governor, he should become the owner of the
establishment—an appropriate and perpetual vindication
over the man who nearly took his and his wife's lives.
Running the saloon and publishing the newspaper would
occupy Hannah's time after he turned in his badge.

Taliff's vision was to call the establishment the
Boar's Head Tavern, after a pub in Shakespeare's *King
Henry IV*. After securing the finances to buy the estab-
lishment and finish its construction, Hannah re-named it
the Black Hat Saloon, a more fitting name for a James
Hannah venture.

The invited guests filed into the new building. The
tavern had a magnificent bar with a huge mirror behind it
and shelves stocked with all manner of bottles and liba-
tions. The glorious main room had yet to be filled with
smoke or used in any other fashion. The tables and chairs
still untouched. The Black Hat Saloon gleamed with
newness.

"Ho-lee damn," Orion exclaimed to Holt. "This may
be the prettiest place I've ever had a drink in."

Under Hannah's direction, the Black Hat was going
to have a more sophisticated atmosphere than the other
bars in town. In addition to the usual poker and drinking
elements, the saloon would be offering faro, chuck-a-
luck, and grand hazard gambling games, as well as
billiards and bowling. The Black Hat also featured a
small stage for performances, can-can girls and skits.
Hannah added this to the original plan, favoring the
opportunities for entertainment and culture.

At the announced start time, Hannah appeared. He

was well dressed as he usually was, spotless Victorian black suit coat, crisp white shirt, only today he wore a deep maroon silk ascot. Before climbing up on hidden crates behind the grand new bar, he took off his thick spectacles and gave them a quick cleaning. Now perched up on the bar, stood waving his arms in the air to bring the room to order, his bowler hat in hand.

"Thank you all for joining me on a most momentous day!" Responding applause from the gathered crowd followed. "I soon will no longer be your sheriff. It is my hope and goal that my new enterprise will become renowned not only as a first-rate establishment, but also a significant part of the fine town of Wilkon." He paused to allow another round of applause. "Not to mention a money-making affair, my creditors will be happy to note."

The crowd laughed appropriately.

"Good thing he knows who owns the bank. " Holt smirked to Orion. The older Ranger chuckled.

"In addition to games of chance and other skill amusements, we hope to entice customers with performances and exhibitions both entertaining and intriguing. In keeping with the reputation of a superior establishment, once we are open to the public, no guns will be allowed inside." The announcement met with polite applause from the group.

"We will have lovely waitresses serving some of the best drinks and food," Hannah continued. "What you will not find here is sporting women. That kind of entertainment will not be allowed here." A larger amount of applause rippled through the assembled group.

"That's a Rebecca decree, to be sure," Holt noted

quietly. "But it's a headache I know James did not want to deal with."

Orion nodded in agreement.

"I had looked high and low for the right person to run my establishment," Hannah said. "Someone who is honest and hard-working…and might someday even consider becoming a part owner."

A smattering of soft comments murmured their way through the array of guests.

"My time was running out before this grand opening and I had yet to find that person," Hannah continued. "But then, just recently, I was fortunate to find such an individual, someone who happened to just show up, out of the clear blue sky."

Another round of chortles was coaxed from the gathering.

"I could not be happier and prouder to introduce my new manager…"

A woman appeared from a pantry door next to the bar and joined Hannah up on the dais of crates. She wore a long-sleeved cornflower blue dress with black ribbon at the neck and hem; practical, but on her, alluring. Her brown hair was swept back into a tight bun, a black, flat-brimmed, manly-looking hat perched smartly atop her head.

She was greeted, at first, with polite, surprised applause, until Hannah continued, "Who says a woman can't do a man's job?"

The woman's bright blue eyes flashed. A strand of sunlight caught her face, accenting a long scar that ran down the right side of her face, from her cheekbone to her jawline.

"I give you the perfect person for this job…Laudie Kate Hart!"

The applause grew in an appreciative crescendo.

Holt had largely ignored most of what Hannah had been saying, thinking about the appropriate time to duck away from today's celebration and start his journey back to Stebbins and the Blue Sky. Suddenly, he thought he heard his friend say, "Laudie Kate Hart."

That can't be right.

He focused his attention up at the bar where Hannah was standing and was stunned with what he saw.

Laudie Kate.

The woman of his dreams…The woman who shot him…The woman he thought wanted nothing to do with him…was standing right there, beaming with happiness.

And she was looking straight at Holt.

"My honored guests," Hannah called out, ending his speech. He ceremoniously pulled the sheriff's badge from his lapel and tossed it to Mayor Cooke. "I'm officially no longer sheriff. Welcome to my Black Hat Saloon! The first round is on me. Please enjoy yourselves!"

As Hannah and Laudie Kate were stepping down from their perch, Mayor Cooke scrambled up and tried yelling over the crowd that the official start of the celebration would commence outside in one hour.

Holt and Orion were swallowed by the milling crowd. They had been cornered by Mayor Cooke's wife, who wanted the handsome young Ranger from Wilkon to tell a portion of his exploits to a few of her special guests. At the same time, Laudie Kate was searching through the crowd, looking for Holt. Suddenly, she turned to the sound of his voice.

Just like magic, the crowd parted, and all at once,

Laudie Kate had a clear view of Holt. He was in mid-story when he saw her.

Her smile was an invitation.

Orion noticed the moment and took over the conversation, subtly nudging his young partner in her direction.

Holt walked up to her, his eyes full of wonder and questions. "Wh-What…h-how…" He shook his head in frustration and took a deep breath. "Can a Ranger buy you a drink?" he asked with a smile.

"That depends on the Ranger," she said coyly, putting her arm through his. They made their way to the far end of the main bar where a woman serving drinks smiled as they approached.

"You know, I don't even know what your favorite drink is," he said.

"Bourbon."

"Two please." He smiled at the bartender.

They took their tumblers and stole away to a quieter corner.

When they were finally alone, Holt started to speak, but Laudie Kate quickly admonished him, "You left without saying goodbye."

"But…"

"Do you know how much I've missed you?"

"But what…"

"You've been on my mind constantly."

"But what about…"

"I had to find you."

"But I *heard* you…"

"You heard Evie and I talking like our mothers. You know, *joking*? We were *making fun* of them." She wrinkled her brow at him. "You need to be careful eavesdropping on women like that."

404   SCOTT F. SMITH

"I, uh…"

"Holt Corrigan, I'm not sure how much plainer things can be." She put down her glass and took Holt's away to set next to it.

He smiled and his eyes caressed hers. His forever blue sky was standing right in front of him.

"This is when you kiss me," she scolded.

"Oh, right. I-I j-just get…"

She pushed against him, and her mouth found his. They held each other and kissed…and kissed.

"You're better at this than talking," she purred.

"Sshhh. So are you," he said, gently taking her face into his hands and kissing her deeply once more.

Laudie Kate took a step back, smoothing her dress to compose herself and gather her breath. She produced a bright red cardinal feather that was tucked into her sleeve and held it out for Holt. "For your hat. It's good luck, I hear."

He grinned. "My luck has already changed."

A LOOK AT BOOK SIX
PLAY FOR BLOOD

Scott F. Smith, son of acclaimed Western author Cotton Smith, returns with another hard-hitting chapter in the Corrigan Brothers saga.

Texas Ranger Holt Corrigan has faced rustlers, killers, and more gunfights than most men survive. But he has never hunted anyone like Calista Theriot. A legendary river pirate turned frontier power broker, Calista has left the waterways behind and ridden into Texas cattle country with a bold new prize in mind. The booming Texas railroad trade.

Beautiful, ruthless, and cunning as any cardsharp, Calista does more than rob men. She ruins them. With newspapers spreading lies and her gang ready to spill blood, she is turning towns against Holt and the people he holds dear. To stop her, Holt must outplay a woman who treats every scheme like a high-stakes poker game and always plays for blood.

Can Holt Corrigan beat the most dangerous gambler in Texas before Calista Theriot takes everything he is sworn to protect?

AVAILABLE APRIL 2026

ACKNOWLEDGMENTS

It's said that if you're lucky, love gives you a fairy tale. The journey my wife and I are on is more of a treasured long-running TV show with laughter, hijinks, and devotion. I can't look away or change the channel. Cindy, thank you for being my cart partner and best friend. All my love forever.

To my sisters, Laura Faulkner and Stephanie Kissick and their outlaws Owen and Rob. From Elmer Bricks and cryin' pigs to cinnamon rolls and Rocky Mountain dawn patrols, my heart brims over with amazing memories. I was blessed to have such a wonderful family. Thank you for putting up with all the shenanigans. With love from your big brother.

Thank you to my friends at Wolfpack Publishing. I am grateful to you all.

Thank you to the Lost Boys, my endless gratitude for the brotherhood and everlasting friendship.

And finally, to my parents, Sonya and Cotton Smith. I feel your love and presence every single day. I miss you more than words can say.

ABOUT THE AUTHOR

Scott F. Smith continues the spirit of the Old West created by his father, Cotton Smith, author of the first two books of the Corrigan series and other wonderful Western adventures, such as *Pray for Texas* and *Behold a Red Horse*.

Vengeance Wears a Star is Scott's debut novel and is rooted in the elements that made Cotton's books great—grand themes, moral conflict, and courage. He grew up with a love of American history, reading, and Western movies and is an Eagle Scout and recipient of the Boy Scouts of America's Silver Beaver Award. He continues to volunteer with Scouting to help develop tomorrow's leaders.

As a youth, Scott was introduced to the ceremonies, customs, and traditions of the Plains Indian. Research for Western storytelling heightened his appreciation for and spiritual connection to the land. For many years, he participated in the Desert Caballeros trail ride, covering a hundred miles in a weeklong trek through the Arizona mountains each year.

Scott is an award-winning writer and producer for corporate clients and relishes the experience of staring at a blank piece of paper or computer screen and creating a story within an easy-to-imagine world. He previously taught high school media and video production, having enjoyed sharing his storytelling expertise as well as helping students bring their own tales to life.

A member of the Western Writers of America, Scott and his wife, Cindy, are global explorers but call Lawrence, Kansas, home.

You can find Scott's work at www.ScottSmithWesterns.com.